The Ordinary Grit

Courage Under an Unforgiving Sky

by Rocky Matson

Dedication

For Melwood "Chris" Matson

You were my first map of what a man could be —
steady in hard weather, generous with hard-won wisdom,
and full of stories about the people who came before us:
the farmers, the ranchers, the schoolteachers
who pressed their hands into unfamiliar soil and held on.

You were the ordinary grit in my life.
I didn't always recognize it as courage.
Now I do.

I miss you, Dad.

Chapter 1: The Red Stake

Elias

The well woke me. Not a sound — a weight, the cold certainty that what I'd find at the rope's end would not be enough. I lay still a moment, listening to Sarah breathe. Her shoulder rose and fell against the thin sheet, steady as something I could count on, and I held to that rhythm a few seconds longer than I should have. Then I got up before the thought could settle into dread.

I dressed by touch in the dark. Ten years of mornings had trained my fingers — the rough denim on the peg by the door, the heavy flannel beside it, the leather belt with its notch worn smooth. No match struck. Kerosene was a commodity I tallied by the drop, same as flour, same as salt, and I knew every corner of this house the way I knew my own calluses — by feel, by repetition, by the cost of building it. The dirt floor was cool under my bare feet. I pulled on my boots at the doorframe, the left one cracked along the heel where I'd patched it twice with harness leather.

Outside, the air held that brief mercy the drought allowed before dawn — almost cool, almost kind. It wouldn't last. By seven the heat would sit on the land like a debt come due. The dry rattle of corn husks carried from the North Field, papery and dead, and somewhere in the dark a coyote tested a single high note, then thought better of it.

I rested my hand on the rough-hewn windlass timber. The wood was parched, grain standing up like tiny ridges under my palm. I listened to the rope creak as I lowered the bucket, each slow revolution of the handle ticking off what felt like the last of something. The waiting was the worst of it. I counted the seconds the way I counted everything — against what I could afford to lose.

The splash came shallow. Hollow.

When I hauled it back up, the bucket was light. Wrong-light. The water that coated the bottom was a muddy gray slurry, barely enough to wet my palm. I dipped two fingers in and rubbed them together. Grit. I set the bucket on the lip of the well and looked at it a long time, the way you look at a column of figures that won't balance no matter how many times you run them. Then I looked at the North Field. The wheat should have been thigh-high by now, turning gold in the early light. What stood there was a field of stunted yellow stalks, heads down, like men waiting to be told the verdict they already knew.

This land was supposed to be the end of something. The end of Kansas, end of the banks, end of the horizon being a threat. I'd promised Sarah that. I'd promised myself. I'd built it with my own hands out of the same dirt it sat on — cut the sod, stacked the walls, sunk the posts for the barn until my shoulders seized and wouldn't straighten for two days. But the earth was closing its fist, and that slurry at the bottom of the bucket told me how much time I might have left before the grip got serious.

I picked up my shovel and walked the North Field perimeter. Mostly checking wire, looking for sag where the posts had shifted in the dry ground. The boots kicked up rust-colored dust with every step, and I could feel the fine grit working into the creases of my lips, coating my tongue with that flat, mineral taste that had become the flavor of the season. A meadowlark sat on a fence post, watching me pass. It didn't sing. Even the birds had gone quiet, as though the land had used up whatever was worth singing about.

That was when I saw the color — bright, unnatural, about fifty yards inside my property line. Not a rock. Not a piece of stray timber.

A stake, milled clean and smooth, driven into the dirt. Tipped in red.

I stopped. The air went peculiar — too still, the kind of still that precedes not wind but something worse. I walked toward it slowly, the shovel gone heavy on my shoulder. Grasshoppers crackled away from my boots in small brown arcs. Up close, the stamped seal of the railroad company pressed into the wood read the way a brand reads on a hide. Cold. Decisive. The lumber was pale and factory-clean, not a thing that belonged in soil a man had worked with his own sweat. It had no business here.

I dropped the shovel and grabbed hold of the stake. My hands were shaking — not from fear but from the pressure that had been building since the well went shallow, the kind of pressure that needs somewhere to go. I yanked. The hard-packed earth held fast. I growled somewhere low in my chest, put my weight behind it, and the stake came free with a sharp crack that sat me down hard in the dust. I sat there with the red-tipped wood in my fist, the stamped seal digging into my palm, and I could smell the paint — sharp, chemical, wrong against the honest dry scent of dirt and dead grass. They hadn't sent a letter. Hadn't knocked. Just driven their mark into the ground as though I were already gone.

I didn't go back to the house. I carried the stake to the barn and buried it under a pile of old burlap. I needed to think without that painted red point staring at me. The barn was dark and close, smelling of old hay and the warm breath of animals, and the familiar creak of the roof timbers steadied me some. I sat on a hay bale and turned my hands over, studying the torn skin where the stake had fought me. The memory of Kansas had a way of surfacing whenever I was already carrying too much — the bank men who'd never once gotten their boots dirty, looking at my brother's farm with eyes that saw only a decimal point on a ledger. Their coats had been clean. Their shoes had been polished. And they'd spoken in a language of percentages and default clauses that amounted to the same thing as a gun. I'd sworn to myself, standing in that foreclosure dust with my brother's face gone hollow beside me, that I'd never give another man the chance to clear me from my own ground.

Dinner that night was quiet. Sarah's stew, wilted greens, the last of the salted pork. It tasted like nothing. The kitchen was close with trapped heat, and a single moth circled the lamp, throwing its tiny shadow against the wall in frantic loops. Samuel, the lad who'd been helping with chores, sat at the end of the table with his eyes moving between us, reading the silence the way a young man does when he knows something is wrong but hasn't learned what to do about it. Good boy. Green as new wood, and just as easy to split. He kept his fork moving but he wasn't eating, just pushing the greens in slow circles.

"Larson says the creek is down to a trickle," Sarah said. She didn't look up from her bowl. "He says some of the folks are talking about hauling from the river. Two days' ride each way."

"We aren't hauling from the river." I heard the stone in my own voice, harder than I'd intended.

She set down her spoon. "Elias —"

"I'll dig deeper. I'll go through the bedrock if I have to."

"The bedrock won't give what it doesn't have." She lifted her eyes then. The worry in them was the kind that had been there so long it had grown roots, deep ones, the kind you couldn't pull without tearing something. "The stock needs water. If we lose the ewes —"

"We won't." The word came out sharp, and Samuel flinched. The moth hit the lamp glass with a tiny ping. I set down my fork and pressed my palms flat on the table, feeling the grain of the wood Sarah had sanded smooth the autumn we'd arrived. "I'm sorry. It's the heat."

She held my gaze a moment longer, then nodded and picked up her spoon again. The scrape of tin on tin filled the kitchen.

The last of the light was dying in the west window, going out in smears of gray. I stared at it and thought about the burlap-wrapped stake in the barn, the red paint bright as a wound even in memory. I should have told her. Should have laid it on the table between us and asked what we were going to do. But I could see how her shoulders already carried the drought — the way they rounded forward just slightly, that small surrender she made every time the sky stayed empty. The tendons stood out on the backs of her hands where they held the spoon. She was thinner than she'd been in the spring, and the light carved her cheekbones sharper than I remembered. I couldn't put a human predator on top of what nature had already sent. Not yet. Not tonight.

"I'm going to check the barn once more," I said, and pushed back from the table. The chair legs barked against the floor.

Samuel half-rose. "I can come along, Mr. Thorne. Help with —"

"Stay and finish your supper." I tried to soften it, but I don't think I managed.

Outside, the stars were hard and distant, scattered across a sky so wide it made a man feel like a single figure in someone else's ledger. I put my palm flat on the sod wall before I went inside. The dry grass pricked my skin — rough and real, the same wall I'd cut from this prairie with my own sweat. I could feel the house breathing, the way sod does on summer nights, releasing the day's heat back into the dark.

Not again, I thought. Whatever came next, whatever those railroad men had in mind for my North Field and the name in my ledger, they would have to come to my porch first.

I went into the dark of the barn and stood there a good while, listening to the horses breathe. Their big lungs filled and emptied in a slow, patient rhythm, and I let it steady me the way Sarah's breathing had steadied me that morning. Somewhere under the burlap, the red stake waited. I left it where it was and stayed in the dark until I'd run the numbers enough times to know that fear was just another column that needed balancing.

Chapter 2: Iron and Bone

Eleanor

I had gone to the smithy for a practical reason — the schoolhouse door hinge had finally given way, the pin sheared clean after months of my students swinging it with the careless enthusiasm of children who have not yet learned that everything out here breaks sooner than it should. Titus Croft was the only man in Oak Haven who could set it right. What I found instead was a lesson in the vocabulary of fear, delivered in iron and old wood.

The hammer's rhythm reached me half a block away, driving up through the packed earth of the thoroughfare before it met the ear — a deep, percussive pulse that seemed less like sound than like the town's own heartbeat made audible. I paused at the threshold. Inside, the heat was immediate and total, a dry searing wave carrying coal smoke and sulfur that tightened my throat and brought tears to the corners of my eyes before I could blink them away. The interior was a cavern of soot-blackened timber and orange shadow, the kind of space that would have terrified me in my first weeks here and now struck me only as vital — necessary, the way a hearth is necessary to a house in winter.

Young Samuel Price worked the bellows, his lean frame folding and unfolding with each stroke, coal-stained and earnest in a way that reminded me of my younger students when they bear down on a difficult passage. Titus stood at the anvil — immense, precise, absorbed — his arm rising and falling with a mechanical grace that struck me, as it always did, as something closer to ritual than labor. He was repairing a plowshare, the broken piece jagged, exhausted object that looked like the land itself had finally had enough of being asked to give.

I stepped just inside the threshold and folded my hands over the hinge fragment in my pocket. Neither man noticed me. I had learned, in my months in Oak Haven, that the forge claimed a man's full attention or it claimed something more permanent — a lesson printed, I suspected, in the pale scars that mapped Titus's forearms.

The rhythm broke when Titus plunged the steel into the brine barrel. The hiss was violent, almost animal, and steam rose in a rolling cloud that smelled of salt and scorched metal. When it cleared, Titus was wiping his hands on a rag — and Elias Thorne was walking through the door behind me.

I moved to the side. Elias didn't see me at first; his gaze was fixed ahead with the narrowed focus of a man who has rehearsed what he will say and fears losing his nerve before he says it. He walked to the anvil and laid a burlap-wrapped bundle on the iron surface. When he pulled the cloth away, what clattered against the anvil was a stake — milled clean, smooth, tipped in aggressive red paint. The stamped seal of a railroad company caught the forge light and threw it back in a small, sharp flare.

Titus's fingers hovered over it without touching, as though the paint were something that might transfer.

"Found it fifty yards inside my line," Elias said. His voice was stripped down, quiet in the way that means a man has been rehearsing his composure since dawn. "They didn't knock. They didn't ask. They marked it."

I recognized what I was looking at then. I had seen survey instruments illustrated in the eastern papers — those crisp, authoritative articles full of words like *progress* and *civilization* and *the march of the age.* I had even taught from such articles, had stood before my students and read aloud the rhetoric of expansion with what I now recognized as an embarrassing lack of scrutiny. None of those articles had ever described what the vanguard looked like from the ground. On the anvil, it looked less like progress and more like an accusation.

Jedediah Stone materialized from the shadows by the wagon tires — I had not known he was there, which was characteristic; the old prospector had a way of being present only when the information required it. He spat into the dirt with the gravity of a judge handing down a sentence, then identified the stake in terms that mapped precisely onto what I had suspected: a surveyor's spike, the kind they used to mark rail grades. His voice was like grinding stone, each word worn smooth by decades of weather and tobacco. He had seen them before, he said. In Kansas. Before the towns started dying.

Kansas. The word transformed Elias's face. For a fraction of a second, something ancient moved behind his eyes — not grief exactly, but its harder cousin, the one that doesn't weep but calculates. His jaw clenched, and he gripped the anvil's edge until his knuckles went white against the soot. I found myself holding my own breath, an involuntary sympathy that startled me. In Boston, I had read about frontier hardship the way one reads about illness in a medical text — with interest, with pity, at a safe diagnostic distance. This was not that. This was a man's history breaking the surface of his face like a bone through skin.

Titus put a hand on Elias's shoulder. Heavy, steadying, with the deliberate pressure of a man who knows his own strength and calibrates it. He said nothing to Jedediah, only looked at Elias with an expression I could not quite read — and then, faintly, I thought I could. It was recognition. Two men who had each survived something, confirming each other's survival across a silence that words would only have cheapened. Titus Croft did not speak of wars, but sometimes a man's posture is the whole story, and his — that squared, weight-bearing stillness — told chapters.

"A marker isn't a track, Elias," Titus said quietly. "It's a question. Not an answer."

Samuel stepped forward then, still gripping the bellows handle, coal-stained and earnest. He asked whether the railroad might bring pumps from the East — real machinery, steam-driven, capable of reaching water the hand-dug wells couldn't touch. He asked it with the bright, guileless hope of someone who has not yet learned that the offer and the price are the same sentence. I recognized the tone; I heard it in my classroom when a student answers with such conviction that the wrongness of the answer becomes almost irrelevant beside the courage of the attempt.

I saw Elias's face change before the words came — the tightening around his mouth, the shift in his shoulders.

"You think they're coming to save us?" He turned on the boy with a force that made me draw a breath. The fear and fury inside him had found the most available opening. He told Samuel about the leash that came with the pumps, about owning your land until you signed it away, about the sheriff who knew the railroad's name and the bank that knew your debts. His voice climbed and roughened. He was not wrong about any of it — that was the cruelest part. He was simply using a boy of seventeen as a target for a shade that was standing somewhere else.

Samuel's face collapsed into confused, stinging hurt. His eyes fell to his boots, and his hand slipped from the bellows handle. The workshop was very still, the coals ticking softly as they settled.

Titus moved then — not quickly, but with the unhurried authority of a wall deciding to take a new position. His bulk interposed between Elias and the boy, and he told Samuel to go find out about the coal shipment at Larson's. His voice was level, almost gentle — a cooling bath poured over heated metal. Samuel vanished into the white glare of the street without a word.

Titus waited until the footsteps were gone.

"He's just a boy, Elias." His voice was flat and patient. "He sees the train. He doesn't see the tracks. Snapping at him won't pull that wood from your field. We need more than a piece of wood before we start digging trenches."

Elias stared at the stake. Something moved in his face — not agreement, not yet, but the beginning of the exhaustion that sometimes precedes it.

I remained where I was, near the door, my fingers still closed around the broken hinge in my pocket. This was not my conversation to enter. But I looked at the stake on the anvil and felt the morning's lesson curdle in my chest. That very morning I had been speaking to my students about Manifest Destiny — the great inevitable tide, I had called it, in the language of the textbook, tracing the westward arrows on the map with a piece of chalk that left white dust on my fingers. And here was the tide's calling card, lying on an anvil, red-tipped and indifferent, waiting to be interpreted. I thought of the Whitman I had quoted to my older students the week before — *Passage to India*, the great hymn to rail and telegraph and the stitching together of a continent — and I felt a flush of something close to shame. The poem had not mentioned Elias Thorne's face.

Elias wrapped the stake back in the burlap. His hands were not steady. "I'm keeping it," he said. "If they want it back, they can come to my porch and ask. But I won't be hiring my own land, Titus."

He walked past me toward the door, his eyes fixed ahead. I don't think he remembered I was there.

The burlap bundle rode under his arm like a wound he was carrying home to tend in private.

I stood for a moment longer in the dimness, looking at the anvil where the stake had lain. A faint impression of the red paint remained on the iron, a ghost of color that the next hour's work would burn away. Titus had already turned back to his plowshare. He lifted the hammer with the same deliberate certainty as before — as if to say that the work in front of him was the only problem that yielded to the tools at hand. I envied him that, briefly and entirely.

Clang! Clang! Clang!

I left without asking about the hinge. It seemed, on balance, a small thing. The larger hinge — the one on which something in Oak Haven had just begun to swing — was not an object that any smith could mend.

Chapter 3: A Cathedral of Sod

Eleanor

Five children.

That was the count this morning. Five out of fourteen. I had already known it before I opened the attendance ledger — the room told me in its own language, the way a half-empty page tells a typesetter the story is running short — but I performed the ritual anyway. Running a finger down the column of names, pausing at each absence as though my attention might serve as a kind of proxy presence for the children who were not here. Sarah Hendricks. Benjamin Cole. Little Clara Marsh, who had been halfway through her first real book and was learning to love the feeling of a sentence that surprised her. Twelve years old and out in the fields now, their hands learning the wrong grammar: the vocabulary of the hoe instead of the pen.

The drought wasn't simply drying the wells. It was editing the future.

I set the ledger down and looked at what remained of my congregation. Five faces, scrubbed and present, and the room designed for fourteen felt enormous around them — the whitewashed sod walls amplifying the particular silence of a space built for noise that doesn't come. The light through the east window fell in a long pale rectangle across the empty front desks, illuminating the fine motes of chalk dust that hung suspended in the air like a slow, indifferent snowfall. Usually these floors were a percussion of scuffed boots and restless energy. Today: a dry, earthen stillness, the only sound the faint scratch of a pencil and the tick of the stove clock that Rachel Parker had donated in September.

In the second row, Thomas Parker was failing to stay awake. He was the oldest of the children left to me — twelve going on forty — and today he looked it. His shoulders curved under the weight of a body that had been bent over a hoe since before dawn, the fabric of his mended shirt pulling tight across his back. His head was nodding, chin drifting toward the scarred desk, his pencil idle between fingers that were cracked at the knuckles and stained the color of the Parker farm's red clay. The silt of that place was embedded in the creases of his neck so deeply that no amount of scrubbing reached the skin beneath. I had noticed it weeks ago and had said nothing, because there is a grammar to poverty that does not welcome correction.

"Thomas."

He jerked upright. For a terrifying second he looked straight through me, his eyes fixed on something I couldn't see — a row of dying corn, perhaps, or the inside of a well that had stopped giving back. Then recognition came, and with it a shame that aged him further. His hand closed around his pencil so tightly I heard the wood creak.

"I'm sorry, Miss Vance." His voice broke at the edges. "The well was low. We had to haul from the creek before the sun got high. Pa says every drop counts now."

Every drop. I looked at the empty desks — the books that sat untouched, the slates unmarked, each one a small monument to a child whose education had been suspended by the weather — and felt the third-level emotion I had come to live with in this place: not sadness, not frustration, but a cold, precise fury at a world that forced a child to choose between his letters and his survival. In Boston, I had read about such conditions in reformers' pamphlets, had even signed a petition once, my pen moving across the cream-colored paper with the easy conscience of the geographically distant. I walked to his desk and touched the corner of his slate. The stone was cool, almost damp, a small surprise in this parched room.

"Focus on the work, Thomas," I said. "The land can take your strength. It cannot take what you put in here." I touched my temple. The words were true, and I believed them, but they were growing harder to say without qualification. They were the kind of words that needed a future to land in, and the future, this season, kept receding like the water table.

Outside, the wind lifted, carrying grit against the windowpanes in a dry, pattering hiss. One of the younger girls — Mary Olsen, seven, small as a sparrow — pressed her palm flat against the glass as though comforting it.

The morning lesson was Manifest Destiny — the irony of which was not lost on me. I stood at the front of the room with the textbook open on my palm, speaking of the great westward expansion, of iron rails and the taming of the wild, and watched the words dissolve before they reached the children. The textbook's language was a thing of confident cadences and triumphant nouns: *settlement, progress, the inexorable advance of American civilization.* How does one describe the inevitable triumph of a nation to people who watched their world contract with each passing season? Thomas was copying, his tongue at the corner of his mouth, but his eyes were glazing. The younger ones fidgeted with the listless energy of bodies that wanted to be anywhere else. I closed the book.

"Recess," I said, earlier than scheduled. The word was mercy, and they received it as such. No cheering — they simply stood and moved toward the door with the deliberate gait of people who have learned to conserve. Even their play had become economical, stripped of the excess that childhood is supposed to afford.

I followed them out into the yard and leaned against the doorframe, one hand raised against the noon glare. The sky was a pale, bleached blue, cloudless, the horizon shimmering where the heat turned the distant scrub into something liquid and impermanent. The air smelled of baked earth and the faint, sweet rot of grass that had died standing. The children sat in the thin strip of shade along the schoolhouse wall and poked at the dust with sticks, drawing shapes that the wind erased before they could finish.

Then Thomas stood up.

He was staring south, toward the main thoroughfare, his hand shading his eyes. I followed his gaze. A dark shape was moving across the flats, trailing a long plume of dust. Not a farm wagon or a buckboard — the outline was too deliberate, too polished. A lacquered black buggy, brass lamps catching and throwing back the sun in sharp flashes that made me think, absurdly, of the gaslights on Tremont Street. It moved with a purposeful clip that felt entirely alien to the sluggish rhythm of our town, as though it traveled on a different kind of time.

The children gathered at the yard's edge, sticks forgotten. As the buggy drew closer the details assembled: a high-stepping horse with a braided mane, a man at the reins who wore a crisp dark suit and a black bowler hat. No duster, no felt brim. He looked as though he had been set down here from a different longitude entirely, a figure cut from one page and pasted onto another. Beside him, propped upright on the seat, a brass theodolite on a tripod caught the sun with the glinting, predatory precision of an optical instrument designed to measure what it intends to take.

The buggy stopped at the schoolhouse gate. The horse snorted, tossing foam into the dust, and stamped once, sharply, as if objecting to the quality of the ground. The man climbed down with a practiced fluid ease — his boots, I noticed, polished to a mirror finish that appeared to actively repel the very dirt they stepped in. He adjusted his hat, shot his cuffs, and looked at the schoolhouse with the expression of a man cataloging a curiosity.

I stepped forward. I felt — and I am not proud of this — the posture of Boston reassembling itself in my spine: the severe, upright line I had spent years trying to soften in myself. I was suddenly aware of the pen stain on my fingers, the grit in my hair, the frayed edge of my collar that I had mended twice and that still would not lie flat. I was aware of how I must look to a man who smelled of expensive tobacco and eastern cities and the particular confidence that comes from never having counted raindrops. I let the sun fall full on my face and refused to blink.

"Good afternoon," he said. His voice was smooth, unhurried, carrying the easy authority of someone to whom the sky had never said no. He tipped his hat with formal precision. "I assume I am addressing the mistress of this charming establishment?"

"I am Eleanor Vance," I said. "And you are trespassing on school property during hours of instruction, sir."

He smiled. It was a warm smile, which was worse than a cold one would have been. Warmth you can trust. Warmth that is also indulgence, that reads your circumstances as charming rather than hard-won — that kind unsettles something deeper than hostility ever could. He produced a card from his vest pocket, offered it between two fingers. Thick cream paper. Embossed letters raised beneath my thumb like a whisper meant to be overheard.

Caleb Voss. Chief Surveyor.

I had no difficulty placing him. He was the answer to Elias Thorne's red-tipped stake — the author of that surveyor's spike I'd seen lying on Titus Croft's anvil not two hours ago. I had been speaking to my students about the progress of the nation, and here was its advance man, standing in my schoolyard, looking at my building with the mild, measuring gaze of a man who calculates worth in grades and right-of-way.

"Mr. Voss," I said. "I believe you are a long way from home. There isn't much here to survey but the bones of the land."

"On the contrary, Miss Vance." He seemed genuinely amused, the way a lecturer is amused when a student raises an objection the lecturer has already accounted for. "The geometry of this valley is quite remarkable, once you look past the current meteorological unpleasantness." He gestured at the parched horizon as one gestures at a minor inconvenience — a smudge on a lens, a crease in a map. His eyes moved to the children. "And you are doing noble work. Education is the bedrock of civilization, after all. Though I confess I haven't seen a sod schoolhouse in quite some time. It's very — quaint. Almost a remnant of a different century."

Quaint.

I have been called that word before in one form or another — when I announced I was going west, when I told Boston acquaintances I intended to teach on the plains. It is the word the comfortable apply to the determined when they cannot quite bring themselves to say *foolish.* I looked at the building behind me — the uneven roofline, the dark rectangle of the doorway, the faded flag I had hung above the lintel on the first day of term. I thought of the hours Titus had spent bracing its timbers, his big hands patient with the joints. Of Rachel

Parker scrubbing the interior walls with lye and a brush until they shone, her knees raw on the dirt floor. Of the books I had hauled across half a continent wrapped in oilcloth, each one chosen as deliberately as a seed for soil I had never seen. What stood there was not a curiosity. It was an argument. It was the proposition that a child in a drought-stricken territory has as much right to Homer and long division as a child in a Beacon Hill parlor.

"It serves its purpose, Mr. Voss," I said. "It keeps the minds of these children from turning to dust along with the crops."

Voss tilted his head, something sharpening behind his eyes — a recalibration, as though he had expected less resistance and was adjusting his instruments accordingly. "You'd be surprised what I account for. I grew up in places not unlike this. I know the value of a book in a wilderness." He paused, and for a moment I thought I saw something genuine flicker across his face — a memory, perhaps, of a schoolroom smaller than mine. Then the polish reassembled. "But a book cannot pull a train. A train is what will truly save these children." He looked at Thomas, who was watching him with the paralyzed fascination of a rabbit watching a hawk. "Wouldn't you rather ride the rails than dig in the mud, young man?"

Thomas said nothing. His fingers worked at the hem of his dirt-caked shirt. His eyes were very large.

I stepped between them. The movement was instinct — the same instinct that moves a teacher to stand between a student and anything that might reduce his world to a simpler, more dangerous shape. "The railroad brings many things, Mr. Voss. It rarely brings freedom. Now — if you have business in Oak Haven, I suggest you tend to it. My students have a lesson to finish."

He nodded, pleasant and entirely undeterred, the way a current is undeterred by a stone it simply flows around. "I do indeed have business. I'm looking for the Thorne property. To the north, near the creek headwaters. A large field — mostly wheat?"

The yard seemed to contract. I looked at the theodolite in the buggy, its lenses catching the sun with cold precision, and understood that he was not asking for directions. He was confirming a target. The red stake in Elias's barn was not a question, as Titus had offered. It was an opening sentence. Caleb Voss was the paragraph that followed, and the theodolite was the punctuation — exact, mechanical, final.

"Follow the track north," I said. "You can't miss it. It's the only land left that's still trying to grow something."

"Thank you, Miss Vance." He climbed back into the buggy, gathered the reins, and tipped his hat one final time. The brass fittings gleamed. "I'm certain we'll have much more to discuss in the coming days. Civilization has a way of making itself heard — even in a cathedral of sod."

He snapped the reins. The buggy surged forward, its wheels churning up a fresh wave of dust that drifted across the yard and settled on the children's faces in a fine new layer of gray. Mary Olsen sneezed. Thomas didn't move.

I stood and watched the buggy diminish down the thoroughfare until it dissolved into the pale shimmer at the road's end. In my hand, the embossed card: *Caleb Voss. Chief Surveyor.* The raised letters pressed into my thumb like a small, insistent argument. I had been teaching Manifest Destiny as theory, as the abstraction of a historical process — the kind of thing one describes in measured sentences to children who copy it into their slates and forget it by supper. But Thomas Parker was standing three feet from me, still staring down the empty road, his fingers still knotted in his shirt hem, his eyes holding the precise expression of someone who has just been told the story he lives in has a different ending than he imagined.

The lesson was not over. It had simply moved outside the building, where the textbook could not contain it and the chalk dust could not soften its edges.

I rang the bell to call them back in. The sound carried across the empty yard and out over the prairie, thin and bright and, for the moment, unanswered.

Chapter 4: Lines in the Dirt

Elias

I saw the dust before I saw the man. A thin, rising spire a mile out, moving steady against the white-hot sky. My hands tightened around the porch railing — the wood hot enough to sting, the sap long since baked out of it. I didn't need to see him to know who it was. I'd felt the pull of that buggy since I'd yanked the red-tipped stake from my soil two days ago, the way you feel a storm building before the first cloud shows.

The air tasted of parched earth and the electric nothing of an approaching storm that meant to deliver heat but no rain. A horsefly circled my wrist once and moved on. My ribs pressed inward from the inside — the old Kansas feeling, the one that starts in the chest and works down into the gut where the numbers live. Not again. I'd built this place out of sod and sheer will. I'd buried a brother in the tallgrass of another state because I'd been too slow to read the circling. I wouldn't be slow this time.

"Sarah." I didn't turn. "Get inside. Take the boy. Stay away from the windows."

The screen door creaked behind me — the dry complaint of hinges I kept meaning to oil and never did. Then I heard the floorboards groan as she stepped up beside me instead. The faint scent of lye soap and dried lavender came with her, soft and out of place in a yard that was slowly turning back to desert.

"I'm staying, Elias." That iron note in her voice — the one she used when the well coughed up silt or the winter ran lean. I looked at her. The sun had engraved new lines around her eyes, a decade of squinting at empty horizons doing what time alone could not. Her apron was faded stiff, and her hands were reddened at the knuckles from the morning's washing. But her jaw was set in a line that matched my own. "This is my home as much as yours. I won't be hid away like a shame while a stranger walks our dirt."

I wanted to argue. Men like the one in that buggy don't take stock of a woman's resolve — they look at grade percentages and right-of-way. But I looked at the North Field, at the way her eyes moved to the stunted wheat with the same proprietary weight as mine. She knew each row. She'd helped me seed half of them, walking the furrows with the bag on her hip until her back seized. She was witness to this. She was the reason the ledger had a purpose beyond debt. I gave one short nod and turned back to the road.

Caleb Voss stopped the buggy exactly where my property began. Not at the gate, not past the gate — exactly at the line. A measurement, not a courtesy. He sat there a long moment adjusting his bowler hat, assessing my house as though he were checking the plumb of the walls. I could see his eyes moving over the dry troughs, the barn with its sagging roof, the fence posts I'd shimmed with flat stones. He was cataloging weakness the way a man catalogs inventory. He was too clean. Dark wool suit, not a drop of sweat on him. He might as well have been made from a different sky.

He flicked the reins and brought the horse into the yard and stopped ten feet from the porch. The dust cloud he'd trailed drifted over us in a fine choking veil, settling on Sarah's apron, on the porch boards, on the backs of my hands. I didn't cough. I held still and watched him climb down — fluid, unhurried — and reach into the buggy for a leather satchel. Every movement he made said the same thing: this man had never once had to move with the heavy-limbed exhaustion of a body that had been working since before light.

"Mr. Thorne, I presume," he said, stepping forward. His voice was smooth, carrying the easy assurance of a man whose numbers always balanced. "And Mrs. Thorne. A pleasure. My name is Caleb Voss. I believe Miss Vance may have mentioned my arrival."

"You're trespassing, Mr. Voss." I didn't move from the railing. Hands loose, visible. "The road ends at the gate. Everything else you're standing on belongs to the name in my ledger."

He smiled. Not a cold smile — that I could have used. It was the smile of a man who has decided your situation is an inconvenience he can heal. He looked around the yard, noting the dry troughs, the barn roof we couldn't afford to fix, the cracked ground where the garden patch had been before we stopped being able to spare the water. "It's a hard year, Elias. May I call you Elias? I've seen the reports. The creek at its lowest in twenty years. Your neighbors at the Parker place — their well has gone to mud, I hear. To work this hard and have the sky turn its back on you. A tragedy, truly."

The sympathy was a tool. I could feel it probing for the crack the way you test a fence post with your boot. He stepped closer and leaned one hand on the hitching post — easy, familiar, as though the post were his. "I'm not here to trespass. I'm here to offer a hand up. The railroad — the Chicago and North Western — isn't just iron and steam. It's a lifeline. It brings the water you can't find in the ground. It brings seed you can't afford to buy. It brings a market for that wheat, assuming it survives another week."

"We aren't for sale." The words came out harder than I meant them to. Sarah's warmth at my shoulder was the only thing keeping the rest of the sentence from being something I couldn't take back. "We've endured drought before. We'll endure this one. We don't need a lifeline with a bill attached."

Voss sighed the way a man sighs when he's performing patience. He opened the satchel and unrolled a heavy parchment against the side of his buggy. The lines on it were sharp, black, and perfectly straight — the clean geometry of a man who has never had to contend with the organic, disobedient shape of actual land. My North Field was a rectangle on that map, bisected by a double line. A scar drawn in advance. I could smell the ink, fresh and chemical, the smell of decisions made in offices far from the dirt they intended to cross.

"Not bills, Elias. A fair price. For the right-of-way through the North Field — a hundred-foot strip along the grade — the company is prepared to offer five hundred dollars in gold. Cash. Today."

The number hit me like a fist to the sternum. Five hundred dollars. More money than I'd turned in five years of farming. I ran it the way I run everything — against what I owed. The mortgage: settled. A new pump for the well: bought and installed. A winter without sitting up in the dark running columns that wouldn't balance. Feed for the stock. Shoes for Samuel. A dress for Sarah that didn't need mending. I looked at the North Field and the invisible line Voss wanted to make permanent. My best soil. The only ground that held moisture deep enough to give the wheat a fighting chance.

"Five hundred dollars," Sarah whispered, barely more than air.

I didn't look at her. I knew what I'd find — the same calculation I was running, the same terrible arithmetic of survival. I looked instead at Voss. At the way he was watching me. Patient. Still. The way a man watches a scale when he knows which way the needle is tipping. He wasn't looking at a man. He was looking at a barrier about to be cleared. I thought of the hours I'd spent hauling rocks from that field until my fingernails tore and the blood mixed with the dirt. He saw a grade percentage. He saw a decimal point.

"If I sell you that strip, the field is gone," I said, steadying my voice. "You'll bring crews and blasting powder and iron. You'll kill the soil for fifty yards on either side with smoke and grease. Then you'll put up a fence, and my cattle can't reach the creek without asking your permission. I didn't come out here to be a tenant on my own land."

Voss shook his head slowly, as if disappointed in a student who can't follow a simple proof. "Elias. Progress isn't an option. It's a tide. You can build a pier and profit, or you can let it wash you away. That five hundred is salvation. Without it, how long can you hold out? Two months? Three? If the rain doesn't come by August, you'll walk away with nothing but the clothes on your back. I've seen it happen to better men. Men in

Kansas, in Nebraska — they held onto their pride until they were starving, and then they sold for pennies to the banks."

Kansas.

The word detonated. The foreclosure notice on my brother's door, nailed up in the damp morning while the birds still sang. The smell of that paper — pulpy, official, soaked with dew that had more water in it than our well. The cold flat eyes of the sheriff who'd stood aside while the bank men walked through the rooms, touching nothing, owning everything. I felt the copper edge of it at the back of my throat, and my hands found the railing again and gripped. Voss saw it. I know he did — he stepped closer, dropped his voice to something neighborly and intimate, the voice a man uses when he's closing a sale and knows the buyer is almost broken. "Take the money. Pay your debts. Buy a new team. You can still farm the rest of the acreage, and when the train stops here, your land will be worth ten times what it is now. Do it for her. Do it for your son."

I looked at Sarah. She was gripping the porch post, her knuckles gone pale, her eyes fixed on the map. The tendons in her wrist stood out like wire. She looked at me, and I saw the longing in her face — the bone-deep exhaustion of a woman who has been fighting the sky for years and would like, just once, to stop. She wanted to say yes. I could see it the way I can see rain coming — in the shift of the air, in the softening of something that had been holding. But then her gaze dropped to my hands — the dirt-stained, scarred hands that had built this house and planted these crops — and I saw her jaw set again, slow and deliberate, like a gate closing.

"No." The word was small. It sat on the air like a piece of iron dropped on stone. "The North Field stays as it is. No tracks. No right-of-way."

Voss didn't flinch. He rolled the parchment slowly, the dry paper rasping in the heat, and buckled his satchel with a deliberate click. He looked at me, and the warmth was gone. His eyes were the color of winter morning sky — pale, flat, a long way from mercy.

"I was hoping you'd be a practical man. It would have made things much easier." He climbed back up into the buggy and gathered the reins, but didn't snap them yet. He let the silence build the way a man lets a fire draw before he sets the bellows to it. "The company has a large department in Chicago. Lawyers. Men who spend their lives studying the fine print of land grants and territorial charters. They handle the obstinate cases. Eminent domain is a very powerful tool, Mr. Thorne — a legal way of saying that the needs of the many outweigh the stubbornness of the one."

A brief sharp smile. "I'll be in town a few weeks. If you change your mind before the lawyers get involved, the offer stands. But every day you wait, the price goes down. Progress doesn't like to be kept waiting."

He snapped the reins. The buggy swept in a wide arc and was gone, leaving a fresh cloud of dust to settle across the porch boards. The horse's hooves faded into a rhythm I couldn't unhear — steady, mechanical, the cadence of something coming that didn't care whether you were ready.

I stood there long after it cleared. The North Field was still standing, the wheat bending in the hot wind, but it looked different now — not a harvest waiting to happen, but ground being disputed. Lines had been drawn across it by a man who'd never planted a seed, and the worst of it was that some of those lines ran through my own chest, dividing what I wanted from what I could afford. I felt the weight of that office in Chicago: hundreds of men in suits who had never touched my dirt but knew exactly how to take it with a stroke of a pen.

A hand found mine. Sarah's. Rough, warm, shaking with a fine tremor she couldn't suppress. I took her hand and laced my dirty fingers through hers, trying to give back something steadier than I felt. Her thumb pressed against my knuckle — once, twice — the small, wordless code we'd developed in the years since words started costing too much.

"We did the right thing," she whispered. "Didn't we? Elias?"

I looked at the sky — that enormous, indifferent sky — and then at the dry cracking earth beneath my boots. The wheat rustled. A crow lifted from the fence line and banked west, riding the updraft with an ease I envied.

"I don't know," I said. The words tasted like the dust that coated everything out here — flat, gritty, honest. "But it's our dirt. And for today, that's enough."

Chapter 5: The Dry Well

Elias

The morning came in gray and grudging, the color of old ash. I was already standing at the edge of the North Field when the light was still uncertain, Voss's words from the day before sitting cold and heavy in my gut like a meal that wouldn't digest. The wheat hung motionless, heads down, the stillness wrong in a way I couldn't name. Not the quiet of a field at rest. The held breath of something waiting. A grasshopper ticked once in the stubble at my feet and went silent.

A mile south, a thin plume of dust lifted from the Parker homestead. Too early for a social call. Too fast for a wagon going to town. In this country, a man doesn't run his horse unless the house is on fire or the soul is leaving the body. The plume widened as it rose, a pale smear against the gray sky, and I could just make out the dark dot of a buggy beneath it, swaying hard.

I turned toward the house. Sarah was already on the porch, hand up against the glare, watching the same thing. Her lips were parted, and I could see the question forming before she spoke it. She didn't speak it. She just looked at me.

"Elias!" The voice carried thin and sharp across the flats, and then Rachel Parker's buggy was swaying dangerously at our gate, the pony lathered and blowing, ribs heaving. She didn't wait for the wheels to stop. She half-fell from the seat, her bonnet hanging by its strings, her face a sweating, gray-white mask of terror. Her dress was stained at the hem with something dark and wet — well mud. "Elias, it's gone. It's all gone."

I caught her by the arms. She was shaking — the deep, fine tremor of a body in shock, like a bird in the hand. Her sleeve was rough under my fingers, the wool stiff with dried sweat. "Rachel. Slow down. What's gone? The stock?"

"The water." She looked past me, her eyes unfocused, fixed on the flat horizon as though looking for something that had already left. "I went to draw the morning bucket. I dropped the stone. It hit — it didn't splash. It thudded. Like dropping a rock on a barn floor. I hauled it up and there was nothing but thick gray mud. Slime and pebbles. I kept dropping it, thinking I'd hit a shelf, but there's nothing. The well is dry."

The air went out of me.

A dry well is a death sentence on the plains. You can lose a crop and survive on grit. You can lose a barn and rebuild it with neighbors. But when the earth stops giving water, the clock starts — and it's a clock with no winding key. I thought of my own well, the daily ritual of measuring the drop, the thin splash I'd been tracking with a sick precision, charting the decline in my head the way I charted debts in the ledger. Three inches less this week. Five less the week before. I looked at the smear of wet silt on Rachel's cheek where she'd touched her face, and the panic in her eyes landed somewhere below my ribs and stayed.

"Thomas tried to dig," she said, her voice climbing toward the edge. "He's down there now, clawing at the bottom with a hand-trowel. He's screaming that he can smell the damp. But it's just dust, Elias. My boy is down in the dark breathing dust."

"Sarah." My voice came out rough and dry as the ground. But my wife was already there — stepping off the porch with two heavy stoneware jugs, no questions asked. She'd seen the gray mud on Rachel's skirts and read the rest herself. Her face was set in that way she has when the numbers have turned bad and the only thing left is to move. She put the first jug in Rachel's hands with a firm, decisive nod. "Drink. Then we're going to Larson's. If your vein has collapsed, the others need to know. We can't have people digging blind in this heat."

Rachel took the jug with both hands. Water slopped over her wrists and she looked at it — at the waste of it running off her skin into the dirt — with an expression I hope I never see again.

The ride to Oak Haven was a blur of shimmer and the hollow clatter of the buggy. I sat in the back, hand on the handle of my shovel. It felt like the wrong tool for everything that was coming. The road was hard-packed and rutted, each jolt traveling up through my spine. We passed the schoolhouse — Eleanor Vance was outside ringing the bell for stragglers — and she stopped mid-pull when she saw our faces. The bell clanged once and fell silent. She knew the look of a funeral procession before the body was cold. She put her hand on the bell rope and watched us pass, and I thought I saw her mouth form a word — *who?* — but we were already beyond earshot.

Larson's Emporium had the smell it always had — cured hams, floor wax, the press of bodies — but the atmosphere was already wrong when we pushed through the door. Half the town was there, clustered around the cold potbellied stove in the posture of men who need a center to stand near even when there's no fire in it. Anders Larson behind the counter, his face the color of old flour, finger tracing his ledger edge the way a man traces a scar. Titus Croft at the window, massive, still, arms folded over his leather apron, blocking the light. He looked like he had been cast from the same material as the anvil. His eyes found mine when I walked in, and he gave the smallest nod — the kind that says *I know* and *go on.*

"The Parkers' well has gone," I said.

The room stopped breathing.

"Mud in the bucket," Rachel added, stronger now that there were walls around her. She stepped forward, hands clasped hard enough to whiten the knuckles. "We have five head of cattle and two horses that won't make it to sundown without a soak. I'm asking for help. We haul from the creek — it's low, I know it's low, but it's still moving back by the ridge."

Jedediah Stone spat into the brass spittoon. The ping rang out like a shot. "Creek won't hold the whole town, Rachel. It's a trickle over a sandbar. You start dipping a hundred buckets a day, you'll be drinking tadpole spit by Tuesday."

"Then we dig deeper!" Pete Higgins shoved his way forward from the back, eyes wild, the cords in his neck standing out. He'd been running on anger and no sleep for a while now, and it showed — his shirt was dark with sweat at the collar, his beard gone ragged. "I'm down to forty feet and the air down there is a furnace. My wife's boiling the wash water three times just to keep it for the hogs. And now Voss is out there with his steam pumps — I saw 'em on his supply wagon. Could pull water from the center of the earth."

The name ignited the room. Voices erupted — overlapping, sharp, climbing. I felt the Kansas ghost stir, that cold, familiar current, the one that rises when fear finds a crowd and the crowd finds a cause. I looked at the faces around me. Neighbors. Men who had helped raise my barn, women who had sat with Sarah during the fever winter. They were changing in front of me, the edges of them going sharp and inward. Fear does that. It turns a man's gaze away from the person standing next to him and fixes it on whatever door is closest.

"Voss says if we sign the right-of-way, the railroad brings in the tankers!"

"They have the equipment! They have the money!"

"They have the leash!" I stepped forward, boots loud on the floorboards. Every eye in the room swung to me. "You think that water is free? Those pumps come with a price that'll hang around your neck for twenty years. Look at his map. He's not looking for water — he's looking for a grade. He'll give you a drink today and own your dirt tomorrow."

"It's easy for you to talk, Thorne!" Higgins put himself in front of me. I could smell the sourness of a man who hadn't slept — stale sweat, stale fear, the two indistinguishable. "You've got the deep vein. You've got the North Field. My kids are crying because their throats are too dry to swallow cornmeal. You want me to tell 'em to die for your pride?"

The words stung. They stung because the arithmetic behind them was real. I looked at Titus, wanting an anchor, but the blacksmith's eyes were fixed on the street. His jaw worked once, but he said nothing. The town wasn't just thirsty. It was cracking along the fault lines we'd spent years filling in with neighborly silence, and the sound of the cracking was louder than anything I could say.

"We organize a water council." Rachel stepped up onto a crate of dry goods, her voice cutting clean through the argument. Her authority in this moment was absolute — a woman who had just lost her well, standing taller for it. The mud was still on her skirts, and she wore it like evidence. "Anders, you have the ledger. We list every head of stock, every soul in this town. We ration the creek. One wagon at a time, twice a day. Elias, you have the strongest team — you and Titus coordinate the hauling for the widows and the far-out places. No one sells. No one signs anything while they're too thirsty to read the fine print."

For a moment the room held. The plain sense of it landed like cool water on hot stone. Men looked at their boots. Anders opened his ledger and licked the tip of his pencil. The argument subsided into a hollow, grim-eyed settling. But as the gathering broke up — people filtering out to wagons, preparing for the first creek run — I saw what remained. I saw Pete Higgins's hand linger on the doorframe as he left, like a man afraid to release the last solid thing. I saw the way his wife waited for him by the wagon, her face closed and still, a child on each hip.

Outside, the midday sun hit like a flat palm. The air didn't move. It just sat.

Jedediah was on the edge of the porch whittling a piece of dry cedar, the shavings curling off in pale strips that dropped into the dust and didn't stir. He didn't look up. "You heard 'em, Elias. They're scared. And a scared man is just a man waiting for a reason to be a coward."

"They're neighbors. They're trying to survive."

"Surviving ain't the same as living." He squinted up at me against the glare. His eyes were like old leather, creased and faded but still sharp. "Saw Pete talking to Voss's driver this morning. Over by the livery. Wasn't talking about the weather. He was looking at those pumps like they were the Pearly Gates."

I looked down the main street. Voss's black lacquered buggy sat outside the hotel, polished and alien in the gray-dust world, throwing back the sun in hard bright flashes that hurt to look at. I thought of the red-tipped stake in my barn. I thought about the way it had felt in my hand — smooth, manufactured, indifferent to the soil it had pierced. A thing made in a factory by men who had never planted a row.

Pete came out of the store, head down. He didn't mount up. He stood beside his horse with one hand on the animal's dry, matted neck, stroking it in a slow, absent rhythm. The horse leaned into his hand, and the tenderness of that — a man comforting his animal when he couldn't comfort himself — tightened something in my chest. I walked over.

"Pete," I said. "We'll get the water moving. Start with your place after the Parkers."

He turned to look at me, and what was in his face wasn't anger anymore. It was the hollow, used-up look of a man who has let out all the rope and found the end. His eyes were rimmed red. His lips were cracked. "I can't wait for a council, Elias." His voice broke on the last word. "I can't wait for you to decide what my kids' lives are worth. Voss made me an offer. The back ten acres. Just enough for the track to curve."

"Pete. You sign that, he'll have the rest by Christmas. You know how they work."

"I know how it feels to hear my daughter cough and watch dust come out!" The anger flared back, bright and brief, then guttered. He put his boot in the stirrup and climbed up, his hands shaking with the reins. He looked at me — and I saw a stranger where a neighbor used to stand. Ten years of barn-raisings and shared harvest meals and borrowed tools, and the drought had burned through it in a season. "You keep your dirt, Thorne. Keep your pride and your deep well. I'm keeping my family. If that makes me a sell-out in your ledger, write it down. But write down that you were the one who wouldn't help when the world went dry."

He rode out. The dust he kicked up hung in the air long after he was gone, a pale curtain that settled slow.

I stood on the boardwalk and held very still. Copper taste at the back of my throat. The sun bore down on the back of my neck, and I let it, the way you let a weight sit that you've earned. Through the Emporium window I could see Rachel and Sarah still talking to the other women, holding together what could be held. Sarah had her hand on Rachel's arm, and Rachel was nodding, and for a moment the simple sight of two women choosing each other over panic was the only solid thing in the world.

I thought about the ledger in my desk — the columns of what I owed and what I owned. I'd been adding to it for ten years, trying to make the numbers say: this land is mine, this work has meaning, this ground will hold. But the ground was shifting. Sand and nothing underneath. And the wind that carried it offered nothing back — just the steady, faceless pressure of progress marching toward my gate, indifferent as weather, patient as thirst.

I went to get the wagon. We had water to haul.

Chapter 6: Shadows in the Sage

Titus

The coals were low by the time Samuel came in. I knew something was wrong before he opened his mouth. The boy's posture said it — shoulders caved, weight back on his heels, like a green joint that hadn't been properly set. His hands hung at his sides, opening and closing on nothing.

I kept working. The bar I was drawing out needed another heat. I watched the color run from cherry to bright orange, let it reach the right depth, then carried it to the anvil. Three strikes. Four. The metal spread the way I wanted — clean, even, obedient to the shape I had in mind. I set it back in the fire and turned.

"You're supposed to be with the herd, Samuel," I said.

He stood in the doorway, dust-caked and hollow-eyed, the forge light catching the soot streaks on his face. He looked like he'd been standing out there a while, working up the nerve. His jaw moved once before the words came. "Two are gone," he said. "Two calves. Rachel's calves. I heard something last night, Titus. On the ridge. Riders." He dropped his eyes to his boots. The leather was scuffed white at the toes. "I thought maybe I was imagining it. Like the books. But they're gone, and I'm afraid to tell Mr. Thorne."

I looked at him. Sixteen years old, maybe seventeen. Thin arms, thin face. Green wood. But the fear in him was real — not the soft kind, the kind that makes a man lie down. This was the harder kind that makes him walk into a smithy and say what he'd done. That kind has iron in it, even when the boy carrying it doesn't know it yet.

I pulled the bar from the fire and quenched it. The steam rose fast, sharp with the smell of brine. I set the piece on the rack, wiped my hands on my apron, and walked to the water barrel. I plunged my arms in up to the elbow. The cool hit the heat in my skin, and the day settled into its proper weight. I held them there a moment. The boy watched. Waiting.

"Tell me about the riders," I said, arms still in the water.

He swallowed. "Three of them. On the northern ridge, maybe an hour past midnight. They sat high — not like the men here. They moved along the skyline and dropped into the draws toward the Badlands. I didn't light the lantern. I just watched."

"Good. A light would've made you a target." I pulled my arms out, dried them slow. The water darkened the leather of my apron where it dripped. "Get your horse. Show me where you saw them."

★ ★ ★

We reached the creek as the sun was baking the last shadow out of the draw. Samuel had left the herd secured at the Parkers' fence. Smart. The boy had more sense in him than he gave himself credit for. The creek bed was empty now — just gravel and dried silt and the confused stamps of forty head of cattle going in circles. What water remained pooled in a few low places, brown and still.

I didn't look at the ridge first. I looked at the mud.

Near a stand of willow roots, the silt was still soft enough to hold an impression. I crouched. My knees popped — loud in the quiet — and I braced one hand on the bank. The print was a crescent shape, sharp edges, nail head at the heel. I traced it with my thumb. The iron was thin. Light. Not a farm horse — farm teams in Oak Haven go barefoot because shoes cost money and the sod is soft enough for it. This shoe was built for speed. Built for roads that didn't end at a fence line.

I moved a few feet and cleared away a layer of dry leaves. Another print. Then a third. A line of them, climbing out of the creek bottom and heading northwest toward the draws. The stride was long and even. No hesitation.

"What do you see?" I said.

Samuel crouched beside me. His breathing had steadied since we'd left town. "A horse. Big one."

"Shod. Thin shoes. Built for distance, not pulling." I stood and scanned the horizon. The ridge where Samuel had seen his shadows was empty now, just sagebrush and pale sky and the flat, hard line where the land met nothing. The tracks ran straight and deliberate toward the Badlands. A man who knows where he's going doesn't wander.

These weren't local men. A local man who needed beef would've taken from his own neighbor, quietly, and hoped no one counted for a week. These men rode in and rode out fast. That was professional work. That was men who knew the ground before they came. I studied the spacing of the hoofprints. Whoever shod this horse knew his trade — the nails were set clean, no deviation. I respected the work even as I marked the man for a thief.

"They didn't wander off," Samuel said. He'd figured it already. Good.

"No." I walked the track line another twenty yards, confirming the direction. Two sets of prints for the calves — small, cloven, pressed deep into the silt by the weight of young animals being pushed faster than they'd choose to move. One horse, maybe two, flanking. Driven, not followed. "These are men who ride for a living. Scouts, or thieves with a buyer. The town's been watching Voss and his surveyors, and we left the back side open."

Samuel was quiet. I could see him working through it — what he'd done, what he hadn't done, what it meant. His shoulders had straightened some since we'd started reading the tracks. Doing a thing — even a hard thing — is easier than standing still with the weight of not knowing.

"I was practicing with the rope," he said finally. His voice was low, ashamed. "That's when they came."

"They would've come whether you were watching or not. The rope had nothing to do with it." I said it because it was true, not to make him feel better. The boy needed fact, not comfort. Comfort bends. Fact holds. "We have to tell Elias."

The boy stiffened. "He'll think I failed him."

"You didn't fail." I looked at him straight. Eye to eye. He needed to hear it plain, and he needed to see it in a face that didn't look away. "You found the prints. You came to me. You didn't hide it or make up a story. That's not failure, Samuel. But Elias has to know because this isn't just two missing calves. It's somebody testing the fence. And if we don't answer, they'll come back and push harder."

That landed. I watched it settle into him the way a proper weld settles — not flashy, just solid. His chin came up. His hands stopped fidgeting. He wasn't a different boy, but the one he already was had firmed up some.

We mounted up and rode for the Thorne homestead. The Badlands were a dark shape to the west, cut into the land like a scar the earth had given itself. Somewhere in their draws, men were eating beef that didn't belong to them. I thought about the prints. I thought about the thin shoes built for speed. I thought about how the strike pattern of a well-shod horse tells you something about the farrier, and how the farrier tells you something about the outfit.

Men who rode for someone, or men who were simply desperate. Didn't matter which, not yet. What mattered was that the tracks existed, and now they were ours to answer.

The sun climbed. The gravel road stretched ahead. Two horses and two riders under a sky that had no particular opinion about any of it. Samuel rode beside me and said nothing, which showed better judgment than most grown men I knew. His back was straighter than it had been when he'd walked into my shop this morning. Not much. Enough.

The boy was learning. That was something. That was a start.

Chapter 7: The Law of the Sod

Elias

I was cleaning the Winchester when they came over the rise.

The rifle lay across my knees, the stock warm from the porch boards, the barrel catching the morning light in a long bright line. I'd been at it since before coffee, running the oiled rag through the bore with the slow, deliberate care of a man who doesn't intend to use a thing but wants it ready. The smell of gun oil mixed with the dry, mineral scent of the yard. Sarah had left a cup of chicory on the railing. It had gone cold.

I knew before they pulled up. Two riders at this hour meant bad news. Good news walks to your door and knocks. Bad news rides in with a purpose. I kept my thumb on the hammer and watched them come — Samuel on his roan, leaning forward the way a boy does when he's carrying something he wants to be rid of, and Titus behind him, silent as a fence post, riding that big bay of his with the stillness of a man who's already done his thinking. The morning grit had already settled into the creases of my neck. My hands smelled of lye soap and gun oil.

I stepped off the porch. "Samuel. You're early from the graze." My eyes went to Titus. "And you brought the smith."

Samuel swallowed. I could see the knot in his throat work. He gripped the saddle horn with both hands as though it might steady his voice. "It's the stock, sir. Two calves. Rachel's yearlings. They're gone."

The Winchester went still in my hands.

Gone. I stood there and let the word do its work, turning it over like a stone to see what was underneath. The wind came through the dry cornfield behind the barn. That hollow rattle of dead stalks — the sound the land makes when it has nothing left to give. A meadowlark took off from the fence wire, and the wire hummed after it, a thin metallic note that faded into the heat.

"Gone," I said. "Wandered?"

"Stolen," Titus said. His voice was flat, certain. The way a man states a measurement. "Samuel saw riders on the ridge last night. Shod horses. Light shoes for speed. I read the tracks myself. They went north through the draws. Those calves didn't wander, Elias."

The weariness I'd been carrying since first light cracked open into something harder. I looked past them toward the North Field, where Voss's red-tipped stakes stood in a row like a tally of everything I was losing. Shod horses. Men who ride distance. Men who've done this before. I ran the arithmetic: two calves meant less than thirty dollars in normal times, but nothing was normal. Rachel's herd was already thin. Those yearlings were the seed of next year's stock — the margin between holding on and going under.

"Men who don't care for the law of this sod," I said, almost to myself, "because they've got a bigger law behind them."

"You think it's the railroad?" Samuel said. His voice was careful, testing.

I turned on him. Maybe too fast. "Voss makes us an offer we can't swallow, and when we say no, our fences get tested. Our cattle walk off in the night. You think that's a coincidence?" I heard myself talking and knew some of it was the anger I'd been banking all season, finally drawing on its own. But the anger had a ledger behind it, and the ledger added up. "This is how it worked in Kansas. My brother's place. They don't always use a gavel first. Sometimes they use the dark. Make a man desperate enough and the railroad money starts to look like salvation instead of a collar."

I started pacing. The Winchester cradled against my chest. The porch boards creaked with each pass. "I won't be bled out by men in bowler hats. Not calves. Not land. Not one inch of it."

"Elias." Titus stepped forward. Not aggressive — just present, the way an anvil is present. His shadow fell across the yard, long and solid. "We don't know it's Voss's men. Hungry men do ugly things in a drought year. Half the territory's on its knees."

"I know what I see." But even as I said it, I felt the heat in me drop a degree. Titus had a particular way of making the temperature in a room go reasonable. You couldn't shout usefully in his direction. The man absorbed anger the way iron absorbs heat — took it in, held it, let it cool.

I stopped pacing. I looked toward the road, where the dust from their arrival was still settling in pale drifts. "Samuel. Ride to the Parkers. Then the Higgins place. Tell them we meet at the schoolhouse at sundown. Every man with a horse." I paused. "And tell them to bring their rifles."

Samuel's eyes widened, but he nodded and reined his roan around. Titus watched him go, then looked at me. He didn't say anything. He didn't need to. The look said: *Be careful what you light.* I held it a moment, then went inside to tell Sarah.

⋆ ⋆ ⋆

The schoolhouse smelled of tobacco and gun oil by the time the sun went down.

Eleanor Vance stood at the front of the room with a brass bell in her hand and an expression that said she'd use it. She looked like a woman trying to keep a lantern lit in a crosswind. The kerosene lamps threw long shadows across the blackboard, across the neat chalk lines of arithmetic that would have meant nothing to most of the men filing in. Someone had pushed her desk to the side. The children's slates were stacked in a corner, and in their place stood the hard geometry of grown men with weapons — rifles propped against desk legs, shotguns across laps, the dull gleam of oiled metal catching the yellow light.

I stood near the center of the room, watching them come. Anders Larson, jaw set, eyes down, his ledger book clutched to his chest like a talisman. The Higgins brothers, both flushed and raw, their faces carrying the look of men who have been awake too long. Pete Higgins with the look of a man who has been adding up small losses for so long the total has finally become intolerable. He caught my eye and held it — not hostile, not friendly, just the flat acknowledgment of a man measuring another man's resolve.

"Gentlemen," Eleanor said. "This is a house of learning. Let us speak with the order this community deserves."

"Order?" Pete's chair scraped. "My well's a mud hole, Eleanor. And now there are thieves on the ridges." He looked at me. "What's the law say about that?"

The law says whatever the men with the most ink decide it says. But I kept that to myself.

I stepped into the center of the room. The floorboards were gritty underfoot. I told them what Titus and Samuel had found — the tracks, the shod shoes, the angle of the trail heading north into the draws. I told them what I believed it meant. Some of them already suspected it. I could see it in the way they nodded before I finished the sentence. A few didn't want to believe it, and I watched their faces work through the arithmetic — the slow, grudging calculation of men who are being asked to accept that the trouble has more than one direction.

"We ride a patrol," I said. "Four men a night. Armed. If a shod horse on the ridge doesn't belong to a neighbor, we don't ask for papers."

The room rumbled. Men shifted their hands toward familiar stocks. The sound of agreement grinding together like millstones.

Then the back door opened.

Caleb Voss stepped into the lamplight. Clean linen coat. Polished bowler. Leather folio under his arm. No weapon — but his confidence was its own kind of armament. He didn't hurry. He walked to the edge of the light like he'd been invited, and the room contracted around him the way water closes around a stone.

"Mr. Thorne," he said. "I heard the alarm. A hard season brings hard men." He looked around the room with what I supposed was meant to look like sympathy — the practiced warmth of a man who has studied concern the way other men study contracts. "The lawless elements of the territory have sensed your vulnerability."

"Vulnerability," I said. The word sat in my mouth like grit. "Meaning the hole you've been digging for us."

Voss sighed. He looked past me to the other farmers, and when he spoke again it was to them, not me. That was deliberate. He was cutting me out of my own meeting. "My friends — why would a railroad corporation risk a federal investigation to steal scrub cattle? We deal in steel. Not hides." He let that settle, counting the silence the way a man counts cards. "These thieves are the very reason you need what I'm offering. Sign the right-of-way. Take the company's gold. Buy yourself a sheriff and a telegraph wire. Civilization brings the law. Isolation only brings the dark."

A few heads went down. I saw it — the hook catching. Anders Larson staring at his hands, his thumb rubbing the spine of his ledger. Pete Higgins leaning back, eyes half-closed, the fight leaking out of him like water from a cracked jar. When a man is bone-tired and his children are drinking silt, the promise of a sheriff doesn't sound like surrender. It sounds like sleep.

I opened my mouth, but someone else moved first.

Titus stood up.

He'd been in the corner, near the back, which is where Titus always sat, because he could see everything from there and his back was to the wall. The floorboards groaned under his weight. He didn't look at Voss. He looked at the men he'd shod horses for, the men whose wagon axles he'd replaced in the dark after the harvest runs. The men he'd worked beside every season for a decade. He let them see him looking, and the looking was enough to stop the room from tilting any further toward the surveyor's voice.

"I'm no orator," Titus said. His voice was the kind that doesn't need to be loud. It went through the walls of a room the way heat goes through iron. "I don't much care about the politics of iron rails. But I know the soil here. I know the men in this room." He let that lie for a moment. "We don't need a sheriff from the county seat to teach us how to be neighbors. And we don't need to sell our birthright to earn a night's sleep."

The room had gone still in the way a forge goes still when the bellows stop.

"I'll lead the patrol," Titus said. "Not to fight. To deter. One man on a ridge sees shadows and waits. Forty men on the ridge — that's a different calculation. A thief thinks twice when he knows the whole township is watching."

That was it. Just that. No fine language. No performance. The panic that had been building — the sharp, electric charge of communal fear — began to cool and settle. Not gone, but shaped. The way iron settles when you take it from the fire and stop hitting it.

From near the stove, Jedediah Stone spat into a bucket and stepped forward. The man looked like something the Badlands had discarded and then reclaimed. He smelled of campfire and long years, and his hat was so sun-faded it had no color left, only a memory of color.

"I'll track for you, Blacksmith," he said. "I know every dry wash from here to the northern draws. If those shod horses are still moving, I'll find their beds." He swung his squinting eyes toward me. "But hear me, Thorne. Ride out with iron in your hands, you're inviting the law whether you want it or not. Once the lawyers and marshals get a taste of our dust, they stay. And the law out here falls on the side with the most ink. You start a war, and the railroad hides behind the smoke."

I looked at Jedediah. Then at Titus. Then at Sarah, who was standing in the back doorway, hands folded over her apron, her face quiet. The look she gave me wasn't fear. It was the patient, steady look of a woman who has weighed out enough flour to know the difference between a full measure and a desperate one. I held her eyes a moment. She gave the smallest nod — not permission, but agreement. The same answer she'd been giving me for ten years: *I trust you, but I'm watching.*

I nodded. One motion, sharp and decided. "Then we ride for deterrence. We watch. We wait." I looked toward the door where Voss was still standing, his folio tucked under his arm, his hat catching the lamplight. "And we let Mr. Voss know that while his civilization may be coming, Oak Haven is already here."

Voss adjusted his bowler. He smiled the small, patient smile of a man who believes he can outlast any weather. "A noble sentiment, Mr. Thorne. I hope it's enough to feed your children when the frost comes. Goodnight to you all."

He walked out. The door closed behind him with a soft click that somehow carried more weight than a slam.

The silence he left wasn't peaceful. It was the quiet of a field after hail — everything still upright, but you'd need to look close to tell what was damaged. Men began to rise, gathering their rifles, talking low. I watched Titus move to the corner with Jedediah, the two of them bending over a rough map Jedediah had pulled from inside his coat, Titus's hands moving steady and precise over the lines. The same hands that bent iron, now drawing out a plan for the ground we had left to defend.

Eleanor came up beside me. She didn't speak for a moment, just stood there with the brass bell still in her hand, watching the men file out. Then she said, quietly, "You'll need the schoolhouse again. For the rotation schedule. I'll leave the lamps."

"Thank you, Eleanor."

She nodded and went to straighten the desks the men had shoved aside. I watched her hands set each slate back in its place — neat, precise, as though order itself were a form of resistance.

I thought about my North Field. The red-tipped stakes. The ledger back at the house where every column was either debt or drought. We'd held tonight. I didn't know yet what that was worth — whether the holding was strength or just the last reflex of a man too stubborn to open his hand.

But we'd held.

Chapter 8: Echoes in the Canyon

Elias

The Badlands don't apologize for themselves. The soil turns to red clay and powder, the wash of alkali bleaching the rocks white as old bone. No grass. No sage to speak of. Just the land showing you what it looks like when the water is finally gone — the honest face of the earth with nothing left to hide behind.

We rode single file down a dry wash that narrowed as it went, the walls rising up like the sides of a trough. My hands were tight on the Winchester and I made myself loosen them. Tight hands mean a man's ahead of himself, and I'd learned years ago that you can't outrun what's coming — you can only meet it with a clear head or a clouded one. The stock of the rifle was warm from the sun, and the walnut grain was slick with the sweat from my palms. I wiped them on my trousers, one at a time, and put them back.

Jedediah led. He'd been born to read ground the way I'd been born to read weather. Every few minutes he'd lean low over his mule, touch a stem of broken sagebrush or trace a scuff mark in the hardpack, then straighten and ride on without a word. The mule picked its footing like it knew the weight of the errand. The story of my missing calves was written in the dust, and Jedediah was turning pages — silent, methodical, following a trail I wouldn't have seen if it had been painted in whitewash. Behind him I tracked the angle of the sun and calculated the distance. Two hours, maybe three. The thieves weren't expecting pursuit, or they wouldn't have stopped to butcher.

That thought put an iron bar across my chest. Not weight — more like the clamp I use when I need to hold something in place before it sets wrong. My jaw ached from clenching.

"Easy, Elias," Titus said, riding up alongside me. He looked at my knuckles. Then at my face. He didn't say anything else. Didn't need to.

I didn't answer. I thought about Rachel Parker instead — her calves, the ones she'd been nursing since March, the ones her youngest boy Thomas had given names to. Patch and Cricket, I think. I thought about what those calves were worth against a dry season, against a ledger that had more red than black. Two calves: the margin between a family that eats through February and a family that doesn't. And I thought about Voss and his red-tipped stakes and the particular kind of patience a man needs to destroy something slowly — how you didn't have to burn a house down if you could starve it out instead.

The canyon mouth narrowed. Red rock walls came up on both sides, trapping the heat and throwing it back at us doubled. The horses' breathing grew labored, the sound bouncing off the stone and coming back to us distorted, larger than it should have been. Somewhere overhead a hawk turned circles on nothing, riding a thermal we couldn't feel down here. I envied it. There's a simplicity to a hawk's hunger that a man can't match.

Jedediah raised a hand.

We stopped. The only sound was the click of cooling metal in the saddles and the distant cry of that hawk. Jedediah dismounted easy as a man stepping off a porch, crouched near the base of the cliff wall, and put his nose to the air like a hound. His fingers touched the rock face where a smear of soot darkened the sandstone. Fresh.

"Smoke," he said. Barely above a breath. "Old grease and cedar-rot. They're in the box canyon, just around the bend. Three men. Couple of horses. They aren't watching for company, or they wouldn't be burning this high in the day."

I was off my horse before he finished. The lever of the Winchester made its sound — clack-shuck — and the echo came back off the canyon walls and died. My boots hit the sand and I moved toward the bend.

Titus stepped in front of me. Didn't say anything. Didn't need to. His shadow covered most of the trail. The man was a wall when he chose to be, and he'd chosen.

"Out of my way, Titus," I said, my voice coming out lower than I intended. "They took from Rachel. They have our lifeblood sitting over a fire."

"We go in together," Titus said. "But we don't go in shooting. Not yet. A dead yearling thief doesn't bring that calf back, and a dead man's blood doesn't fill an empty pen." He held my gaze. His eyes were steady in a way that reminded me of bedrock — the kind of thing you can't move because it was there before you and will be there after. "Let me lead. Let them see what's in front of them before we decide what kind of day this is."

I looked at him. The anger in me was a banked fire — hot enough to work iron, hot enough to make mistakes. I thought about my brother's place in Kansas, the way things had gone wrong there — the neighbor who'd fired a warning shot at the bank men and how the county had come down on his head like a rockslide, and how the bank had used that shooting as license to clear the whole valley. The shape of a decision that couldn't be walked back. I thought about the way Sarah looked at me that morning when I'd strapped on the rifle — not afraid of what I'd find, but afraid of what I'd become while finding it.

I let out a breath. Nodded. Titus reached out and pushed the barrel of my Winchester toward the ground, gentle as setting down a piece of fragile work. I didn't fight him, but I didn't let go of the stock either.

We left the horses with Samuel and Jedediah and went forward on foot. The sand was soft and deep, muffling our steps. The canyon walls threw shade on one side and glare on the other, and we moved in the shade, close to the rock.

The smell reached us first. Roasting meat. Rich and fatty, obscenely good in all that barren rock. My stomach tightened with hunger and then immediately with fury — those two things arriving at the same moment, which is a particular kind of misery. The smell was so strong and so honest that it cut through everything else: the dust, the alkali, the dry rot of the canyon floor. It smelled like a meal. It smelled like theft.

We came around the sandstone boulder and looked.

The canyon dead-ended in a sheer rock wall, making a natural corral no rancher could've designed better. Three men sat around a low fire. They were ragged — clothes white with alkali dust, hair matted, faces gaunt as old leather drawn too tight over a frame. One was working a hunk of meat with a knife, his wrist turning in slow, mechanical passes. Near the canyon wall, the remaining calves huddled in the shadow, eyes wide, breath shallow. They'd pressed themselves against the rock as far as they could go. The slaughtered yearling lay in the dirt nearby, the hide peeled back and the ribs exposed. The smell of iron and raw hide was heavy in the still air. Flies already, thick and dark, doing their work.

That was Rachel's winter. That was her children's meat, going to grease over a sagebrush fire.

The anger spiked. My thumb moved toward the hammer.

Titus stepped out from behind the boulder.

He didn't announce himself. He simply walked into the center of the canyon mouth, and the sun hit his back and laid his shadow across the entire camp. He carried his sledgehammer in one hand, the head hanging low, the hickory handle resting easy against his thigh. No rifle. No pistol. Just the hammer and the fact of him — a mountain of a man, standing still in the light, saying nothing. The silence was the loudest thing I'd ever heard.

The three men at the fire froze.

One of them reached for a revolver at his hip. He stopped halfway, his hand hanging in the air, his eyes fixed on Titus. The silence in the canyon was absolute. Fire crackle. Wind threading through the rocks above. Nothing else.

"Drop it," Titus said. A statement. Not a command — a statement of what was about to happen regardless.

The revolver hit the dust. The other two backed away with their hands up, eyes tracking the boulders for the rest of us. I stepped out of the shadows with the Winchester raised, and the leader — the one with the knife — stood up slowly. He was thin. Not lean, not trail-worn, but truly hollowed out, the way soil goes when the topsoil's blown off and nothing's left but clay and rock. His cheekbones looked sharp enough to cut. His shirt hung on him like a sack on a fencepost. He stared at the sledgehammer in Titus's hand and his mouth opened but nothing came out.

"You took from the Parkers," I said. The words came out like shards of something broken. "People who have nothing but the dirt they stand on. For a belly full of meat that wasn't yours to kill?"

The man looked at the carcass. Then at me. His eyes were sunk deep in his skull, and the whites had gone yellow. "The wells are dry, mister," he said, his voice a stripped-out rasp. "Ain't seen a crop in two seasons. My brother's back in the hills, too weak to ride. We was just trying to stay alive. We didn't mean harm to your town."

"You meant harm the moment you cut that calf's throat." I stepped forward, the barrel close. The man flinched and closed his eyes. My finger was inside the trigger guard and the distance between a decision and the end of it was about the width of a breath. The hammer was half-cocked. One pull. The canyon would swallow the sound and give it back twice.

I looked at his face. The shut eyes. The hollow cheeks. The hands — cracked and filthy and shaking — that looked too much like the hands of a man who'd spent three seasons fighting the same drought I had. His boots were split at the soles. His belt was cinched to a hole he'd punched himself. I looked at the slaughtered yearling, the blood black in the dirt, and the thought came at me sideways: that I was looking at a mirror. A man who'd lost more, or been dealt less, or started later, and had nothing left but the choice I was about to punish him for. The ledger in my head ran the column and came up with a number I didn't like.

I lowered the rifle.

The silence held another second. Then I said, "Get out. Take your horses and go. If I see you within ten miles of the creek, I won't spend time on reasons. Run."

They ran. Three men scrambling for their mounts, not looking back, not grabbing anything but the reins. They were out of the canyon in dust and gone, the hoofbeats fading fast into the draws. The fire crackled on. The calves shifted in the corner, lowing — a low, bewildered sound, asking for something no one could give them.

I stood in the center of the camp and stared at the fire. My legs felt like they'd been plowing all day. The anger was still there, but it had gone cold, and cold anger is a different thing — quieter, heavier, the kind you carry home instead of spending.

Titus walked over and kicked sand over the embers, killing them. The smoke rose in a thin gray thread and disappeared. "We can save the meat if we move fast," he said quietly. "Rachel will need it. Samuel, bring the horses. Jedediah, check the brands on the others."

We worked the next hour without talking much. Titus dressed out the carcass with his heavy knife — precise, steady, no wasted movement, the blade finding the joints the way his hammer found the weld. Jedediah and Samuel gathered the remaining stock and checked each animal. I walked the perimeter of the canyon and looked at the ground and thought about nothing in particular, which was itself a kind of relief. The canyon walls turned from red to purple as the sun dropped. The shadows filled the space like water filling a basin, slow and cool.

When the work was done, I sat on a low rock and looked at my hands. They were the same hands that had gripped the Winchester. The same dust on them, more or less, as on the hands of the men who'd ridden away. The drought didn't pick sides. It just pressed, and what happened next depended entirely on what a man was made of and how much of it he had left.

Titus came over, wiping his blade on a tuft of dry grass. I looked up at him.

"I wanted to kill them," I said. "I had the sight right on. I could feel the rightness of it."

He crouched down and looked at me level. His face was tired, but the tiredness didn't reach whatever it was inside him that stayed steady. "I know, Elias. I've felt that weight before. It's a heavy thing to set down once you've picked it up." He paused. "But look at your hands. Clean of blood today. That's a better return than any meat we're hauling back."

I looked at my palms. The creases were dark with dust and the calluses had cracked at the edges from the dry air. Then I looked at the mouth of the canyon, where the shadows were stretching long across the red rock. I reached out and touched the handle of Titus's sledgehammer — just a brief, flat touch, the hickory smooth and warm from the sun — and then stood up and swung into the saddle.

We rode out as the first stars came through, the calves' lowing echoing off the stone walls behind us. The railroad was still on my land. The drought hadn't broken. The ledger hadn't changed. But I had not pulled that trigger, and that was a column in the account that would take me a long while to fully understand —

whether it was profit or loss, or something the ledger didn't have a name for yet.

Chapter 9: A Fragile Victory

Samuel

The kitchen smelled like something alive again, and I didn't realize how much I'd missed that until I was standing in the middle of it with flour all over my hands.

Rachel was working the dough like she had a grudge against it, her wooden spoon clicking against the ceramic bowl in a steady, punishing rhythm. Every now and then she'd blow a strand of hair out of her face with a sharp little puff that made her look like she was arguing with the bread itself. Sarah Thorne was at the stove stirring the pot and watching everything at once the way she always did—her sleeves rolled up past her elbows, the flush on her cheeks making her look younger than she usually did. Eleanor Vance was across the table from me, slicing dried apples into thin crescents, her paring knife moving with a small, exact rhythm that reminded me of the way she wrote on the chalkboard—deliberate, precise, nothing wasted. The whole room was warm and close and it smelled like yeast and scorched sugar and the sharp sweetness of those shriveled apples coming apart under Eleanor's blade, and I thought: this is what I came west for. Not the box canyon. Not the rustlers. This.

Though I wasn't going to pretend the canyon hadn't happened.

My shoulder ached where the old Pinkerton wound tightened up in the heat. I rolled it back, trying to work the stiffness out, feeling the scar tissue pull like a seam stitched too tight. My mind went to the three men at the fire—the way the thin one's hands shook when Titus stepped out of the shadows, the hollow look in his eyes that wasn't anger but something worse, something starved. I kept seeing it. The revolver dropping into the dust. Elias's finger inside the trigger guard. The whole moment stretched out like a rope going taut, and me behind that boulder with my Winchester feeling too heavy and my breath coming too fast.

I hadn't run. That was the thing I kept coming back to. In the dime novels, the hero runs toward danger because he's brave and strong and the story needs him to. I'd stood behind a boulder with my stomach turned to ice and my palms soaked through and I hadn't run, and maybe that was a different kind of thing. Braver, even. Or just slower on my feet. I'd stopped trying to decide, because every time I poked at the question it shifted on me like sand.

"Samuel." Sarah's voice cut through the noise in my head. "Stop staring at the wall and make yourself useful. You can stir the pot."

"Yes, ma'am." I crossed the kitchen in three steps, nearly catching my boot on the braided rug, and took the wooden spoon from her. The handle was warm from her grip.

"Slow circles," she said. "You stir it too fast, the bottom scorches."

"I know how to stir a pot," I said, though honestly I wasn't sure I did.

Sarah gave me a look that said she wasn't sure either, but she stepped aside. The stew bubbled thick and slow, and the smell of it hit me so hard my eyes watered—onion and salt pork and something earthy underneath. Weeks of dry cornmeal and bitter coffee, and we were going to eat actual food tonight and hear a fiddle, and I had to keep my face calm because I was so glad I thought I might embarrass myself.

Rachel glanced over from her dough. "Don't you cry into that stew, Samuel Price. We've got enough salt."

"I'm not crying," I said. My voice cracked on the word, which didn't help.

Eleanor looked up from her apple slices. She caught me grinning at the pot and smiled back, small and knowing. "The community that forgets how to celebrate has already surrendered," she said, like she was quoting herself. Maybe she was. She had a way of saying things that sounded like they belonged on a page somewhere.

"Yes, ma'am," I said, and stirred my slow circles, and tried to memorize the way the kitchen looked right then—the four of us working, the steam rising off the stove, the late-afternoon light coming through the window in a warm gold slant that made everything look like it mattered.

* * *

By the time we carried the pots out to the Parker barn, the sun was going orange and the light was going soft and the whole township was arriving in their best clothes—mended and brushed, hair combed back, children scrubbed pink and fidgeting in collars that were clearly too tight. I stood in the doorway with the stew pot braced against my hip and watched them come and couldn't quite make my face stop doing whatever it was doing.

Old Man Peterson had his fiddle out before the lanterns were fully hung. He sat on a three-legged stool in the corner, the instrument tucked under a chin that looked like gnarled oak, and when he pulled the bow across the strings, the first note came out thin and tentative and I thought: maybe it's been too long and we've all forgotten how. Then his hand found the reel and the tune leapt out of him loud and stomping and the whole barn floor seemed to vibrate with it, and people started moving before they'd even thought about it—boots shuffling, hands clapping, a whoop from somewhere near the back.

I got pulled into a group of boys near the center post—Jake Larson and the Higgins twins and a couple of others—and they all wanted to hear about the canyon. I'd told the story twice already but I found I could tell it better each time, the words getting smoother, more sure. I kept Titus in the right proportion: big enough to be true, which was already plenty big. I told them about the shod prints in the silt and the smoke rising from the box canyon and the way Titus just walked into the middle of the camp with nothing but the sledgehammer across his shoulder. Jake's mouth was open the whole time. One of the Higgins twins kept punching his brother's arm at the good parts.

"What'd you do?" Jake asked, his eyes huge.

"Covered the left flank with my Winchester," I said, which was true if you counted crouching behind a boulder as covering a flank.

"Were you scared?" the other Higgins twin asked.

I thought about lying. In the dime novels the hero never admits it. But these boys would know the lie, or they'd learn it later. "Yeah," I said. "Scared cold. But I stayed."

They looked at me the way I used to look at the men on the covers of the dime novels. I wasn't sure how to feel about that. Good, mostly. A little bit scared of getting it wrong. I noticed my voice was getting steadier as I talked, like the telling of it was pressing the fear out and leaving something firmer underneath.

Across the barn I spotted Elias and Sarah dancing, Elias with his boots going heavy and determined and Sarah laughing, her head thrown back, her whole body moving differently than it did when she was worried. I'd seen her worried a lot lately—the way she watched the sky, the way she counted jars in the pantry with her lips moving. Seeing her laugh was something I almost had to look away from, it was so good, so sudden.

Then I saw Titus.

He was standing near the cider barrel, arms crossed, watching the dancers with the careful expression he used when he was evaluating a piece of ironwork. He'd traded his soot-stained apron for a clean linen shirt that looked dangerously tight across his shoulders, and he smelled of soap instead of coal smoke—I'd noticed that when I passed him—and the change made him seem almost approachable, the way a bear seems approachable when it's sleeping. Eleanor

Vance was a few feet away in a dress of deep forest green, her hair pinned up, watching the music with that intense listening expression she wore even when it was a fiddle instead of a recitation.

Elias caught Titus's eye from the dance floor and I saw him say something, a grin cracking through the farmer's usual line-set jaw. Titus shook his head once, but there was something in the set of his mouth that wasn't a refusal.

Titus walked over to Eleanor. No flourish, no ceremony. He just stopped in front of her and held out one of his massive hands, palm up, steady as a shelf. Eleanor looked up at him and her eyes went wide for just a second—not fear, not surprise exactly, more like the look you get when something you've been thinking about suddenly happens—and then she placed her ink-stained fingers in his palm and they moved onto the floor together. Titus danced like a man who was afraid of breaking the floorboards, each step deliberate and exaggerated and careful, and Eleanor kept up with a patient grace that was almost funny except it wasn't funny at all, it was the most human thing I had ever seen either of them do.

Something knotted up behind my sternum. Not sadness. More like standing in a room where something real was happening and knowing you were lucky enough to be in it.

* * *

We ate the apple tarts and the stew and the flavors hit me so hard after weeks of cornmeal that I had to sit down on a hay bale after the second serving and just breathe. I danced once with Rachel's youngest daughter, who was nine and entirely too confident on her feet, and she spun me twice when I was only expecting once and my bad shoulder seized up and I staggered into Jake Larson, who laughed until he had to hold the post for support. My shoulder throbbed after that, a deep nagging pulse along the scar, but I didn't care.

The barn got warm. The air went thick with sweat and hay and the sweet-sour smell of cider, and the lanterns threw long amber shadows that swung whenever someone brushed the rafters. At some point I stepped outside to get my breath back and cool down. The night air hit my damp skin like a cold cloth and I shivered once, hard, and it felt wonderful.

The night was silver and cold after the heat inside—dark sky, bright moon so sharp I could see the craters, the prairie stretched out flat in every direction. The music came through the barn walls as a soft, muffled pulse. I stood in the yard and breathed and felt the sweat dry on my neck and thought: this is real. The canyon was real. This dance is real. Both of them are part of what this place is and neither one cancels the other out.

Then I noticed Elias.

He was about thirty feet away, near the fence line, standing very still. A figure had come out of the dark to meet him—a man I recognized even before the moonlight caught the polished bowler hat and the white gleam of a collar that had no business being that clean this far from a city.

Voss.

My stomach dropped. I didn't move. Didn't breathe, or felt like I didn't. Voss reached into his coat and pulled out a long cream-colored envelope and held it toward Elias, the paper looking unnaturally white in the moonlight, and even from where I stood I could see Elias's posture change—the way a post changes when you've sunk it wrong and the ground heaves. He didn't take the envelope right away. His fists were at his sides.

Their voices came to me in pieces, too low and too far for full words. I caught "eminent domain" from Voss—heard it clear, those two words carrying a flat, legal weight that cut through the night air different from the rest—and I didn't know all that it meant yet, but I knew from the sound of it that it was a different category of bad than thieves on a ridge. This was a paper. This was something that didn't care how many men rode patrol or how big your blacksmith was. This was something you couldn't track through the draws.

Elias took the envelope. Even from thirty feet I could see his hands, and they weren't steady.

Voss tipped his hat—a gesture so polite it looked like a slap—and walked back into the dark. Just like that. Gone.

Elias stood alone in the dirt, holding the paper. Inside the barn, the fiddle reached a high, soaring note and the dancers whooped and the sound poured out through every crack in the wood and into the cold night air. Elias didn't move. He was looking at the envelope and looking at the barn and I could see him calculating something, the way he always calculated things, running numbers that weren't coming out right.

I wanted to go to him. I didn't. This was something he needed to carry back in himself, at his own pace, on his own terms. I was seventeen years old and I had flour under my fingernails and a scar on my shoulder and none of that made me the right person for that moment.

But I watched him, because somebody should.

He tucked the paper into his belt and turned toward the light. His walk was slower than it had been an hour ago, heavier in the shoulders. But he walked back in. And I followed a minute behind, my boots crunching in the cold dirt, my breath making small clouds that vanished before they were fully formed.

The fiddle was still going. The lanterns were still burning. Rachel's children were still dancing with too much enthusiasm and not enough coordination and making everyone around them smile, and Anders Larson was clapping along from the corner with his hat pushed back on his head.

I found a spot near the back wall and leaned against it and watched the room and thought about what I'd just seen. The canyon, the dance, the paper. This was all one thing. Not separate pieces—one real, complicated thing that didn't fit the shape of any story I'd ever read. In the dime novels, you won or you lost and then the chapter ended and you knew where you stood. Here, you won the canyon and lost the field, and then you went back inside and danced anyway, because the fiddle was playing and the stew was hot and there was nothing else a person could reasonably do.

I didn't know if that was brave or just stubborn.

Standing there in the warm, noisy barn, with my shoulder aching and the music winding down toward something slow and quiet, I thought it might be both.

Chapter 10: The First Frost

Titus

I left the smithy before the sky made up its mind.

That's the only warning you get on the high plains: the sky going a certain kind of gray, flat and low, the air dropping its temperature like a man setting down a heavy load all at once. I banked the forge coals and hung the draw tongs on their peg. The iron I'd been working—a hinge pin for the Larson gate—sat half-formed on the anvil, still warm, the orange gone out of it. It would keep. Iron doesn't go anywhere you don't take it.

But Elias was three miles out on the North Field with a legal paper in his house and the first real snow of the season building on the horizon, and a man like that... in a situation like that... needed somebody nearby who wasn't afraid of him.

I rode heavy and I rode fast. The bay knew the road to the Thorne place without much direction. She was a solid animal, wide in the chest, the kind that doesn't flinch at wind. I let her have her head and hunched into my coat collar and watched the sky thicken.

The first flakes found me a mile out—wet, fat, the kind that stick. They landed on my sleeves and melted slow. By the time I came over the last rise and saw the homestead, the sky had gone white and the ground was starting to match it. The North Field was already disappearing under a fine, pale gauze. Elias was on the porch side of the house, nailing boards over the parlor window. He was swinging the hammer the way a man swings when he's working out something that won't leave him alone. Too hard. Not controlled. The wood was taking punishment it didn't need.

I pulled up and watched him work one minute without saying anything. The nail went crooked. He pulled it, started over. His breath came in thick white clouds. His coat wasn't buttoned and the wind was putting color into his neck that had nothing to do with effort.

I tied the bay at the post, looped the reins twice, and walked over. My boots left deep prints in the frost-stiffened grass.

"You're driving them crooked," I said.

He didn't look up. "Then it'll hold crooked."

"It won't hold at all. Crooked nail splits the grain." I kept my voice even. Not a lesson. A fact.

He hit the nail. The pine board settled into the frame, and the house went half-blind. He stepped back and looked at it, chest heaving, the hammer hanging loose at his side. His knuckles were white around the handle.

"Come inside," I said.

He looked at the field. The surveyors' stakes were still out there, red tips visible against the white for now. Another hour and they'd be gone too—buried under something that didn't care about courts or railroads or the lines men drew on paper.

"One more," he said.

I picked up the next board and held it flat against the window frame while he drove the nails. His hands were shaking slightly—not from cold, from something colder than cold. I held the board steady and didn't mention it. A good joint doesn't need discussion. You brace what needs bracing and you let the other man do his work.

When the last nail was in, I put my hand on his shoulder. He stiffened, then went still. That was Elias—he'd fight a wall, but he'd accept a hand if you gave it without ceremony.

"Inside," I said again.

He set the hammer on the porch rail and followed me in.

* * *

The house smelled of woodsmoke and something sharp from the stove—vinegar maybe, or the iron tang of a kettle that had been on too long. Sarah was standing by the fire, her hands tucked in her apron, her face carefully composed. She'd been waiting. She knew what he'd been carrying since the dance, same as I did. She looked at me when I came in and gave a small nod—not thanks, exactly. Recognition. One load-bearing member acknowledging another.

Samuel was in the corner on a low stool, hunched over his knees, listening to the wind pick up outside. The boy's face was pale, and his good hand was gripping the edge of the stool hard enough that the tendons stood out along his wrist. You could see the storm was getting through to him in a way the rustlers hadn't. Guns and men he understood from his books. The prairie in winter was something different. Something that didn't need a reason and didn't carry a weapon and couldn't be outrun or outfought.

Elias went straight to the table. The cream-colored envelope was there under an iron candlestick, the paper looking wrong in this room—too smooth, too clean, like a piece of a different world that had been left behind by mistake. He picked it up, unrolled it, and stood reading it for what couldn't have been the first time. The lamp threw orange light across the parchment and across the deep lines of his face, making the hollows under his eyes look darker than they were.

I pulled out a chair and sat. The chair was solid—pegged joints, no nails. Whoever built it knew what they were doing.

The wind slammed into the sod walls. The lamp flame bent sideways and righted itself. Fine silt sifted down from the ceiling, dusting the table. Elias kept reading, his eyes moving over the same lines they'd already traveled a hundred times. Looking for the crack in the language. There wasn't one. I'd seen enough official papers in my life to know when a wall had no gap. This one was built to hold.

"Eminent domain," he said, to no one.

"I know," I said.

"Thirty days to settle on compensation, or the court sets it."

"I know."

"They don't even have to wait for me to agree. They just take it."

I didn't answer that. Some facts don't need confirmation. They just sit there, heavy and true, like cold iron on an anvil.

He set the paper down flat, both hands pressed against it, fingers spread wide. He was a man trying to hold something in place that had already shifted. I've seen that—a joint that's lost its fit, a frame that's torqued out of true. You can press it all you want. Without the right repair, pressing just wears you down.

A sound outside. Heavy, slow steps in the snow. We all went still. Samuel's head came up. Sarah's hand went to her apron pocket. I was on my feet before the sound resolved itself into hoofbeats—mule hooves, not horse. Heavier. Slower. I knew that gait.

I moved to the door and looked through the crack. The cold came in through the gap like a blade drawn across my face.

Jedediah Stone, wrapped in so many furs he looked like something the prairie had grown. He was leading his mule toward the barn, head down against the wind, one hand on the animal's halter and the other holding his hat. He didn't look up. He didn't knock. He just moved toward shelter the way an animal moves toward it—because this was where shelter was, and that was the whole calculation.

"Barn's open, Jedediah!" Elias shouted past me.

The old man disappeared into the barn. The mule's tail vanished last into the white.

Elias closed the door and dropped the crossbar. The sound was heavy and final, oak dropping into iron brackets—the kind of sound a weld makes when it's set and there's no backing out. He stood with his hand on the bar for a moment, his back to us, his shoulders pulled up near his ears.

Sarah moved. She walked to the table and placed her palm flat over the parchment. Then she took it from under his hands, folded it once with a sharp, decisive crease, and put it in the hutch drawer. She didn't ask permission. She closed the drawer and the latch clicked shut.

"The law can't travel in this," she said, her voice steady and low. "Voss is in the hotel in town. The Marshal isn't riding for a piece of paper in a storm. Tonight it's just us."

Elias turned from the door. He looked at her, then at the hutch, then at the room—as if seeing it for the first time. Or the last time. Hard to know which, with Elias. He pulled out a chair and sat, and the fight went out of his shoulders by slow degrees, the way metal cools when you pull it from the coals.

Sarah set the Bible on the table and pushed the lamp close. The leather cover was worn smooth, dark at the spine where generations of hands had held it open.

I looked at Samuel. The boy had straightened on his stool, watching Elias open the book with stiff, cold hands. The pages smelled of old paper and some dried flower pressed between the leaves a long time ago—something fragile that had lasted. Elias found the passage—same one I'd heard in rooms like this before, in other years, other storms—and began to read.

The Lord is my shepherd; I shall not want.

His voice was rough at first, catching on the words like a file on cold stock. Then it steadied. The wind hit the house again, a serious blow that made the rafters groan and dusted snow through the eaves. Nobody flinched. The lamp held.

I sat across from Samuel and we both listened.

The boy's color was coming back. He wasn't gripping his knees anymore. He was watching Elias read the way he watched me at the anvil—like the act of it was teaching him something he didn't have words for yet. His lips moved slightly, following the psalm without sound.

I thought about the iron bar I'd been drawing out when he walked into the smithy two mornings ago. Green wood, I'd thought then. But green wood bends without breaking. That's not nothing. In the right hands, with enough heat and patience, it becomes something you can trust to hold weight.

Outside, the storm had nothing to say that interested me. I'd heard it before. It was just pressure. Weather. The kind of thing a properly built structure endures without comment. The walls were thick. The crossbar was set. The stove had coal enough for the night.

The stove hummed. Elias read on. Snow stacked up against the boards I'd watched him nail, and the house held, and we stayed inside it—four people in a warm room while the cold did what it would.

Some nights that's enough. Sometimes it's everything.

Chapter 11: Cabin Fever

Elias

The ink had skinned over in the well. I pressed the nib through the crust anyway, harder than I should, and the tines splayed against the page. A blot spread across the column—black, ragged, growing. There was nothing to write. Three weeks of blizzard had swallowed the fence posts and erased the horizon. My columns—bushels of wheat, gallons of well-water, price of seed—were a graveyard of empty space. Numbers I'd carried in my head for years had stopped meaning anything.

The room smelled of woodsmoke, damp wool, and the sour bite of too many bodies breathing the same used air. Everything had been touched and retouched and rearranged until we'd run out of ways to pretend the walls weren't closing.

Across the table, Samuel was trying to sharpen a slate pencil with a paring knife, his movements clumsy and slow, his breath fogging in the thin air near the far wall. He slipped. The pencil clattered to the floor and the knife bit the table with a dull thud.

Something in me snapped.

"Can you not sit still for five minutes, boy?" The words came out sharp and jagged. I didn't recognize my own voice—thin, brittle, like ice on the creek that gives way before you hear it crack. Samuel froze. The hurt flared across his face and was quickly buried beneath a stare at his boots.

"I was just..." The rest dissolved into a whisper. He pulled his hand back into his lap and sat very still.

I stared at the ink blot until it looked like a hole in the world. My hands were shaking. Not just from the cold. From the suffocating weight of being the one who was supposed to keep the walls standing and the fear at bay and the voices level, and who was failing at all three. If I couldn't keep the peace within these sod walls, how could I hold the land against the iron and the lawyers waiting for the thaw?

Sarah set her mending down with a soft sigh. She didn't look at me, but her judgment was there, quiet and weary, which was worse than anger. Anger I could have met with my own. Weariness just sat on me.

"Barn check," I said, before she could speak. I pulled the heavy coat from the peg near the door. The leather was stiff, frozen into a shape that resisted my arms. I wrapped the wool scarf tight. "Drifts are piling high against the north side. Need to see the door hasn't buckled."

"I'll come with you." Samuel scrambled up, eager for the chance to be useful—to erase the sting of my snap. I gave one curt nod.

The moment I lifted the crossbar, the door shoved back against me like a living thing. Snow swirled in, coating the floor in seconds. We wrestled it shut behind us. The world narrowed to five feet of visibility around the lantern I carried, its flame bending and guttering in the wind. Cold found every gap in collar and cuff. We moved by memory, boots sinking knee-deep into drifts that had turned the yard into jagged dunes. The barn was thirty yards off, a dark shape climbing out of the blur.

Inside, the air was marginally warmer—thick with hay and the humid breath of livestock. Animals shifted in the stalls, eyes catching the lantern with a dull, nervous gleam. I walked the aisle, trailing a hand along the partition boards, looking for the soft spot. The structure groaned under the wind. Best timber I could buy, and tonight it felt thin.

"Elias." Samuel's voice was low. Strained. He stood at the far pen, where we kept the ewes.

I moved toward him. The lantern swung and caught a patch of wool that wasn't moving. One of the older ewes on her side, legs drawn up as if she'd been trying to fold herself smaller against the cold. Still as stone. I knelt. Her fleece was cold under my glove. The life had gone out of her hours ago, leeched away by a draft I hadn't found or a weakness I hadn't patched.

One sheep. A small number in the tally of a farm. But right now it felt like the first stone in a landslide. I had boarded the windows, filled the larder, done everything a man could do. And still the world was taking what was mine, piece by piece. The urge to put my fist through the wall rose and fell in the same breath, left behind by something heavier: the plain fact of my own smallness against the size of what was coming.

"We'll have to move her," I said. My voice came out flat. "Before the others spook."

Samuel reached for the ewe's hind legs without a word. Together we lifted the stiff, heavy weight, settled her behind the plow, and covered her with a burlap tarp. I stood over that hump of canvas, the lantern throwing my shadow long across the barn floor. The oil was running low, the flame shrinking toward the wick.

I looked at Samuel. He stood watching me, waiting. I could feel the apology sitting in my chest like a stone I couldn't cough up. But apologies were currency I didn't have right now—not while the barn groaned and the drifts climbed and the column of losses kept growing. I turned for the door.

"Come on. Sarah will be waiting."

We walked back out into the screaming white. The house was a smudge of yellow lamplight, barely there. The wind drove ice into our faces, and the thirty yards felt like a mile. I thought about the ewe stiffening behind us in the dark barn, and the ones still alive in the pen, and the drifts that would be higher by morning. The balance was still moving. I had no way to stop it.

Chapter 12: The Teacher's Vigil

Eleanor

From the schoolhouse window, through the one corner of glass not yet claimed by frost, I had watched them that morning—Elias and the boy, Samuel, crossing back from the barn in the half-light before the storm closed its fist again. They moved slowly, leaning into the wind, and at one point the boy stumbled and Elias caught his arm without breaking stride, the gesture so automatic it might have been involuntary, the body's grammar overriding whatever quarrel the mind was still composing. They did not speak—or if they did the wind swallowed it—but there was something in the way they walked, shoulder to shoulder, hunched against the same blow, that arrested me. A small, inadvertent portrait of what people become to one another when the country strips away every decorative reason for proximity and leaves only the structural ones. I held the image a moment longer than I should have, the way one lingers over a well-made sentence before turning the page. Then the white curtain drew itself shut between us, and they were gone, and I was alone again with the cold and the question of what to burn.

Three days into the storm, I stood before the empty woodbox and could think only of Milton.

Not of warmth. Not of survival in its blunt, practical terms. Of Milton—the particular cruelty of it, the way the cold had driven me back through three years of westward reasoning until I was standing in a sod schoolhouse at the edge of the known world, considering which pages of Paradise Lost I could afford to burn. The irony was not lost on me. It was, in fact, the only thing keeping me company, and poor company it was.

The box held nothing but bark grit and the ghost of cedar. I straightened, joints popping in the dry cold, and tucked my fingers into my armpits. The tips had gone waxy white, the nails almost blue—a color I associated with porcelain, not flesh. The stove had lost its heat hours ago; the cast-iron sides were cool to the touch, and the firebox held nothing but a sift of gray ash that stirred when the wind found the flue. The corners of the room held a cold so complete that frost was etching itself up the walls, crystalline ferns spreading across the sod with a patience that felt almost botanical, almost ornamental. Beautiful and lethal, as so much of this country was. In Boston, one might have framed such a pattern and hung it in a gallery. Here, it was a death sentence in miniature.

I turned toward the back of the room—my private quarter, partitioned by a heavy wool curtain that smelled of lanolin and woodsmoke—and made myself look at the bookshelf. Here was my civilization. Here was every argument I had made to my father, to the women of the Ladies' Literary Society, to anyone who had tried to persuade me that the frontier was no place for a woman who had read Cicero. The spines stood in their ranks: geography, rhetoric, poetry, grammar. A bridge I had constructed over a thousand miles of prairie between the parlors of Beacon Hill and this whitewashed room. Each volume was a small act of defiance, carried west in a trunk that the stage driver had cursed for its weight.

My hand stopped over Paradise Lost. The gold lettering had long since faded to a ghost of itself, the cloth binding softened by years of handling until the corners were frayed to threads.

To burn it would be desecration. It would also mean three hours of warmth.

The frontier does not negotiate. That was the first lesson it had taught me—more efficiently than anything I had taught my students. It does not accept promissory notes of culture or character. It does not recognize the cadence of the classics or the authority of a well-constructed argument. It accepts only what keeps the body at the temperature required for thought.

I took a heavy geography text from the bottom shelf instead. Its maps were already obsolete—the borders of empires redrawn, the iron rails advancing faster than any cartographer could track. I opened it. The spine cracked like a small bone. I looked at the woodcut illustrations of rivers I would never see, mountain ranges I would never climb, and allowed myself precisely one moment of grief—measured, contained, the way I had been taught to grieve in a parlor where tears were considered a failure of composure—before I tore out the first page.

A map of the Mediterranean. All deep blues and ancient names. I crumpled it against my palm—the paper stiff, resistant, as though the knowledge itself objected to the use—and struck a match. The sulfurous bite stung my nostrils. The flame curled orange along the coastlines of Greece and Italy, blackening them before the page erupted into light. I fed it more pages. The heat was pathetic at first, a suggestion rather than a warmth, but I leaned forward with my face near the grate and breathed the acrid smoke as though it were something fine.

One by one. The Principles of Rhetoric. A collection of Victorian essays whose margins I had annotated in pencil during my first year of teaching. The Latin grammar I had carried since my own schooldays—its pages dense with my younger handwriting, the careful notes of a girl who had believed that mastery of the subjunctive was a kind of armor against an ungrammatical world. Each volume represented something I had fled: the decorative expectations of my father's household, the silk-caged social performance of Boston drawing rooms. I had come west to be necessary. To build something that mattered with my own hands and my own mind. And here I was, making arguments for survival out of dead men's prose.

Three hours of warmth for the thoughts of a dead man. The logic was cold and perfectly sound. I wondered, watching the leather bindings curl and hiss, whether this was what the frontier always demanded in the end—not that you abandon what you love, but that you learn to hold it more loosely.

The stove's glow had just shifted from a flicker to something steadier when the wind changed.

Beneath the storm's shriek—beneath the door rattling in its frame—something deliberate. A rhythmic, muffled percussion that the wind could not account for. Not a branch. Not the random complaint of the eaves. Metal on frozen earth. A shovel, moving with intention.

I went to the window and scraped a circle clear with my fingernails, the frost coming away in cold curls that fell to the sill. At first, only the white wall of the storm, a void so featureless it might have been the blank page at the beginning of the world. Then a shape resolved out of it—a massive, dark form that seemed not to walk through the drifts but to displace them, one heavy shovelful at a time. Titus Croft. Shoulders working with slow, deliberate force, carving a trench through four feet of packed snow. A burlap sack across his back, straining his coat at the seams. Every few yards he would stop and lean his full weight on the spade, his breath rising in clouds the gale tore away before they could fully form.

I could not move. I stood at the frosted window with my hand against the glass, watching him the way one watches a sentence resolve itself on the page—with held breath, waiting to see how it ends. A warmth started somewhere behind my sternum that had nothing to do with the burning books—a grounding, almost frightening recognition of what it meant that he was there. That he had come not because anyone had asked, but because he had read the situation the way he read iron: seen the fracture, and moved to brace it.

He reached the door and slumped against it, head down, his labored breathing audible through the sod walls.

I unbolted the door. The storm screamed in with him, ice needling my face and coating the floor in a fine, glittering powder. He nearly fell across the threshold, the sack dragging him to his knees. He did not speak. He knelt on the floorboards, his beard a mask of frozen mist, his eyelashes crusted white, his eyes unfocused in a way I had never seen in him—the look of a man who had used everything he had and was surprised to find the cupboard empty.

I slammed the door and leaned against it. The room fell into the sounds of crackling books and his ragged breathing, each exhale a small labor in itself.

"Titus," I said. His name felt strange and weighty, as though I were pronouncing a word in a language I was still learning—the syntax familiar, the meaning not quite arrived at.

I knelt beside him. He smelled of coal smoke, wet horsehair, and the sharp mineral heat of the forge—a smell so thoroughly him that it was almost startling, like encountering a familiar sentence in an unexpected context. I had catalogued it before, at the dance, but here in this small room with the frost climbing the walls, it was more concentrated, more real. He looked up at me, and for a moment something raw moved across his face. A man surprised to find himself still alive.

"Coal," he managed. The word came out ruined, scraped raw. He gestured toward the sack. "From the smithy. Thought you might be running low on the green wood."

I looked at the sack. Then at the stove, where the last of my Latin grammar was curling to ash—a conjugation table dissolving into gray flakes that floated upward. The sharpness of that—the small shame of it—

cut more cleanly than the cold had. He had fought his way through a lethal white void to bring me coal, and I had been burning Cicero.

I took his hand to help him up. It was enormous, the skin a topography of old scars and labor, and burning hot with a feverish heat that made my numb fingers ache. I guided him toward the stove, his movements heavy and uncoordinated, and he sank onto the low student bench with a sound like a load of timber settling. The bench was made for children; he overfilled it the way a paragraph overfills a margin, but he sat, and the bench held.

I opened the sack. The coal clattered into the grate, each piece black and dense and smelling of the forge, and the fire transformed—from the wavering orange of paper to a deep, intense blue-white that radiated heat in solid, pressing waves. I sat on the floor near the stove and watched the light move across his face, carving shadows into the lines of it, and I thought: here is a text I have not yet learned to read, though the syntax is simpler than I expected.

I brought him water in a tin mug. When I held it out, our fingers touched—briefly, almost incidentally, the callus of his thumb against the back of my hand. He drank without ceremony, throat working, water spilling into his beard. When he set the mug down and closed his eyes, the exhale that followed was the longest sound I had heard in three days.

"You shouldn't have come," I said. My voice was steadier now than it had been all morning, steadied perhaps by having someone to direct it toward. "The Marshal said the drifts would swallow a horse. You could have died out there, Titus Croft."

One eye opened. The iris was a dark, stormy gray. "And you could have frozen with your nose in a book, Eleanor Vance." His gaze moved to the bookshelf, where I had carved gaps like missing teeth in an otherwise orderly jaw. He didn't say anything more. His jaw tightened once, and that was sufficient. He understood the arithmetic. He had always understood arithmetic—the kind that dealt not in abstractions but in the weight of what you could carry and the distance between here and warmth.

"Cold logic," I said. "The frontier doesn't leave room for the things that don't help you breathe. I thought I was stronger than that. I thought a few boards and some whitewash would be enough to keep the world out."

Titus shifted. The bench groaned beneath him. He held his palms toward the grate, and the firelight found all the old damage in his knuckles—split skin healed over, burn scars gone silver, the permanent swell of joints that had absorbed ten thousand hammer-blows. "Strength isn't about keeping the world out," he said. His voice dropped into the low, resonant register that seemed to come from somewhere deeper than his chest—from the same place the forge's heat came from, bedrock and patience. "It's about knowing what's worth keeping inside when the walls start to fail. I was three years in the cavalry, Eleanor. I watched men burn whole libraries to keep a wounded captain warm for an hour. Melt down their own medals to make bullets." He paused. "You do what the dirt demands. There's no shame in survival."

I looked at him—really looked, in the deepening glow of the coal fire. A man who had become a pillar because he knew what it was to have everything collapse around him. The observation was not new, but it was newly felt, the way rereading a passage years later yields a meaning the first reading missed.

"Is that why you came to Oak Haven?" I asked. "To find a place where the dirt demands less?"

He laughed. A short, dry sound without any mirth in it. "I came because the hammer and the anvil are the only things that don't lie. You hit the iron, it changes. You give it heat, it softens. In the war, nothing worked that way. You'd follow an order that felt like a prayer and end up standing in a field full of ghosts. I wanted a life I could measure in pounds and inches. Something I could fix when it broke." He looked at me, direct and unhurried. "But the wind finds you. No matter how far you run from the noise."

I leaned my head against the warm iron of the stove. The metal radiated through my temple, a dull, steady comfort. "I ran from the silence," I admitted. "In Boston, rooms are full of people saying nothing that matters. All performance—the right dress, the right quotation delivered at the right pause in the conversation. I wanted to be necessary—not decorative. I wanted to teach children who understood the value of a single page because they'd had to fight the cold to read it." I glanced at the bookshelf again. The gaps looked back at me, unadorned, truthful. The sense of loss had not gone, but something quieter had settled beneath it. A resolve with no flourish attached. "I suppose I got what I asked for."

We sat without speaking for a long time. The coal fire's rhythmic pulse. The storm's muffled assault against the walls. The schoolhouse had contracted around us until there was only this circle of warmth and the two of us within it, and I felt something I had not felt since I crossed the Missouri—the sensation of being seen, not for the dresses or the degrees, but for the grit required to simply remain standing. It was, I realized, the first honest conversation I had had in months that was not conducted through the careful scaffolding of the classroom.

Titus broke the quiet. "Samuel. He's got the hands for the forge, but something else in his head. Asks me about the stars. Asks how the iron knows it's supposed to be a plow and not a sword." The ghost of a smile. "I tell him to ask the teacher. I tell him I only know the heat and the weight."

"He's a bridge," I said. "Like all of them. They're the ones who'll have to decide what to do with the railroad when it cuts through. They'll need the hammer, Titus, but they'll need the logic too. They'll need to read the maps before the company redraws them."

He nodded. His head dropped back against the wall, and his breathing slowed and deepened, exhaustion claiming what it was owed. His hands loosened in his lap, the fingers uncurling one by one the way hot metal relaxes as it cools.

I went behind the curtain and returned with the heavy wool blanket my mother had pressed into my arms the morning I left—soft, fine weave, the color of claret, a relic from another world that still smelled faintly of her lavender water. I draped it over his shoulders. His hand came up and caught mine. He didn't pull away. Neither did I. His palm was warm and rough, a map of labor, and in that moment the storm's isolation felt less like confinement than like the particular silence that falls when something important has been decided—not spoken aloud, not formalized, but recognized, the way one recognizes the thesis of a paragraph before the argument is complete.

"Stay, Titus," I whispered, though he was already half asleep. "The path is buried again anyway. The schoolhouse is strong enough for two."

His grip tightened once around my fingers, then loosened.

I sat back down on the floor. The coal fire soaked into my skin, the warmth almost painful after the hours of cold, the way a thawing hand aches before it feels whole again. I picked up the arithmetic textbook I had spared—the one that would teach Samuel and the others the geometry of their own futures—and held it without reading it. Its weight was a kind of promise. A book I had chosen to keep not for sentiment but for use. Outside, the storm continued its furious, pointless assault, a composition of wind and ice performed for an audience of no one. But inside, the vigil had changed. We were no longer merely waiting for the thaw. We were holding what we had claimed.

Chapter 13: The Thaw and the Mud

Elias

The thaw came from the south, smelling of wet earth and something ancient beneath it—the smell of ground waking after a long, indifferent sleep. I had expected relief. What I got was mud.

For months, the winter had held Oak Haven under a crust of white so complete you could hear your own blood moving. The ledger sat empty through all of it, page after page of nothing, columns I couldn't fill because the land was sealed and the markets were frozen and there was no commerce left to measure. Then the wind shifted, and inside three days the drifts began to sag and weep, gray rivulets gathering in the hollows where the soil was lowest. The fence posts emerged from the snow like bad news delivered one line at a time. I stood on the edge of the porch, the boards already slick underfoot, and watched the North Field turn itself into a quagmire—not a cradle for wheat, not a field ready for seed, but a vast, sucking soup of silt and rot that smelled of things that had been dying slowly all winter underneath.

The road into town had become a wound in the prairie. Black, viscous mud, alive in the way that only spring mud can be—heavy and shifting and patient, pulling at whatever touched it. At the bend near

Larson's, a freight wagon sat tilted at a hopeless angle, its bed of supplies canted toward the ditch. The oxen were belly-deep, heads hanging, breath steaming in the raw air. The driver was a small, frantic shape, his whip cracking uselessly at nothing. The mud held the iron-rimmed wheels with a wet, slurping grip and didn't care in the least.

My stomach tightened. The mud was the physical twin of the legal knot Caleb Voss had cinched around my neck before the first frost. The court order, the eminent domain threat—the blizzard had suspended all of it, frozen in the same white amber as everything else. But the heat was bringing it back to the surface. Paper and sod, the Marshal had said. I looked at my hands—knuckles scarred, skin etched with the grit of fifteen years—and felt the land sliding away in the muck. The numbers in my head ran themselves without my asking: thirty days on the notice, six weeks to planting, twelve head of cattle too weak to drive, and a well that hadn't been tested since November. Every figure came up short.

"Elias?" Sarah's voice through the screen door, soft and edged. "Samuel's back from the smithy. Says the wagons are backed up to the ridge. Nothing is moving."

"The land's too soft, Sarah." I didn't turn around. Couldn't bear to let her see my face, the way the skin around my mouth had gone tight and hard. "It's taking everything down with it."

She was quiet for a moment. I heard the screen door creak as she leaned against the frame. Then: "Come eat something."

"In a minute."

The minute stretched. It was still stretching when the hoofbeats broke through the drip of the eaves—heavy, splashing, deliberate. Two riders on the main track, horses laboring through the sludge, lifting their legs with a wet, sucking effort at every step. They weren't neighbors. Neighbors moved with the easy rhythm of people who knew the terrain, who leaned into the ruts and let the horses find their own footing. These men rode with a stiff formality that ignored the difficulty of the ground. One wore a bowler hat so clean it looked like an insult against the gray sky. The other—broader, older—wore a heavy duster that flared back from a silver star pinned to his breast.

Something locked up in my chest like a gate dropping.

Caleb Voss. And beside him, the law.

I stepped off the porch, boots sinking to the ankle in cold muck that gripped my soles and sucked at them when I pulled free, and went out to meet them. I didn't wait at the gate. A man who waits at his own gate has already conceded something.

Voss reined in, his bay heaving, flanks streaked with sweat and grit. Flecks of mud clung to the animal's belly like dark coins. He looked down at me with a mask of professional indifference. "Mr. Thorne. I trust you survived the winter with your health intact."

I said nothing. I was looking at the other man. Marshal Dillon—carved out of cedar and old leather, eyes two points of flint under a sweat-stained brim. The kind of face that has seen enough that it doesn't bother arranging itself into expressions anymore. A man who didn't enjoy his work and finished it anyway. He reached into his duster and produced a cream-colored envelope, the paper impossibly dry and white against the sodden world around it.

"Elias Thorne?" A voice like stones turning in a riverbed.

"You know who I am, Marshal. You've sat at my table for Sunday dinner three years running."

Dillon's expression didn't change. He didn't look at the house. He held the envelope out with a slow, deliberate movement, the way a man extends something he wishes he didn't have to offer. "This is a formal notice of eviction for the parcel designated as the North Field, under the authority of the United States District Court. The Chicago and North Western Railroad has been granted immediate right-of-way for track expansion and supply staging."

I kept my hands at my sides, fisted tight, the nails cutting into the heels of my palms. "The North Field is mine. The deed's in my ledger. I've paid the taxes every year they were due. I've bled into that soil until it's more mine than it is God's."

"The law don't much care about blood, Elias." The Marshal's voice dropped to something close to pity—the worst thing he could have offered me. Worse than the paper, worse than the badge. Pity from a man you'd fed at your own table. "It cares about the public good and the commerce of the nation. You've got thirty days to clear your equipment, livestock, and any standing structures. After that, the company has the right to remove what remains by force."

Voss leaned over his pommel. His eyes had the bright, cold quality of a man who had never once been afraid he'd lose. "It's progress, Mr. Thorne. Take the compensation. Move to the south ridge. You'll have capital for a real house, maybe a deep-bore pump so the next drought doesn't break you."

The south ridge. Thin soil, scrub brush, nothing but sage and shale. They wanted my heart and offered me a stone in return. I reached out and took the envelope from the Marshal's hand. The paper felt oily, unnatural—a different kind of material from anything that belonged in this yard. I didn't open it.

I tore it. A sharp, dry crack in the wet air. Again. Again. The white fragments drifted from my fingers and landed in the black mud at my feet. The ink began to run—the formal letters blurring to gray smudges as the water claimed them, pulling the law down into the dirt where it belonged.

Voss's mask slipped. The steel underneath was colder than the mud. "That was a legal document, Thorne. Tearing it doesn't change the county records. You're only making this harder on yourself."

"Bring your papers," I said. My vision blurred at the edges but my voice held. "Bring your badges and your maps. You're going to have to dig me out of this dirt like a stump. I'm staying."

Dillon sighed. He adjusted his reins, his horse shifting and sinking, one hoof disappearing into the muck with a wet sound. "Thirty days. I've known you a long time. I'd hate for the last thing I do in this town to be hauling you off your porch in irons."

"Then don't do it. Turn that horse around and tell them the law stopped at the mud."

"Paper is stronger than sod, Elias. It's a lesson a lot of men learned the hard way back east. Don't let your pride be the thing that buries you."

They turned their horses and fought their way back to the main road, the animals slogging through the mire with their heads low. I stood in the muck and watched until they were nothing but dark shapes against the weeping sky, shrinking, and then gone. The quiet returned, heavier than before, broken only by the world melting around me—the drip from the eaves, the far-off sound of the swollen creek, the settling of snow giving up its hold. I looked down. The fragments of the notice were already disappearing, pulled down into the dark, indifferent earth. Gone, but not gone. A man can tear the paper. The record remains in some office in a town he's never visited, written in ink that doesn't care about rain.

I turned toward the house.

Inside, the air was warm and smelled of lye and stewing onions, but the comfort of it felt dishonest, like a balance sheet with a number missing. Sarah stood by the stove, her hands frozen over a bowl of dough, the knuckles white. Samuel sat at the table, shoulders hunched, eyes fixed on a knothole in the boards. They had heard. In a house made of sod and thin timber, a man's ruin travels on the air.

"Thirty days," Sarah whispered. She kept her gaze on the dough, her fingers beginning to work it again with a jagged, frantic rhythm that wasn't baking—it was holding on. "Elias, what are we going to do? The cattle are still weak. We can't move the north fence in thirty days, not with the mud like this."

I walked to the table and dropped into my chair, the wood groaning. My hands were trembling—a fine, involuntary vibration I couldn't stop. I put them under the table and gripped my knees. "We aren't moving anything, Sarah. Not a post. Not a head of stock."

Samuel looked up. His face was pale, the eagerness drained out of it, replaced by a hollow, flickering fear that made him look younger than he was. "The Marshal... he wasn't joking. I saw the way he looked at the barn. He was measuring it. Like he was already seeing it gone."

"Let him measure. A man can measure the sky, but that don't mean he owns the wind. We hold. That's what we do. We hold until the ground dries, and then we plant. If they want this field, they're going to have to plow me under with the seed."

Sarah looked at me then, really looked. Her eyes were red-rimmed, but the old Kansas fire was still in them—the fire that had kept us alive when the grasshoppers took the first crop and the fever took our neighbors and the well went dry and we hauled water three miles in buckets that cracked in the heat. "You're talking like a man who wants to die, Elias Thorne. This isn't just about the land. It's about us. About Samuel. If you fight the Marshal, they won't just take the field. They'll take everything."

I looked away. Through the window the North Field was a smear of gray and brown under the low sky. I thought of my brother back in Kansas—the way he had stood in the doorway of a house that no longer belonged to him, hands empty, his ledger on the table behind him with the last page blank because there was nothing left to record. I had promised myself I would never be that man. I had built these walls to be a fortress. But the world was here now, and it was wearing a badge.

"I'm going to the smithy," I said, pushing back from the table. I needed the sound of Titus's hammer. The smell of hot iron. The sight of something being mended instead of taken apart. This kitchen felt too small, the air too full of the words we weren't saying. "The plowshares probably cracked in the frost."

"Elias—" Sarah said, but I was already at the door, pulling on my coat, feeling the cold leather resist my arms the same way it had all winter.

I couldn't stay. A man who breaks in front of his people is no use to anyone.

The ride into town was a slow, grinding crawl. Every hundred yards my horse stumbled, its legs sinking into hidden pockets of slush. I talked to the animal in a low, steady murmur—easy now, easy—more for my own benefit than his. Oak Haven looked like a shipwreck—the main street a canal of liquid filth, storefronts dark, the windows reflecting the leaden sky.

A broken crate lay half-submerged near the watering trough. I dismounted at the smithy, mud splashing to my knees, and tied the horse to the rail with fingers that wouldn't quite cooperate.

The forge fire was low—a dull orange glow that barely pushed back the shadows. Titus stood by the anvil, not working. He held a piece of scrap iron, his thumb tracing a jagged crack across its surface, studying it the way another man might study a wound. He looked up as I came in, and from his expression I knew the news had traveled faster than the Marshal's horse. In a town this size, a man's misfortune is common property before he even knows he's lost anything.

"They served you," Titus said. Not a question. He set the iron on the anvil with a heavy, metallic clack that rang in the rafters.

"Thirty days." I walked toward the heat of the forge and held my hands out to it. The warmth was a relief so sharp it almost hurt. "He says the North Field belongs to the railroad now. Says I'm a squatter on my own dirt."

Titus picked up his sledgehammer. Slow, practiced grip. He didn't look at me. He looked at the coals. "The law is a strange thing, Elias. Supposed to keep the peace. Most of the time it's just the tool the big man uses to break the small one. I saw it in the war. I saw it in the territory. A badge don't make a man right. It just makes him hard to argue with."

"I'm not giving it up, Titus."

He turned then—his frame blocking the light from the door—and looked at me with those stormy gray eyes. A flicker of the man he had been before he laid down the rifle. A man who understood the cost of a lost cause and the cost of not fighting one. "Then you'd better start thinking beyond plowshares. When that thirty days is up, the Marshal isn't bringing more paper. He's bringing men who get paid to not have a conscience. And the mud won't keep them out forever."

I reached out and put my hand on the anvil. The cold iron was a grounding weight against my palm—solid, certain, the one thing in the room that didn't shift. "I know," I said. "I know."

I left the smithy and stood in the doorway. On the porch of Larson's Emporium, a knot of men had gathered, their voices low and urgent, their breath making small clouds in the damp air. They looked my way—faces I had worked beside, eaten beside, prayed beside. Anders Larson had his arms crossed, his mouth set in a line I couldn't read. I could read the rest of them without crossing the street. They were wondering if my defiance was going to pull the railroad's attention down on all of them. Whether I was the anchor that would drown the whole community.

The isolation settled over me like a second coat. Heavier than the first.

I climbed back into the saddle and turned for home. Before I left the edge of town I looked at the North Field one last time. The sun was trying to break through—a thin, sickly yellow light spilling over gray, dissolving snow. The land lay still and patient beneath it, neither promising nor refusing. I breathed the smell of the wet earth. I was not going to lose it. I was made of the same dirt as this prairie, and if they wanted to take it, they were going to have to break the man along with the soil.

I kicked the horse forward, sinking back into the mud, and headed home.

Chapter 14: Iron Arguments

Titus

A hammer is for building or breaking. Not for talk.

I stood outside the boarding house, hands heavy at my sides, soot still ground into every crack in my knuckles. The place smelled of damp cedar and stale grease—the smell of a building that trapped air instead of moving it. The door frame was warped from the thaw, the hinges pulling away from soft wood. I noted that the way I note everything: structurally. A building that can't hold its own door together is not a serious place. But Voss was inside it, and Elias was drowning in his own stubbornness, and someone had to reach into the mire and pull him out before the Marshal came back with more than paper.

I pushed through the door. My shoulders brushed the frame on both sides. The floorboards flexed under my weight.

The back room Larson had set aside for the railroad's business looked like it had been set down from somewhere else entirely—clean surfaces, polished desk, no grime, no heat, no coal. No evidence that anyone in the room had ever made anything with their hands. The kind of space that made you feel like an intrusion just by standing in it. Maps covered the walls.

Precise, geometric drawings that turned our hills and creeks into ink and calculation—the land reduced to lines that could be argued over by men who had never walked the ground they were drawing. Caleb Voss sat behind the desk, his white shirt a blinding contrast to the gray world outside, his pen moving with the steady, practiced ease of a man who had never doubted the authority of what he was writing. The scratch of the nib was the only sound in the room, dry and purposeful.

He didn't look up when I came in.

I stood there and waited. A mountain of grime in his sanctuary of order. I could feel the dirt on my boots darkening the floorboards. Didn't bother me. Dirt is honest.

"Mr. Croft," he said finally, setting his pen aside with a small click. He looked at me with clear, untroubled eyes—no fatigue in them, no winter. The kind of eyes that had never stared into a forge wondering if the coal would last the week. "I didn't expect the town's mechanical heart to stop beating long enough for a visit."

"You're killing a man, Voss." My voice came out rough, a file on soft metal. "Elias Thorne. You're taking the only piece of the world he has left. Move the line south of the North Field. It's a mile. Maybe less. For the railroad that's a rounding error. For Elias it's everything."

Voss leaned back, his chair making a small, human creak that was the most honest thing in the room. He smiled the way a man smiles when he's explaining rain to someone who's never been wet. "Mr. Croft, you're a man of iron and coal. You understand that structure requires precision. You know that if one gear is misaligned, the machine fails. The railroad is a machine. It requires grade tolerances the locomotives can actually pull against—or the entire venture is unprofitable."

He stood and gestured toward the largest map. I moved closer. My shadow fell over the drawing, blotting out a county's worth of ink.

He traced the line through the Thorne homestead with one clean finger. The nail was trimmed, the cuticle pale. A hand that had never gripped a handle. "Here. The grade through Thorne's North Field is near-perfect. Flat, stable, minimal earthwork. To detour south, we encounter a four-percent rise over a quarter-mile. We would have to blast through a limestone ridge or build a trestle. Fifteen thousand dollars. Three months of labor." He looked at me. "Do you understand what fifteen thousand dollars means, Titus?"

"I know it's a number," I said. My jaw ached from clenching it. I could feel the tension running down my neck and into my shoulders, the same tension that builds before a heavy strike. "I also know that fifteen years of a man's sweat isn't on that map. You talk about tolerances, but you don't see the wheat. You don't see the well he dug when the rest of the town was ready to quit. You're looking at the dirt, Voss. You aren't looking at the man."

Voss sighed. Genuine. Patient. As though I had misunderstood a simple thing—a child confusing iron for steel. He reached into a drawer and slid a document across the desk—heavy paper, the railroad's seal embossed at the bottom like a brand on a hide. "I am bringing progress to this dust bowl, Titus. That is a procurement contract. The Chicago and Northwestern will need tens of thousands of spikes, rail-plates, structural brackets—and a local smithy capable of specialized repair work. I've seen what you build. You're not a farrier. You're the best ironworker between here and the Missouri."

I looked down at the paper. The numbers were there in dark, bold ink. More money than I'd see in ten years of shoeing horses and mending busted plowshares. It was clean shirts and coal that didn't have to be rationed. It was new tongs, a proper trip-hammer, stock iron that wasn't salvaged from broken wagon rims. The end of a particular kind of grinding. I could feel the weight of the forge in my mind—the iron's honest response to heat and force—and for a moment I let myself see what it would mean to build something that mattered beyond this small, starving settlement. A moment. That's all I gave it. The way you let a piece of metal cool in your hand just long enough to test the temper before you decide if it holds.

I let the moment pass.

"This contract lowers your ore and coal costs by forty percent once the line is operational," Voss continued. "You wouldn't be scraping for scraps. You'd be an industry. A pillar of a new Oak Haven." His voice dropped to something rhythmic, persuasive—the voice of a man who has closed deals before and knows where the joints are weakest. "All I need is for you to talk sense into Elias. Help him understand that his land is a relic. He takes the compensation, buys the south ridge, and with what we give him he can be a wealthy man. He's fighting a ghost, and you're the only man he trusts enough to hear it."

I touched the edge of the map. The paper was cold.

No grit in it. No weight. I thought of Elias's ledger—that thick, cracked book where he recorded every birth and death of his stock as though they were his own blood. To Elias, the ledger was testimony. To Voss, a ledger was a way to make people disappear into columns. They both lived by the record of things. But Elias lived in the soil, and Voss lived in the ink. The distance between those two lives was not fifteen thousand dollars. It was something that could not be measured in the terms on that map, or any map. It was the kind of distance you feel in the handle of a tool—the difference between iron that's been worked right and iron that's been forced into shape too fast.

I pulled my hand back, leaving a faint smudge on the clean surface. Good.

"I've seen men like you before, Voss." I looked him straight in the eye. My reflection in his spectacles was a dark, irregular shape that didn't fit the room's geometry. "In the war, we had officers who looked at maps and saw strategic positions. They didn't see the boys in the tall grass. They didn't see the mud turning red. They saw the objective." I stepped back from the desk. "You think you're bringing civilization. You're bringing a different kind of hunger. One that doesn't care if it eats a man's heart as long as the train runs on time."

I left the contract on the desk. The thought of touching it felt like touching iron that had been quenched wrong—brittle under the skin, liable to crack at the first real load.

"I won't take your money. I won't talk Elias into a grave of his own making. You want his land, you take it with the Marshal. But don't tell yourself you're doing him any favors. You're the storm that happens to carry a pen."

Voss's expression settled back into its professional mask—smooth, cool, the kind of finish that comes from long tempering. Nothing rough left on the surface. "A storm is an act of God, Mr. Croft. The railroad is an act of man. One is inevitable, and the other is merely expensive. I'm sorry we couldn't reach a more civilized arrangement. Talent is no substitute for foresight. Eventually, the hammer has to stop, and the train has to go through."

I walked out. Didn't look back. A man who looks back at a room like that is already measuring himself against it.

The mud of the street hit my boots with a familiar weight. Honest weight—the kind you can feel and trust. I looked toward the North Field. The sun was dropping, dragging long shadows across the prairie, turning the wet ground into something that looked almost like dark metal, hammered flat. I stood with my hands at my sides—scarred, stained, mine—and let the cold air run through me.

There was grief in it. Not anger at Voss—he was doing what he was made to do, same as iron left in the rain will rust. Not a flaw. Just a property. Not quite fear for Elias, either. Something heavier. The exhaustion of watching something solid get worn away by water and paper, a little at a time, until there was nothing left to brace against. I knew that feeling from the war. I knew it from watching good men hold a line that was already gone. The body knows before the mind does. The hands go still. The jaw unlocks. And you stand there, not because you think you can win, but because your boots are planted and you haven't been given the order to move.

I turned toward the smithy. The forge was waiting—coals banked, the anvil cold but patient. The iron knew what it was for, and so did I. As long as I could hold a hammer, I would not let my hands be turned into ink.

Chapter 15: Seeds of Doubt

Elias

I planted anyway.

The iron plow handles were cold against my palms, and the North Field stretched out ahead–a vast, open skin of land that had survived the winter's grip and the drought's long squeeze. It was still my land. The deed said so. The calluses on my hands said so. The fifteen years of sweat I'd poured into the dirt said so, though dirt doesn't keep records in any language the courts understand. Now the field was marred. Red-tipped surveyor's stakes stood in a line against the horizon like a row of bad crop markers, smooth and manufactured, foreign to every irregular, earned thing on this property. Every time my eyes caught that line, something tightened between my shoulder blades, a slow pull like a leather strap cinched one notch too far.

"Steady, girl." Whether I was talking to the mule or myself, I couldn't say. The mule didn't answer. She put her head down and pulled, and the harness creaked, and the blade cut into ground that was still cold two inches beneath the surface.

The soil was stubborn–holding onto the memory of the frost the way a man holds onto a grudge, tight and unreasonable. But I leaned my weight into the handles and let the blade bite deep. The fresh-turned earth came up dark and wet, smelling of roots and iron and things that had been sleeping. This was more than planting. Each furrow was a word in a sentence I was writing against the world. This is mine. I am still here. You will not take it.

Behind me, Samuel was working to clear the rocks we'd churned up, tossing them one by one into the wooden sledge with a dull, rhythmic clatter. A lanky boy, all knees and elbows, and today his movements were hesitant. I could feel his eyes on me, then shifting to the stakes, then back again, the way a man's eyes move between a wound and the person who caused it. The silence between us wasn't the comfortable working quiet we usually shared. It was thick with the things we weren't saying. I kept my focus on the rhythm—the jingle of harness, the wet tearing sound of earth being opened, the smell of ancient, disturbed soil rising up to meet my face. It was the only thing keeping the panic from climbing up through my chest and into my throat.

"Elias?" His voice was small against the openness of the field, swallowed almost before it reached me. "Do you think we should be planting this close to the markers? The man in the bowler hat said the line goes right through here. Right where we're standing."

I hauled on the handles and turned the plow at the end of the row. My boots sank into the fresh-turned mud, the cold seeping through the leather and into my bones. I looked at him—and saw the fear in his eyes. Not just for the land. For me. He was looking at me the way you look at a man standing too close to an edge, and he was right to. My hands were locked in a white-knuckled grip on the iron, and I didn't trust what I'd do with them if I let go.

"The markers are just wood, Samuel. The land is bone and blood. We plant because it's spring, and we plant here because this is Thorne land." I set my feet in the next row, the mud sucking at my soles. "Caleb Voss can draw all the lines he wants on a piece of paper, but he can't grow a single stalk of wheat with a pen. We do the work. The rest is in God's hands."

He nodded. But he didn't look convinced. He bent back to his task with his shoulders hunched, as though waiting for something to fall from the empty blue sky. I turned the mule into the next furrow and didn't say anything more. The harness jingled. The blade cut. A meadowlark called from somewhere near the fence line, two clear notes that sounded too bright for the day we were having.

I knew what he was thinking. I knew what the whole town was thinking. Every time I looked at those stakes, I didn't see progress. I saw the bank in Kansas. I saw my brother standing in a doorway that no longer belonged to him, his ledger on the table behind him, the last page blank.

By the time the sun had started to drop, casting the stakes' shadows long across the furrows like dark fingers pointing east, I knew I had to go for seed. My stores were low—a quarter-bushel left in the barn, maybe less, and the planting window was closing the way a door closes when you can feel the weight of it but can't stop the swing. I left Samuel with the stock and started the long, heavy walk toward town. The mud clung to my boots with each step—a deliberate, exhausting resistance, as if the field didn't want to let me leave. Or perhaps it was trying to tell me something I didn't want to hear. The air turned colder as the sun dropped. Coal smoke drifted from Oak Haven's chimneys, flat and gray across the flats, smelling of the kind of warmth I didn't have time for.

Larson's Emporium was the heart of the settlement—low-slung, smelling of brine, dry flour, and the sharp, woolly musk of men who lived their days under the open sky. Usually the bell above the door was a welcome sound, a signal that the community was still holding together, that there was still a place where a man could walk in and be known. Today it sounded like an alarm. The warmth of the potbellied stove reached me, but it didn't touch the cold spot lodged beneath my breastbone. Anders Larson was behind the counter, hands on a bolt of calico, but the smile he gave me didn't reach his eyes. The expression of a man about to deliver bad news and wishing someone else were there to do it.

"Elias. You're out late. Figured you'd be half-buried in the North Field by now."

"I'm trying to be, Anders." I leaned against the counter. My hands had started their fine trembling again; I tucked them in my pockets where they couldn't give me away. "I need the winter wheat seed. Two bushels. On the book until first cutting. You know I'm good for it. Six years, not a missed payment."

Anders stopped moving. He smoothed the calico with a slow hand, working the fabric flat against the counter the way a man works a thought he doesn't want to say out loud. His knuckles went white. The clock on the wall ticked through the silence—each tick loud enough to feel. Finally he let out a long breath that seemed to deflate his whole frame.

"Elias, I've been looking at the ledgers. With the drought last year, and prices shifting... my suppliers are demanding cash up front for the seed shipments this season."

The blood left my face in a rush, a sudden draining cold that spread through my limbs and settled in my fingers. "Cash? Anders, nobody in this valley has cash until harvest. We've always operated on credit. That's how we survive."

He leaned in, his voice dropping to a whisper that felt like a door being shut. "I talked to Calcb Voss. He told me the railroad's offering a fair price for that right-of-way. More than fair. He said if you took the settlement you'd have enough cash to pay off everything here and buy the best seed from back east. You could pay me today, Elias. You could be clear of it all."

I stepped back. The floorboards creaked under me. The betrayal was a taste on the back of my tongue, flat and dry, the taste of dust in a room where you expected water. "You're asking me to sell my land so you can balance your books. That's what our friendship is worth. A few columns in a ledger."

"It's not just my books!" His voice cracked, the careful front giving way. He gestured at the window, at the town beyond it—the dark storefronts, the empty street, the mud. "The railroad brings jobs. It brings trade. It brings a future that doesn't depend on praying for a cloud that never comes. If you hold out, they might bypass us entirely—go ten miles north, and Oak Haven dries up and blows off the map. The whole town is waiting on you to be reasonable."

I looked at his hands. Pale, soft—the hands of a man who measured his life in yards of cloth and pounds of sugar. Clean nails. No scars. He couldn't understand.

To him, land was a commodity to trade for security, a line in a ledger that could be balanced or struck through. To me, it was the only thing that stood between my family and the drifting nothingness that had swallowed my brother.

"I'm not being unreasonable, Anders. I'm being a farmer. If you won't extend the credit, I'll find another way. But I won't sell."

I turned toward the door.

The store wasn't as empty as I'd thought. In the shadows near the grain scales, Jedediah Stone stood against a post, face unreadable beneath his battered hat. By the stove, Parker and two other farmers were huddled, their voices dropping to nothing the moment I looked their way. The room tightened around me like a collar. Parker—a man I'd helped pull a calf for two winters ago, a man who'd sat at my table and eaten Sarah's bread—found something interesting in the floorboards and kept his eyes there. None of them looked up. They shifted their feet. Adjusted their hats. Stayed silent.

These were the people I had bled for. The community I had built my life around. They looked at me now the way you look at a stump that's blocking the road—something that needs to be dealt with, not spoken to.

I was no longer a neighbor. I was the obstacle.

I pushed the door open. The bell chimed once, mocking and clean.

Outside, the wind lifted dust from the street and threw it in my eyes. I stood there and breathed—cold, thin air, the smell of wet soil riding in from the North Field. My shadow stretched long and thin before me on the muddy ground, a lonely shape in a landscape that felt less familiar than it had that morning. I started the walk back, one boot in front of the other, the eviction notice sitting in my pocket with its paper edges sharp against my thumb.

The whole town is waiting on you to be reasonable.

The furrows were open behind me, empty, waiting on seed I didn't have. First stars were beginning to show—faint, far away, indifferent to ledgers and deeds and the small desperate calculations of men who lived below them. I kept walking and didn't look back at the lamp-lit windows of the emporium, where the warmth was, where the community I'd known was rearranging itself around the shape of my absence.

A man could survive on grit. I had done it before.

But I had never done it with the community watching, waiting for me to fall.

Chapter 16: The Schoolhouse Trial

Eleanor

The schoolhouse smelled of beeswax and cedar shavings and the lingering metallic bite of the coal Titus had brought for the stove. On ordinary evenings, those combined scents reassured me—they said: warmth, learning, shelter from the open country that pressed in from every direction. Tonight, they said nothing of the kind. Tonight, the whitewashed sod walls felt less like sanctuary and more like the walls of a courtroom in which I was both judge and defendant, and the jury had not yet decided whether to attend.

I moved the desks myself. Dragged them scraping across the floorboards, arranging them in a circle rather than the neat rows I kept during the school day. My arms ached from it—the desks were heavier than they appeared, crude pine affairs weighted with years of children's restless energy, their surfaces carved with initials and small gouges where pencils had pressed too hard during examinations. I did it deliberately. A classroom's hierarchy—teacher at the front, students arrayed by rank—was exactly the wrong architecture for what needed to happen. People had to see one another's faces, not the backs of one another's heads. They had to speak as equals. Whether they were capable of it was a question I could not answer in advance, and I confess I had spent the better part of the afternoon drafting and discarding opening remarks that might tip the balance.

My hands, still faintly stained with berry ink from the afternoon's lesson on penmanship, smoothed the edge of the last desk into alignment. "Dialogue, Elias," I said, without looking up. My voice caught slightly on the dry air. "Not shouting. If we are to remain a community, we must speak as one, even if the words are hard to swallow."

He didn't answer. He stood by the heavy oak door with his hands shoved deep into his coat pockets, and I could see from the set of his jaw that he was already composing a speech rather than listening for one. Elias Thorne was a man whose silences were not empty—they were dense with calculation, with seasons tallied and losses weighed, the way a page of prose can be dense with meaning even when the sentences are short. I had learned, in the months since coming to Oak Haven, that when he went that still, he was not reflecting. He was bracing.

The door creaked open, admitting cold air and the first of the townsfolk. They came in with the slow, reluctant shuffle of people who had been told to attend a meeting they already dreaded—the gait of students entering a classroom where a difficult examination awaits. Anders Larson entered first, his eyes cutting to

Elias and then away, his mouth a drawn line. He smelled of the emporium—dry flour and wool and the faint sourness of brine. Behind him: Rachel Parker and her husband John, their faces carrying the exhausted arithmetic of people who had spent too many nights calculating the same impossible sum. Rachel's hands were already working at the fabric of her apron, a habit I had noticed in her before, the way some students twist their pencils when they cannot find the answer. The room filled by degrees, each new arrival bringing a stronger scent of cold wool and fear, and each choosing a seat with the careful deliberation of someone who understood that where you sat said something about where you stood.

Then came a different kind of entrance entirely.

Caleb Voss did not shuffle. He walked in with the measured tread of a man who knew the precise value of every step—the cadence of a practised rhetorician, though his rhetoric was conducted entirely without words. He removed his bowler hat—but only after he was well inside the room, and the gesture had the quality of something rehearsed, a performance of humility that implied its own opposite. He did not seek a chair in the circle. He retreated to the shadows along the far wall and folded his arms, and the effect was of a man watching a play whose ending he had already read. His presence altered the room's atmosphere the way a dropped coal alters a pail of water—quietly, and all the way through. I noted that his coat was brushed and his collar was white, and that these small details of grooming were themselves an argument: that the world he represented was orderly, prosperous, and inevitable.

I took my place in the circle and waited until the settling sounds—chair scrapes, heavy exhalations, the particular silence that falls when people are afraid to speak first—had run their course. Then I stood.

"We are here because the world is changing faster than the rain can fall," I said. I looked at each face in turn, letting my gaze rest a moment longer on Elias than on the others. His expression did not change. "The railroad is at our gate. The drought is at our throats. We can either tear ourselves apart, or we can find a way to endure together. Anders, you asked for this meeting. Speak your mind."

Anders rose with a slow creak of knees and conviction. He gripped the edge of the desk before him and stared at the grain of the wood rather than the faces around him—a man reading his confession from a surface that could not judge him. "It's the debt, Eleanor. Not just the seed anymore—it's the everything. My ledger is full of red ink. The drought has taken the marrow out of this valley. We're starving on our feet, and we're too proud to say so out loud." He looked up, his eyes bright and hollow at once, the look of a man whose argument has finally outrun his shame. "The railroad—Voss is offering cash. Real money. If the tracks come through, the prices on coal and flour drop by half. We could buy mechanical pumps. Reach the deep water. We wouldn't have to watch the cattle die one by one in the creek bed."

Rachel Parker did not stand. She leaned forward, her hands working her apron into a tight knot, and when she spoke, the rawness in her voice silenced the room more completely than any formal appeal could have. "My Thomas is twelve years old. He's got the back of a man of forty. He spends all day hauling buckets from the creek because our well is nothing but mud. He hasn't been to school in three weeks because he's too tired to hold a pencil." Her voice broke on the word pencil, and the smallness of that object—the mundane, essential tool of a child's education—made the breaking worse. "Is that what we're protecting? The railroad is a lifeline. It is the only one we've got. Please. Just step aside."

Something compressed in my chest—not grief, exactly, but the pressure of holding two true things at once, the way one holds two contradictory passages from the same text and cannot dismiss either without falsifying the whole. Rachel was not wrong. Elias was not wrong. And this room, which I had arranged so carefully into the shape of dialogue, was filling with the kind of anguish that resists rearrangement.

A farmer named Henderson rose next, his voice stripped of patience. "We're all paying for your pride, Thorne. You talk about stewardship, about the land being sacred, but you can't eat soil. You're holding out for a ghost, and you're dragging us all into the grave with you."

Voss stirred in the shadows—a slight tilt of the head, the silver chain of his pocket watch catching the lamplight with a brief, precise flash. He said nothing. He did not need to. He had found a far more efficient instrument than argument: he had recruited the people Elias loved. The observation chilled me more than the draft from the door. It was the strategy of a man who understood that the most effective pressure comes not from the hand that pushes but from the ground that gives way.

Elias stood. The chair scraped back with a sound that made Rachel flinch. He walked to the center of the circle—the place where I had stood—and when he looked out at his neighbors, his voice came out low and grinding, like millstones working.

"You talk about money like it's rain," he said. "Like it's going to wash away the dust and make everything green again. But money doesn't have roots. It doesn't know the smell of the earth after a frost, and it doesn't care whose blood is in the soil." He reached into his coat and pulled out the eviction notice—the paper he'd been carrying for weeks, worn soft at the folds, the creases darkened by the oils of his hands—and held it up against the lamplight. "I've seen this before. In Kansas. My brother wasn't much older than Thomas when we lost the first homestead. He believed in the progress too. He signed the papers because the bank promised him a harvester and a future not tied to the mercy of the clouds. When the harvest failed, they didn't come with water. They came with more paper. They took the harvester, the barn, and then the house. He died in a rented room with nothing but the clothes on his back."

He turned to Rachel. His voice dropped, and the dropping of it was more eloquent than any oratory—the way a diminuendo can say what a fortissimo cannot. "I want Thomas to have an easier life too. But I want him to own the life he has. If you sell a piece of the whole, you've admitted the whole has a price. And once the railroad owns the path, the banks will own the town. They'll own the wells you want to build. We're not just farmers—we're stewards. If we give this up for a quick breath of air, we leave them a desert of debt."

He paused, something working behind his eyes that he would not name. I recognized the shape of it—the moment when a man has said everything he can say and knows, even as he says it, that it is not enough. The same moment I had witnessed in a hundred classrooms, when a student reaches the limit of what language can carry and stands there, exposed, waiting for the silence to do the rest.

He was right about the principle. He was right in ways I could trace all the way back to Locke and Jefferson, to the argument that a man who works the land is bound to it by something more durable than a deed. But principle, as I had learned in the years since Boston receded behind me, does not always speak the language of necessity. He had given them a sermon, and they needed bread.

Voss stepped forward into the light. His face arranged itself into an expression of careful concern—a mask so well fitted it was almost indistinguishable from the genuine article, and I found myself admiring the craftsmanship even as I recoiled from the purpose behind it. "Mr. Thorne speaks with passion, and I respect his history. But history is a heavy thing to carry when you're trying to walk into the future. The company isn't the bank. We're the engine of growth. We want Oak Haven to thrive, because a thriving town means a profitable line." He looked around the circle, his smile thin and entirely certain of itself. "The offer stands. The Marshal will be here in a week to finalize the eminent domain filings. I would much rather provide you with the means to save yourselves."

The impasse was not dramatic. It was simply impenetrable—a wall with no door in it, no rhetorical passage through which argument could travel. I stood, my hands not quite steady, and looked at the faces I had been trying to hold together: Rachel's tear-tracked cheeks, Anders' sunken shoulders, Elias's rigid stillness. Titus, in the corner, sat unmoving, his face unreadable, his hands resting on his knees like tools set down between tasks. "It seems the words are not enough tonight," I said. "The meeting is adjourned. Go home safely. Think on what has been said. Think on what it means to be a neighbor."

They rose and filed out in silence, the sound of their boots against the floorboards marking a rhythm like a slow and reluctant departure from a church where the sermon had offered no comfort. No one spoke to Elias. No one touched his shoulder. They moved past him the way water moves past a stone—around, not through. Anders paused by the stove at the last, reached out and touched the iron with his fingertips, then withdrew his hand as if burned. He left without looking back. The door swung shut behind him, and the cold air that rushed in carried the smell of the open prairie—dust and distance and the absence of shelter.

I stood at the edge of the empty circle and did not move for a long time. The hurricane lamps were burning low, their wicks shortening toward the end of the oil, the light contracting around us. Outside, the wind had taken up its customary address to the prairie—restless, unceasing, answering nothing.

I thought of a sentence I had once written on the board for my students: *A community is a text that every member writes together.* I had meant it as encouragement. Now it seemed to describe something darker—the possibility that a story can be written by its absences, by everything left unsaid, and that even the most carefully constructed circle is no protection against a room full of people who have stopped reading from the same page. I had arranged the desks. I had opened the dialogue. And the dialogue had revealed precisely what I feared: that the grammar of this community was fracturing along lines I could not diagram.

Elias walked out without a word. The door closed behind him, and the cold swallowed the lamplight.

I began returning the desks to their rows.

Chapter 17: Sparks

Elias

Sleep was thin and useless. I lay in the dark and traced the uneven patches of the sod ceiling the way a man runs his thumb along the stitching of a worn harness — not to learn anything, only because the hands need something to do. The room smelled of dried clay and the faint lavender Sarah kept in a muslin pouch under her pillow, a scent that belonged to a gentler life. Her breathing beside me was shallow and slow. I had not told her about Henderson's words. I had not told her about the way the circle of neighbors had looked at me by the end, like men calculating the cost of a tool they no longer want.

The eviction notice was in my coat pocket, hanging by the door. A single sheet of legal paper that weighed more than anything I'd ever carried out of a field. I could not stop thinking about it even in the dark. My mind kept running the figures — the filing fees I didn't have, the lawyer's retainer I couldn't afford, the timeline that left no margin for error. The arithmetic of ruin is a specific kind of insomnia. Every number leads to the next, and none of them balance.

Then the light came. A faint, dancing pulse of orange against the far wall — the wrong color for moonlight, the wrong angle for the lamp. I lay still for two full seconds, forcing my mind to work rather than react. Not the house. The smell was wrong for the house. It was sharp, acrid, already mixed with pine pitch — the smell of something built and cured and dry for months, going up all at once.

I sat up. Through the small window, the horizon north of the depot was alive. A ragged crown of fire against the black sky, wide and climbing. I knew that ground. The railroad crews had staged their timber there — thousands of pine ties stacked in great dry columns, waiting to be spiked into my soil. They were burning now, and the scale of it put a cold knot between my shoulder blades that had nothing to do with the night air.

"Sarah." I put my hand on her shoulder, gentle but firm. Her nightgown was damp with the sweat of restless sleep. "Sarah, wake up."

She came up slowly, the way she always did since the hard winter — reluctantly, as if sleep was the only place she still held something in reserve. She sat up and the silver tangle of her hair caught the strange light. She saw the glow and went quiet, watching it. In the firelight coming through the glass, the lines of her face were deep and still. She didn't gasp. She didn't cry. She just held herself very straight, the way she did when she was deciding how much fear to let past the gate.

"Is it the house, Elias?"

"No. The depot. The ties." I was already pulling on my boots, fingers fumbling at the laces. The leather was cold and stiff and I had to force my feet in. I reached for my coat, and the crinkle of legal paper stopped me cold. I had stood in the schoolhouse hours ago and laid my hatred for that railroad out in front of the whole town. And now the horizon was answering in fire. The coincidence was not lost on me. It would not be lost on Marshal Dillon either.

"Don't go," Sarah said. The panic in her voice was controlled, which made it worse. She caught the sleeve of my coat, her fingers twisting into the rough wool. "If you're there, they'll say it was you. They'll say you did it to stop the line."

"And if I stay here, I'm a coward hiding in the dark." The words felt incomplete in my mouth.

"You're not a coward." Her grip tightened. "You're a man with a family. There's a difference."

I looked at her, and behind her face I saw Kansas — the orange sky over the first homestead, the way smoke rises straight up on a windless night. She had watched one home burn already. Now she was watching me walk toward another fire. What I didn't say was the real reason I had to go: Jedediah. The old prospector was the only man in Oak Haven with enough bitterness and enough nerve to strike a match on my behalf. I had to know whether his loyalty to me had finally turned into a weapon I couldn't put down.

"I'll be back before light," I said. It was a poor promise and we both knew it.

The cold outside hit hard. The night air smelled of woodsmoke and the dry mineral scent of the drought-cracked earth. I didn't take the horse — hoofbeats would bring Voss's Pinkertons down on me before I got fifty yards. I ran across the cracked face of the North Field, the fissures of the drought catching at my boots in the dark like the land itself was trying to hold me back. Twice I stumbled, once going down on one knee hard enough to feel the jolt in my teeth. The air had changed direction; it tasted of ash now, dry and bitter at the back of my throat. Above, the smoke had blotted out a third of the stars and was working on more, a dark curtain being drawn across the sky from north to south.

The fire's sound grew from distant roar to something physical — a deep percussion I felt in my sternum before I heard it in my ears. The heat reached me next, drying the moisture from my eyes and tightening the skin of my face. The stacks were collapsing, great skeletal frames folding inward in showers of sparks that rose fifty feet and hung like a second sky. The smell of hot pine pitch was so thick I could taste it — bitter, resinous, final. And at the edge of the staging area, silhouetted against the hellish light, stood a man I recognized by the set of his coat alone.

Jedediah. His long duster flapped in the thermal wind. He wasn't moving. He stood with his head tilted at an odd angle, listening rather than watching, the way he listened to hoofbeats before he could see horses. His hands hung open and empty at his sides.

"Jed!" The fire swallowed my voice. I pushed forward, shielding my eyes with my forearm against the heat. The air shimmered and bent, distorting the ground so it looked like the earth was breathing. I grabbed his shoulder — the coat was hot to the touch, the wool almost singeing my palm. "What have you done?"

He turned. His eyes were clear. Not guilty-clear, not the flat look of a man suppressing knowledge, but genuinely clear — the clarity of a man who has nothing to hide and knows it. "I didn't do it, Elias." He pointed into the darkness beyond the firelight, his gnarled finger steady. "I heard brush snapping and came running. Thought a calf had got into the timber. But the match was already dropped. Three men on shod horses. They didn't ride like railroad men — they were running, hard. West, toward the Badlands."

"You see their faces?"

"Too dark. But I know the sound of shod horses on hardpan, and I know men who ride like they've got the devil behind them. These weren't amateurs, Elias. This was planned."

I looked at the fire. Thousands of dollars in lumber. The town's argument against me, its hope for mechanical pumps and falling prices, turning to gray ash and wasted heat. Who burns the railroad's timber? Not a farmer trying to protect his land. Not a prospector arguing about water rights. Men who wanted chaos — who wanted Oak Haven too busy blaming itself to watch the western ridgeline. The rustlers we'd tracked into the canyon. They needed this town looking inward.

Before I could speak, I heard the lever-action. A clean, metallic click that cut through the roar of the fire the way a single word cuts through a crowded room. I went still. Every muscle in my body locked at once.

Marshal Dillon stepped out of the smoke. His badge caught the firelight. His face was a slab of grim certainty, and behind him three men in dusters spread into a half-circle with their repeaters up. The nearest one had a jagged scar across his chin and eyes that held no curiosity at all — only the flat patience of a man paid to point a rifle and wait.

"Don't move, Stone." Dillon's voice was the voice of a man who had already written the report. He was looking at Jedediah. "I found tracks leading straight to where you're standing."

"I was tracking the men who set it!" Jedediah's voice cracked. "They went west into the Badlands — shod horses, three of 'em. You move now, you can still pick up the trail."

"The only trail I'm picking up ends right here." Dillon reached for the shackles at his belt. The iron links clinked dully as he pulled them free. "You've been muttering about this railroad since you drifted in, Stone. Voss told me you'd try something desperate once the legal road was closed."

"Voss is the one you should be asking questions of," Jedediah shot back. "He's the one burning his own timber to claim the insurance and blame the settlers — "

"Enough." Dillon's jaw tightened. "I've heard enough stories from you to fill a library, and not one of them has ever come with proof."

The injustice of it worked through me like a blade going slow. I stepped between them. "He didn't do this, Dillon. I know this man. He's a tracker, not a saboteur. He came because he heard noise, the same as I did."

Dillon shifted his gaze to me. It was a cold, professional assessment — the look of a man checking the strength of a joint. "And what about you, Thorne? You're the one who stood up tonight and promised blood and soil. You've got the most to lose. Maybe you sent your prospector here while you sat home with your alibi." He stepped closer. The smell of tobacco and leather cut through the smoke. "You're lucky I didn't find the match in your pocket. Now get out of the way before I decide this cell needs two occupants."

The rage came up fast and hot, a different heat than the fire — unreasoning, the kind that makes a man forget his own arithmetic. My hands balled into fists. "You're letting the real criminals ride free while you arrest a witness!"

One of the Pinkertons stepped forward and pressed his Winchester into my sternum. The cold steel was a plain fact, hard and indifferent. "The Marshal told you to move, farmer," the man said. His breath smelled of stale coffee. "Unless you want to test how patient I am."

I looked at Jedediah. He wasn't fighting. He had the face of a man who had been inside a cage before and knew that truth was a crop that rarely germinated in iron. He met my eyes and gave a small, slow shake of his head. Don't. Your wife. Your boy. The message was clear as water.

I stepped back. The backward step was the hardest thing I'd done since the Kansas foreclosure — harder than signing that paper, harder than loading the wagon. I stood with my jaw locked and watched Dillon spin Jedediah around and slam his wrists into the iron.

The clink of the shackles was a small sound. It shouldn't have been as final as it was. They led him off into the smoke, his boots dragging, his head down — a grizzled man being folded into the machinery that had no use for him except as a culprit.

I stayed until the fire had eaten its way down to the lower stacks. The heat faded to a dull, residual warmth that meant the worst was over and nothing could be undone. Ash drifted through the air like dirty snow, settling on my shoulders, my hat brim, the tops of my boots. I looked at my hands — soot-black, the grit worked into every crease and callus — and thought of Sarah telling me that if I went, they would say it was me. She was right. To everyone watching, these were the hands that had lit the match.

I didn't go home. I walked toward the rhythmic heartbeat of Titus Croft's smithy. Even at this hour, the forge was awake. The town had no real jail — no stone walls, no cell. There was only one structure in Oak Haven solid enough to hold a man against his will: the smithy. Titus had built it to last.

The smell of sulfur and hot iron reached me before the door did. Inside, the hearth burned low, a red eye in deep shadow. The walls were lined with tools hung on iron pegs — tongs, files, punches, all of them catching the faint light in dull gleams. Titus stood at his anvil but wasn't working. He was leaning on the long handle of his hammer, staring at the corner of the room. His massive shoulders were slumped in a way I had never seen. I followed his gaze.

Jedediah sat on a low bench, his ankles chained to the base of the anvil. The chain was short — six inches of play at most. The woodsmoke smell was still heavy on his coat, and his long hair hung forward, hiding most of his face. His hands lay loose in his lap, palms up, like a man who had surrendered something he couldn't name.

Titus didn't turn when I came in. He worked the bellows with a slow, even pull, the coals hissing and brightening. "They forced me," he said. The words came up from somewhere deep, the way sound travels up from a well. "Dillon said the smithy was the only secure place. Said I was the only man strong enough to hold a watch. He swore out a deputization on the spot." He looked at me then, and in his eyes was a conflict so old and heavy it had its own specific gravity. Titus, who had laid down his rifle to pick up a hammer, was now a jailer. The forge he'd used to build this town was now the weight that kept his friend in the dark.

"He's innocent," I said. "He saw the men. Three on shod horses, riding west. Rustlers. They need the town distracted and fighting itself."

Titus nodded once, slowly. "I know. He ain't a burner. He's got too much respect for wood to waste it on a fire he didn't build for warmth." His knuckles tightened on the hammer handle, the tendons standing out along his forearms. "But Dillon needs order. Voss is screaming about lost time and corporate property, and the town needs a name to put on the fire so they don't have to look at their own desperation. Jedediah is the easy mark. Man with no land and no name."

"So we find the proof ourselves," I said. "We find those tracks before the wind takes them."

"Wind's already up," Titus said. "And Dillon's boys are watching the road. You ride out at dawn, they'll follow you. You stay here, they'll say you're conspiring with the prisoner." He set the hammer down on the anvil with a finality that echoed off the stone walls. "Every move we make now costs something, Elias. Make sure you can afford the price."

I crossed to the corner and crouched down in front of Jedediah. The heat from the forge pressed against the side of my face, and up close I could see the red marks where the shackles had already bitten into his wrists. He was tracing the chain links with one finger, slow and methodical, the way a man reads a familiar text. He didn't look up. "I'll get you out of this, Jed. I'll talk to Eleanor. She knows the law. She can find a way to show the tracks."

Jedediah made a sound — a short, dry exhalation that wasn't quite a laugh. "Tracks are gone, Elias. Fire took some and the wind'll take the rest by sunup. And the law is just a different kind of fire. Once it starts, it doesn't stop 'til it's consumed everything in its path." He looked up at me, his eyes sharp and bright in the low light. "Stay clear of this. You've got a wife and a boy. You've got a crop to plant. You tie yourself to me, they'll pull you under too. I've been in holes deeper than this one."

"Not with iron around your ankles, you haven't."

He almost smiled. "Fair point."

I stood. The forge heat was oppressive now, pressing against the skin of my neck and hands. Titus had gone back to staring at the coals, a man caught between a badge he'd been forced to acknowledge and a friend chained to his own anvil. The smithy, which Titus had built to be a place of making, had become a place of keeping. Every slow breath of the bellows sounded like a clock measuring out the hours until something broke that couldn't be mended.

I walked out into the gray pre-dawn. The air was cold now, biting at my sweat-soaked shirt, and the ash was settling soft and even across the North Field and the road and the surveyors' stakes with their red tips. I could see the first pale suggestion of light in the east, thin as a knife edge. Somewhere a rooster crowed, confused by the wrong light, and the sound was so ordinary it hurt.

The fire had not just burned the railroad timber. It had burned the narrow margin of doubt the town had extended to me, and with Jedediah in chains, there was no one left to speak for the truth except a man everyone had already decided to disbelieve.

I had the land, still. But the ground under my feet felt different — less like property, more like evidence.

Chapter 18: The Blacksmith's Dilemma

Titus

The forge breathed with a low, hungry rasp. I pumped the bellows. Orange sparks danced into the soot-heavy air. The charcoal groaned as the heat intensified, color shifting from dull red to white-hot. I didn't look away. The center of that heat was a length of iron rod going soft, its stubborn edges blurring as it surrendered. A simple hinge for a cellar door. I worked it the same as I'd work a cavalry saber — metal doesn't lie. It has no past. It doesn't care for the law. It only answers to the weight of the hand and the honesty of the heat.

Behind me, chain clinked. A high, sharp note through the bass thrum of the forge. I didn't turn around. I knew that sound now. It was the sound of a man being reduced.

Jedediah Stone sat on the low wooden bench, shackled to the base of my main anvil. Three hundred pounds of iron. His anchor. Marshal Dillon had called it a temporary measure, security until the circuit judge could arrive. To me, it was a stain on my floorboards. I'd spent years turning weapons into tools, trying to wash the copper memory of blood out of my hands with the clean scent of coal smoke. Now my shop was a cage. I was holding the key.

"That fire's gettin' awful bright, Titus," Jedediah said. His voice was like dry husks rubbing together, worn thin by the smoke he'd breathed at the depot. "You lookin' to melt that iron or just scare it into shape?"

I pulled the rod from the coals with the tongs. It was translucent, quivering with heat. I laid it across the anvil face and swung.

Clang. The vibration ran up my arm. Solid. Good.

Clang. Clang. I drew the metal out, tapering the end. Each blow sent a fine spray of scale off the surface, gray flakes that floated and winked out on the dirt floor. I didn't speak until the orange glow had faded to cherry red — the end of the working heat.

"The heat's fine, Jed." I set the rod aside on the brick ledge. "It's the world outside that's turned into a furnace. You know what they're saying at Larson's? They're saying you're the match-strike. That Elias put the idea in your head and you put the flame to the wood."

The chain rattled against the anvil foot. "Let 'em talk. Talk's cheap when the well's dry and the belly's empty. But you were there, Titus. A man don't burn what he might need to survive. Those ties were the only thing bringing the train, and the train's the only thing bringing the pumps. I'm a fool maybe, but not a suicidal one."

"No," I said. "You're not."

I thrust the iron back into the coals. Watched the fire take it again.

He was right. The Law of the Sod held this place together — the unspoken agreement that your neighbor's life is your life, because out here, that's the only law that holds weight. Water is for everyone. Survival is a communal act. Burning railroad timber was a strike against the town's own breath. Jedediah, for all his drifting and grumbling, had a soul tied to the land's rhythm. He hadn't done this. I knew it before he said a word — he'd been with me not an hour before the glow started, helping me pull a stone from a mule's hoof. His hands had been steady and patient with that animal. Not the hands of an arsonist. Innocent. But Dillon didn't want alibis from a blacksmith who preferred silence to testimony.

"I saw 'em, Titus." Jedediah leaned forward as far as the chain allowed. The firelight caught the deep creases of his face — old cedar, worked by weather. "Three riders. Shod horses. Canyon boys, the ones we chased in the summer. They dropped the match and rode west into the Badlands before the first stack even started to roar. I told the Marshal. He wasn't listening."

"He never listens."

"No. He takes what Voss gives him and calls it evidence." Jedediah's jaw tightened. "I could hear the shoes on hardpan, Titus. Ring of iron on rock. No mistaking it. Those horses were shod recent — good work, tight clinches. Not range stock."

My hand stopped on the bellows.

The rustlers. Desperate men made brutal by the drought. If the town was busy blaming Elias and Jedediah, nobody would be watching the western ridge. A calculated chaos. It was working. I'd seen this before — the war was full of it, men herding your attention toward the noise while the real damage was being done elsewhere. A flanking maneuver dressed up as a campfire. A cold anger settled in my gut. Not hot. Not explosive. The heavy, leaden kind. The kind an old soldier carries when he's recognized a trap and has already stepped in it.

The door opened. Harsh morning light and a swirl of fine dust. Samuel Price came in carrying a tin pail and a cloth-wrapped bundle. He looked smaller than he had yesterday. Shoulders hunched. Eyes darting from the anvil to the man in chains. He was my apprentice — came west looking for a legend, found only the sweat of the forge, and now was seeing the ugly seam beneath the dream. The soot on his face hadn't been washed. He'd been up all night, same as the rest of us.

"Miss Rachel sent this," he said. His voice cracked. He set the pail on my workbench, away from the heat. "Stew. And some bread. She said even a man in trouble needs to eat, though she didn't look me in the eye when she said it."

"How's the stew?"

"Thin, sir. But hot."

I set my hammer down. "What's the word, Samuel? Plain. I need truth, not polish."

He wiped his hands on his trousers, nervous and repetitive. The boy had a habit of wringing his fingers when he was scared. He was doing it now. "It's bad, Mr. Croft. Anders Larson is outside the Emporium telling anyone who'll stand still that the railroad's pulling out because of the fire. He's calling Jedediah the 'criminal element' — says Elias brought him into town like a plague. People are scared. And when they're scared, they start looking for something to break."

I looked at Jedediah. He was staring at the dirt floor. Unreadable. I'd seen this before too — in the war, the way fear turns neighbors into wolves inside a single night. They didn't want justice. They wanted the uncertainty to end. If hanging a prospector made the railroad stay, plenty would provide the rope.

"Elias is under town arrest," Samuel continued, dropping to a whisper. He glanced at the door as if someone might be pressing an ear to the oak. "Dillon's got a Pinkerton posted at his gate. Sarah's inside, won't come to the window. Feels like a siege, only the enemy is us."

"And Eleanor?"

Samuel blinked. "Miss Vance is at the schoolhouse. She's been writing letters since dawn. I saw the ink on her fingers when she came to the well." He paused. "She looked angry, sir. The kind of angry that comes with a plan."

Good. Eleanor had a mind like a set of calipers. If anyone could find a legal angle, she could.

"Thank you, Samuel." I kept my voice hard and even. "Go back to the Emporium. Ears open, mouth shut. If anyone asks, tell them I'm working on the Marshal's business. Go."

He nodded and vanished back into the dust. The door swung shut behind him and the smithy went dim again, the world reduced to the coal-glow and the shadows.

I unwrapped the bundle. Bread still warm. The smell of yeast and flour — a sharp reminder of what we were trying to hold together here. I tore off a hunk and handed it to Jedediah. He took it without ceremony. Ate with slow, mechanical precision, the way a man eats when he doesn't know where the next meal comes from. I poured some of the stew into a tin cup and set it on the bench beside him. He drank it one-handed, the other wrist resting on the chain as if it were a familiar weight.

"They're gonna come for me, Titus," he said, when the silence had stretched long enough. "Maybe not today. But once the depot cools and they see the timber's gone for good, they'll want a payment. I'm the only coin in the pocket."

I didn't answer him. I walked to the door and dropped the heavy oak bar into its sockets. The shop went dim. I stood in the low light and looked at my hammer. I'd made a vow when I came to Oak Haven — not to God, not to a court, but to myself, which is the only vow that actually holds. The vow was this: the hammer builds. It doesn't break. I'd killed men in the war — in the high mountain passes, in the dusty flats where you couldn't tell the living from the dead until you were standing over them — and I had carried those ghosts for twenty years. I was not interested in adding to the count.

But you can't mend a broken town with a hinge.

The day went slow and gray. I worked through the orders that had piled up. A plowshare for the Parkers — the old one had cracked along the landside, cheap casting, and I had to draw new steel to reinforce it. A set of horseshoes for a teamster. Every strike of the hammer was clean and necessary. The rhythm held me together the way it always did. Strike, turn, strike, cool.

The simple honesty of shaping metal. Jedediah sat quiet, watching the shadows move. Sometime in the afternoon he hummed a tune I didn't recognize — low, tuneless, something from a place I'd never been. Then he stopped. The silence was worse.

The sun went down. The town settled into a watchful stillness — not peace, but the held breath before something breaks. I sat on my stool near the forge, the fire nothing now but a faint red pulse. I could hear the wind through the sagebrush outside. The smell of ash still coming from the depot, a quarter mile off. The air had that taste of aftermath — charred wood and wet cinder and something chemical underneath, probably the creosote they'd treated the ties with.

I looked at the key on the edge of the anvil. Piece of brass. Small. Light.

It sat there like a loaded rifle.

I stood and walked to Jedediah. He was asleep, or making a good show of it — chin on chest, breathing slow and even. The firelight caught the edge of the shackle around his ankle, and the metal had already worn a raw line into the skin above his boot. I studied it. A man shouldn't wear marks from my iron. Not in my shop.

I went to my tool chest and took out the fine-nosed pliers and a length of tempered wire I used for delicate clockwork repairs. My pulse was steady and unhurried. This was not a decision I was still making. I had made it the moment I let them put the chains on him in my shop and said nothing. That silence had been my first error. This would be my correction.

I knelt in the dirt. The smell of horse sweat and old iron was thick — the floor of a smithy holds every job ever done on it, pressed into the packed earth like a record. The padlock was a heavy industrial thing, but I knew its geometry the way I know the shape of a horseshoe. I inserted the wire. My fingers were surgeon-steady. I'd picked locks before, in another life. The skill hadn't left. Skills like that never do.

Click. A small sound. Barely audible over the wind.

Scrape. The tumblers moved, one by one. The lock snapped open.

I did not remove it. I took the pliers and marred the keyhole — gouged the brass to look like it had been worked by a piece of scrap iron. Scratched the chain links to suggest a struggle. The deception had to be physical. Dillon would inspect every surface. I made sure the story the metal told was convincing.

Then I put my hand on Jedediah's shoulder and shook it once.

He came awake instantly. Eyes sharp and bright. He looked at the open lock, then at me. His mouth moved but no sound came. His throat worked. I gave him the time.

"Titus," he finally whispered. "What are you doing?"

"The Law of the Sod." My voice was low and rough as slag. "You said it yourself. We don't refuse water to a traveler, and we don't let a man hang for a crime he didn't commit. Not in this town. Not while I'm holding the hammer."

I pulled the chain away from the anvil. The links scraped across the iron base with a sound like a long exhale. He stood, legs stiff and shaky, a man relearning the weight of his own body. He swayed once. I steadied him with a hand on his arm. The muscle underneath was thin. He hadn't been eating enough, even before the chains.

I reached into my coat and took out a small leather pouch — dried beef and a handful of silver coins, everything in the shop's till. Not much. Enough to keep a man moving for a week if he was careful.

"Go west," I told him. My hand on his shoulder was firm. "The Badlands. Those rustlers did this — find proof. That running iron. A surveying flag. Anything that ties them to that fire. You bring it back, or you stay gone. Because if Dillon finds you empty-handed in open country, he'll shoot you where you stand."

"And if I find it?"

"You bring it to Eleanor. Not to Dillon. Eleanor will know what to do with it."

Jedediah took the pouch. His fingers were rough as file-work, a life of scratching at the earth written into the skin. "Why are you doing this, Titus? You're a pillar of this town. You do this, you're throwing away everything you built."

I looked at the dark forge. The coal bed had gone to ash and the hearth was nothing but a black mouth. "A town that hangs an innocent man to please a railroad company isn't a town worth building. It's just a collection of houses held together by fear." I stepped back. "Use the creek bed going west. It'll cover your tracks until you hit the rocks. The moon's behind a cloud. Move now."

He didn't say thank you. No need. He gave one short nod and disappeared through the back door. The night swallowed him whole — one moment a shape in the doorframe, the next just the sound of boots on dry grass, and then nothing.

I stood in the center of the dark shop and listened to him go. The chain lay coiled on the dirt floor like a dead snake. The marred lock sat on the anvil edge where the key had been. I picked up my hammer and held it, feeling the familiar weight settle into my palm. The hickory handle was smooth from years of grip, shaped to my hand and no one else's. I had broken the lock. I had not broken the truth.

In the morning I would tell Dillon I'd fallen asleep. That the prospector must have had a tool hidden in his boot. I would take the suspicion. That was the deal. A man does a thing and he carries what comes after. That's the weight of the work.

The shop was clean again. The air felt different — less like a cage, more like a forge. I could build in a forge. I couldn't build in a cage.

I sat down on my stool, set the hammer across my knees, and waited for the dawn.

Chapter 19: Tracks in the Ash

Elias

The morning light didn't break so much as bleed through — a gray shroud of soot and low-hanging dust that turned the whole world the color of old newspaper. I stood on the porch in my stockinged feet, the wood cold and grit-slicked under my soles, watching the horizon. I expected the heavy stillness that follows a fire, the kind of quiet that feels like the land itself is taking stock. What I got instead was motion.

The supply wagons came in a long, rattling line. Canvas covers flapped. But these weren't supply wagons. The men unloading from them didn't carry shovels or picks. They wore long dust-colored dusters, hats pulled low, and across their laps lay the cold dark glint of repeating rifles. The belts at their waists were heavy with brass. Ten wagons. Twenty. More. They spread into the town square with the practiced, efficient movement of an army taking ground — tents going up around the skeletal remains of the depot, men fanning out along the road. White canvas bloomed in the dirt like sores. Caleb Voss stood at the center of it all, his bowler hat a dark smudge against the gray sky, directing the operation with short, stabbing gestures. He looked less like a surveyor now. He looked like a general.

The town went small under that many eyes. You could feel it — the way the buildings seemed to shrink, the way the familiar sounds of morning (a rooster, a pump handle, a door banging) were swallowed by the rattle of equipment and the low murmur of men who had no stake in this ground beyond what they were paid to take.

I stepped off the porch and walked to the north edge of my fence line, watching. Forty men, at least. All of them looking at Oak Haven the way you look at a problem you've already decided how to solve. The smell of the burnt depot was still thick on the air — charred pine and scorched earth and something chemical underneath, probably the creosote they'd treated the ties with. It coated the inside of my throat and I couldn't swallow it away.

A single horse came at a gallop. I turned. Marshal Dillon, riding hard, didn't slow until he was nearly on the fence rails. Dry dirt sprayed against the lower boards with a sound like buckshot. He was off the saddle before the horse had finished stopping, his boots hitting the ground in a heavy double thud, and the look on his face dropped something cold and heavy into the pit of my stomach.

He didn't greet me. He crossed the distance between us fast, the heels of his boots punching into the cracked dirt. "Where is he, Elias?"

"Where is who?"

"Don't." His voice was a low growl, close to violence. He got near enough that I could smell the stale coffee on his breath and the iron tang of his badge in the cold air. "Where's the prospector?"

I kept my eyes level. Held myself still the way you hold still when a rattler is deciding whether to coil. "I haven't seen Jedediah since you took him to the smithy in chains. I've been on my land, same as you ordered."

"Titus claims he fell asleep and the old man picked the lock." Dillon's hand moved to rest near his sidearm — not drawing, but making the presence known, the way a man lays his cards face down on the table to remind you he's still in the game. "That lock didn't yield to a piece of scrap, Elias. It was handled. And we both know whose shadow was seen near the smithy last night. You've been whispering in his ear from the start. You helped him run."

"I did not." The words were plain and steady. I let them stand without embellishment. Three words. All of them true. "If Jedediah is gone, he's gone because he knew he wouldn't get a fair hearing in a town that's already looking for a ghost to hang. I didn't see him. I didn't help him. You're hunting for a culprit because you let the real ones ride west while the depot was still hot."

Dillon's eyes narrowed until they were just slits of cold certainty. The skin around them creased like old parchment. He had already decided. I could see it in the way he was holding himself — the decision already made, the conversation merely a formality, the verdict written before the trial. He reached into his duster and produced a folded sheet of paper. He shoved it toward my chest.

"Voss has brought in the Pinkertons to secure the line's interests, and they have long memories for men who obstruct the law. Until Jedediah Stone is back in chains, or until I'm satisfied you had no part in his flight, you are under house arrest. Effective immediately. You don't cross the fence line. You don't go to the smithy. You don't go to the Emporium for a pound of flour without a guard at your side. If I see your shadow on the road, I'll treat you as an escaped felon."

I let the paper fall to the dust between us. It lay there, white against the brown earth, the legal print too small to read from standing height but the meaning plain enough. "House arrest. On my own land. For the crime of being right."

"For the crime of being in the way," Dillon said, and there was a honesty in it that caught me. He mounted up. For one moment, at the top of his swing into the saddle, something showed through the set of his face — not regret exactly, but an awareness of cost that he was choosing to ignore. Then it was gone, replaced by the hard mask. "Stay inside, Elias. For your wife's sake, if not your own. The mood in town is building into something I won't be able to hold back. You understand me."

"I understand you fine, Marshal. I just don't believe you understand yourself."

He spurred the horse and rode back toward the square without looking back. I stood in the settling dust and watched the surveyors' stakes in the North Field, their red tips catching what pale light the sky could manage. Those stakes had started all of this — the first inch of a line that would swallow everything. I counted them out of habit. Fourteen visible from where I stood. Each one a small wound in the earth.

I walked back toward the house. Sarah's face was at the window, pale and blurred through the glass, her hand pressed against it. The gesture was so still it could have been a daguerreotype — the farm wife waiting for news, the same image in a hundred homesteads across a hundred hard years. I didn't want to go inside. Going inside meant explaining that the fence was no longer a boundary but a wall. I stopped at the gate and gripped the sun-bleached wood, and a splinter drove itself deep into my palm. I let it sit there. It was the sharpest, most honest thing I'd felt all morning.

Then I saw the guard.

He stepped out from behind the corner of my barn — dark duster, repeater cradled in his arms with the easy, boneless grip of a man who'd been doing this kind of work long enough that it required no effort. He was young, maybe twenty-five, with a thin blond mustache and a jaw that hadn't seen a razor in days. He didn't speak. He leaned against the post of my own gate and looked at me with eyes as empty as a dry well. Took a slow, deliberate bite of hardtack. The crunch was loud in the still air. He chewed with his mouth open, unhurried, watching me the way a barn cat watches a mouse it hasn't decided to chase yet.

He wasn't there to protect me. He was there to watch.

"You've got a nice place here," he said. His voice was flat, Midwestern, carrying no opinion. "Be a shame if anything else caught fire."

I didn't answer. The words would have cost more than they were worth. I went inside and closed the door. The click of the latch sounded final. Sarah was standing by the stove, not cooking, just standing with her hands wrapped around a cold cup of coffee. She looked at me and I saw the question in her face — all the questions, really, compressed into a single look.

"House arrest," I said. "Until Jed is found."

She set the cup down on the counter. Her hands were steady but her mouth pulled tight at the corners. "And the guard?"

"Pinkerton. At the gate."

She crossed the room and looked through the window. The guard hadn't moved. A dark column of a man against the flat, wide-open country, standing on my land as if it were his. Sarah watched him for a long moment. Then she pulled the curtain shut.

"I'll heat water," she said. "You've got ash in your hair."

I sat at the kitchen table while she filled the kettle from the indoor pump. The familiar sound of water on iron. The hiss as she set the kettle on the stove. Small, domestic sounds that should have been comforting and instead felt like they were happening on the other side of a wall.

The Bible sat on the sideboard. The ledger next to it — the book where I kept the seasons' true accounts, crop weights and debt columns, the numbers that told the story of this place better than any words. Both of them sitting there like objects from a world that was still operating under rules that no longer applied.

I opened the ledger. The columns were in order. Seed costs, yield projections, the fall's grazing tallies. Everything I had held onto through the drought years, through the Kansas foreclosures, through Sarah's long silences and the winter that took the north herd. All of it reduced, this morning, to the record of a man who was locked out of the very ground the ledger described. The numbers were still true. They just didn't matter anymore — or they mattered in a way that had nothing to do with farming. They were evidence now. A paper trail of a man's desperation, ready to be read by hostile eyes.

Every time I looked up, the guard was there. Every sound from the square — a Pinkerton's shout, the clink of equipment, the ring of a hammer on a tent stake — made the room contract a half-inch. I was the master of these fields, the man who had outlasted the '89 drought and the Kansas banks and every offer of progress that came dressed up as salvation. I had survived by refusing to be moved.

Now I was sitting at my own table with a splinter in my hand and a hired man at my gate, and the land outside was full of other people's plans.

Sarah brought me a basin of warm water and a clean rag. I washed my hands and face, the water turning gray with ash almost immediately. She stood behind me and brushed the soot from my hair with her fingers, slow and careful, the way she used to brush the flour from her apron at the end of a baking day. Neither of us spoke. The tenderness of the gesture was almost unbearable.

I worked the splinter out with my thumbnail, a thin sliver of the same gate-wood I'd put in the ground eight years ago. A small thing. Not much of a return on the labor. I held it up to the light from the window — a sliver of pale wood, tapered to a point, the grain still tight and sound. Good wood. I'd chosen it well, back when choosing wood for a gate was the kind of decision that mattered.

I set it on the table beside the ledger.

Outside, the guard finished his hardtack and started on another piece.

Chapter 20: The Cold Forge

Titus

The forge was dead. Not banked. Dead. I hadn't fed it since the night I let Jedediah go.

I stood in the dark shop and listened. Wind against the planks. The creak of the bellows chain where it hung slack. Somewhere outside, boot heels on packed earth — a Pinkerton making his circuit past the smithy for the third time since midnight. The rhythm was regular. Every nine minutes. I had counted.

The air in the shop held the smell of cold iron and old sweat. No coal-smoke. No heat. A forge without fire is just a hole in a stone. Useless. I had let it go out on purpose. A cold shop draws no visitors. A dark window asks no questions. I needed both.

I ran my hand along the anvil face. The steel was cold under my palm. Five hundred pounds of cast and ground metal, and in this temperature it pulled heat from the skin like a leech. The surface was true — no dishing, no sway. I had dressed it last month with the grinder. Good tool. Patient tool. It would wait.

The lock sat on the workbench where I had placed it after Dillon's inspection that morning. Marred brass. Scratched keyhole. He had turned it over in his hands, held it to the light, run his thumb across the gouges I had cut into the metal. His eyes had come up to mine. I gave him nothing. He took the lock and left. The story the metal told was the story I had written into it, and Dillon did not have the craft to read the forgery beneath the forgery.

But he suspected. A man doesn't need proof to suspect. He needs only the shape of the thing.

Boot heels again. I counted. Nine minutes. The Pinkerton passed the door without slowing. His shadow cut across the gap beneath the oak — a brief darkening, then gone. I waited until the footsteps faded toward the Emporium before I moved to the window.

The town looked wrong.

White canvas tents lined the square in rows. Firelight from their camp threw long shapes across the storefronts. The depot was a black skeleton against the sky — charred uprights, collapsed roof beams, the iron rail-ties twisted and bowed from the heat. I studied the wreckage the way I study a failed weld. The fire had started low, at the base of the stacked ties where creosote had pooled in the grain. That was an accelerant point. Deliberate. No accident leaves that signature.

The crossbeams had fractured where the grain ran diagonal — weak wood, green-cut, the kind a railroad buys cheap when it's building fast and counting on replacement. The iron ties had warped but not melted. Twelve hundred degrees, maybe. Hot enough to buckle but not enough to slag. A controlled burn. Whoever set it knew what they were doing. They had read the structure and found its failure point.

I stepped back from the window.

The Emporium across the square had its shutters drawn. Larson's place was dark. The whole street had the look of iron left too long in the quench — brittle, contracted, all the flexibility shocked out of it.

Twenty Pinkertons. Maybe more. Repeating rifles, new leather, polished brass. They moved through Oak Haven with the weight of men who had done this before — occupied a town, squeezed it until it gave up what they wanted. I had seen that weight before. Different uniforms. Same mechanics. You take the ground, control the movement, isolate the ones who might resist. Elias was penned on his own land. Jedediah was running. Eleanor was writing letters that would reach no one who could act in time.

And I was standing in a dead forge, counting a sentry's footsteps.

The back wall of the shop held my failures. Every smith keeps them. A cracked axle head. A set of hinges where the weld didn't take. A length of bar stock I had drawn too thin, the grain stretched past its limit, ready to snap under any real load. I kept them as reminders. Iron tells you what it can bear. You have to listen. Push past the limit and the metal doesn't warn you twice.

The town was at its limit. I could feel it the way I feel a piece of steel approaching critical temperature — not by color alone, but by the way the air changes around it. The heat coming off it. The sound it makes when you tap it. Oak Haven was making that sound now. The high, thin ring of metal about to fail.

I crossed the shop to the quenching tub. The water was still. A skin of coal dust floated on the surface, undisturbed. I put my hand in. Cold. The kind of cold that makes the joints ache. I held it there and let the sensation climb my wrist, my forearm. A test. The body tells you things the mind won't.

My hands were steady.

The door opened. No knock. I turned. Samuel stood in the frame, barely visible against the dark. He was breathing hard. Sweat on his forehead despite the cold.

"Two more wagons came in." His voice was low. Controlled, but only just. "From the east road. Graves is with them. They're setting up a command post at the depot."

"I saw."

"Titus." He stepped inside and pulled the door shut. The dark swallowed him to the shoulders. "They're talking about a sweep. Pinkerton captain told the Marshal they'll search every building in town by morning. Every shop. Every cellar."

I looked at the floor. The trench was sealed. The floorboard sat flush. No sign of disturbance. But a man who knows what he's looking for will find it. Graves had that look — the flat, cataloging gaze of a man who takes inventory before he takes action.

"Let them search."

"But — "

"There's nothing here, Samuel." The words were hard and flat. I made them that way. The boy needed a wall to lean against, not a door to walk through. "Go back to the boarding house. Sleep if you can. Stay clear of the Pinkertons."

He didn't move. His hands were working at his sides — that wringing habit, fingers knotting against each other. I had been trying to break him of it. A smith's hands need to be still when the work is hot.

"Are you afraid?" he asked.

The question was honest. He had earned the right to ask it.

"No." I picked up a rag from the bench and began wiping down the anvil face. The motion was automatic. "Fear is a warning. I'm past the warning."

He stood there another moment. Then he nodded once and went out. The door closed behind him. I listened to his footsteps move away toward the east end of town — quick and light on the packed earth. A young man's walk. He still moved like someone who believed speed could solve a problem. The Pinkerton's circuit would bring him past the smithy again in four minutes. Samuel would be clear by then. The boy had good instincts, even if he didn't trust them yet. Green iron. Sound grain. He just needed tempering.

I set the rag down.

The shop was quiet. The anvil was clean. The tools hung in their places on the wall. Everything in order. I had spent five years building this order — peg by peg, tool by tool, the slow accumulation of a life that meant something other than what came before. Every hinge I forged was a sentence in a new language. Every plowshare was a word I didn't have to speak. The work held me together the way a good weld holds a joint — not by force, but by the fusion of two surfaces that had no business being separate.

The Pinkertons didn't care about my welds. They cared about the chain on the floor and the empty bench where Jedediah had sat and the lock with marks that might be read a second way by sharper eyes.

I went to the forge. The coal bed was gray and dead. Ash on ash. I cleared the clinker with the rake — slow, deliberate strokes, scraping the fused slag from the firepot until clean coal showed beneath. The sound of the rake on iron was thin and dry. No heat to give it resonance. I laid fresh coal around the edges. Built the fire the way I always build it — small at the center, banked tight, air channels open underneath. Structure first. Then heat.

I struck a match. The sulfur flare lit the shop in a brief yellow flash. I touched it to the tinder at the base of the coal pile. A thin curl of smoke. Then a glow. Faint at first. The color of rust. I worked the bellows — one slow pump, then another. The glow brightened. Orange crept through the coal like a vein of copper through basalt.

The air in the shop shifted. Temperature rising. The anvil would warm. The tools would warm. The iron in the rack would lose its brittleness and remember what it was for.

I pumped the bellows again. The fire answered.

There was a thing I had to do and I was done waiting for someone else to do it. The decision wasn't new. It had been forming since I heard the chain fall from the anvil and watched Jedediah walk into the dark. Since I marred the lock. Since I looked at the depot wreckage and read the fire's handwriting. The decision had been cooling in me the way a quenched blade cools — heat driven inward, locked in the grain, invisible from the surface but present in every molecule of the steel.

I reached for the bellows handle and pumped it to full draw. The coal flared white at the center. Heat pushed against my face and forearms. The forge was alive again.

I took a bar of good steel from the rack. Three-quarter inch. Clean stock, no pitting, no rust. I laid it in the coals and watched the color climb. Black to red. Red to orange. The metal started to glow from the inside out, the way conviction does.

I would find them. The men who burned the depot and framed this town against itself. I would find them the way I find a flaw in a piece of iron — by testing it, by striking it, by listening to what the metal says when the hammer falls. And when I found them, I would do what was required. Not more. Not less. The tool doesn't choose. The man does.

The steel reached working temperature. I pulled it from the fire with the tongs and laid it on the anvil. Lifted the hammer. The hickory handle settled into the groove my palm had worn over five years of building.

I swung.

The ring of the first strike filled the shop and went out through the walls into the dark town. Clear. Certain. The sound of a forge that was no longer cold.

Chapter 21: The Midpoint Storm

Elias

The air didn't just go still. It died.

I stood at the window, forehead against the glass, watching the Pinkerton at my gate. He had stopped pacing. His head tilted back, reading something the rest of us hadn't caught yet — some shift in the pressure, some animal knowledge buried under the duster and the badge. The sky, flat pewter all morning, was curdling at the horizon. Not the heavy purple of a rain cloud, but a deep, suffocating black that started at the edge of the world and moved inward. A wall of solid earth, torn loose and marching. I had seen this before. You don't forget the shape of it. Kansas, 1882 — the duster that buried our first fence and left a half-inch of grit inside the coffee pot. This one looked worse.

Pressure dropped in my ears — a sharp, stabbing ache that made the house feel like it was being squeezed by something enormous and indifferent. The light turned jaundiced, the color of old grease, casting everything in a sepia tone that made the room look like a photograph of itself. The surveyors' stakes in the North Field flashed red against the darkening sod. Then the wind hit.

Not a gust. A blow.

The sod walls shuddered on a frequency I felt in the joints of my hands. The kettle on the stove rattled. A glass jar on the shelf walked itself to the edge and tipped over, rolling across the boards with a dull, hollow sound. Gravel and dry soil pelted the glass — clack-clack-clack, like birdshot. Out at the gate, the Pinkerton was fumbling with his duster, the long coat whipping around his legs. He looked toward the square, then back at the house. The certainty was gone from him. He wasn't a hired enforcer anymore. He was just a man standing in the open when he shouldn't have been.

The first wall of grit hit solid. He flinched, covered his eyes, turned, and ran for the lee of the barn. Gone. House arrest, overruled by the sky.

I should have stayed inside. Sod walls two feet thick — built for exactly this. But the kitchen meant the table and the ledger and the clock counting off the minutes of my confinement. The ticking had become a kind of torture, each second a small accusation. Sarah was in the cellar, where she belonged. I had guided her down the steps myself, her hand cool and dry in mine, her face composed in that way that meant she was more afraid than she was showing.

"Bolt the trap," I'd told her.

"You bolt the door," she'd answered, which was her way of saying come down with me. I didn't.

I grabbed my hat, jammed it low, wrapped a wet rag around my face, and stepped out.

The air was solid with silt — gritty, abrasive, tasting of old dust and decades of drought baked into the topsoil. I couldn't see the gate. Couldn't see the barn. The world had reduced to a screaming ochre void navigable only by feel. The porch railing was slick under my hands. I gripped it until the wood bit into my palms. The wind pushed against my chest like a hand.

A fence wire snapped — that high, singing ping of overstretched metal letting go, followed by the whip-crack of the loose end whipping free. The sound was swallowed in an instant by the roar. I was about to go back inside when I saw the shape.

Darker than the dust. Moving wrong. Something lurching, bent at the waist, dragging a leg. Twenty yards out, moving toward the schoolhouse. It went down, a heap of shadow in the churning dirt. Clawed back up. Went down again.

I knew that coat. The mismatched fur, the particular way it swung, one side longer than the other where he'd patched it with a different hide. I had watched it for years.

Jedediah.

The wind had him. He was clutching something to his chest with both arms, knuckles white, losing ground with every step. He moved like a man who had been moving for a very long time and was running on the last of something that couldn't be replenished.

I didn't think about house arrest. I didn't think about Dillon's threats or the Pinkerton or the paper lying in the dust by my gate. I went off the porch.

The wind caught me like a sail. I stayed low — bent double, weight forward, one foot at a time. The drifts were already building against the fence posts, fine silt piling up in soft ridges that gave way under my boots. Every breath was a fight against the rag clogging with mud. The grit found every opening — collar, sleeves, the gaps between my fingers — and worked its way in with a patient, grinding persistence. I found the road by the change in the ground underfoot, packed earth harder than the field, and followed it until I reached him.

He was on his knees ten yards from the schoolhouse fence, hands buried in the dirt, head down. When I grabbed his shoulder he flinched hard and his head came up. His face was a mask of red mud and blood — the dark, wet stain spreading across his coat was not new. Old, dried in patches, fresh in others, the layered look of a wound that had been bleeding, crusting, and bleeding again. He had been shot, and he had been walking with it for a long time. Days, maybe. The coat was stiff with it.

He still had the bundle. Iron and cloth, arms clamped around it. The grip of a man who has made a decision about what matters and will not let go until the decision is taken from him.

I tried to say his name. The word went nowhere — the wind tore it apart before it left my teeth.

He looked at me. Through the mud and the blood, his eyes were focused. He was still in there. He tried to speak and only a wet cough came out, a sound that carried the taste of copper even through the storm. He held the bundle tighter and jerked his chin toward the schoolhouse. The message was clear: get me inside.

I hooked my hands under his arms and heaved. He sagged against me, slack and half-conscious—the dead heft of a man who'd spent the last of himself. He reeked of blood, sagebrush, and the harsh mineral sting of Badlands hardpan. I dug my heels in and pulled. The schoolhouse was ten yards away and each of those yards cost the full work of a furrow-length. My lungs burned. I breathed mud. The muscles along my spine screamed, and I felt something pop in my lower back — not breaking, but warning. The schoolhouse came out of the blackness — walls, porch, door. I kicked it with everything left in my legs.

The wood groaned and gave.

We went through together, Jedediah's boots dragging across the threshold, and the door slammed behind us with a bang that shook the frame.

The quiet inside hit like a hand on the chest. The roar dropped to a moan — still there, pressing against every surface, rattling the windows in their casings, but muffled now by two feet of sod and the heavy oak door. Amber lamplight and chalk dust and woodsmoke. The air smelled of slate and kerosene and the particular warmth of a small room holding too many bodies. I lay still for two full seconds just breathing. The floor was hard-packed dirt, cool against my cheek. Then I looked up.

Eleanor in the corner with three of the Parker children — the two girls and the youngest boy, their faces pale and wide. She had her arms around the smallest one, her hand cupped over the child's ear as if she could block the sound of the world ending. Her eyes found mine and held, assessing the situation the way she assessed everything: rapidly, completely.

Titus near the stove, hammer in hand, face set like worked iron — his body angled between the door and the children, the way a man stands when he's been waiting and knows something is coming. He saw Jedediah and his jaw tightened, but he didn't move. He wouldn't — not until he understood the whole picture.

And by the chalkboard: Caleb Voss.

Bowler hat on the nearest desk. Fine wool coat caked with dust. Holding his brass theodolite in both hands, the way a man holds something useless and knows it. Caught on the line when the duster hit, run to the nearest solid structure same as everyone else. His cravat was loose and his hair, usually oiled flat, stood in wild tufts. He looked diminished — not the general of the morning but a man who had been reminded that the land he was trying to tame had opinions of its own. His eyes moved from me to Jedediah. The calculation in them stalled. For the first time since he'd arrived in Oak Haven, the numbers weren't adding up.

We were all of us there: the farmer and the teacher, the smith and the drifter, and the man who had come to take what the rest of us built. Outside, the storm drove black dirt against the windows and screamed down the chimney and erased the world beyond those walls. The lamp flickered. A draft found the flame and it bent sideways, sending shadows leaping across the alphabet chart on the wall and the children's drawings pinned above the slate board.

Jedediah still had the bundle — iron and cloth, arms wrapped tight, blood from his coat seeping slowly onto the schoolhouse floor. He looked at me through the mud, and his eyes were sharp enough to cut. He tried to speak again and this time managed a single word, barely a rasp:

"Proof."

He had found something in the Badlands.

Whatever came next was going to happen in this room.

Chapter 22: The Eye of the Needle

Eleanor

The schoolhouse was lying. Its four sod walls held their usual quiet, but the quiet was a fiction — a thin page of wood and packed earth stretched over a world that had become a grinding machine. Wind screamed at the shutters, high and keening, shuddering the floorboards under my boots. The lamp on my desk guttered with each gust, the flame bending sideways as if flinching. What struck me first was not the sound but the smell: chalk dust, the metallic sweetness of blood, and the low sulfurous breath of the kerosene. Three scents that had no business occupying the same sentence, yet here they were, mingling in the thick air of my classroom like a grammar of crisis.

Elias stood gasping in the doorway, Jedediah sagging across his arms, the man's breath coming in ragged, wet hitches against Elias's chest. Both of them were caked in red mud, the color of old brick, and the wind behind them clawed at the doorframe as if trying to follow them in.

"Titus, help me." Elias's voice rasped like torn fabric.

The blacksmith moved. He dropped his sledgehammer — its thud on the floorboards a single, blunt exclamation — and crossed the room with a quiet grace that had no business belonging to a man his size. Together they hoisted Jedediah onto the center table, my lesson-plan table, sweeping aside Grammar, Arithmetic, the worn Bible with its cracked spine. I had arranged those books that morning with the particular care I always give to the instruments of learning. Now they lay scattered on the floor, pages splayed, making room for the broken man who had stumbled out of the blackness.

I reached them in an instant. The sight of Jedediah's coat, matted with dark viscous blood that had soaked through to the table's surface, was enough to turn a stomach, but my hands did not shake. I thought of the children before I thought of anything else. "Thomas." The oldest Parker boy looked up from the back stove, his siblings huddled against him — Mary with her face pressed into his shirt, little James with his thumb in his mouth and his eyes enormous. "Keep them here. Don't let them look."

He nodded, that terrible gravity of a child forced to be older than his years, and drew his brother and sister deeper into the shadow behind the stove. Mary whimpered once, a sound like a kitten, and Thomas shushed her with a murmur I couldn't hear. I made a note to myself — the kind of note a teacher makes instinctively — that Thomas Parker had a steadiness in him that would serve him well, or break him, depending on what the world demanded of it.

Caleb Voss had not moved from the chalkboard. His fine wool coat was gray with silt, his knuckles white around the brass theodolite, and the arrogance had drained entirely from his posture. He was simply another soul caught in the teeth of the storm — a fact I noticed and filed away. In Boston, I had seen powerful men diminished by circumstance before: a professor caught in a lie, a deacon found drunk on a Sunday. The expression is always the same — the naked bewilderment of someone discovering that the rules they counted on have been temporarily suspended. I had no patience for it just then.

"He's hit in the shoulder." Elias began peeling back layers of fur coat. The smell of copper and unwashed wool was stifling. "Eleanor, I need water and clean rags."

The schoolhouse held no clinic. There was the small basin near my desk, the water already lukewarm from the morning's washing, and for rags — there were none. The only clean cloth in the room was on my person. I did not deliberate. I reached down, gripped the hem of my white petticoat, and pulled. The fabric gave with a sharp, decisive sound — the sound of a sentence being ended mid-clause — and I tore strip after strip, the rending of cloth cutting through the roar of the storm like punctuation. The cotton was good quality, dense-woven, something I'd brought from Boston in a trunk that now seemed to belong to another woman's life. It would serve better as bandage than as modesty.

The children did not look. Voss did. I let him.

"Here." I pressed the white strips into Elias's hands. His fingers were shaking — not with fear, I thought, but with the tremor that comes after sustained physical effort, the body's delayed accounting of what it has spent. "Titus, bring the lamp closer. I can't see the depth of the wound."

We worked in the jaundiced circle of the light. Jedediah groaned and arched as the cloth met the wound — a shallow furrow across the deltoid, a rifle shot that had grazed him blind in the dust. It bled freely, bright arterial red that darkened almost immediately in the lamplight. I dipped a rag in the basin and cleaned around the edges, watching the water in the bowl turn pink, then crimson. Each time the wind drove itself against the building, the lamp guttered, throwing long shadows across the maps of the world pinned to the walls: Africa, the Pacific coast, the empty-looking expanse labeled "Great Plains." The maps had always seemed provisional to me — approximations drawn by men who had never stood where the land they described actually lived. Tonight they felt like a joke.

Voss watched. He had not moved to help, but his expression had shifted into something I could only describe as study. He observed the way Elias pressed cloth to the wound, the economy of Titus's hands on the lamp, the rhythm of our shared, wordless labor. He was seeing something he had not accounted for — the communal grammar of survival, the sentences people form when the alternative is silence and death. I thought, not for the first time, that his iron tracks could be mapped and graded and financed, but what they could not purchase was the thread we were working with that night. You cannot lay rail across a bond forged in blood and lamplight. The gauge doesn't exist.

"Is he going to live?" Thomas Parker's voice, cracking on the last word. He was trying to keep the fear from his younger siblings, doing imperfectly what adults do imperfectly every day — hiding the truth behind a tone that says everything will be fine.

Titus looked back over one massive shoulder. "He's too stubborn to die tonight, boy. The dust is just making him meaner."

A small, fragile laugh from Mary, muffled by her brother's shirt. The sound was so unexpected and so human that it pierced the room more cleanly than the wind.

Jedediah's eyes fluttered open then — bloodshot, glazed, but sharpening by the second. He looked at

Elias, then at me, then at the ceiling, as though he could feel the weight of packed earth above us. His lips moved, shaping words that didn't quite arrive. He tried to speak; I pressed him back down, my palm flat against his chest, feeling the uneven percussion of his heart through the coat. "Quiet, Jed. You're in the schoolhouse. You're safe."

His fingers closed around my wrist. Iron. "Elias," he wheezed. "I found it — the truth of it. Before the black took the light." A cough, a spray of red dotting his beard. His eyes rolled toward the shadow. He was not finished, but the strength was spent. The sentence trailed off the way a student's essay trails off when the bell rings — mid-thought, urgent, unresolved.

Outside, the storm reached a new register, a physical concussion that shook the door in its frame and sent a fine rain of dirt sifting from the ceiling onto my hair and shoulders. I became acutely aware of the room's composition: a farmer, a blacksmith, a teacher, a surveyor, and three frightened children, all threaded onto the same needle by one bleeding man. Whatever we had been to each other before the duster struck, we were this now. A single paragraph, punctuated by wind.

The gale eased, slightly — not stopping, but catching its breath, the way a storm pauses between movements as if consulting a score. Voss finally moved. He set the theodolite on a student's desk with a deliberate click, reached into his frock coat, and produced a silver flask. The scent of aged brandy cut cleanly through the copper smell of blood. It was a good brandy — I could tell by the nose, the way you can tell good paper by its weight.

He did not drink. He walked to Titus and held the flask out — not with the flourish of a gesture, just an offering. The simplicity of it surprised me. "It won't fix his shoulder," he said. His voice, stripped of its boardroom authority, was surprisingly quiet. "But it might take the edge off the cold."

Titus studied the flask, then the man. A long beat. I watched the play of calculation cross the blacksmith's face — the old soldier's wariness, the pragmatist's assessment, and beneath both, the exhaustion of a man who had been standing between other people and harm for longer than anyone had thanked him for. Then he took it, drank slow, and handed it back. "Thank you." Two words that seemed to cost him something real, a hairline fracture in the armor he had worn since the railroad's scouts first appeared in the valley.

Voss turned the flask toward me; I shook my head, my hands still at the bandaging. He sat on the edge of a student's desk, his legs dangling with an incongruous boyishness, and looked toward the shuttered windows where gravel rattled the wood. "I've seen gales strip a roof in the East," he said, his voice distant. "Floods that swallowed whole blocks. But this — I never expected wind to have weight."

Elias looked up from Jedediah. "Weight?"

"In the city, wind is just air moving too fast. Here it is the land itself rising. I was out at the grade when it hit. I couldn't see my own hand. I have the maps. The elevations. The soil surveys. But I had no accounting for the wind."

It was genuine — or as close to genuine as the man could manage. An admission of ignorance, a recognition that the country he intended to reorganize had declined to be measured. I understood what I was hearing: not sympathy, but a shared enemy. The prairie does not negotiate with surveyors any more than it negotiates with farmers. To the dust, we were all equally temporary. I caught myself thinking of a line from Emerson — something about nature not being amenable to the plans of any single mind — and then I caught myself catching myself, the Boston reflex that still fired unbidden in moments of stress. Out here, Emerson is not useful. Out here, the text is the land, and it writes its own commentary.

"The land here doesn't like to be measured, Mr. Voss," I said, wringing out the last rag. The water in the basin was the color of rust. "It likes to be known. There is a difference."

Voss met my eyes. "The railroad is coming regardless, Miss Vance. You can't stop history with a petticoat and a prayer."

"History is only the story men tell to excuse the things they've taken," Elias cut back, and his voice carried an anger I recognized — the kind ground down to something beyond simple resentment, fine as the dust in the air. "Progress just died in the dirt out there. We're the ones still breathing."

Voss did not argue. He recapped the flask and looked at Jedediah. The truce between us was fragile — a bridge built of nothing but shared exhaustion — but it held. For that hour, the geography of our conflict had shifted. Farmer and surveyor and teacher and blacksmith: just people waiting for the world to stop screaming. I watched the lamplight play across their faces and thought that this was the truest classroom I had ever stood in — no lesson planned, no text assigned, just the raw curriculum of survival.

Jedediah's breathing had settled into a heavy rhythmic rasp. The bandages were a mottled crimson, and the bleeding had slowed to a dull seep. Then he moved — good arm flailing, eyes snapping open with a lucid, terrible focus, staring at the ceiling as though reading something there. His voice came out dry, like tinder catching: "It wasn't a mistake. Not a wandering calf or a hungry man."

"Jed, lie still — "

He ignored me. His trembling fingers worked at the inner lining of his coat, tearing at the stitching with a desperation that spoke of hours spent protecting whatever lay inside. He pulled free a bundle wrapped in red silk — the exact shade of the railroad's surveying flags that had haunted Elias's North Field. Inside the silk: a small, portable running iron. It struck the surface of my desk with a metallic clink that rang through the room, a sound as clear and final as the period at the end of a sentence.

A running iron. Designed for one thing: altering a brand. A thief's tool, the kind that earned a man a rope in this territory without formality. But it was the wrapping that silenced us. The red silk flag bore the stamped mark of the Chicago and North Western. The letters were crisp and official, the ink barely faded — this was not something salvaged from a trash heap. It had been taken deliberately, recently, and used as camouflage.

"Found it in the canyon," Jedediah whispered, his voice failing. "The camp — they weren't just rustling. They used your markers, Voss. Tore up the lines, wrapped their tools in your colors. They wanted us to think it was you. Wanted you to think it was us. Chaos is what they're selling. While we're at each other's throats, they're cleaning out the valley."

Elias looked at the iron, then at Voss. The surveyor had risen, his face the color of candle tallow. "That flag was from the south depot," he said, the precision gone from his voice. "Stolen three weeks ago. We assumed local vandals."

I watched the understanding move through the room — not like a wave, but like ink spreading across wet paper, reaching each person at a different speed. The fires, the missing cattle, the stakes pulled from the North Field — none of it had been the railroad pressing its thumb down, and none of it had been Elias resisting. There was a third party, a predator that fed on friction, that had been using our mutual suspicion as cover. A town at war with a railroad is a town that cannot watch its own perimeter.

Titus's hand moved to the hammer on the floor. He had read it the same moment I had.

"They're framing us both," Elias said, the words slow and deliberate. "Every stake I pulled, every time I saw red in my fields, I thought it was you breaking me. And you thought we were sabotaging your grade."

Voss looked at him — and for the first time, the calculation in his eyes was not about land value or legal leverage. It was survival arithmetic. "If they're using our flags and running irons, they're not common thieves. They're organized. They want this town to burn so they can pick through the ash."

The room contracted around that word: ash. I looked at the running iron lying on the desk where Thomas Parker had learned his multiplication tables last Tuesday, its cold weight pressing a dent into the pine surface, and understood what Jedediah had carried through the storm. Not just evidence. A demand. We could go on fighting each other and be picked clean, or we could stop. The text was plain enough for even the most reluctant reader.

The choice had already been made for us. We were all caught in the eye of the needle, and threading it required all of us — together — to hold the end of the same line.

Chapter 23: Uneasy Truce

Eleanor

Morning did not arrive so much as it leaked through the shutters — a thin, sallow light that carried no warmth, only the announcement of what the night had done. I had been awake for some time, sitting on the edge of my desk with a cold cup of water in my hands, listening to the wind diminish from a roar to a moan to something that might, with charity, be called quiet. The Parker children slept in the corner I had arranged with extra blankets and my coat, their three small bodies curled together like a single organism. Jedediah breathed on the improvised cot, his chest rising and falling in a slow, wet rhythm that I checked every few minutes from across the room.

When Titus wrenched the schoolhouse door open, a wall of packed silt reached his waist. The drift had formed against the door in a smooth, sculpted curve, as if the prairie had spent the night pressing its face to our threshold. I stood behind him, one hand on the doorframe, and looked out at a landscape so thoroughly rearranged that the familiar grammar of Oak Haven had been erased. Fences were suggestions beneath the drifts. The road was a rumor. The storm had rewritten the town in a language of gray, leaving only alien geometries where the prairie had decided to relocate itself. It reminded me of nothing so much as a palimpsest — the original text scraped away, a new one inscribed over the faint traces of what had been.

We stepped out one by one. Elias, then myself, then Titus. The air was thick and gritty, a suspension of fine powder that coated the tongue and settled into the creases of clothing instantly. Voss followed, his polished bowler hat clutched in both hands, the boardroom composure not quite restored. His hair stood in tufts, his cravat hung loose, and there was a quality to his expression that I had not seen before — not humility, precisely, but the echo of it, the way a bell continues to vibrate after the strike has passed. The Pinkerton guards who had sheltered in the lee of the building shook themselves like hounds, dust rising from their heavy coats in clouds that drifted past us without apology.

Voss found his authority first, though it was thinner than yesterday's. "My supply line," he said, looking toward where the main road had been. His eyes tracked the obliterated grade, the buried ruts, the landscape that declined to acknowledge any plan that had been laid upon it. "The wagons won't move an inch. The whole grade will be buried." He turned to the Pinkerton captain — a man whose face resembled cured leather, all texture and no expression. "Get your men on shovels. We clear the main thoroughfare first. The iron doesn't come in, the project stalls."

It was a pragmatic calculation, nothing more — the railroad's ledger demanding action — but Voss executed it with a theatrical awareness that interested me. In another moment, the armed men had set their rifles against the schoolhouse wall and accepted borrowed spades. There was something instructive in the sight: the instruments of coercion replaced, however briefly, by instruments of labor. Repeating rifles leaning in a neat row against the sod wall of my school, their barrels catching the wan light, while the men who had carried them bit into the drifts with the same mechanical rhythm they would have used to dig a trench. I watched Voss position himself where the townspeople emerging from their homes could see him directing the work — his arm sweeping with a grand deliberateness, as though this were a project he had commissioned rather than a catastrophe he was obliged to address. He was performing generosity while purchasing goodwill. The reading was not difficult.

"He's a clever one," Titus remarked, leaning on his hammer beside me. His voice came from low in his chest, a register that had nothing theatrical in it. "But the dirt doesn't care about his intentions. It just needs moving. Let him play the hero for an hour if it opens the way to the Emporium." A pause. He shifted his weight, watching the Pinkertons dig. "The red flags for markers will put Elias's teeth on edge."

"They already have," I said. I could see Elias across the square, standing apart from the work party, his eyes fixed on the small red pennants Voss's men had planted to mark the cleared sections. His jaw was set in a way I had come to recognize — the farmer reading the land, finding it occupied by a vocabulary he hadn't consented to.

The sound of a horse struggling through the drifts pulled us toward the center of town. Marshal Dillon appeared, his mount heaving, the animal matted with gray sludge. He looked like a man who had not slept since the wind started — bloodshot eyes, grit in the creases of his face, the posture of exhaustion held upright by duty. Before he had fully dismounted, Voss was at his stirrup — producing from his coat the running iron Jedediah had brought in, the red silk flag still wrapped around it. He held it out to the Marshal with the precision of a man who has rehearsed the moment.

"Proof, Marshal. Found at the rustlers' camp. They've been using our markers — framing the company and the town alike. Sabotage and theft, conducted under the cover of our dispute."

I noticed how Voss said "our dispute" — the possessive pronoun doing quiet work, positioning himself as a partner in the suffering rather than its architect. It was a rhetorical move I might have admired in a debate. Here, against the backdrop of the buried town and the blood still drying on my schoolhouse table, it struck me as something closer to obscene.

I watched Dillon take the iron, turn it in his gloved hands. His eyes moved from the silk to Voss, then to Elias, who had stepped forward with a look of raw, unspeakable relief — the expression of a man whose innocence had been waiting in a locked room for someone to find the door. The Marshal studied him with the professional coolness of a man who was not yet willing to surrender a theory.

"This changes the nature of the hunt," Dillon said. He surveyed the assembled faces — the townspeople who had gathered, drawn by the horse and the voices, their own faces gray with dust and the particular wariness of people who have spent the night wondering if the world will still be there in the morning. "I'll need men who know the breaks and the badlands. I'm deputizing a small party. We track them before the next wind covers the trail."

Elias reached for his hat. "Count me in, Marshal."

Dillon raised one hand. "No, Thorne. Not you."

The silence that followed was precise and terrible. Elias stared, his throat working. I could see the words forming and dissolving behind his eyes — the argument, the protest, the appeal to reason — all of them considered and discarded in the space of a single breath.

"Proof of a third party doesn't erase your standing as prime suspect for the arson," Dillon said. He had the decency to look at the ground as he said it. "A running iron in a canyon doesn't explain who struck the match in town. Until the circuit judge clears you formally, you're under town arrest. You don't cross Oak Haven's boundaries. You do, I treat you as a fugitive." He looked at Voss, then at the Pinkerton captain. "Voss, your men provide the muscle. Titus, I'll take you if you're willing."

Titus gave a single nod that carried the economy of a man who does not waste motion.

I did not step forward. It was not my place to argue law with the Marshal, and I knew it would do Elias no good to see me try. What I could do — what I did — was remain beside him as the posse arranged itself, as Titus saddled his bay and Samuel appeared, pale-faced and determined, to insist on going. The boy's shirt was untucked and there was a smudge of soot across his forehead, and he argued his case with a breathless urgency that made Titus look at him for a long moment before nodding once. I watched Elias watch them leave — the dust of their departure settling over the already-buried road — his hands balled at his sides, prisoner of his own community.

He turned without a word and walked in the direction of Larson's Emporium.

I returned to the schoolhouse. There were three Parker children still inside, stirring now, rubbing their eyes against the gritty light. The room smelled of blood and kerosene and the particular close warmth of people who have weathered something together. I opened the shutters to let the gray morning in, the hinges protesting with a screech that made little Mary flinch. I cleaned the basin, stripped the ruined bandage rags from the table, scrubbed the wood with lye soap until the surface was merely stained rather than covered. Jedediah was breathing slowly on the cot we had improvised from two benches. I pressed my fingers briefly to his wrist — pulse steady, color returning. He would live. The knowledge settled in me with a quiet satisfaction that had nothing to do with triumph and everything to do with craft. We had kept him alive with torn cloth and warm water and the stubborn insistence that a man who carried evidence through a storm deserved to survive the delivery.

I fed the children from the small store of cornbread and dried apples I kept in the schoolhouse cabinet. They ate silently, with the focused concentration of children who have been frightened and are not yet sure the frightening thing is over. Thomas watched me with eyes that asked questions his mouth wouldn't form. I answered the ones I could by being steady — by moving through the room as if the day were any other day, by setting the chalk on the ledge of the board, by smoothing the maps back against the wall where the wind had curled their edges.

By mid-morning, when Elias had not returned, I locked the schoolhouse and went to find him.

He was coming out of the Emporium. I recognized the set of his shoulders before I saw his face — the particular stiffness that means a man is holding himself upright by decision rather than ease. He was carrying nothing; he had gone in for supplies and come out empty-handed. When I fell into step beside him, he did not seem surprised to see me. Perhaps he had expected it. Perhaps he had simply stopped being surprised by anything.

"Anders closed my credit," he said. His voice was even, which meant it cost him something to keep it that way.

I did not ask for details. I had seen it in the store before I reached him — the way conversation died, necks turning, eyes relocating themselves to shovels and rake-handles when Elias Thorne's name came up.

It is a particular kind of exile, the kind that does not require walls or locks. A community can imprison one of its own simply by withdrawing its attention. I had seen it in Boston — the cut direct, the social death — but there it was performed with calling cards and turned shoulders in drawing rooms. Here it was performed with averted eyes and shelves of goods that remained behind the counter. The mechanism is the same. Only the scenery differs.

"Larson said trade has dried up since the depot fire," Elias continued, his voice carrying the flat evenness of a man reciting facts he has already processed and found wanting. "That the Pinkertons are scaring people off, eating their stores. That I brought the trouble."

"You brought the resistance," I said. "They're calling it the same thing."

He stopped walking. A muscle moved in his jaw. The street around us was mostly empty — a few men still shoveling, a woman shaking out a blanket in a doorway, a dog nosing at the base of a buried fence post. I had taught children long enough to know when someone needed the words to be different from the truth, and long enough to know that offering them the wrong version was no kindness. "It isn't the same thing," he said finally. "I know that."

"Yes. And the law will clarify it, when the judge comes."

"When." The word was flat. Not a question. He looked down the street toward his own property, invisible behind the drifts. "I needed nails, Eleanor. Cedar shingles. The storm peeled back a section of barn roof, and if I don't fix it before the moisture turns, the hay rots. And I can't buy a nail in my own town."

The specificity of the complaint — nails, shingles, hay — moved me more than any broader statement of injustice could have. This was not a man raging against the machine. This was a man trying to keep his barn standing.

"I'll speak to Anders," I said. "My credit is still good. We'll call it a loan between neighbors."

He looked at me sharply. "I don't need charity."

"It isn't charity. It's commerce. You'll repay me at harvest." I held his gaze. "The same arrangement you had with Anders for ten years. The only thing that's changed is the counter it crosses."

He considered this. The muscle in his jaw worked once more, then stilled. "Thank you, Eleanor."

We stood on the dusty street, the gutted town around us, the Pinkerton shovels still ringing somewhere behind us. A neighbor named James Parker — father of the three children who had slept in my schoolhouse — emerged from the hardware bins of the

Emporium and passed us without acknowledgment, his eyes on the middle distance. He carried a paper sack of something under his arm and walked with the hunched gait of a man who does not want to be noticed. Elias watched him go.

"They need someone to blame for the drought, too, if they could manage it," I said quietly.

He almost smiled. It did not reach his eyes, but it was something — a fracture in the set expression, a momentary acknowledgment that the absurdity of the situation had at least the merit of being recognized.

I did not tell him it would pass, because I did not know that it would. I did not offer optimism as a remedy. What I could offer was the company of someone who was reading the same page clearly, without the distortion of want. We walked back through the silt-heavy streets together, and the silence between us was at least honest — two people holding the truth of a difficult morning without needing to translate it into comfort.

The schoolhouse waited at the end of the road, small and resolute under the gray sky, its walls bearing a new coat of dust that made the sod look almost white. My children would be back in the afternoon, silt in their hair and hunger in their faces, and I would open the door and set the chalk to the board and we would continue the lesson. That was the work. Whatever else was burning, whatever truces held or failed, the lesson continued. It was the one thing I could offer that the storm could not bury.

I left Elias at the gate of his property — the Pinkerton guard had returned to his post, hardtack in hand, as if the storm had been a minor interruption — and walked back alone.

Chapter 24: The Hammer's Weight

Titus

The forge was cooling. The banked coals had faded from orange to a resentful gray, and the smithy held only residual heat — the kind that presses against the skin without warming it. The air smelled of old ash and sulfur and the faint iron bite of the quenching tub. I stood by the anvil and looked at my tools on the wall. Tongs, punches, fullers, the drawing knife, the cold chisel. Every one of them hung on the peg I'd driven for it. Order. Purpose. I was not looking for a plowshare. I was looking for the man I had promised God I would never be again.

Samuel stood near the quenching tub, watching me. His lanky frame was a silhouette against the open doorway, the gray light behind him turning him into a shadow with anxious hands. I could feel his attention on my back the way you feel cold air coming under a door. He didn't know about the years before the smithy. He knew me as the man who showed him how to hold a striker and read the color of iron. That was all I'd wanted anyone to know.

"Titus." His voice was thin. "The Marshal's waiting."

"I know what he said."

I went to the back corner. The shadows were deepest there, under discarded iron scrap and coal dust. I began to clear it — each piece of iron thrown aside rang hollow against the stone hearth. A broken hinge. A length of strap iron. The head of a mattock with a split eye. Five years of debris covering what lay beneath. I cleared it all until the floor was bare.

I took a pry bar from the rack. Cold steel. I wedged it into a seam of floorboard that had no business being loose. The wood splintered and gave with a groan that sounded like a confession.

Samuel came closer. I didn't look at him.

The trench was shallow. I'd dug it five years ago, the first week I arrived in Oak Haven, before the roof was on, before the bellows were hung. Oilcloth, buried under the spot where I'd spent every day since trying to build something worth keeping. I reached in. The bundle was heavy, and the smell hit before I had it fully clear: lanolin, mineral oil, cold steel. The smell of the war. Once you've breathed it that way — breathed it over the bodies of men who were standing a moment before — it never fully leaves the back of the throat. It doesn't fade. It waits.

I set the bundle on the anvil. The oilcloth peeled back with a sticky, wet sound. The Spencer lay there, terrifyingly well-maintained. Brass receiver, short barrel, the lever that promised seven rounds. I had kept it clean every year — a habit, the kind of thing hands do without asking permission from the brain. Oiled it in the dark, wrapped it back up, buried it again. A ritual I didn't like and couldn't stop.

I lifted it. Balance was immediate and familiar. It fit my arm the way the hammer fits. That was the trouble.

I looked up. Samuel wasn't looking at the rifle. He was looking at me. Fear in his eyes — not a boy's fear of something loud, but the specific fear of seeing someone become a stranger. He took a half-step back, his hand brushing the quenching tub. The water inside rippled.

"You know how to use that?" he asked.

"I know how." No ornament in the answer. I took a rag and began wiping excess oil, the motion the same as striking — rhythmic, deliberate. I checked the action. Each click of the mechanism echoed in the vault of the smithy. Clear. Sound. Ready. The lever moved with the smooth, oiled precision of a thing that has been maintained by a man who does not want to need it but cannot bring himself to let it rust.

"Were you a soldier?" Samuel asked. The question had been building in him for a long time. I could hear it in the way the words came out — not casual, not sudden, but carefully placed, like a piece of iron laid on the anvil before the first blow.

"I was." I didn't look at him. "A long time ago."

He waited for more. I didn't give it.

I walked out into the morning.

The street was a study in wreckage. Silt covered everything to a foot or more. The sun pressed through the lingering haze, pale and unconvincing, and the ochre light turned every surface the color of old brass. Fence posts leaned at angles. The Emporium's porch was a ramp of packed dirt. The Pinkerton horses were already being readied near the Marshal's post. The guards moved with a practiced arrogance — men who wore violence like a tool belt, unaware of the weight of it over time. Their boots were polished. Their holsters were stiff and new. I noticed these things the way I notice a weld that hasn't been struck right — by instinct, by habit, with the quiet certainty that it will fail under stress.

Before I reached the horses, Eleanor stepped out from the shadow of the schoolhouse. Heavy shawl. Rigid posture. Her eyes fixed on the rifle.

"Titus." My name, spoken that way, was both a prayer and an argument.

She stopped a few feet from me. The dust moved around the hem of her skirts, lazy eddies stirred by a wind that had not fully died. "You don't have to do this. The Marshal has the Pinkertons. He has men paid for this work."

"He needs men who know the land."

"He needs men who will come back whole."

She looked at me. I looked back. She had treated this town like a cathedral since the day she arrived, and the line of her jaw said she would defend it as one. Her eyes held no tears. Eleanor wasn't the kind of woman who used tears as arguments. What she used was clarity — the hard, clean clarity of a mind that sees the cost of a thing before it's spent.

"I've watched you for years," she said. "I've seen how you look at your hands when you think no one's watching. You trace the scars. You flex the fingers. You've worked hard to find a quiet place in yourself. If you go out there with that — if you do what they expect — you'll lose that quiet."

I looked down at the Spencer. The weight of it had changed since she started talking. Not heavier. Different. Like a tool that's been reforged and doesn't quite fit the old handle. I thought of the forge. The ring of the hammer, the hiss of quench, the slow conversion of raw iron into something useful. Five years of building. Five years of proving to myself that the hands could make instead of break.

"Sometimes a hammer builds," I said. "You use it to shape the plow, to set the hinge, to make something that lasts. But sometimes the structure is rotting and the threat is at the door, and that same hammer has to break. The tool doesn't choose. The man does. Right now, the breaking is the only way to keep the building."

"But the tool is changed by the work." Her voice was steady, not pleading. "You can't break things indefinitely and expect to still be a builder when it's over. Look at your hands, Titus."

I looked at them. Soot, grease, the small burn maps of twenty years at the forge. The knuckles thick with callus from the hammer. But underneath, I could feel the old knowing — where the safety lived, how to scan the horizon for the glint of a hostile barrel, the exact angle of a rifle when the eye drops to the sight. The muscle knowledge that doesn't die. You bury it under floorboards and five years of honest work and it lies there, patient as iron, waiting for heat.

I was afraid. Not of the rustlers. Afraid of how easily the old habits were returning, how the body remembered without being asked.

"I'll come back," I said. "I'll pick up the hammer again. I have to believe that. If I don't, the rustlers have already won." I adjusted the Spencer strap. Leather creaked against my coat.

Her face settled into resignation. Not acceptance — resignation, which is a different thing. She didn't try again. She stood in the silt and shadow — a single figure of grace against the battered wall of the schoolhouse — and watched me turn my back. Each step away felt like a measurement of the distance between who I had become and who I was being asked to be again. Ten steps. Twenty. The forge behind me. The breaks ahead.

The posse was seven: the Marshal, five Pinkertons, myself. Samuel was there holding the reins of my bay, face pale and set. He had insisted on coming. He was green, but the stubbornness he'd learned from Elias would not be reasoned out of him. I looked at him and saw a boy who still believed you could ride into the hard country and come back the same person you left as. I didn't disabuse him. He'd learn it or he wouldn't.

I swung into the saddle. The bay shifted under my weight, settling into the familiar balance. I felt the Spencer against my thigh. It lay there with the casual patience of something that has been waiting a long time to be used.

The Pinkerton captain was a man named Mordecai Graves — hatchet face, eyes that cataloged rather than saw. He took in the Spencer, my worn leather, the grime on my face, and dismissed them all in a single glance. "So this is our tracker?" He turned to the Marshal with an entertainer's timing. "I thought you said professional. Not a coal-shoveler."

"Titus knows these breaks better than any man alive." Dillon's voice was tired but firm. "He can handle himself. You'd do well to listen."

Graves laughed — dry, rattling, meant to be heard. "We've handled worse than cow-thieves in the Badlands. My men train on the latest tactical method. We don't need a stable hand to read trail." He spurred forward, his horse kicking up a cloud of silt that coated the rest of us. His men followed, laughing.

Old heat rose in my neck. I pushed it down. Anger is expensive in the field. It buys nothing and costs everything.

"Ignore him," Dillon muttered as we moved. "Peacock. But he has the guns."

"Guns are only as useful as the eyes behind them, Marshal."

The prairie was rolling dunes under silt, landmarks buried or distorted. The air was still thick with suspended dust, making the distance shimmer and blur. A mile out, and the Emporium was already invisible. Two miles, and the last fence was behind us. The Pinkertons rode as if on a parade ground — loud, inattentive, their gear bright and clean. One of them had a flask out. Another was whistling. They did not understand what the land required: respect. Nothing more, nothing less. It didn't care about their training or their contracts. It didn't care about the repeaters slung across their saddles. It cared about nothing. That was its power.

I kept my eyes on the ground.

Miles out, I found it. A patch of disturbed silt — not wind-work, too directional. The grain of the disturbance ran counter to the storm's pattern. I dismounted. Knelt. Pressed my fingers to the earth. A hoofprint: deep, sharp edges, not yet filled by the shift of dust. Shoeing pattern I didn't recognize as local — the nails were set wide, a farrier's style I'd seen on trail horses out of Abilene, not range stock. Behind it, the churned signature of a small herd moving fast. Twenty head, maybe more. The earth told the story clearly.

I stood. "They went west. Toward the breaks. Looking for cover."

"Breaks?" Graves pulled up. His horse sidestepped, nervous from the unfamiliar ground. "Marshal said canyon."

"Canyon is a trap and they know it. They're using the storm's aftermath to lose a trail, the breaks to lose pursuit. We follow the canyon road, we're chasing ghosts." I pointed at the hoofprint. "That shoe was set wide. Trail work. These men have been moving cattle through rough country for months. They know what they're doing."

Graves looked at the Marshal. I could see the struggle — arrogance versus evidence. Evidence won, barely. He spat and turned his horse. "Fine. We follow the blacksmith for now. But if we don't find them by sunset, I'm taking command."

"You take command when you can read a track, Captain. Not before."

Dillon shot me a look. I didn't care. The words were out. Wasted anger, maybe. But the ground had told me what I needed to know, and a man who can't read it has no business leading men across it.

We turned west. The sun descended. The haze turned the light copper-gold, and long shadows stretched over the silt like dark fingers reaching east. Cold was beginning to come up from the ground — the stored chill of the night, released by the weakening sun. Samuel rode close beside me. He wasn't talking, but his presence said everything — a young man riding toward something he'd imagined from books, finding out what the real version felt like. His hand kept drifting to the pistol at his belt, then pulling away, as if he were checking and rechecking that it was there. I wanted to tell him to go back. I didn't have the right. The boy had earned his place.

The Pinkertons muttered among themselves. They watched me and Samuel with the quiet contempt of men who have confused expense with competence. Their horses were better fed than ours. Their coats were thicker. Their rifles cost more. None of it would matter if we found what we were tracking in the dark.

I kept my distance and my eyes on the horizon. Every mile deeper into the breaks was a mile further from the forge, a mile back toward the man under the floorboards. The Spencer rode easy against my leg. The balance was good. The weight was familiar. That was the problem — it should have felt strange, and it didn't.

I kept riding. The hammer was in my hand. The breaking had not yet begun, but the ground was prepared for it. Iron knows when it's close to the fire.

Chapter 25: Fool's Gold

Elias

Each nail strike vibrated up through the handle into my wrists, my arms, the hinges of my shoulders. The barn roof is no place for a man under town arrest to be doing his best thinking, but the storm had peeled back a section of cedar shingles like a tin lid, and if I left it open to the first moisture, the last of my hay would rot. So I was up there, in the thin haze left by the duster, driving nails into wood, when I saw it.

The sun was a pale coin behind the overcast. Air smelled of scorched earth and dry heat and the faint chemical bite of alkali blowing in from the breaks. Every strike echoed flatly across the empty yard — a sound that should have been satisfying, the sound of a thing being mended, but instead felt hollow. House arrest. The Marshal's word for it. My word for it was something else — something involving the sixty acres to the north and the fact that the men who might be clearing my name were out in the breaks without me. Titus, Samuel, that pack of overpaid Pinkertons with their clean holsters and their ignorance of the ground — all of them riding through country I knew better than any man in the county, while I sat on my own roof driving nails.

I wiped my brow with a hand that wouldn't stop trembling. Not the heat. The waiting. The helpless arithmetic of a man who can see the numbers going wrong and can't touch the ledger.

I looked toward the North Field.

The red-tipped stakes were still there, geometric cuts across my best ground. I was used to them by now the way you get used to a stone in your boot — still there, still wrong, a dull ache you've stopped bothering to curse but haven't stopped feeling. My gaze moved past the boundary of the homestead, further, toward the jagged ochre lip of the Badlands where the alkali flats wavered in the haze. I squinted. A glint — sharp, rhythmic, unnatural. Not a tin can or quartz vein. This was the steady flash of polished brass and glass working the sun, a signal thrown off by a theodolite or a survey rod. Deliberate. Precise. The kind of light that comes from an instrument designed to measure the world into parcels.

My breath stopped.

I dropped the hammer. It skittered down the cedar slope and caught on a batten. I left it. I scrambled up to the ridgepole, the rough wood biting into my palms, and shielded my eyes against the glare. Two miles west, where the communal grazing land rolled into the broken coulees. A tripod. Two assistants with survey rods, moving toward the dry creek bed with a deliberateness that had nothing improvised in it. They moved the way men move when they've been told exactly where to go and how fast to get there.

They were not on the North Field. They were not even on the original line Voss had staked.

They were on the creek access. The commons.

My mouth went dry, a copper taste rising from somewhere deep. The taste of the old fear, the Kansas fear, the taste that comes before you lose something you can't replace. Voss. The truce in the schoolhouse had not been a truce. It had been a diversion — a way to keep the town's hands busy while he moved his instruments somewhere new. He'd waited for Titus and the guns to ride away. Waited for Oak Haven's attention to go with them. And now he was moving through the afternoon like a man who had already won, measuring ground that didn't belong to him but didn't, technically, belong to anyone.

I ran the numbers fast, the way I always do when the fear comes. If he took the creek access, he wasn't taking a field — he was taking the water. Every farm in the valley ran head of cattle on that grass when their own turned to dust. The creek was the only reliable water left after the wells went low. Take the grass, take the water, take the commons, and you don't need to burn a single barn. You don't need a foreclosure or an eviction notice or a marshal with shackles. You just wait. The farms go fallow one by one, quiet as a debt coming due, quiet as a column of numbers adding up to nothing.

I slid down the roof. The shingles tore at my palms; I didn't feel it. The ground hit my boots with a jolt that ran up to my knees. I went straight for the stable, the Marshal's warning about breaking parole already fading behind the arithmetic I was doing. Start the calculation: what is my land worth without the creek? What are my neighbors' lands worth? What is left of Oak Haven if the commons are fenced and graded?

Zero. Zero down the ledger. Every line.

The stable smelled of horsehair and old leather and the particular mustiness of a building that hasn't been properly aired since the storm. The mare was in her stall, ears pricked, watching me with the calm attention of an animal that knows something is wrong before you do. I reached for the saddle and began working the cinch, my fingers clumsy with the speed of it.

"Elias?"

Sarah's voice, from the barn doorway. She was holding a dampened cloth, likely for the dust that had settled over every surface in the house. She'd been cleaning since dawn — I'd heard the brush on the floorboards, the clink of plates being wiped. Her eyes were on the saddle in my hands. She didn't ask where I was going. She could read the answer in the way I was moving.

"He's in the Badlands," I said. My voice came out rough, the words feeling like gravel pushed through a narrow gate. "Voss. Surveying the creek grazing. The commons, Sarah."

She was quiet. I braced for the logic she carried — the careful, hard-won endurance that had been our only armor. The cautious voice that says: wait, let the law work, breaking parole gives them the excuse they need. I had heard that voice a hundred times. It was usually right. It had kept us alive through Kansas, through the drought, through the long winter. I loved that voice, even when it held me back.

She stepped into the barn. Walked past me. Her skirts brushed the mare's flank and the horse shifted but didn't startle — Sarah had that effect on animals, the same steadiness that calmed children and frightened men. She went to the tack room. When she came back, she was holding my heavy tin canteen, freshly filled. Cool to the touch. She pressed it into my hands. Her grip was steady — hands mapped with the same labor as mine, roughed by the same seasons, the same rope burns and lye and sun.

"I saw the glint from the kitchen window," she said. Her voice was hard and cold, the way frost comes on a clear night without warning. "A man doesn't build a life just to watch it be choked out while he hides under the bed. If they take the creek, there's no reason to stay in this house anyway."

I looked at her. She looked back. Her jaw was set the same way it had been the day we'd left Kansas — the look of a woman who had already lost everything once and had made a private accounting of what she would and would not tolerate again. No preaching. No easy comfort. Just the stark truth of a woman who knew the arithmetic as well as I did and had arrived at the same sum.

I took the canteen. The weight of it was solid and real — cold water and cold tin, the most useful thing in the world when you're heading into dry country. I swung into the saddle and the mare moved under me with a willingness that said she was tired of standing still too.

"Be careful," Sarah said. Not a plea. An instruction. The way she'd say check the gate or watch the weather — practical, final, not interested in argument.

I rode.

The ride to the Badlands edge ran through low draws, keeping me off the skyline and out of sight of the town. The silt from the storm had softened the ground so that the mare's hooves made almost no sound — just a muffled thud, thud, thud, like a heartbeat heard through a wall. I kept low in the draws, following the contours of the land the way a man follows the lines of a ledger — reading the terrain, calculating the angles, staying in the margins where the numbers worked in my favor.

The air thickened as I approached the breaks — alkali and ancient baked mud rising from the ground, a mineral smell that coated the tongue and made the eyes water. The land here was beautiful in the way of cruel things: creamy white bluffs, deep shadow-filled coulees, the knuckled ridges of limestone that belonged to no deed and therefore belonged to every man who needed grass and water. Bunch grass grew along the creek banks in tough, gray-green tufts. Cottonwoods — the only real trees for miles — lined the creek bed, their bark pale as bone in the haze. This was the safety valve of Oak Haven. Open range. The one unencumbered thing left.

I crested a ridge and found them.

Voss stood near a pile of red-painted rocks, his bowler hat absurdly clean against the rugged landscape, consulting a map that he held open with both hands. His coat was buttoned despite the heat — the man's vanity extended even into the wasteland. Two assistants worked the creek bed below with survey rods, driving stakes into the soft bank at measured intervals. The

Pinkerton guard near the buggy saw me first — hand dropped to his holster — but Voss looked up and raised a palm in dismissal. He didn't look surprised. He looked like a man who had been expecting a certain appointment and was mildly gratified that it had arrived on schedule.

I pulled the mare up ten feet from him and did not dismount. I wanted the height. I wanted to feel the horse under me — living, warm, a piece of the land I was defending. The mare's ears flicked forward, reading the strangers the way I was reading them.

"You're a long way from the North Field, Voss," I said. "And a long way from any agreement we reached last night."

Voss sighed and folded his map with the agonizing patience of a man who has all the time in the world. He tucked it into his coat with two fingers, precise as a card trick. When he looked up, the calculated charm was gone. What replaced it was colder: pure pragmatism. "The North Field is a legal quagmire. Your resistance, while tenacious, has made that route expensive. The railroad loathes inefficiency. We needed a secondary option."

"This isn't an option." I gestured toward the creek bed, where one of his men was pounding a stake into the bank not thirty feet from the water line. "This is the commons. Every man in Oak Haven runs cattle here when his own grass burns. You take this, you kill the town. You're not building a road — you're building a fence around our lives."

Voss stepped closer. His eyes were doing arithmetic — the same kind of arithmetic I did, the same cold computation, only his ledger had different columns. "I'm building a future that doesn't depend on the luck of a single harvest or a dry creek's charity. Yes, this route is harder to grade. The engines work harder. But it has no individual deeds to fight through. It's unencumbered ground."

He paused, and when he spoke again his voice dropped to the register of a man explaining something obvious to someone slow. It was the voice of a man who has confused patience with generosity. "And as for the town — Oak Haven is already dying. You simply haven't read the balance sheet. The railroad doesn't need a village of struggling farmers. It needs a depot. If the town can't adapt to the new geography, it was never meant to last the century. I'm not strangling you. I'm choosing which parts of the landscape are worth the investment."

There it was. Not a monster. Something worse: a man who believed people were variables, and that some variables had to be struck from the account. He stood there in his clean coat and his polished boots, on ground that had never known a plow because it was too precious for plowing — ground that existed so that men who had nothing else left could still feed their stock and water their families — and he saw a line on a map. A grade. A percentage of return.

He'd used our fear of the rustlers — the whole dark machinery of the last week — to buy himself the time to move his instruments to a new line. The truce had been a strategic pause. The schoolhouse had been a waiting room. The brandy he'd poured for Titus, the moment of shared humanity in the storm — all of it had been real, perhaps, in the moment, but it had not changed the arithmetic. Voss's arithmetic didn't have a column for shared humanity.

"You think because we're quiet, we're beaten," I said. My voice was low. Something had settled in my gut — not hot anger anymore but the cold kind, the kind that has been in the ground a long time and doesn't burn off. It was the anger of a man who has run out of other feelings. I thought of Sarah handing me the canteen. The look on her face. The steadiness of her hands. A steward doesn't let the wolves in just because they speak in a civil tone. "You think this land is empty because there's no fence on it. We are the fence, Voss. We know every inch of this dirt. You can map it. You can stake it. But you'll never own it, because the land knows who belongs to it, and it isn't you."

Voss tilted his head. A small, pitying smile — the smile of a man who is certain the other man is wrong and finds the wrongness almost touching. "Passion is a poor substitute for iron, Mr. Thorne. You've broken your parole. The Marshal will need to be informed."

"He will be," I said. I turned the mare back toward the homestead. I didn't look at the Pinkerton. I didn't look at the theodolite. I looked west, where the sun was descending toward a deep, fiery horizon that turned the tops of the bluffs the color of heated iron.

"We understand exactly what you are now," I said, and put the horse to a walk. "You're going to find out exactly what we are."

The glint of the brass followed me, steady as an eye, as I rode back into the draws. I could feel it on my back like a finger pressed between the shoulder blades. The fear was gone. Not replaced by hope — hope is a thin crop, and I'd watched too many thin crops fail. What had taken its place was something harder. Something that had been growing in the bad soil all season without my knowing it, the way a root system spreads underground before the first green shoot breaks the surface: the decision to stand, regardless of yield.

The mare's hooves were steady on the packed earth. The canteen knocked gently against the saddle horn. Sarah's water. Sarah's faith. The simplest equation in the ledger.

I wasn't going back to hide in my barn. I was going back to ring the bell.

Chapter 26: Blood on the Sage

Titus

The Spencer lay across my thighs, cold and familiar, the walnut stock nested into my arm as though nothing had changed in twenty years. Nothing had. That was the trouble.

The gun oil smell rose faint from the receiver—old intentions preserved in mineral grease. I had cleaned the carbine the night before by lantern light, working a rag through the bore with the same deliberate rhythm I used to draw out a weld. My hands remembered. They remembered everything: the fit of the trigger guard against the second knuckle, the balance point just forward of the breech, the way the stock warmed to body heat after ten minutes of carry. I had told myself I was cleaning a tool. The lie had the thin, bitter taste of the lye soap I'd used to scrub the grease from my fingers afterward.

Beside me, Halloway kept adjusting in his saddle, his horse skittish under the pressure of restless hands. He was the Pinkerton captain—not Graves, who'd stayed back with the supply line, but cut from the same cloth: authority worn like a brand-new suit, eyes hunting for the next citation in his record. The kind of man who reads the field for promotion, not survival. His hat was too clean. The brim hadn't bent to weather yet. I'd shod enough officers' horses during the war to know the type—polished brass on a green frame.

We had been tracking since before first light. The sagebrush held a thin, bitter dew—not the smell of life, just evidence that the night had not been dry. The air carried the sharp alkaline edge of the canyon floor, and above us the rimrock caught the first gray suggestion of dawn, the stone layered in bands of ochre and rust like the strata of a forge wall after years of heat. Behind me, Samuel rode in a silence that said more than chatter. I could feel his gaze on my back. He was watching a version of me he'd never seen in the smithy—a man who moved through rimrock shadow with a rifle as an extension of his arm. He didn't know what to do with it. Neither did I.

"Smoke." Halloway's hand snapped to his sidearm. He pointed toward a notch in the canyon wall where a pale thread of gray drifted against the ochre cliffs. "Cottonwoods. That's them."

I pulled my horse up. Leather creaking. The woodsmoke reached me now—juniper, sharp and peppery—and under it, the rhythmic shift of horses in a corral. Tired horses, from the sound. No stamping. Just the slow, resigned shifting of animals that had been ridden past their limits.

"Let me go in first, Captain." My voice came out like gravel ground between stones. "I know this country, and I know what starving men do when cornered. If I can talk to them, we get the truth about the depot fire without turning the dirt red. No need for lead if a word will serve."

Halloway's lip curled. He looked at his four Pinkertons—men who read the world as bounties. "You're a blacksmith, Croft. Stay with the hammers. We have a company mandate: secure the property, neutralize the threat. You don't negotiate with a wolf once it's inside the fold."

"They're men."

"They're property liabilities," he said, adjusting the leather gloves on his hands, pulling each finger tight. "And we're the company's solution."

I held his gaze for a count of three. He looked away first. That told me what I needed to know—he wasn't afraid of the rustlers. He was afraid of the paperwork if they talked.

"Samuel." I turned in the saddle. The boy's face was pale in the predawn light, drawn tight with a tension that made him look younger than his years. "Stay back with the horses when we dismount. Behind the limestone ledge. You don't move until I call for you."

His jaw was set—Elias's stubbornness, borrowed and put to use. He nodded once, a quick, firm motion.

"I mean it," I said. "You hear shooting, you get lower. Not higher."

"Yes sir."

The "sir" caught me. He'd never called me that in the smithy. I turned away before he could see what it did to my face.

We went in on foot. The crunch of gravel was too loud. I kept my thumb on the Spencer's hammer, not to cock it, but to feel the cold certainty of it. The canyon walls narrowed, funneling us toward the notch, and the air grew warmer in the compression—trapped heat from yesterday's sun still bleeding out of the stone. We crested the rise and the camp opened below: three lean-tos made of juniper poles and canvas scraps, three men around a small guttering fire. They looked smaller than I remembered from the standoff weeks back. Their coats were tattered. The horses picketed nearby were gaunt, ribs pressing through their hides like barrel staves.

A coffee pot sat at the edge of the coals, steam curling from its lip. The smell of it—thin, burnt, stretched too far—mixed with the juniper smoke and the rank closeness of sweat-soaked clothes. These were not dangerous men. These were men at the end of a rope, trying to boil one more cup from grounds that had already given everything they had.

I stepped into the open. Rifle lowered. Palms visible.

"Halloway, hold—" But he was already bringing his men up into position, spreading them along the ridgeline with hand signals he must have practiced in a mirror.

I took three slow steps down the slope, the scent of parched earth rising to meet me. "Morning, boys. It's Titus Croft. We've come for the stock and for answers. Put the iron down and nobody bleeds today. There's a law in Oak Haven. It's a law of mercy, if you let it be."

The man by the fire—jagged scar across his cheek, a face that had been weathered past his years—froze. He reached for a Winchester leaning against a saddle. Slow. Exhausted. The motion of a man going through a reflex, not a decision. He looked at me with the hollow terror of a man who had run out of horizon. "We didn't burn nothing, Smithy! We just took the calves. We were hungry!"

"Then come in and say so to the Marshal. Put it down, son. This doesn't have to end here."

His hand wavered on the Winchester's stock. I could see the arithmetic working behind his eyes—the calculation of odds, of distances, of how fast three starving men could move against six armed riders.

"You've got my word," I said. Quiet. Steady. The way I spoke to a horse before I drove the first nail.

The shoulders sagged. His hand released the rifle. He started to raise his arms, his eyes finding mine with a flicker of desperate hope. The other two men stayed where they were, still as rabbits in a field, waiting to see which way the wind blew.

"Now!" Halloway's voice shattered it. "Fire!"

The volley was instantaneous. The air went thick with black powder and the scream of lead. The man I had been talking to was slammed backward by three rounds, his chest erupting dark in the dim light. He had no time to cry out. His arms were still raised. The second rustler took it in the throat as he dove for cover, his breath bubbling out in a wet whistle that I would hear in my sleep for years. The third was cut down where he knelt, his body pitching forward into the fire, scattering coals across the dirt.

"Stop!" My voice was lost in the rhythmic crack-crack-crack of repeaters. "They were surrendering! Halloway, they were down!"

I stood in the clearing. Smoke drifted in ribbons, curling around the lean-tos, threading through the cottonwood branches. My ears rang. The coffee pot had been knocked over in the volley, and its contents spread in a dark stain across the packed earth, mixing with what was darker still. Three men who'd been alive thirty seconds ago. Three men who had carried the truth about the depot fire. Not questioned. Not judged. Struck from the ledger to satisfy a captain's impatience.

The Pinkertons came out of the brush—faces flushed, chests expanded. Halloway was smiling. "Clear and efficient, Croft. That's how the company handles liabilities. No lawyers, no delays."

"He was surrendering," I said. The words were flat. Iron on iron.

"He was reaching for a weapon."

"He let it go. You watched him let it go."

Halloway straightened his collar. "That's not what my report will say."

I looked at him. The old shadow moved in my mind—the ghost of the cavalryman who had seen too many mornings like this one, too much red on too much grass. My grip tightened on the Spencer. What I wanted to do with the butt of it I did not let myself think through.

Then: a sound that cut through the ringing. A sharp, high gasp. Not from the camp.

I turned.

Behind the limestone ledge, Samuel was slumped over, both hands clutching his shoulder. A stray round—ricochet off the canyon wall, or simply a careless shot—had found the one thing I had told myself I could protect. He was sliding toward the dirt, his eyes wide with a sudden, agonizing incomprehension. His mouth moved but no sound came.

"Samuel!"

The world closed to a single point. The blood blossoming through his shirt was bright—a crimson so vivid it looked wrong against the gray-washed canyon. He hit the ground, and the dust puffed up around him in a small, indifferent cloud.

A fourth figure emerged from the high rocks above the camp. A lookout we had missed, shielded by the rim. He was levering a fresh round into his carbine, eyes fixed on the boy. His face was twisted with the blind vengeance of a trapped animal whose den has been destroyed.

The Pinkertons were still congratulating each other. They didn't see him. They didn't see the muzzle coming to bear.

The muzzle was there.

The blacksmith was gone. Not decided, not discarded. Simply gone, in the time it took the lookout's finger to tighten on the trigger. I moved. Not a run—a charge, the kind that the body produces when calculation has no time to interfere. The Spencer barked once; the round caught the lookout in the shoulder and spun him. But distance was wrong. I threw the rifle aside—it clattered against the limestone, stock cracking—and went forward with what God gave me.

I went up the limestone with my hands. Fingers digging into stone, chest heaving, boots finding purchase on the jagged face. Twenty years of swinging a four-pound hammer. Twenty years of bending iron that didn't want to bend. The rock gave me holds where a lighter man would have slipped. The lookout was trying to lever another round, his face a mask of pain and panic, blood spreading from his shoulder in a dark bloom. I reached him before the hammer fell.

I took the barrel of his carbine and wrenched it clear. A crack of bone in his wrist—sharp, like a dry branch. Then I drove my shoulder into his chest and pinned him against the cliff. He looked at me. Whatever he saw made the fight leave his body before the blow landed. I hit him once—short, precise, efficient—and the conversation ended. He dropped into the scrub brush and was still.

I stood on the ledge. My chest worked hard. Below, the Pinkertons stared up. Mouths open. Rifles slack. The laughter was gone from them entirely. They were looking at something they hadn't expected and did not have a category for.

I looked at my hands. Shaking—not with cold. With a heat that belonged to a different decade. There was blood on the knuckles, and grit worked into the creases of my palms, and underneath it all, the same calluses that shaped horseshoes and door hinges and the iron bands of water barrels. The same hands.

"Titus..."

Thin as thread. Barely audible. But it broke what needed breaking.

I scrambled back down, shale sliding under my boots, until I reached the boy. Samuel lay in the dust, the color of ash. The blood came steadily, rhythmic, soaking through the cloth I pressed against his collarbone. High wound. Too close to the lung. I could feel the pulse of it under my palm—quick, too quick, like a bird's heart.

"I've got you," I said. My voice had something rough in it I didn't try to clear. "Look at me, Samuel. Keep your eyes on me."

His pupils were wide, reflecting the blue sky overhead. "It burns, Titus. Like the forge."

"I know it does." I pulled my shirt over my head, wadded it tight, pressed it hard against the wound. He winced, and the sound he made was small and young. "The fire's going out now. You're going to be fine." A lie. I told it anyway, the way you tell a horse easy, easy while you set a broken leg.

I looked up at Halloway, who stood ten feet back, face pale, eyes calculating—property, mandate, report. He opened his mouth.

"Get the horses," I said. The words came out at a register that made the captain flinch. "Now. If this boy dies because you were slow, I will show you exactly what twenty years of restraint feels like. Move."

They moved. They moved with a frantic, fumbling speed that told me they finally understood something no report would contain.

I stayed on the ground. Hands locked over Samuel's wound. Feeling the warmth of his life trying to escape into the canyon dust. I did not close my eyes. I did not look at the bodies in the camp. I did not look at the man on the ledge. I looked at the boy's face and held pressure and waited for the horses, and the waiting was worse than the charge had been because in the waiting there was nothing for the hands to do but hold.

The ride back was long and hollow. I carried Samuel on my own horse, his body against my chest, his head on my shoulder. His breath came shallow, hitching, vibrating against my ribs. I had wrapped the wound with my shirt, tied with a leather thong from my saddlebag, but I could feel the dampness working through to my bare skin. I kept one arm around him and held the reins with the other, my forearm braced against his sternum so he wouldn't slide.

The horse knew the way home. Horses always do. I let it pick the path and kept my attention on the rhythm of the boy's breathing—counting the intervals between each inhale, watching for the gap that would mean the lung had filled. Two seconds. Three seconds. Two seconds. The count was all I had.

I had made a vow after the war. After the Missouri border, after the blood and the burning. I had turned my strength to the hammer and the anvil, and I had believed—genuinely believed—that if I built enough useful things I could balance the scales. Five years of plowshares and hinges and horseshoes. Five years of the ring of iron against iron. Five years of honest heat, and then five more, and then five more after that, until the man who had ridden with raiders was buried so deep under soot and sweat that even I couldn't find him.

The vow was broken. I had known it would break the moment I pried up that floorboard.

Samuel moaned—a soft, thin sound, like a nail drawn across tin. I pulled him tighter. "Nearly there," I said, though we were still miles from the Thorne gate. "Eleanor's waiting. She'll have everything ready."

I was not talking to him alone.

The Pinkertons rode ahead, keeping their distance. They had their report: four dead rustlers, recovered stock. Heroes in the ledger. I knew what I was in the same ledger. I was the variable that had refused to be efficient. The entry that didn't balance.

They would write it up clean in a Chicago office, and the ink would be dry before the blood was.

The land passed on either side—gray-green sagebrush, pale limestone outcrops, the slow roll of the high plains stretching to a horizon that offered nothing. The afternoon light came in low and copper-red, cutting long shadows across the ground. Beautiful, the way this country always is, without any interest in what has happened beneath its sky. I did not look at it. I looked at the back of Samuel's head—the pale, thin neck of a boy who deserved better than the morning we had given him.

Two seconds. Three seconds. Two seconds. Still breathing.

The victory we were carrying back to Oak Haven was not a triumph. It was an accounting. The rustlers were dead. The boy might live or might not. I had killed a man with my hands. The peace I had spent half a lifetime building—quiet, careful, anvil by anvil—was gone, and I was the one who had brought it down.

The forge would still be there when I returned. The hammer would hang in its place. But I knew what the hands remembered now, and the hands would not forget.

I kept riding. Samuel breathed. The light went red, then dark.

Chapter 27: Fever Dreams

Elias

The guest room smelled of carbolic acid and something I didn't want to name. I stood at the window with my hands locked between my knees, watching the light die across the North Field. Outside, the wheat stood in rows straight as a ledger column, the heads just beginning to bow with the first weight of grain. Inside, the only sound was the wet, hitching rattle of Samuel's breathing.

He lay in the center of the bed, swallowed by Sarah's best linens—the ones with the blue stitching at the edges that she only brought out for company. His skin was the gray-yellow of a guttering candle. Every few minutes, a low moan escaped him—not a cry for help. Something further away than that. A sound from a room I couldn't enter. His hands lay flat on the quilt, the fingers curling and uncurling like a man searching for a grip on something that kept sliding away.

Eleanor stood over him, her silhouette sharp against the lamplight. She moved with a clinical precision that terrified me in its steadiness, wringing out a cloth in a basin of cool water. The splash sounded wrong in the quiet room—too loud, too ordinary for the thing that was happening three feet from the basin. Rachel Parker worked beside her, sorting clean rags with the practiced calm of a woman who had seen sickness before and refused to be broken by it. She stacked them by size—long strips for binding, small squares for dabbing, a pile of old flour sacks torn into patches. The two of them moved in a rhythm I had no part in. I sat by the window and tried to make myself useful by staying out of the way.

"His fever is climbing again," Eleanor said. She pressed the cloth to Samuel's forehead. He flinched, his eyes rolling beneath thin, translucent lids. "He keeps talking about the forge. Titus. He says the iron is too hot."

I didn't answer. I looked at my hands. I'd scrubbed them twice at the pump, working the bristle brush until the skin went pink, but the grit was still there—packed into the creases, under the nails. Not gun oil. Not powder. Just the ordinary dirt of a man who had been in the wrong canyon at the wrong hour. The same dirt that was on my boots when I walked the rows each morning, checking for cutworm. Same hands. Different failing.

Titus stood near the door, filling the frame. He wasn't a man built for rooms like this—too much mass, too much silence of the wrong kind. His shirt was gone, given over to bandaging, and someone had found him one of mine. It pulled tight across his shoulders and hung loose at the waist, and the wrongness of it made the room feel more wrong. After a time, he spoke. "Halloway's telling everyone they've secured the town. That the rustlers are gone. Calling it a victory."

"Victory," Rachel repeated. The word came out sharp enough to cut. She looked up, her eyes gone hard. "My Thomas saw the way you rode in with this child. The town isn't listening to Halloway. They're looking at that boy's blood and wondering what kind of progress requires a child to take a Pinkerton's bullet." She turned back to Samuel's bandages. Red was already blooming through the fresh white cloth—a small, insistent fact that no amount of talk could cover.

I watched it spread and thought about the yield calculations I'd been running all week. How many rows of wheat per acre. How many acres to the North Field. How many dollars per bushel if the harvest came in clean. Numbers that had seemed life-or-death this morning now sat in my head like stones at the bottom of a dry well—still there, still heavy, but no longer the thing that mattered. I tried to run them anyway. The mind reaches for what it knows when the ground shifts. Three dollars a bushel. Forty acres. A hundred and twenty dollars, minus seed cost, minus—

Samuel coughed. A wet, torn sound. The numbers scattered like quail.

Eleanor leaned close and whispered something—a prayer or maybe a line of text from some book she kept in her head. She brushed Samuel's cheek with the back of her fingers, and the gesture was so careful, so deliberate, it turned something over in my chest. This boy had showed up at our gate with nothing but a rope and a dime novel and a hunger to be useful, and we had taken him in the way you take in a stray calf—not because you can afford it, but because the refusing would cost more than the feeding. Now the cost was being tallied in a currency I had no way to pay.

Eleanor was holding the line with a basin of water and a refusal to let go. The rest of us were just furniture around her.

Titus cleared his throat. "I'll be at the smithy. If the fever breaks—or doesn't—someone come for me."

He walked out through the kitchen without waiting for an answer. I heard his boots on the porch boards, then the yard, then nothing. I understood the impulse. A man who doesn't know his purpose in a room should find a room where he does. The smithy was cold and dark, but at least the anvil didn't ask questions a man couldn't answer.

I stayed. Not because I had more purpose than Titus, but because the North Field was visible from the window, and as long as I could see it, I could hold on to the thread of the thing I was supposed to be protecting. The wheat moved in the wind, catching the last of the copper light. Forty-eight hours. The Judge's deadline had the clean finality of a number I couldn't dispute. Forty-eight hours to file the injunction, or the survey became permanent. Forty-eight hours while a boy lay bleeding in my guest room and the town split itself into camps and the Pinkertons walked our main street like they'd bought it at auction.

The murmur of voices drifted from the porch—neighbors gathering, not from nosiness but from the gravity of a shared loss. Jedediah was out there. I could hear the low scrape of his voice, talking to someone about water rights or fencing or one of the dozen small arguments that held a community together like stitching on a quilt. They hadn't just come for Samuel. Something had shifted in the town's accounting. The Pinkertons had arrived with maps and the promise of order, and what they'd delivered instead was a boy with a hole near his lung. The margin between what Voss had promised and what he'd delivered was Samuel Price, lying here among Sarah's good linens, fighting for every breath.

Sarah appeared in the doorway, her face composed in the way she composed it when composure cost something. Her hands were dusted with flour—she'd been baking, because Sarah baked when she couldn't fix a thing any other way. Bread for the neighbors on the porch. Bread for the women in the sickroom. Her answer to every crisis was to feed it, and

I loved her for the stubborn practicality of that even when it broke something behind my ribs to watch her carry a tray past a boy who might not wake up to eat.

She didn't speak. She looked at Samuel, then at me. Her expression asked a question I didn't have an answer to yet. I shook my head—not a refusal, just an honest inventory. I don't know. She set the tray on the bureau and left without a word, and the smell of fresh bread filled the room and mixed with the carbolic, and I had to turn back to the window because the combination was unbearable.

I put my palm flat against the glass. Cold. The North Field lay dark under a sky going black at the edges. The wheat was still there, still standing. What grew in this country took root hard and held. I had to believe that meant something—about the wheat, about Samuel, about all of it.

* * *

Across town, the Emporium was lit up past its usual hour. I learned later what had happened there—Larson told me the next morning with the flat, deliberate cadence of a man confessing a debt.

Anders Larson stood behind his counter with his hands flat on the polished wood and his face wearing the particular look of a man who has finally tallied a column he'd been avoiding. Jedediah Stone was there, and the Parkers, and the smallholders from the southern ridge. Even a few of the men who'd been talking about railroad money sat in the corners with their hats pulled low.

"I was wrong," Larson said. The words hit the floor of the room like dropped tools. "I told you Voss was the future and Elias was just a stubborn man holding a ghost. I thought the company brought order." He paused. His hands pressed harder against the counter, the knuckles whitening. "I saw that boy's face. I saw those Pinkertons and the way they moved through our street like they owned it. That isn't law. That's a bigger breed of thief."

"Occupiers," Jedediah said, his voice the dry rasp of a man who had learned certain things in camps far from here. "It starts with maps. Then the repeaters. Then they start deciding who's a liability."

Thomas Parker shifted on his crate by the stove. "What do we do about it? We can't outgun them. We've got squirrel rifles and single-shots against Spencer repeaters."

"We don't outgun them," Larson said. "We outspend them. Or rather, we stop spending on them entirely."

What followed wasn't dramatic. No speeches. No clenched fists raised to the ceiling. A farmer from the south ridge stood up and said what most of them were thinking: that he'd rather die of thirst on his own land than live as a tenant to a company that shot surrendering men. Larson said he was pulling credit for the Pinkertons. Supply double-priced or not at all. A message to the Marshal. Jedediah offered his wagon for a supply run to Fort Pierre, bypassing the rail depot entirely.

It was the shift I'd been working toward for months, and it happened in a back-country dry-goods store while I was sitting by a window watching wheat in the dark. That's how it usually goes. The things you fight for don't turn when you're watching. They turn when you're looking the other way, and you find out about it the next morning over coffee, and the man telling you can't quite meet your eyes because he's admitting he should have been there all along.

* * *

I fell asleep in the chair near midnight, my forehead against the cold glass. When I woke, the North Field was still there, gray under a quarter moon. Samuel's breathing had steadied. Not well—not by any measure—but the hitching rattle had smoothed to something closer to sleep. The blood had stopped spreading through the bandage. A small mercy, but I'd learned to take the small ones and enter them on the right side of the ledger.

Eleanor sat at his bedside, her back straight, her hands folded in her lap. She hadn't left. I didn't know if she'd slept at all. Her Boston dress was rumpled and damp at the cuffs, and a strand of hair had come loose and hung along her jaw, and she hadn't bothered to push it back. She looked up at me when I stirred, and what passed across her face wasn't exhaustion or despair. It was the expression of a woman who had decided to outlast the difficulty, whatever it cost her.

"He asked for water," she said quietly. "An hour ago. He knew where he was."

I nodded. That was worth more than any number I could run.

I put another log on the fire—the split oak we'd stacked in October, dry and ready, one of the hundred small preparations that kept a homestead breathing through the hard months. The bark caught and the flames rose and the room warmed by a degree, and I sat back down.

The numbers were still in my head. Forty-eight hours. North Field. Acres. Dollars. Voss's name, which I'd started filing under a different column than railroad or progress or even enemy. The column I was building for it was simply: cost. A cost that had to be met or refused, and I hadn't yet decided which. But the margin was narrowing. Every hour that Samuel breathed, the calculation tipped a little further toward the side that said: refuse. Pay whatever it costs to refuse.

Outside, somewhere on the far side of town, a dog barked once and went quiet. The prairie settled into its nighttime stillness—not silent, never truly silent, but eased down to the small sounds that the day crowded out: the creak of the windmill, the rustle of grass, the slow tick of the cooling stove. Samuel breathed. The fire ticked. I watched the North Field until the black sky began to gray at the rim, and I started working out what we had left to spend.

Chapter 28: The Paper Tiger

Eleanor

The corridor outside the schoolhouse door was not a corridor at all — it was three feet of packed earth between the building and the fence, where the mud had been trampled into a surface that resembled, in its aspiration if not its execution, a vestibule. Someone had propped the door open with a chunk of limestone, and the voices inside carried through the gap in fragments: the rustle of legal papers, the scrape of a chair leg against pine floorboards, a man clearing his throat with the self-conscious formality of someone about to speak on the record. I paused there, adjusting the collar of my dress against the early chill, and listened to the language already filling the room — "right-of-way," "eminent domain," "public utility" — words that moved through the morning air with the blunt confidence of instruments designed not to describe the world but to replace it. I had spent enough years in the company of such language to recognize its particular music: the passive construction that erases the actor, the abstract noun that dissolves the human cost into policy. I smoothed my skirt, tucked the folder of county records under my arm, and stepped inside.

The Little Red Schoolhouse did not smell of chalk and cedar that morning. It smelled of wet wool, tobacco, and the particular sourness of men who had not slept. When I arrived before dawn to arrange what chairs remained, I stood for a moment in the doorway and tried to recognize the room. The children's desks had been pushed to the walls to make space for a heavy oak table — Larson's, brought over sometime in the night on a cart that had left ruts in the schoolyard — and where I had tacked up the multiplication tables and the map of the territories, someone had hung a railroad survey that made the room look like a surveyor's office rather than a schoolhouse. The survey's lines ran in confident diagonals across the paper, indifferent to the contour of hill or creek, as though the land were merely a problem of geometry.

It was the small violations that accumulated into injury: the muddy boot-print across the threshold I had swept clean two days before, the tin cup of dried sage I kept on my desk now shoved to the corner behind the stovepipe, the chalk ledge — worn smooth by two years of small hands and daily lessons — dusted with tobacco ash. I had seen rooms repurposed before. In Boston, after the fire of '72, the lecture halls at the Women's Educational Association had been converted to triage wards, and I had helped carry out the cots and replace them with chairs when the crisis passed. But that had been an emergency yielding to restoration. This felt like an occupation pretending to be an improvement.

I pressed my back against the sod wall and watched the men settle into the children's seats. They filled them with a discomfort that was almost comic — grown men with their knees pressed against the undersized desks, their hats in their hands, elbows drawn in as if afraid to take up too much room — but there was nothing comic in their faces. Worry had etched itself so deeply into the corners of their mouths that it looked like a permanent feature of their physiognomy, like the lines in old leather. Rachel Parker sat in the second row, her hands twisting the hem of her apron in a slow, rhythmic motion she probably wasn't aware of. Anders Larson was pale, his jaw working as though rehearsing words he hadn't yet decided to speak.

Judge Miller sat behind the oak table as though he had been deposited there by some bureaucratic force of nature and expected to be retrieved shortly. He was a gray man: gray suit, gray complexion, gray manner. His skin hung in tired folds around a sharp jaw, and his eyes scanned the room with the administrative indifference of a station master checking luggage. He looked at us the way an exhausted professor looks at a class he has long since given up on — with the patience of a man who has learned that the time between a question and its predetermined answer need not be wasted on genuine deliberation. He kept pressing his fingertips to his temples, a gesture I recognized from my own years in Boston, in rooms where powerful men were asked to confer dignity upon decisions already made. The gesture said: I know how this ends. Can we not simply arrive there?

To his left stood Caleb Voss. I had been observing Voss since he arrived in Oak Haven, cataloguing his patterns the way I might study a difficult text — reading for structure, for rhetorical strategy, for the assumptions buried beneath the polished surface. What struck me most, again that morning, was not his confidence but its texture. He was clean in a way that communicated effort — the collar crisp, the suit precisely dark, the sheaf of papers held with the ease of a man who knows the weight of a document is not in its pages but in who has signed them. He did not look at me. I was furniture to him, or perhaps something less neutral: a potential complication, a woman who had access to the old county records and the will to read them. He held his papers and looked at the judge, and I watched the language of their bodies settle into a dialogue that excluded everyone else in the room. A slight forward lean from Voss. A near-imperceptible nod from Miller. The grammar of the foregone conclusion.

Elias stood near the front, his shoulders carrying the particular set of a man who has not slept and does not intend to show it. I had known him long enough to read the grammar of his posture: the weight forward on the balls of his feet, the jaw tight, the hands — those scarred, calloused hands — shoved into his pockets where they couldn't betray him. He was translating his fear into anger, which was the only conversion his nature allowed. Beside him, Titus filled the doorway like a keystone in an arch, his arms crossed, his face unreadable. I wondered what it cost him to stand in this room after the canyon — to trade the terrible simplicity of violence for this slower, colder violence of papers and precedents.

"Order," said Judge Miller, though the room was already silent. He tapped a brass ring against the table. The sound was flat and final, a period at the end of a sentence he hadn't written yet.

"We are here to conclude the matter of the Right-of-Way for the North Western Extension. Mr. Thorne, I understand you have objections to the final assessment and the notice of seizure."

Elias stepped forward. The floorboards groaned. Every head turned, but it was the quality of the attention that interested me — not the curiosity of people watching a dispute but the held breath of people watching someone go over the edge.

"It's not just an objection, Your Honor." His voice was steadier than I expected, though I could hear the effort beneath it, the way a taut rope hums. "It's my land. I've recorded every drop of rain and every failed crop in my ledgers. The North Field isn't acreage. It's the buffer between my family and the wind. We're not occupants. We're the ones keeping this land alive while the drought tries to take it back."

I had heard Elias speak of his land before, in the schoolhouse and at Larson's counter, and his language never varied: always the ledger, always the yield, always the wind as adversary. He spoke the way he farmed — with a plain, deliberate economy that trusted the thing said rather than the way of saying it. It was, in its own fashion, a kind of eloquence. The eloquence of a man who has never had the luxury of ornament. But I had spent enough time in rooms with judges to know that plain truth, plainly spoken, was not always what the law required. The law had its own dialect, and it did not bend toward the vernacular.

Judge Miller didn't look up from his papers. "Stewardship, Mr. Thorne, is a noble sentiment. Truly. But it is not a legal standing. This court is not here to weigh the depth of your sweat or the sincerity of your attachment to the soil. We are here to determine the legality of eminent domain as it pertains to a project of vital public utility."

"Vital to whom?" Elias's voice had an edge now, fine and sharp. "The people in this room are the public.

We're the ones who will be cut off from the creek. How is it a utility if it destroys the community it claims to serve?"

A murmur passed through the room — not agreement exactly, but recognition. The sound of people hearing their own thought spoken aloud.

Voss stepped forward. His voice was the voice of a man trained to be the most reasonable person in any room — smooth, measured, with the quality of good leather, soft until you found the structure beneath it. "Mr. Thorne's perspective is understandably narrow. He sees a fence line; the state sees a network. The railroad brings the mail, the coal, and the markets that will ensure Oak Haven survives the next drought. Without this line, this town is an island of dust."

An island of dust. He used the phrase deliberately, knowing how it landed on men whose crops were failing and whose wells were low. I had heard that rhetorical move before — in Boston, in the newspapers, in the voices of men who had perfected the art of folding a threat into a gift. The form was impeccable: conditional salvation presented as inevitability. You couldn't fault the grammar of it. You could only note what it omitted, which was everything that mattered.

Elias turned to the judge, bitterness sharpening every word. "You can't put a price on the years I've lost.

Nations are built on the word of a man and the sanctity of his home. You're not building. You're harvesting us."

"Spare us the oratory," the judge said, with the particular cruelty of a man who mistakes brevity for wisdom. "Mr. Voss, your legal citations, please. I have a train to catch."

Voss nodded. His lawyer — a young man from back East whose hair looked painted on, whose shoes had never touched unpaved ground — opened a heavy leather volume and began to read. His voice had the toneless, rhythmic quality of someone who has concluded that the words themselves are irrelevant; it is the authority behind them that does the work. Kohl v. United States. The Pacific Rail Act. The Territorial Statutes regarding the expansion of transport infrastructure. I knew the precedents. I had encountered them in the county records three weeks earlier and had spent the better part of two nights searching for the crack in the wall they made.

Each citation was a door closing. I watched Elias's face as the lawyer read, and I watched what happened to a man when the language he has always trusted — the plain language of deed and labor and promise — turns out to have no standing in the language that governs it. He was not being shouted down. He was being translated out of existence, one Latin phrase at a time. The law was using his own belief in words against him, and I felt the cruelty of that acutely, as a teacher who had spent years telling children that words were the truest tools they would ever own.

"The precedent is clear," the lawyer continued. "The necessity of the line outweighed the sentimentality of the homestead. The North Field is a primary grade requirement. To divert it would cost an additional fourteen thousand dollars and delay the project by six months."

I had been a teacher long enough to recognize the moment when a student stops listening because he has grasped the shape of the answer and found it unbearable. Elias had gone very still. His eyes were on his hands. The room was silent except for the scratch of the judge's pen against his notepad — a preparatory sound, the sound of a conclusion being drafted before its conditions had been met.

"Does the defendant have any further legal arguments?" asked the judge.

Elias raised his eyes. He looked at Titus, at Jedediah, at the men beside him. They were looking at the floor — not from cowardice but from the particular helplessness of honest men confronted with a system that has no use for honesty. Then he looked back at the judge, and his voice came from somewhere far back in his chest: "I have no more words, Your Honor. If the law says my sweat has no value, then I suppose the law and I have nothing left to say to one another."

The judge reached for his pen. "Based on the evidence of public utility and the established precedents of eminent domain, the court finds in favor of the Chicago and North Western Railroad Company. The right-of-way through the Thorne North Field is hereby granted." He did not hesitate. He did not perform deliberation. The words came out with the fluency of something rehearsed, perhaps even written in advance on the ferry from Pierre. "Mr. Thorne, you are hereby ordered to vacate the specified acreage within forty-eight hours. Any structures, fences, or crops remaining after that time will be cleared by the company at your expense. Construction will commence at dawn on Thursday."

The brass ring struck the table. The hearing was over. The total elapsed time, by my estimation, was less than twenty minutes.

The room began to empty with the shuffling silence of people trying not to look at Elias Thorne. I understood that silence. It was the shame of a community that had believed, for a time, that a unified stand at Larson's Emporium was the same as a legal victory. They had been broken by a signature, and they did not know how to carry that knowledge past each other. Some men paused at the door, turning as if to speak, then thought better of it and stepped out into the light.

Titus set his hand briefly on Elias's shoulder — the heavy, bruising grip of a man who has no adequate words and does not pretend otherwise — and walked out. His footsteps echoed in the hollow room long after he was gone. Elias stood where the judge had left him, his hands at his sides, staring at the table as if the brass ring were still vibrating.

I did not leave immediately. I stood at the back after the men had filed out and looked at what remained of my classroom. My desk had been pushed aside. The tin cup with the dried sage sat behind the stovepipe, tilted at an angle. The multiplication table I had lettered on butcher paper was half-hidden behind the railroad survey. Everything I had assembled here — the primers, the maps, the chalk ledge worn smooth by two years of use — had been shuffled to the margins to make room for a table and a judge who wanted to be elsewhere by noon.

I straightened the cup. I took down the railroad survey, folded it, and set it on Larson's table. I moved my desk back to its place and wiped the tobacco ash from the chalk ledge with my sleeve. These were small gestures, nearly meaningless. But I had learned in Boston, and confirmed here, that civilization consists of small gestures maintained under pressure, and that the moment you stop making them is the moment the room becomes something else entirely.

I walked out into a morning that was too bright and too indifferent. The sun had no opinion on eminent domain. The dust reflected it without comment. A meadowlark sang from the fence post by the road, its voice absurdly beautiful against the ugliness of the hour.

* * *

Elias's wagon had reached the edge of the homestead by the time I came around the schoolhouse's north side, and I watched him climb down with the movements of a man twice his age — slow, deliberate, as though each joint required separate permission. Sarah was on the porch. She had not asked the question yet; it was written in the set of her shoulders, in the way her hands had drawn into her sleeves. She knew. The body reads the answer before the mouth delivers it.

He stopped at the bottom step. "We lost, Sarah. The Judge — he didn't even listen. He gave them the field. We have forty-eight hours."

She did not cry. She stepped down and took his hand, her fingers rough and warm against his cold ones. "The house is still here. The well is still here. We're still here."

"For how long?" His voice broke at the seam — a sound I had heard only once before from him, the night Samuel was carried in. "I brought you here to be safe. To own something no one could touch. And I failed. I've lost it all again."

"You haven't lost us," she said. Her voice was quiet, steady, and carried the particular authority of a woman who has decided that the ground she is standing on is the ground she will defend, regardless of what any judge has written on any paper.

I turned away before he answered. That moment was not mine to witness, though I knew I would remember the geometry of it — the two of them on the porch steps, the wheat field stretching behind them, the morning light catching the dust that rose from the road where the judge's buggy was already disappearing toward the county line.

I walked back toward the schoolhouse, my mind already moving through what I had read the night before — the county charters, the territorial maps, the old survey from 1824, its lines shaky and the script flowing in the hand of a clerk who had probably written it by firelight in a canvas tent. A navigable waterway. A federal easement. One hundred yards on either side. The words had been buried under sixty years of amendments and refilings, but they had not been struck. They were still there, like old writing beneath new paint, waiting for someone with the patience to look.

The law, I had learned in many years of studying it from the outside, is not a fixed text. It is a palimpsest — layered, contradictory, full of old writing beneath the new. Voss had read the top layer and concluded he had the whole document. But documents have history. Texts have contexts. And I had not yet stopped reading.

I went back inside, lit the lamp, and spread the maps across my desk. The chalk ledge was clean. The sage stood upright in its cup. The room smelled, faintly, of cedar again. I picked up a pencil and began to trace the line of the creek where it bent toward the North Field, following the shaky ink of a surveyor who had been dead for half a century, whose handwriting might yet save a farm.

Chapter 29: Embers

Elias

The kerosene lantern sat on the dirt at the edge of the North Field, its light making a small yellow country in the dark. The wheat swayed in a low wind. In the moonlight, the stalks looked like silver ghosts — pale, whispering, already half-gone. My boots had sunk an inch into the parched ground. It gave way like ash.

Forty-eight hours.

I turned the matchbook over in my fingers. The sulfur smell was sharp, a thin prick of violence against the quiet. I thought of Kansas — the way the wind had carried the smell of char across my brother's fields when the bank took the fence. I had sworn I would never be on the wrong side of a fire again. But here I was, crouching in my own wheat with a match in my hand and nothing left that felt like mine.

The survey stakes stood at the field's edge, their red tips catching the lantern's glow — small, insistent flags planted in the center of everything I'd built. If the law said this land was a utility, if Voss meant to lay his iron over the furrows I'd cut with my own hands, then he would find nothing but blackened earth and bitter smoke. Let him grade burnt wheat. Let him explain to his investors why the right-of-way smelled like a funeral. The numbers made a grim kind of sense: forty acres at zero was the same as forty acres burnt. The harvest was already taken from me. The fire would just be the honest version of what the judge's pen had already done.

I crouched and pulled a single match free.

"It's a fine crop, Elias. Be a shame to see it go up in a hurry."

My thumb froze against the striking strip. The voice came from the deep shadow of the cottonwood at the field's edge — gravel and patience, the voice of a man in no hurry at all. I didn't need to look. Jedediah moved through dark ground the way water did: by finding the paths no one thought to block. The faint smell of old campfire smoke and the metallic tang of his prospecting gear reached me before his footsteps did.

I didn't turn. "They're taking it anyway, Jed. Thursday morning, the engines come. I won't let them have the satisfaction of clearing it themselves."

"Might be so." His footsteps came slow, the crunch of dry silt. He didn't reach for my arm or blow out the lantern. He just stood a few feet off, his silhouette blending with the cottonwood's trunk, and his being there had a weight to it — not judgment, but witness. A man who had seen a hundred fires and knew none of them had ever truly warmed a soul.

"A man burns his own crop," he said, quiet, "he's telling the world he's finished. That what he's saying, Elias?"

I didn't answer right away. The match sat between my thumb and forefinger, and I could feel the grain of the wood, the thin ridge of the sulfur head. One stroke and the North Field would be smoke by morning. One stroke and the column in the ledger marked yield would read zero, and the column marked cost would read everything.

The urge to strike it was still there, a coal in my gut, but it was being cooled by the sheer fact of being seen. To burn the field was to prove the Judge right: that I was a man of clay and fury, unfit for the order they were bringing. To burn it was to hand Voss the story he wanted — the stubborn farmer who destroyed what he couldn't keep, who chose ash over compromise.

I looked at the match a long time. The wheat whispered around me. Somewhere out in the dark, a coyote called and got no answer.

Then I closed the matchbook and shoved it deep into my pocket. I stood, my knees popping, and blew out the lantern. Darkness rushed in. Only the moon remained, laying its cold light across the field in long silver bands. Jedediah said nothing. He turned and walked back into the sage, his footsteps fading until there was only the wind through the dry stalks and the slow, stubborn creak of the windmill turning on the hill.

I stood there another minute, breathing the night air. It tasted of dust and the faint sweetness of ripening grain — a taste that didn't know about judges or deadlines or survey stakes. The wheat was still growing. It didn't know it was condemned. I envied it that.

* * *

I went back to the house. The kitchen smelled of dried lavender and the cold ghost of the stew Sarah had made for a dinner I hadn't touched. The pot sat on the stove with its lid off, the gravy congealed to a skin. The clock on the mantle worked away at the dark, tick by tick. Each tick was a second closer to Thursday.

I sat at the table and opened the ledger. The leather cover was cool and cracked under my thumb, the binding starting to separate at the spine from a year of nightly use. I turned through the pages: rain counts, calf births, seed costs, the price of baling wire. April: two inches. May: half an inch. June: nothing. A history of a man trying to hold a line against fate, column by column. I ran my finger down the last page of figures — the tally of what the North Field was supposed to yield this season, the number I'd been carrying in my head for weeks, the number that was supposed to balance everything else. Now the columns just looked like marks in a dead man's book.

My forehead went down to the table. The wood grain pressed against my skin, smooth and cool, worn by years of plates and elbows and Sarah's hands wiping it clean after supper. The clock ticked on. At some point, the tick pulled me back to myself — but it wasn't the clock. The sound was a fist on the door, hollow and frantic, and then a voice I knew.

"Elias! Open the door!"

I was on my feet before I'd decided to stand. The shotgun was in my hands, the cold steel barrel steadying me the way it always did — not a threat but a fact, like the weight of a fence post when you need something to lean on. I threw the bolt and pulled the door open, and the night air came in with a gust of cold ozone and spent exertion.

Not Pinkertons. Eleanor.

She was leaning against the doorframe, her hair loose from its pins, her face white as fresh paper. She clutched a bundle of documents to her chest, fingers stained dark with ink. Her chest heaved. She'd run from the schoolhouse — a mile and a half in the dark, over ground that would turn an ankle if you didn't know it — and she was still gripping those papers like they were the deed to salvation. Her eyes were sharp and bright with something I hadn't seen in her before — not fear but its opposite: the feverish light of a person who has found the thing she was looking for.

"Eleanor—" I took her by the shoulders. She felt small, vibrating. "Is someone hurt?"

"No." She shook her head, stumbled past me into the kitchen, and spread the papers across my open ledger before I'd shut the door. "I found it, Elias. I was going through the original county charters — the ones from before the territory was organized. The maps Larson kept in the basement. I didn't stop until I saw it."

Sarah appeared in the bedroom doorway, blinking against the lamplight, her nightgown white in the dark. She pulled her shawl around her shoulders and stepped into the kitchen without a word, her bare feet quiet on the boards. "Eleanor? What's happened?"

Eleanor didn't look up. She pointed to a yellowed map — a survey from sixty years back, the lines shaky, the script old and flowing. The paper smelled of mildew and dust, the smell of a thing that had been waiting in a basement for someone to need it. "The creek. Look at the designation. The 1824 charter — the one the federal government used to grant the first land parcels. They designated Oak Creek as a navigable waterway."

The air in the kitchen went thin. Sarah moved closer, her hand finding the back of my chair.

"The creek has been dry since the year I got here," I said. "It's a gully for tumbleweeds."

"It doesn't matter." Her voice had risen to something fierce — the voice of a woman reading a verdict she'd been searching for, the voice of the teacher who has found the answer and will not let the class move on until everyone understands. "Under federal maritime law — the statutes brought over from the East — a waterway designated as navigable is protected land. The government holds a permanent easement for one hundred yards on either side. No private entity, not even a railroad with an eminent domain order, can build within that zone without a direct Act of Congress." She looked up at me. "Voss's new route — the one through the Badlands he was surveying this week — it crosses the creek bed three times in five miles."

I looked at the map. The lines seemed to shift — the shaky ink of a surveyor who'd probably drawn them by firelight in a canvas tent, sixty years ago, not knowing or caring what they'd mean to a farmer standing in a kitchen at midnight with a matchbook in his pocket.

"You're saying," I started, careful, the way you say something when it's too big to say all at once, "if we can prove the creek is legally a river — even if it hasn't seen water in a decade—"

"I'm saying the law is a tool," Eleanor said. Her voice had dropped to something quiet and certain, the voice she used when she wanted a thing remembered. "Voss used the law to take your field because he saw the land as a number. He forgot this land has a history. If Oak Creek is a navigable waterway, his entire southern route is a legal impossibility. He cannot lay a single tie without violating federal protection. A territorial judge's order cannot override a federal waterway designation. The Judge doesn't have the standing."

Sarah crossed the kitchen and set her hand on Eleanor's shoulder. She squeezed once — not a word, just a pressure that said what Sarah always said without speaking: we are here, and that is enough.

I reached out and touched the edge of the old charter. The paper was dry and brittle, the color of old straw. Beneath my thumb, it felt as solid as the floor of the North Field after a good rain — the kind of solid that holds weight, that takes a root, that doesn't give when the wind leans on it.

We weren't finished. The Judge had taken the field from us with ink and precedent, and now Eleanor had brought us ink and precedent of our own. The matchbook was still in my pocket. I could feel its weight against my thigh — a reminder of what I'd almost done, what I'd almost become. I wouldn't need it.

The drought had taught me one thing about water: it goes where you give it a path. All we had to do was give it a path.

I pulled a chair close to the table, angled the lamp so the light fell clean across the old map, and started reading. Sarah brought coffee. Eleanor turned the pages. Outside, the North Field stood in the dark, unburned and waiting.

Chapter 30: The Water Logic

Elias

The sky above the schoolhouse belfry had not quite given up on the night — a deep gray pressing against the eastern rim, the first light still a rumor. My hands found the bell rope in the dark, the braided hemp rough against my palms, the fibers catching on the calluses the way a harness catches on a cracked yoke ring. Below, Oak Haven lay quiet under a waning moon, the sod roofs low and featureless as furrows from up here. I took a breath of cold air — it tasted of dust and the thin, metallic edge that comes before dawn on the high plains — and pulled.

The first clang was a physical blow — a bronze shudder through the rope and into the marrow of my arms. It broke the stillness flat, a desperate sound, nothing like a call to prayer. I found a rhythm and kept it. Hard. Demanding. Clang. Clang. Clang. My shoulders burned with the kind of ache that belongs to a plow harness, the old punishment of seasons resurfacing in the predawn chill. I didn't stop until the lights came on.

Yellow pinpricks bloomed in the dark, one by one — Larson's store, the Parker place, the low shape of Jedediah's dugout on the south ridge. Shadows moved in the windows. I came down the ladder, my knees popping on each rung, the worn rungs flexing under my boots, and stood on the schoolhouse porch as the town arrived.

Anders Larson was first, coat thrown over his nightshirt, eyes squinting against the lantern Eleanor held beside the door. Titus followed, moving through the gloom like a slow landslide, coal smoke and cold iron coming off him even at this hour, as though the forge never fully let go of the man. Rachel Parker clutched a shawl around her shoulders, her face set in the hard patience of a woman who has been woken by bad news before and knows how to stand in its presence. Jedediah stood at the edge of the lantern's reach, arms crossed, waiting to be unpersuaded. Even Samuel had come — his arm still bound tight against his chest, his face pale as flour paste, his eyes wider than his strength could account for. I wanted to tell him to go back to bed. I didn't. He'd earned the right to be here.

They looked hollowed out. All of them. The drought had done it first — thinned their faces, put the particular dullness in their eyes that comes from watching a well drop week by week. Then the Judge had finished the job, stripping away the last belief that the system they'd built their lives around might protect them.

"Is it the Pinkertons?" Anders asked, his voice thick with sleep and a thin edge of dread. "Have they come early?"

"No." I reached into my pocket and pulled out the charter — the yellowed scrap Eleanor had unearthed, its ink dark against the old parchment. The paper was brittle between my fingers, light as a leaf, heavy as the deed to the North Field. "We aren't done. Eleanor found a loophole. Oak Creek is designated as a navigable waterway in the 1824 federal charter. If there is water in that bed — actual flow — Voss can't touch it. Federal law overrides the Judge's order." I looked at them — every tired face, every pair of eyes. "But we have to make it a river again. Not tomorrow. Today."

The silence that followed was thick enough to cut. The wind moved through the dry sunflower stalks at the schoolhouse edge, a sound like something hollow being scraped. A dog barked somewhere on the south side of town and was hushed. Then Jedediah laughed — short, dry, a bark of disbelief. "That creek hasn't run since the grass turned. You're asking for a miracle, and God's been stingy with those."

"Not a miracle." I stepped into the lantern light, the charter held at my side like a deed of trust. "Sweat. Up at the headwaters — four miles into the ridge — there's a spring that's been diverted into a sinkhole since the rockslide two years back. We dam the sink.

We dig a channel back to the old bed. It'll be muddy and shallow, but it'll flow. That's all the law needs."

Anders looked at his boots. A calculating man, a man of credit and inventory, a man who added columns before he added his name. "Elias, that's backbreaking work. Half of us are already running short. We've got nothing left in the pantry and less in the legs."

The cold anger came up fast, and behind it the fear — the clawing kind, the kind that knows exactly what it's afraid of and has already calculated the loss. "Then pack the wagons!" The words jumped out before I could weigh them. I heard the sharpness and didn't take it back. "But don't call this place a home if you won't pick up a shovel to save it. Voss wants us to think the law is a mountain we can't move. Eleanor's found the crack. We just have to drive the wedge."

A hand came down on my shoulder — heavy, steady, the kind that doesn't move once it lands. Titus stepped into the center of the light. He looked at the townspeople without hurry, his eyes passing over each face the way he inspected a piece of stock iron before deciding what it was good for. Then he looked at me. "I've got three dozen shovels in the forge," he said, his voice low and level, a sound like an anvil being set on stone. "And a dozen pickaxes. I'll start sharpening the edges."

Anders looked up. His jaw tightened. He glanced at Rachel, then at the dark horizon where the railroad camp sat, the faint orange glow of their watch-fires visible against the ridge. He let out a long breath — the kind that marks the end of one calculation and the beginning of another. "I've got spades at the store. Two kegs of nails if we need a flume. I'll pledge my stock, Elias. And my back."

That was all it took. Not a speech. Just two men saying what they'd do. Rachel set her jaw and said the women would bring water and food. Thomas Parker stepped forward, hands balled tight. The tools gathered themselves in the dark, the clink and scrape of ordinary preparation — shovels lifted from porches, picks pulled from shed walls, rope coiled over shoulders. The sound of people who had stopped waiting for the rain and decided to go find the water themselves.

* * *

By the time the sun bled over the eastern rim — an orange smear through the haze, reluctant and thin — we were already moving. A line of wagons and men on foot, snaking toward the northwestern ridges with a shovel over every shoulder. I led the way. The grit was between my teeth from the first step, the dry taste of the land that had taken so much already. Dust rose from the wheels and hung in the still air behind us like the wake of a slow boat. I didn't look back at the North Field. I couldn't afford to. Every time I looked at that wheat, the matchbook in my pocket got heavier.

The headwaters were four miles of uphill slog over gray stone and stunted cedar, and they made us pay for every foot. The trail — if you could call it a trail — switched back and forth across the face of the ridge, the wagon wheels catching on exposed roots, the horses blowing hard by the second mile. By the time we reached the spring, our shirts were plastered to our backs and our lungs had that high, thin burn of overworked bellows. The spring itself was a disappointment that I'd prepared myself for and still wasn't ready to see: a silver thread of water weeping from a crack in the limestone, vanishing almost immediately into a jagged maw of sun-cracked scree. It looked like trying to fill a wagon tank with a dripping rag.

But the law didn't care how much water there was. Only that it followed the path you gave it.

"Here!" I pointed to the line of the old gully, choked with tumbleweeds and dry silt. "We dig from the spring to the bed. We dam the sinkhole with stone and clay. Move!"

The first pickaxe strike jarred up my arms to the shoulder socket. The ground was three years of drought compressed into a crust — sun-fired clay that resisted every blow the way a locked vault resists a fist. I swung again, and again. The shock traveled through the handle and into my elbows, my shoulders, the base of my neck. Beside me, Titus worked the larger boulders with his sledgehammer, each fall sending a ring through the stone that I felt in my back teeth. We didn't talk. There was only the rasp of breath and the clinking of metal on stone and the occasional grunt when a root or a buried rock refused to give.

The heat rose quickly, a pressing, airless weight that settled over the ridge like a wool blanket soaked in warm water. Salt stung my eyes until I was squinting through a red blur. I wiped my face with my sleeve and the sleeve came away dark with grime. Children — Samuel working one-armed, William, the Larson boy — hauled buckets of dirt from the trench, their small faces streaked, backs bent under loads they shouldn't have been carrying. No one complained. The work had a feverish quality, a shared understanding that we were digging our way out of a grave and the clock was the only enemy we couldn't outfight.

Around noon, I straightened to wipe my face and looked down the line. The sun was a white eye directly above, and the air over the rocks had that wavering, unsteady quality that made the ridges look painted rather than real. There was Eleanor — her fine dress ruined past repair, her hem caked to the knees with red clay, her hands muddy as she helped Rachel haul stones for the dam. She moved without complaint, placing each stone with the deliberate precision she used when writing on the chalkboard. There was Anders Larson, a man of books and credit, standing knee-deep in a trench with a face gone purple with effort, his store coat folded on a rock behind him like a life he'd temporarily set aside. The sight of them kept my own shovel moving when my arms had gone to rope.

We weren't just moving dirt. Every cubic foot we threw was a page of argument against the maps Voss had drawn.

⋆ ⋆ ⋆

The channel we'd carved by midafternoon was a ragged scar in the earth — barely two feet deep, three feet wide. Shallow enough to look like a joke. I stood in it with my boots sinking into the new moist silt near the spring, and tried to find the logic of water in the numbers: the grade of the slope, the volume of the spring's output, the length of the channel to the old bed. The dam was holding, the sinkhole blocked by stones and packed clay that Titus had tamped down with his own weight. A dark pool had begun to form at the spring's edge, spreading slowly, the surface catching the light in small, trembling flashes. The smell of wet earth rose from the channel — sweet, heavy, a scent I hadn't breathed in longer than I wanted to count. It smelled like the morning after a rain that hadn't come.

"Keep digging!" The words came out cracked and dry. "We're halfway! Don't let the sun beat you!"

Titus paused, chest heaving, and looked up at the ridge. I followed his gaze.

High on a limestone outcropping, two figures stood against the sky. Even without binoculars, the silhouette of the closer man was unmistakable — straight back, the line of a bowler hat, the way he held himself like a man surveying property he already owned. Voss. Beside him, a glint of polished metal: the Pinkerton Captain's rifle. They stood there for a long time, two men watching from above with the patience of people who believe they have already decided the outcome.

Titus said nothing. Neither did I. I gripped my shovel until the handle bit into the groove of my palm and drove the blade back into the earth. Let them watch. Let them see what a town looked like when it decided to stop being polite about survival. I wanted Voss to understand, up on his rock with his maps and his orders, that the Law of the Sod was written in sweat, and it wasn't a law he could find in any volume his lawyer carried.

We dug.

★ ★ ★

The shadows had gone long and thin across the trench before anyone saw the riders.

"Elias!"

Eleanor's voice — sharp, stripped of everything but alarm. I straightened from the channel and turned, the shovel still in my hands, the new blisters on my palms splitting open against the wood.

At the top of the ridge, silhouetted against the dying sun: a line of horsemen, moving in a slow, deliberate trot, dust lifting behind them in a pale cloud. Long dusters. Brass tacks on the saddles catching the last light. The jingle of bits and the heavy thud of hooves on packed earth. The Pinkertons had come down off their hill.

Work stopped. The men climbed out of the trench one by one, their faces pale under the grime. We stood in a ragged, exhausted line, shovels in hand, chests heaving. The air had that electric quality — the stillness before a duster, when the world holds its breath and even the insects go quiet.

Titus had moved to the dam without being told. His sledgehammer rested on his shoulder like something growing there. His face had closed up into the flat, hard expression I'd seen once before, in the canyon. Not anger. Readiness. The kind of readiness that doesn't ask permission.

The Pinkertons stopped twenty yards out. The Captain sat his tall black gelding with the ease of a man who had been doing this for years — running smaller men off land they loved. He looked down at us and let the silence work for him, the way powerful men do, before he was ready to spend his words. His eyes moved along our line, counting, measuring, finding us wanting by every arithmetic he knew.

"Nice bit of gardening," he said at last. His voice was smooth, unhurried, the voice of a man who has the numbers on his side and knows it. He surveyed the trench, the dam, the pooling water. "But you're trespassing on railroad right-of-way. Interfering with the development of a public utility. That's criminal, last I checked."

I stepped forward, the loose shale crunching under my boots. My legs were dead weights; I moved on something past exhaustion, something that lives deeper than muscle — in the part of a man that remembers why he's standing here and not somewhere else. "This is a federal waterway," I said. "We're restoring a navigable stream. You touch this dam, and you're the ones in violation. Federal law, Captain. That outranks your judge."

He laughed — dry, rattling, turned back to his men as though I'd said something worth sharing. A few of them grinned, the grins of men who have been told they're on the winning side. Then the smile dropped. "I see squatters with shovels digging a ditch. I see an obstacle." He straightened in the saddle, his hand settling near the butt of his revolver. "Step aside, Thorne. We'll fill this hole and get back to the real work. Go home to your wife before someone gets hurt."

I looked at the pooling water behind the dam — dark, still, catching the last copper light of the day. The silver thread of the spring. The channel running toward the old gully, not yet connected, not yet flowing, but close. So close I could smell the promise of it in the wet silt under my boots. I thought of the North Field. I thought of Kansas, of men on horses looking down at my brother's yard while a bank official read from a paper. The same angle. The same weight in the gut. The same arithmetic: you have nothing, and we have everything, and the law is on our side.

I raised my shovel. Titus shifted his grip on the hammer. Anders stepped up, his face set hard, the storekeeper gone and the man underneath showing through. Even Samuel found a piece of limestone and held it in both hands, his one good arm trembling with the weight.

"No," I said. The word came out clean and final, the way a number comes out when the column is done and the answer is the answer, whether you like it or not.

"The water stays. We stay. You want to fill this trench — you'll dig through us first."

The Captain's eyes narrowed. His hand dropped to the butt of his revolver. The air on the ridge went to nothing — no wind, no sound but the faint trickle of the spring and the cold, high taste of what was about to happen. We were outmanned and half-dead from the work. I could count the cost of a fight in the time it took to draw a breath — the cost in bodies, in families, in everything we'd dug for since dawn.

But I looked down the line and what I saw wasn't a row of beaten farmers. It was roots. The kind that go down past the topsoil, past the drought crust, into something older than any map. The kind that hold even when the ground above them has turned to dust.

We weren't moving.

Chapter 31: The Stand at the Creek

Titus

The Captain's hand settled on his holster. Not a grab. A settling — slow, deliberate, the way a man sets a tool he plans to use. The leather of his glove rasped against the checkered walnut grip. That sound carried. It carried the way the first crack in a load-bearing beam carries — not loud, but final.

I had come up the ridge in time to see the line of Pinkertons fan out behind him — five men, disciplined, spreading like a weld cooling into its final shape. Trained men. Company men. The kind paid to hold a position until the other side breaks. Their horses were fresh, their dusters buttoned against the dust, their rifles upright in the scabbards. They smelled of gun oil and coffee and the particular arrogance of men who have been told the outcome is already decided. I stood at the back of the crowd and assessed the structure of it.

Elias was out front. Shovel raised, boot on the loose shale, looking up at the Captain's gelding like a man who had already decided the outcome and was just waiting on the other party to catch up. He was green wood, Elias — green wood under pressure: it bends, it splinters at the grain, but it does not release the nail. His shirt was dark with sweat and clay, his face streaked, his hands raw on the handle. He looked half-dead from the day's work and twice as stubborn as the morning. Beside him, Anders Larson with his jaw locked, storekeeper's hands blistered and shaking but holding the spade level. Young Samuel clutching a piece of limestone in both hands, white at the knuckles, his wounded shoulder drawn up tight against the strain. Rachel Parker a few steps back, still standing, her chin up, her eyes on the Captain with the flat appraisal of a woman measuring a man and finding him short. Eleanor at the trench's edge, her dress ruined to the waist with red clay, her face pale and set.

I read the geometry of it. Twenty yards between our line and theirs. The Captain's rifle still in the scabbard, but his hand had already traveled to the butt and come back twice — the habit of a man working up to the act. The Pinkertons behind him hadn't drawn. They were reading their captain for the signal. Once he drew, they drew. Once they drew, someone on our side would answer with a rock or a shovel blade, and then we'd have a full fracture on our hands, and a fracture at this load would not hold. It would kill.

"Nice bit of gardening," the Captain was saying. He had the voice of a man who had done this before — smooth, unhurried, built for wearing people down. "You're trespassing on railroad right-of-way. Interfering with a public utility. Criminal, last I checked."

Elias answered him. I didn't listen to the words. I watched the Captain's right shoulder. A man who's about to draw drops the shoulder first. It's the tell — the body beginning the motion before the mind gives final permission. The shoulder was tight but hadn't dropped. Not yet.

"Step aside, Thorne. Go home to your wife before someone gets hurt."

The shoulder didn't drop. But the hand was drifting again, the fingers opening and closing on the grip, and the horse underneath him had begun to shift its weight forward — picking up on its rider's tension, preparing for whatever came next.

I stepped out of the crowd and walked toward the trench.

I didn't run. Running was a different statement. Running gave the horses something to react to, and a spooked horse in close quarters was an unpredictable variable — twelve hundred pounds of muscle with no opinion on property law. I walked with my full weight — three hundred pounds of it, bone and muscle and twenty years of coal work — and the horses felt me before the men did. The ground transmitted it. The Captain's gelding shied two steps sideways, tossing its head, the bit jangling. The horse to the far left danced, its rider snatching at the reins. I kept walking. Each boot fell heavy, flat, square on the stone.

"Hold it, Croft!" The Captain's voice had a new edge in it. Not fear — not yet. A recalculation. The numbers were changing on him, and he knew it. "Stay back! I've got orders!"

I kept walking.

The hot smell of the horses thickened as I moved through their line. Sweat and leather and the sharp, grassy scent of a recent feeding. One of the animals turned its head and blew against my shoulder as I passed, a warm huff of recognition — horses know a farrier's hands, even at a distance. The Pinkertons pulled their mounts aside. Not out of courtesy. Out of the instinct that tells a man to step out of the path of something that will not step out of his.

The trench ran along the base of the ridge, and the dam was fifteen yards beyond it. The red survey stake the company had driven into the shale stood at the path's edge — milled lumber, paint still fresh, driven in by a man who had never felt the resistance of this particular ground. It stood there like an insult — a factory thing, clean-cut and certain, planted in earth that had never asked for it.

I stopped at the stake. Reached into my belt and took out the iron spike I'd brought from the forge that morning.

The iron was the right weight. I'd drawn it out at four in the morning, working by feel in the dark shop, the coals barely glowing, the anvil cold under my hands. I'd heated the stock in the banked fire and drawn it to square — two inches of hardened steel, tapered to a point. The work had taken twenty minutes. I hadn't lit a lamp. Didn't need one. The hands know the iron by sound and resistance, the way they know the difference between a good weld and a cold shut without looking. I had held the spike in my fist all the way up the ridge, the metal warming to my grip until it felt like a part of my own hand.

I set it against the earth at the edge of the dam, right in the center of their intended path, and I drove it.

One strike. The sledgehammer came down with everything — the full weight of the head, the full rotation of the shoulder, the full pull of my back and legs, the ground beneath my boots solid enough to take the force. The iron bit six inches into the sun-baked clay with a crack that bounced off the limestone ridges and came back twice.

The sound did the work I needed it to do.

The Captain's gelding shied hard, nearly unseating him. Two of his men grabbed their reins with both hands. The line broke its shape — a gap opened between the second and third rider, the kind of gap that turns a formation into a collection of individuals. In that moment — three, four seconds — the geometry shifted. They were no longer a wall. They were separate men on separate horses, each one making his own calculation.

I straightened. Turned to face the Captain.

He had the rifle halfway out of the scabbard, the lever half-cocked, the barrel catching the last of the sun. His eyes were on me, and in them I read the calculation: the size of me, the hammer, the distance between us, the fact that no one had fired yet and what it would mean to be the first. I let him do the math. I had time. A man doing arithmetic doesn't pull a trigger.

"This work is lawful," I said. My voice carries without effort. I don't shout. Shouting is for men who aren't sure they'll be heard. "The creek is the life of this town. You touch this dam, and you answer to me. Not the Marshal. Not the Judge. To me."

I had spoken longer sentences than that in my life. But those were enough.

The Pinkertons behind the Captain exchanged looks. Quick, darting glances — the kind men make when they're checking to see if anyone else is willing to go first. They were men hired to press the weak. They were built for resistance of a certain type: soft resistance, the resistance of people who haven't decided yet. They were not built for a man with a sledgehammer who had walked through their line like it wasn't there, and their faces showed it. A man paid a company wage is a different structure than a man standing on the ground he has decided to hold. Company iron goes brittle at the seam, given enough load. I had seen it before, in the war, and in every negotiation since. You find the seam. You put the load there. The structure tells you what it's made of.

The Captain's rifle barrel had dipped. He knew it. He didn't holster it, but he stopped moving it. The muscle in his jaw was working — the visible sign of a man trying to find a line in his orders that covered this particular situation and not finding one.

"You're making a mistake, Croft," he said. The edge had left his voice. What remained was the recitation of a line — something from his orders, spoken because his orders required it. "This line is going through, one way or another."

I said nothing. I let the hammer hang at my side, the iron head resting against the clay. I looked at him the way I look at a joint that I'm not certain will hold: with patience, and without particular feeling about the answer. The answer would come. It always does, if you wait for the load to tell you.

He turned his horse.

Not fast. He gave it the dignity of a slow withdrawal — a man concluding a business call, not retreating. But he turned, and his men pulled their mounts around behind him, and the line that had been pressing us began to draw back up the ridge. The dust rose behind them in a thin curtain. The jingle of their tack faded. One of the horses left a pile of manure on the trail, and the small indignity of it seemed right — the last word of a retreat that had no other words to offer.

I turned to Elias and gave him one nod.

He understood it. He straightened, and whatever had been locked in his chest for the last hour released — I could see it in the way his shoulders dropped, the way the shovel lowered from its fighting angle to its working angle. He turned to the line behind him. "Jedediah! Anders! Break the dam!"

They moved. Not like individuals — like a single mechanism, each part knowing its function. Jedediah shoved the key boulder aside with a grunt that came from the floor of his lungs. Elias drove his shovel into the base of the clay wall. I watched the structure, the load path, the weakest seam — the place where the packed stone met the softer clay. When the moment was right I stepped forward and placed my boot against a section I'd been reading since I arrived. I pushed.

The wall gave.

Not all at once. The first breach was a seam of dark water, thin as a wire, finding the path through the clay. Then it widened. The pressure behind it had been building for hours — silently, patiently, the water doing what water does, which is wait for the weakness and go.

The breach opened into a rush — dark, muddy, cold — and the sound it made was not dramatic. It was the sound of a small thing becoming necessary. A hiss, a gurgle, the low percussion of water hitting dry stone for the first time in years. The stones darkened where the flow touched them. The silt turned from gray to brown. The smell of wet earth rose up — heavy, sweet, alive — and the smell alone was enough to change the way the air felt in your lungs.

The flow moved down the channel, following the grade we'd cut. I tracked it with my eyes the way I track a cooling weld — watching the direction, watching whether it held, watching for the breach that would send it sideways into the scrub. It held. It moved into the old gully and kept moving, brown and shallow and alive, carving the dust as it went. A small thing. But it was running where we'd told it to run, and that was the whole argument.

The people behind me made a sound. Not a cheer. An exhale — long and collective, the pressure releasing from a structure that had been under load for months. Rachel Parker was crying, her hands at her mouth. Anders Larson was laughing, a strange, involuntary sound, the laugh of a man who has just survived something he hadn't expected to survive. Eleanor stood at the trench's edge with her arms at her sides, watching the water with an expression I couldn't read but recognized — the look of a person seeing a thing they had only known in theory become real. Samuel ran along the water's edge, watching it move, his eyes bright with something I didn't have a name for. He would live, that boy. He'd be back on his feet by the end of the week. I had decided that on the ridge and saw no reason to revise it.

I looked up at the outcropping where Voss had stood. Empty. The man was good at disappearing once a situation had turned against him. He'd be in his tent by now, writing a wire. The fight wasn't over. It would move to paper and courts and back again before it was done. Men like Voss didn't stop at the first refusal. They came back with different tools — lawyers, legislators, a revised survey, a new judge. The iron would have to be tested again.

But the water was moving. A shallow, muddy thread of it, threading through the old bed toward the valley. The federal charter said navigable. The charter didn't say deep.

I set the sledgehammer across my shoulder and started down the ridge. My boots found the familiar rhythm of a downhill walk — heel, ball, the weight shifting forward, the hammer balanced. Behind me, the sound of the water grew fainter but didn't stop. The work had held. The joint had not fractured. We would see what the morning brought, but the structure was intact.

That was enough for tonight.

Chapter 32: The Judge's Ride

Elias

The water was there.

That was the one fact that mattered. A coffee-colored ribbon winding through the chalky gully stones, barely deep enough to cover a man's ankles, but moving. The sound was a wet shushing against the banks, a music I hadn't heard on this land in three years. I stood at the creek's edge, boots sunken into the muck we'd spent the night conjuring, and let the silt settle on the back of my tongue. Even tasting like liquid earth, it promised life. A thin promise. A conditional promise. But the only one I had.

The predawn air stung the inside of my nostrils — that thin, biting cold that comes just before the sky gives in to morning. The stars were going out one by one, as if someone were closing ledgers for the night. Along both banks, the gully stones glistened wet, and the smell that rose from the mud was rich and dark and old — the smell of something the land had been holding in reserve, waiting for someone stubborn enough to dig for it.

"He's coming, Elias," Eleanor whispered. She stood beside me, her silhouette sharp against the graying horizon — dress stained with clay at the hem, hair escaping its pins, eyes bright with something past exhaustion. She clutched a leather-bound volume of territorial statutes like a man grips a fence post in a windstorm. "Buckboard just crested the south ridge. Twenty minutes before the sun starts pulling this back into the sky."

Twenty minutes. I looked at the water. The earth was drinking it faster than I wanted to count. The dry silt along the banks was crawling with it, wicking our hard work upward the way a cloth wick draws kerosene — silently, steadily, with no interest in the cost. Every inch the flow dropped was one fewer inch between us and the railroad's red line through my North Field. My hands were wrapped with dried mud that cracked when I pressed my fingers together — old parchment on old skin. The blisters from the shovel had broken and dried and broken again, and the raw places underneath had gone numb sometime after midnight. My throat had gone tight somewhere around the same hour and hadn't loosened since.

I looked up at the sky. The gray was thinning at the eastern rim, a pale band of light spreading like a stain on bleached linen. The sun would be on us soon. Once it climbed above the ridgeline, the shallow water would begin to evaporate in earnest, and our creek would shrink to a damp memory. The arithmetic was simple and merciless: we needed the Judge to see the water before the water left.

The buckboard's rattle grew — a mechanical intrusion into the morning quiet, the squeak of an ungreased axle and the clatter of iron rims on the hardpan road. Judge Miller sat beside the driver, black coat whitened by road dust, face carrying the sour set of a man pulled from a warm bed for a fool's errand. He'd crossed the Missouri on the ferry before dawn to reach us — ridden out of Pierre in the dark, and the journey showed on him. His hat was on his knee, and even from a distance, the angle of his jaw said everything about his opinion of the hour. Behind him, on a chestnut mare, rode Caleb Voss. Even at distance, his shoulders told the story: the rigid posture of a man who believed the world obeyed the lines on his maps and would continue to do so, regardless of what a few farmers had dug in the night.

The carriage creaked to a halt at the gully's edge. Horse sweat and hot leather mixed with the raw, damp smell of the new creek. I stepped forward, knees popping from the night's labor, every joint feeling like it had been set in dried mortar. "Morning, Judge."

My voice came out like gravel in a tin cup. I offered my hand. He ignored it, climbing down with a deliberate grunt that announced his displeasure before his boots hit the ground. They left dark prints in the dust — thick Missouri River mud still caked on the soles, the gray-brown clay of the ferry landing that was nothing like our chalky prairie dirt. He was shorter than I remembered — shorter and grayer, the dust of the road settled into every crease of his coat.

"Thorne." He adjusted his spectacles and looked at the muddy flow, then back at me. His eyes moved from the shovel marks on the bank to the raw clay of the dam upstream to the exhausted faces of the men and women standing behind me. "You've called me out at an ungodly hour to look at a puddle. I hope for your sake there's more to this than a leaky cistern."

"It's no puddle, Your Honor." Eleanor stepped forward with a steadiness that shamed her exhaustion. She moved the way she moved in her classroom — with purpose, with the quiet authority of a person who knows the text better than anyone else in the room. She opened the book to a marked page, her finger tracing the line with surgical precision. "Under Territorial Statute 42-B, designation of a navigable waterway depends not on seasonal volume but on the historical presence of a defined channel and a continuous current flow. Water rights are paramount in this territory. The railroad's charter specifically prohibits construction within one hundred yards of a protected stream to prevent contamination of communal resources."

Her voice was clear and steady, and I watched the Judge's face as she spoke. His eyes followed her finger along the text the way a farmer's eye follows a row to check if it's true. He was listening. Not agreeing — not yet — but listening, which was more than he'd done in the schoolhouse.

The Judge leaned over the bank, boots hovering close to the muck. A jagged bit of sagebrush we'd tossed in upstream bobbed past — slow, spinning in a small eddy, but moving. Undeniably moving. I pressed my fists against my thighs and watched the water's edge. It receded a fraction of an inch as I watched, the wet line on the stones dropping like the mercury in a thermometer. Stay, I thought. Ten minutes. Just stay.

"Navigable?" Voss dismounted and walked toward us, polished boots clicking on the stones. He didn't look at the water. He looked at me, his mouth twisted into that thin, knowing smile — the smile of a man who has already written his version of events and is merely waiting for reality to catch up. "Your Honor, this is a farce. Twenty-four hours ago this gully was a graveyard for cattle. It's a trick of the light and a few desperate men with shovels — an artificial diversion to obstruct progress."

He stepped to the edge, pointing a gloved finger at the raw shovel marks upstream. "Look at those banks, Judge. This isn't the work of nature. You can't let a bucket of mud stop a project that links this territory to the world."

The heat came up in my chest the way it does before I say something I'll have to stand behind — the old Kansas heat, the kind that used to get my brother into trouble and me out of it. "The water is in the bed, Voss." I moved toward him. I could smell the expensive tobacco on his coat, the pomade in his hair, the scent of a man who'd never had to weigh the cost of a dry well against the cost of feeding his family. "Doesn't matter how it got there. The spring is flowing again because we cleared the path the drought choked off. That water is the life of this town. You call it a nuisance because it doesn't fit your ledger. We call it staying alive."

The Judge straightened and looked toward the ridge where the Pinkertons were camped. His gaze settled on the armed men standing by their horses, repeaters catching the first light. He'd met them on his approach — coming up from the river road, still carrying the dust of the crossing, the Captain demanding his credentials with an arrogance that hadn't sat well with a man of the bench. I'd heard about it from the driver afterward: the Captain had blocked the road, asked to see papers, kept the Judge waiting in the dust while he sent a man to fetch Voss. The Judge had sat in the buckboard and said nothing, which, for a man of his temperament, was the most dangerous response possible.

"Ingenuity," the Judge said, almost to himself. He looked back at the creek, then at the weary, mud-caked townsfolk gathered at a respectful distance — Anders with his suspenders over a filthy nightshirt, Rachel with her arms crossed, young Samuel with his arm in a sling, standing because he refused to sit while the rest of us stood. "Mr. Voss, I spent my morning being interrogated by your private guards as if I were a common rustler. The railroad appears to believe its interests override the dignity of the law."

Voss's smile slipped. "Your Honor, the guards are for the protection of company property—"

"The law does not require protection from its own citizens, Mr. Voss." The Judge's voice found its courtroom resonance — a sudden, full sound that seemed too large for the open air, a sound that carried the way a blacksmith's hammer carries across a still morning. He gestured at the water. "You call this a trick. I see a community that labored through the night to reclaim a resource the earth tried to take from them. Whether a shovel or Providence put the water there is irrelevant. The water is present. The channel is historical. The statute Miss Vance has cited is quite clear."

He turned to me, and for just a second, something passed across his face that wasn't legal logic — a flicker of the kind of recognition one survivor gives another. One man who has sat in the dust and counted what he had left, looking at another who was doing the same. "A navigable waterway is a sacred trust in a land this dry, Thorne. The railroad holds the deed to the path. They do not hold a deed to the rain."

"Judge, this is a technicality!" Voss stepped forward, face darkening, the carefully maintained composure cracking at the edges like dried clay. "The costs of delay are staggering—"

"Then the company should have invested in better surveyors and fewer gunmen."

He reached into his coat for a portable inkwell and a fountain pen and used the buckboard's wheel cap as his desk. His hand moved across official parchment in a scratchy, deliberate rhythm — the sound of a pen on paper, which is either the quietest sound in the world or the loudest, depending on which side of the document you stand.

That pen was the loudest thing on the prairie. The sound of a gate slamming shut. My jaw ached; I hadn't known I'd been clenching it since the buckboard appeared on the ridge. Eleanor was biting her lip beside me, knuckles white on the book's spine. Behind us, the townspeople stood in a ragged half-circle, and I could feel their attention like a physical thing — the weight of thirty people who had dug all night, watching a pen move across paper, waiting.

"I am issuing a temporary injunction against all construction and grading within one hundred yards of this waterway," the Judge announced, handing the document to the Marshal. "Construction stops immediately. The company will file an appeal with the High Court in Pierre — given the current backlog, expect no hearing for at least six months."

Six months. The number landed in my chest and settled there, solid as a fence post. Six months was a harvest. Six months was a season of rain or a season of drought, but either way it was time — time to file, time to argue, time to let the water do what water does when you give it a path.

Voss grabbed his horse's reins hard enough that the animal shied, its hooves clattering on the gully stones. "This isn't the end, Thorne," he hissed, leaning toward me. His eyes had gone flat and cold, the polish gone from them, and what remained underneath was just a man who had been told no and didn't know what to do with it. "Water evaporates. Judges leave. The railroad is iron, and iron doesn't care about a muddy ditch. You've bought yourself a season. That's all."

He spurred his horse and was gone. The dust of his departure hung in the air, then settled on the wet stones of the creek bank like a final punctuation mark. I watched him go and felt nothing like triumph. What settled over me was pure fatigue — the kind that lives in the knees and behind the eyes, the kind that makes the ground look like a reasonable place to lie down. I'd spent months working toward this moment, running the numbers and the risks and the what-ifs the way a man runs his finger down a column of figures looking for the error. Now the column balanced, and I was too tired to feel it.

The Judge climbed back into his carriage, his face returning to its mask of weary duty. "Get some sleep, Thorne," he said. "And tell that blacksmith of yours to keep his hammer for tools. I'd hate to come back out here for something less civilized than a water right."

The buckboard rattled away, the axle squeaking, the dust following it back toward the river road and the long ride to the crossing.

I crouched down and pressed two fingers into the mud at the creek's edge. Wet. Real. The flow was shallower now, the sun already beginning to pull it back toward wherever it had come from, the dark stain on the gully stones narrowing as I watched. But it had been here long enough. It had been here when it counted. That was all the ledger required.

Eleanor let out a long breath beside me — the first unguarded sound I'd heard from her all night. Her shoulders dropped, and for a moment she looked less like the teacher and more like the woman underneath —

tired, dirty, relieved, and not quite believing it. She closed the book of statutes and held it against her chest.

"Thank you," I said. The words were too small for what I meant, but they were what I had.

She nodded once, and something moved across her face that might have been a smile if it hadn't been so close to tears.

We stood there in the growing light, watching the brown water trickle through the dust. Behind us, the town began to stir — someone laughed, someone clapped Anders on the back, Rachel called out something about coffee. The ordinary sounds of people who had been given another day.

The North Field was still ours. For now, that was the whole ledger.

Chapter 33: The Negotiating Table

Elias

I set my palms flat against the scarred wood of the teacher's desk and looked at my hands. They were broad, dark with creek-bed silt, the knuckles scabbed from the night's digging. A half-moon of dried blood sat under the thumbnail where I'd caught it on a stone sometime after midnight. They didn't belong in a schoolhouse. They belonged out there, in the dirt. That was the whole problem — and maybe the whole advantage.

The little red schoolhouse smelled of chalk dust, old cedar, and the lye Eleanor used on the floorboards. The afternoon sun cut through the narrow windows in thick bars, lighting the motes of grit that drifted in the warm air. The children's primers sat in a neat stack on the corner shelf, and the multiplication table Eleanor had lettered on butcher paper hung beside the map she'd pinned to the wall — a map that had nothing to do with arithmetic and everything to do with the price of staying. Outside, the world was vast and still. In here, the air pressed close, weighted by everything left unsaid.

Across from me, Caleb Voss sat in a student's chair too small for his frame. His knees were angled up, his elbows crowded by the desk, and the indignity of it showed in the set of his mouth. He'd placed his bowler hat precisely on his knee — a man who controlled what he could when the larger situation had escaped him. His eyes were fixed on the map Eleanor had pinned to the wall, and though the morning's legal defeat had taken the sharp edges off his confidence, the predatory stillness was still in him. He was a man who didn't know how to stop moving forward — only how to find a new path through the brush. I'd seen that quality in drought. The wind doesn't stop because you've built a fence. It just looks for the gap.

"The injunction holds six months, Mr. Voss," I said. "We're not here to hide behind a judge's signature. We're here to offer you a way out that doesn't involve a court clerk."

He leaned back, the wood creaking under his weight. "You've cost my company thousands in delays. You manufactured a river from a dry gully and turned a circuit judge against the progress of the entire territory. If you think I came here to ask for mercy, you've mistaken my fatigue for weakness."

His voice was steady, but I noticed the way his fingers pressed against the brim of his hat — the small, restless motion of a man running numbers he didn't like. I'd seen that motion in myself, sitting at the kitchen table with the ledger open, adding a column and hoping the sum would change.

I didn't answer right away. I looked at Eleanor, standing by the bookshelf, posture straight and unyielding as a fence post. Her dress was clean — she'd changed since the creek — but her hands still showed the rawness of the night's work, the knuckles red and the nails broken short. She gave one small nod. Then I looked at Titus, leaning in the doorframe, arms crossed over his chest. He looked like a stone outcropping that had decided to take up residence in the doorway. He said nothing. The slow blink of his eyes told me he was ready. He'd been ready since before we walked in. Titus didn't prepare for meetings the way other men did. He just arrived, and the room adjusted.

I reached into my satchel and pulled out the rolled parchment.

"This isn't mercy." I spread the map across the desk, anchoring the corners with inkwells. Eleanor had drawn it herself — every contour of the land captured in precise, elegant hand, the creek's winding path traced in careful blue ink, the elevation lines rendered with a draughtsman's accuracy. The North Field was marked in green. The original rail survey crossed through it in red. And beside it, in a firm black line, the new route. "It's a better map."

Voss stood despite himself, drawn toward the desk the way a man is drawn toward a document he knows concerns him. He leaned over it, eyes scanning the lines with the practiced intensity of a man who reads landscape in grades and distances. His finger hovered above the paper, tracing without touching, as though the ink might still be wet. I watched his gaze travel to the North Field — where the original red survey line had been crossed out in a single stroke of black.

"You've moved the right-of-way," he muttered, tracing the new route. "South. Through the ridge."

"Avoids the fertile bottomland entirely." I pointed to the elevation marks, feeling the tension settle into my jaw like grit between the teeth. "Skirts the southern ridge, follows the natural shelf above the flood line, reconnects with your planned path three miles west of the settlement. Keeps your tracks off my wheat. Stays two hundred yards clear of the creek's headwaters."

Voss let out a short laugh — the sound of a shovel hitting stone. "The ridge. Do you have any idea what you're asking? That's solid limestone and shale. Steeper grade, and the blasting alone would triple labor costs. My engineers would laugh me out of the office for trading flat sod for a mountain of rock."

"They might." Eleanor stepped forward, fingers interlaced, her voice carrying the cool, measured cadence of a woman who has spent the last three days reading every statute and precedent she could find and knows exactly how many pages remain. "But they might also consider the cost of an indefinite injunction. The High Court in Pierre is notoriously slow — and the Missouri crossing doesn't get easier in winter. Six months is conservative. If we find further discrepancies in the original charter — and I am still looking — we could tie this up for years. Can the railroad afford a gap in its transcontinental link over a mountain of rock?"

Voss turned to look at her. I saw him recalibrate — not a teacher anymore, but an adversary who understood the power of a well-placed word. His eyes narrowed, and for the first time since I'd met him, I saw something that might have been respect — grudging, unwilling, but real. The silence stretched. Outside, a hawk called, far off and indifferent. The chalk dust settled in the bars of light.

"It's a matter of business, Caleb," Titus said. His voice was a low rumble that seemed to come through the floorboards rather than the air. He hadn't moved from the door, but his shadow fell long across the room, cutting the sunlight in half. "You talk about progress like it's a gospel. But progress eats time as much as it eats coal. Right now, your project is starving."

"The company has deep pockets," Voss replied. "We can outspend a town that's one bad harvest away from eating its seed corn. This line runs east from Pierre, across the Missouri, and links to every market between here and Chicago — that's not a project you kill over a water ditch."

"Maybe you can. But can you outspend bad press?" Titus kept his tone conversational, almost gentle, which made it land harder. "A town of starving heroes fighting the iron horse to save their water. That's a story that travels east. The kind that makes investors in Boston nervous. They don't like blood on their dividends, and they don't like delays that look like bullying."

A muscle twitched in Voss's cheek. He looked back at the map, eyes tracing the difficult terrain of the southern ridge — the contour lines bunched close together where the grade steepened, the hatching Eleanor had used to mark the exposed limestone. He was running numbers now, his mind working the way I work the ledger after a thin harvest — measuring the loss against the greater loss of not acting. I stayed silent and let the logic of the situation settle. A man calculating is a man who hasn't said no. You don't interrupt that calculation. You let the numbers do the talking.

"The rock work is prohibitive," Voss said at last. The fire had gone out of his voice, replaced by something flatter, more practical — the voice of a man shifting from ambition to damage control. "Even if I convinced the board to accept the detour, I'd have to show them a way to offset the cost. Men who know how to swing a sledge and don't demand union wages."

I looked at Titus. He looked back at me. We both knew what was coming. This was the hard bargain — the price the railroad would put on our say in the matter. Not just a different path. Our bodies on that ridge, building the thing we'd fought against. My neighbors who'd already lost weight to the drought, who'd already dug through the night to fill a creek bed, who'd already stood in a line with shovels against armed men on horseback. The thought turned in my stomach like bad water. But I looked at the cold lines of Voss's face and saw the alternative clearly enough: the injunction would expire, a new judge would be sent, the survey stakes would return, and the wheat would be plowed under for railroad ties. It was this, or the eventual loss of everything we'd held on to.

"The town will supply the labor." The words came out slow, like I was lifting each one from the bottom of a dry well. Eleanor's eyes widened slightly, but she didn't object. She understood the same thing I did — that the shortest road isn't always the easiest one, but it's the one that gets you where you need to go. "We will clear the grade. We will move the rock. In exchange, you pull your stakes out of the North Field today, put it down in writing that the creek and its headwaters stay untouched, and give us a depot with a fair freight rate for our grain."

I laid the terms out the way I lay out a season's budget — each item on its own line, each one non-negotiable.

Voss stared at me. For a moment, the calculation left his face and what was underneath was simple surprise — the look of a man who has been playing chess and discovers the other side has changed the game entirely. He'd expected a fight, maybe a bribe. Not a partnership built from desperation and grit. He looked at Titus's hands — loosely curled at his sides, relaxed, but hands that everyone in the room knew could bend iron — and then at Eleanor, watchful and still, the book of statutes within arm's reach on the shelf. He was looking at a single entity, not three people. Three voices, one argument.

"You'd do that?" he asked. His voice had gone quiet, stripped of the boardroom polish. "Break your own backs to help me bring the train through?"

"We'd do it to keep our land." I met his eyes. The sun had moved while we talked, and the light no longer fell between us but on us both, catching the dust on his lapels and the dirt on my collar equally. "We're not doing it for you, Voss. We're doing it for the soil. So that when our children look at that ridge, they see the price of their freedom — not yours."

A long minute passed. The light through the windows shifted, the gold deepening toward something darker as the sun lowered. The hawk called again, closer now, and somewhere on the porch a board creaked — someone waiting outside, listening, too polite or too afraid to come in. Voss took a slim cigar from his coat pocket and rolled it between his fingers without lighting it. He stared at the map. His thumb traced the contour of the ridge one more time, following the black line Eleanor had drawn, measuring it against whatever number he'd arrived at in his head.

"Thirty days." His voice sharpened again, the business edge returning like a blade being resheathed after inspection. He stood straight, his eyes locking onto mine. "I want the first mile of grade cleared in thirty days. Your people fall behind pace, the deal is void — and the injunction won't matter because I'll have enough men here to build through your kitchen. Do we understand each other, Mr. Thorne?"

"We understand."

Relief and dread arrived together, the way debt and hope do in a thin year — you can't have one without the other. We had saved the land. We had traded our peace for a mountain of labor. Thirty days to clear a mile of limestone ridge with hand tools and whatever Titus could forge. The number sat in my chest, heavy and specific, the kind of number that keeps a man awake.

Voss extended his hand. It was smooth, well-manicured, the hand of a man who moved money and maps. I let it hang there for one breath, looking at my own — the scars, the dark under the nails, the calluses that had built up across two decades of raking dry ground. Then I took it. My grip was stronger than his and I didn't soften it. A brief, functional shake that sealed a pact between two worlds that would never truly understand each other. His palm was dry and cool. Mine was rough and warm. The handshake lasted two seconds and contained everything neither of us would say.

"I'll have the contracts drawn up by morning," Voss said, retrieving his hat. He set it on his head with the same precision he'd used to remove it — a man for whom every gesture was a calibration. He nodded to Eleanor and Titus — not quite respectful, but closer than he'd come before. "I suspect I'll be seeing a lot of you on that ridge, Mr. Thorne. I hope you're as good with a pickaxe as you are with a map."

The door swung shut behind him. His bootfalls crossed the porch, descended the steps, and crunched away across the schoolyard. The creak of a saddle. The snort of a horse. Then quiet.

I leaned against the desk and let the quiet settle into the room the way evening settles into a field — slowly, from the edges in. Eleanor put a hand on my shoulder — light, but steadying, the way you steady a fence post before you tamp the dirt around it. "You gave him the only thing he couldn't take by force," she said softly. "Our cooperation."

"It's a hard bargain," I said. My voice sounded thin to my own ears, hollowed out by the day. "After everything they've already suffered, I've asked them to break their bodies for the railroad."

"They'll do it because they trust you." Titus moved away from the door and stopped beside the desk, looking at the map. His eyes traced the ridge line with the appraising gaze of a man already calculating how many sledgehammers he'd need and how many spikes he could draw from a single bar of stock iron. "And because it's the only way to stay. A man will do a lot of hard things if it means he doesn't have to walk away from his own fence line."

I rolled up the map, the parchment crackling under my fingers. It felt like a document of debt — which is exactly what it was. Every deal is. You sign your name and you owe the work that makes the words come true.

"We start tomorrow," I said. I looked at Titus. "Every pry bar and pickaxe you can forge. Heavy sledges, rock drills. The town has to see that we're leading this. We have to be the first ones on that ridge."

"The forge will be hot before sunup," Titus said. A simple statement. No promise, no oath. Just the way things would be, spoken by a man whose word and his action were the same thing. "I'll have the iron ready. You bring the men."

I tucked the map under my arm and walked out into the twilight. The sky was deep and dark at the zenith, turning a fading copper at the western edge where the sun had just gone down. The first few stars showed through — faint, tentative, the way new entries appear in a ledger before the ink has dried. The air smelled of drying grass and the faint, lingering dampness of the creek, carried on a wind that had found its way down from the ridge.

My horse was where I'd tied him, patient as all horses are with the foolishness of men. I swung into the saddle and looked toward the silhouette of the southern ridge against the darkening sky. It was massive, jagged, the limestone teeth of it catching the last light. In thirty days, we'd be up there with pickaxes and sledges, breaking that rock one blow at a time. The thought should have crushed me. Instead, it sat in my chest beside the relief like a second heartbeat — steady, heavy, real.

The North Field was safe. The creek was still ours. I thought of Sarah waiting at home with a lamp in the window, of Samuel with his arm in a sling asking what happened, of the neighbors who'd look at me tomorrow with tired eyes when I told them what the victory had cost. I'd tell them straight. That was the only way I knew.

I turned my horse toward home. The ridge stood dark against the stars. Far off to the east, the Missouri was a faint black seam in the lowland dark — the same river the Judge had crossed before dawn, the same river that separated our world from the courthouses and contracts of Pierre. The road was long and dry and mine.

Chapter 34: Sweat and Iron

Titus

The sky above the southern ridge was slate and iron-grey, the light not yet strong enough to cast shadows. Good working light. Clear enough to see the stone. I stood at the base of the incline, boots set wide on the loose scree, and looked up. Limestone and shale. A hard face, webbed with hairline fractures where the frost had done its slow work over centuries. It would not yield easily. That was fine. Nothing worth keeping ever did.

The morning air tasted of flint and something mineral — the exposed rock itself breathing cold off its face. I could feel the temperature difference between the scree under my boots and the open air at my back, the way you feel the difference between the near side of the forge and the far wall of the shop. My breath came out in thin wisps that vanished before they rose a foot.

I gripped the pickaxe. Hickory handle, fresh-forged head — I'd spent half the night at the anvil on this one, drawing the steel out under repeated blows until the edge was true. The temper had taken clean. I could tell by the color when I quenched it, that pale straw that means the hardness is right — hard enough to bite stone, soft enough not to shatter on impact. I tapped the head against the rock face. It rang clean and high, a sound I trusted more than any man's word. I swung.

The first strike threw sparks off the limestone face, white-hot flecks that died in the grey air. The second cracked it — a sound like a knuckle popping, deep in the grain. The third opened a seam. That was always how it went with stone: find the fault line, work it open, let the iron do the rest. Same principle as the forge. You don't overpower the material. You read it. You find where it wants to break and you help it along.

I settled into the rhythm. Around me, the others were picking up the beat. Anders Larson three feet to my left, swinging with a storekeeper's soft grip, blade glancing wide on every other stroke. His palms were going to pay for that angle before the hour was out. I watched his technique without slowing my own work. The way he choked up on the handle, the way his elbows flared — all wrong. He'd adjust or he'd blister through to the bone by noon. I didn't say anything. A man learns faster from the tool than from being told.

The sun crested the horizon. Dust turned golden. Sweat came fast on the ridge — the stone radiated heat back at you even in the early hour, the way iron holds temperature after you pull it from the coals. The warmth rose through the soles of my boots, and I felt the familiar pull in my shoulders, the deep muscle groups that do the real work. I shrugged deeper into the rhythm without speaking. There was nothing to say. The rock told you everything you needed to know about what to do next — where to strike, how hard, what angle. You just had to listen with your hands.

An hour in, Anders's pick glanced off a buried knot of ironstone. The handle kicked up hard and he lurched sideways, lost the rhythm completely. The shock of it went through his whole frame — I could see it travel from his wrists to his shoulders to the stumble in his feet. He leaned against the shaft, chest heaving, face grey with dust and sweat. His hands were shaking on the handle. He didn't look at me.

He had some things to account for.

I'd watched him through the long months — watched him tilt toward Voss's money when the drought squeezed the Emporium down to its bones. Watched the way he'd stopped meeting Elias's eye in the street, the way he'd started locking the storeroom door when he used to leave it open. Small changes. The kind you notice when you spend your days reading the grain of things. A man could understand fear. Fear was a simple mechanism — pressure applied, material gives. But there were things you did in fear and things you didn't do, and Anders had done some of the wrong ones. The question was whether the failure went all the way through or just to the surface.

I kept working. I let him breathe.

"Elias," he said — then stopped. Wrong man. He turned his head and found me instead, eyes adjusting, blinking the dust and sweat clear. He was hollow-looking. The confidence that usually held his frame upright had gone out of him like heat bleeds out of cooling iron — you could almost see it leaving, the slow sag of it. "I thought the railroad was the only way out. I looked at my ledgers, at the dust, and I couldn't see another path." He wiped his mouth with the back of his wrist. His lips were cracked. "I thought I was being practical."

I set the pickaxe head on the ground and let it rest. Gave him the courtesy of stillness. A man confessing deserves at least that much.

"You were scared," I said.

"Yes." The word came out thin. He looked at the ground between his boots.

"Scared for the store?"

"For everything. The store. The town. Myself, if I'm honest about it." He turned the pick handle in his blistered grip. "I told myself I was thinking about the community, but I was thinking about Anders Larson. That's the truth of it."

"Fear'll make a man into green wood. Bends under load before it should."

He didn't answer. There wasn't much to say to that because it was true. I looked at him straight — took the measure of him the way you measure a piece of stock before you cut it. Checked the grain, checked for cracks that go deeper than the surface. There was still something workable in Anders Larson. The structure hadn't failed all the way through. He'd bent, not broken. Bent stock can be heated and straightened. Broken stock goes to scrap.

"I don't know if this makes anything right," he said quietly. "Being up here."

"It doesn't make it right. It makes it current. Pick it up. Lot of rock left."

He straightened. Rolled his shoulders once, a slow movement that cost him — I could see it in the wince he tried to hide. He picked up the handle. When the blade hit the stone again, it was different — less frantic. Steadier. He'd stopped fighting the rhythm and started following it. His angle was better too, the edge biting into the seam instead of skating across the face. Good. Wasted effort is wasted material. A man who learns to let the tool work is a man who'll last the day.

We worked in parallel. The sun climbed. The air thickened with heat and stone dust, a fine powder that settled on the sweat of our arms and turned us grey as the rock itself. The ridge began to look like something that had been worked — the raw-broken rock a different color from the untouched face above it. Lighter. Fresher. The way a weld joint looks when you've just dressed it, the new metal bright against the old. Progress was visible. That mattered. You can ask a man to work blind for an hour. You can't ask him to work blind for a week. He needs to see what his labor is building.

A sound below. I paused and looked down the slope. A small figure was picking its way up through the loose scree, moving careful on account of the sling. Samuel. He carried a wooden yoke across his good shoulder, two buckets swaying and catching the light where water sloshed over the rims. The boy had learned to compensate for the bad arm — adjusted his center of gravity, shifted the load to the left, found a new way to walk that kept the buckets level. I'd watched him figure it out over the past weeks. No one taught him. He read his own body the way I read metal — tested it, felt where the weakness was, and built around it. He didn't complain. He found the new balance and used it.

"Water!" he called up, voice carrying through the dry air. He set the buckets down with a controlled settling of his knees and offered the dipper to Elias first, then swung toward me.

I took it. The water was cool and tasted of cedar — the bucket's wood still breathing its flavor into the liquid. I drank long and handed it back. Wiped my mouth with my sleeve and tasted dust and salt.

"Thank you."

Samuel nodded, but his attention was already elsewhere. He looked along the cleared stretch of ridge, eyes moving across the broken rock with something close to calculation. He was starting to read terrain — seeing the grades, the angles, the way the stone shelf tilted east and would need to be leveled. Two months ago he'd have looked at that same stretch and seen an obstacle, a thing in the way. Now he was seeing a joint — a place where two things had to connect, where the cleared grade would meet the natural slope and the whole thing had to be true.

"Titus said you'd be halfway to the top by noon," Samuel said to Elias, "but I think he underestimated you."

"Titus said no such thing," I said.

Samuel grinned — that quick, unchecked grin that still had boy in it despite everything else about him that had hardened. He didn't correct himself. He didn't need to. The joke served its purpose. It lightened the air on the ridge, and the men around us needed that.

Elias told him not to be hauling water up the ridge with a healing arm. Samuel held his ground — squared his shoulders under the yoke and told him a man does whatever work he's capable of. Said I'd told him that.

I had. I watched the exchange without adding to it. Elias would either hear it or he wouldn't. The boy was right, and he was steady in being right, which was more important than being right loudly. There was a quiet certainty in the way he stood there, the yoke balanced on his one good shoulder, not asking permission but not defying either. Just stating fact.

"You're doing a man's work," Elias told him finally. The words came out with weight. They landed.

True enough. I looked at Samuel — at the new lean of him, the way the soft boyishness had burned off during the fever and the weeks of slow healing, and left something denser underneath. His forearms were ropy where they'd been smooth. His jaw sat differently. Green wood going to hardwood. It was a good process to watch, even if it was a hard one. The fire that does the seasoning doesn't ask the wood's permission.

Samuel picked up the yoke and moved on up the line toward the Parker boys, his lopsided shadow stretching long across the broken stone. I watched him go. Steady feet on unsteady ground. Then I turned back to the stone face.

I set the pick into a new seam and worked it open. The limestone peeled away in slabs — good flat pieces that could be stacked into retaining walls along the grade. Nothing wasted. I sorted as I worked, kicking the slag to one side, stacking the usable stone on the other. The habit of the forge: everything has a use or it doesn't. Decide fast and move on.

By midday the ridge was loud with it — dozens of picks working the limestone, the sound coalesced into a single rolling percussion that came up through the soles of your boots and settled in your chest. I recognized the rhythm. It was the same steady pulse that lived under everything I did at the anvil — that deep, repeating beat that the body falls into when the work is honest and the tool is right. The whole town was producing it now, not just my shop. Farmers and clerks and boys with slings, all swinging to the same meter. The sound of it carried out across the flats below, and I wondered if the women in town could hear it — that distant thunder of a community driving steel into stone.

I worked my way along the line, stopping where technique was failing. The Parker boys were strong but undisciplined — too much force, not enough angle. Wasted every third swing, the pick bouncing off the stone face instead of biting into it. I stopped beside the older one and held out my hand. He gave me the pick without being asked. I swung once, slow enough for him to see the mechanics — the way the handle drops through the grip, the way the wrist turns at the top of the arc so the blade comes down at the angle the stone wants.

"Let the weight do the work," I said. "You're fighting it."

He took the pick back and tried. First swing, wide. Second, closer. Third, the blade bit clean and a chunk of limestone broke free the size of a dinner plate. He looked at it, then at me.

"Like that," I said.

He got it in four tries. Good. Jedediah Stone needed no instruction. He'd been breaking rock long before today, his crowbar working the seams with the patience of a man who'd spent sixty years learning that the earth gives up its secrets to whoever asks the longest. His face was its own argument against anyone who thought him old. There was no strain in it. Only purpose.

I looked down the slope and saw the buggy on the flat ground below. Voss. He was sitting still in the driver's seat, brass binoculars up, watching the ridge. The dust from his wheels had already settled, which meant he'd been there twenty minutes at least. Maybe longer. I kept working.

He'd expected us to crack under the weight of it. He'd given us thirty days because he figured the labor would split us — farmers against storekeeper against drifter, exhaustion pulling at the old fault lines, opening them wider until the whole structure came apart. He'd figured wrong. He hadn't accounted for the fact that working stone together does the opposite of splitting a town. It welds it. Joint by joint, swing by swing, the seams between us were closing under the heat and pressure of shared labor. The same principle as the forge, two pieces of iron won't bond until you bring them both to welding heat. The work on this ridge was the fire.

I brought the pick down hard and split a limestone face clean through the middle. Two pieces. One became part of the cleared grade — good stone, flat and solid. The other I kicked aside — slag, no use to anyone. The distinction was clean.

Voss lowered the binoculars. He sat a while longer, not moving. I could see the stillness in him from here — the stillness of a man revising his estimate, recalculating numbers that had seemed certain an hour ago. His hands rested on his knees. The reins lay slack in his lap. Then he picked them up, but he didn't drive away. Not yet. He kept watching.

He saw what I saw. Not just a grade being cleared, but a joint being tested under load and holding firm. A structure that was supposed to fail under stress, and wasn't failing.

I raised the pick and brought it down. The stone broke. The dust rose, fine as forge smoke, and drifted east on the noon wind. The ridge kept opening up ahead of us, one strike at a time, and the sound of the work carried across the flats like the ringing of iron on iron — the oldest sound I knew, and the one I trusted most.

Chapter 35: The Golden Spike

Elias

The fence post was humming.

I pressed my palm flat against the rough grain of the post at the edge of the North Field and felt it before I could name it — a low vibration traveling up through the wood from somewhere deep in the earth, a trembling that had no business being there on a still morning. The soil beneath my boots was dry and cracked, as it had been for two years, mapped into the same thirsty geometry I'd spent every season memorizing — the fissures branching like dead roots, the pale crust lifting at the edges where the moisture had long since given up trying. But the post was humming. I kept my hand there, fingers splayed against the grain, and felt it build.

Then came the sound. A high, keening wail that tore through the stagnant heat and rolled across the flats in a wave of impossible iron — close and real in a way the distant construction-camp echoes had never been. A train whistle. Not the ghost of one carried on the wind from miles away. This one was here. This one shook the wire on the fence line and set the sparrows scattering from the cottonwood by the well. The world we had tried to keep out was crying its way into our valley.

In the paddock, the cattle panicked. They bunched against the fence, eyes rolling white, ribs heaving against the rails. The red heifer tried to hook her way through the gap between the gate and the post, and the yearling behind her bawled, a raw sound that cut underneath the whistle's fading echo. They didn't know the sound of progress; they knew the sound of something they couldn't see coming fast. But the children — Thomas Parker and a swarm of others cresting the ridge, their small figures sharp against the early light — ran toward it, arms waving, voices swallowed by the great metallic shriek. For them, it wasn't a threat. It was proof the world was bigger than Oak Haven's horizon. I watched Thomas's bare feet kicking up dust as he ran and thought of my own boys at that age, how they'd have been halfway to the tracks already, elbowing for the best view.

Something cold tightened in my chest, even as the relief came. We were no longer isolated. The wall of quiet had been breached, and as I watched the first smudge of black smoke mark the sky — a dark, greasy thumbprint on the pale morning blue — I knew the Oak Haven I'd spent my life protecting was gone. The hard-scrabble place where a man could disappear into his own labor, where the only sounds were wind and animal and the creak of your own gate — that place was finished. We'd invited the iron in to save us from the dust. Now we'd live with the noise.

I walked toward town with that knowledge sitting heavy on me, the way a full sack of grain sits across your shoulders — you carry it because you have to, but you feel every step.

The new depot stood at the edge of town: fresh-cut pine framing, the resin still sharp and sweet in the boards, the whole skeleton hammered together in a feverish week of labor. Sawdust still rimmed the platform in pale curls. The smell of it mixed with the coal smoke rolling ahead of the engine — two kinds of industry meeting in the air above our heads. As the engine came into view, rounding the last bend where the grade we'd cleared cut through the ridge, the crowd was already gathering — weathered faces, mended wool, women with flour dust still on their aprons, men who'd set down their tools mid-task and walked over without being called. The whole community pressed close together the way livestock will in a thunderstorm, needing the warmth of the herd without quite knowing why.

The engine was a massive, soot-stained thing, hissing steam, venting great white plumes that smelled of coal and hot oil. The ground shook with its approach — I felt it in the boards of the platform underfoot, a rhythmic pounding that traveled up through my boot soles and settled somewhere behind my ribs. It was beautiful in the way a flash flood is beautiful — you can't look away from a force that size, even when it's rolling over your land. The boiler was taller than a man at the shoulder. The drive wheels were black and greased and bigger around than a wagon wheel. I watched them slow and lock, the brakes squealing, sparks jumping from the rails.

The engine groaned to a halt. Steam shrieked from the release valves, a white curtain that rolled across the platform and dampened every face in the crowd. For a moment we were all standing in a warm fog that tasted of iron and water and the deep mineral smell of a boiler under pressure.

Titus stood near the platform edge, arms crossed, watching the pistons with the expression of a man calculating tolerances — measuring the throw, the diameter, the quality of the machining. His jaw was set, but I could see the interest in his eyes. He respected the engineering even if he didn't love what it meant. Beside him, Eleanor tracked the movement of the machine's workings with her scholar's eye — she was reading it the way she reads everything, looking for the grammar of the thing, the sentence structure of piston and connecting rod. She caught my glance and gave me a small, complicated smile that held both wonder and grief in equal measure. We were all witnesses to the end of our old world, and none of us could agree on how to feel about it.

Then the boxcar doors slid open with a screech of dry metal, and the mood shifted from awe to something more immediate. Men in grease-stained caps and heavy gloves began working crates onto the platform, their boot heels ringing on the boards. Deep-reach pump cylinders — cast iron, heavy as sin, the kind that could find the water we knew was hiding far below the parched surface. Rolls of barbed wire in neat spools, the galvanizing still bright. Milled lumber, straight and true, not the sun-twisted wood we'd been making do with — boards with clean edges and honest grain, the kind you could build something permanent from. Sacks of seed that hadn't been thinned by two years of heat, the burlap stenciled with names of places where rain still fell on schedule.

The mechanical salvation we'd bargained for, built with our own blistered hands on the ridge. Every crate that hit the platform was a line in the ledger I'd been keeping in my head for months, and for once the column was showing something on the credit side. The numbers were starting to balance.

One crate was lowered with more care than the others. Through the slats — a flash of deep crimson.

The scent hit me a moment later. Sweet and cold and sharp, cutting right through the coal smoke and sweat like a blade through chaff. Apples. Fresh ones, still holding the cool of some distant, shaded orchard where the air was damp and the trees grew tall without anyone having to fight for it. A smell I hadn't realized I'd forgotten — the ghost of a greener place, a life before the dust took everything. My mouth watered before my mind caught up. I could feel the memory of it in my teeth, in the soft tissue of my throat — autumn in a place where autumn meant abundance instead of the beginning of another dry reckoning.

Rachel Parker stepped forward. She reached out and touched the smooth red skin of one of the fruits. Didn't pick it up right away. Just rested her fingers on it, the way you touch something you're not sure is real — the way I used to touch the first green shoot in the North Field after a hard winter, afraid that pressing too hard would prove it was nothing. Then she began to cry — not loud, not theatrical, just a quiet shuddering that moved her shoulders and made her chin dip toward her chest.

She looked at Anders Larson, who was standing close with a crowbar in his hand and sawdust on his sleeves. He nodded, his eyes bright and wet, his lips pressed into a line that was trying to be a smile and not quite getting there. That crate of fruit was what the water logic had promised: the veins of the country pumping blood back into our withered limb. The suspicion and fear of the past months didn't disappear — you don't un-plow a furrow — but they softened, the way hard ground softens after the first real rain. Something could grow in that softness, if we tended it.

I stood back and watched my neighbors. Sarah came up beside me, and I felt her hand find mine — her fingers warm and flour-dusted, fitting into the spaces between my own the way they always had. She didn't say anything. Neither did I. We just stood there and watched the town receive what it had earned.

They weren't desperate individuals anymore, each fighting alone over a dry creek and a flagging account. They were a community, gathered around the proof that staying had been worth something. Old Jedediah Stone was examining one of the pump housings, running his gnarled hands along the casting marks with the critical eye of a man who'd installed a few in his time. The Parker boys were hauling lumber off the platform, stacking it with a care they'd never shown their own woodpile. Mrs. Henderson was holding an apple in both hands and just looking at it, turning it slowly, as if it were a letter from someone she loved.

Samuel was helping a team of men shift one of the big pumps, his good arm straining against the rope, face set in adult purpose. The sling was gone — I hadn't noticed when he'd shed it. His bad arm hung at his side, not quite right yet, but he was using the good one with a man's economy. The boy who'd arrived with dime novels in his saddlebag had been replaced by someone who understood the weight of iron and what it cost to move it. He looked up, caught my eye across the platform, and went back to work without a word or a wave. That was all I needed to see. The acknowledgment was enough. More would have been too much for either of us.

Caleb Voss stood on the rear platform of the last car, bowler hat straight, coat somehow free of the dust coating the rest of us. The crease in his trousers was still sharp. He had a clipboard, his pencil moving with a clinical efficiency — checking off items, recording quantities, the practiced motions of a man who understood that everything was inventory. Then his gaze drifted over the crowd and settled on me.

He paused. The pencil stopped.

No warmth. No triumph. Just the cold, professional recognition of a task concluded. Two men who had spent the better part of a year trying to break each other, standing thirty feet apart with a locomotive between them, neither willing to pretend it had been anything other than what it was.

As the engine built steam again — sharp, rhythmic huffs that sounded like something enormous catching its breath — Voss stepped down onto the bottom stair. He didn't come into the crowd. He stayed on his island of iron and steel, one hand on the rail, his boots on the step. He looked at the depot, then at the tracks stretching back toward the horizon — that long silver line bisecting the prairie like a seam in the earth — then at me. With a slow, deliberate motion, he reached up and tipped his hat. Not friendship. Not apology. The salute of one survivor to another across a field they'd both lost pieces of.

"Mr. Thorne," he called, barely carrying over the boiler's growing roar. "Schedule is set. Every Tuesday and Friday. Don't let the pumps rust."

My throat was too tight for words. The grit, the dust, the weight of everything we'd done and lost to get here — it all pressed up against the back of my tongue and held it still. I nodded once, sharp and curt. Sarah's hand tightened on mine.

The train lurched forward, couplings clanging — a chain of iron jolts running car to car like a shudder passing through a body. One final whistle, a sound that shook the glass in the depot windows and sent the last of the sparrows scattering, and the engine began pulling its long tail of steel out of our valley. Black smoke trailed it like a banner, thinning as it went, until it was just a grey smudge against the morning sky.

I stood there after the smoke had faded into the haze, listening to the quiet return. But it was different from the old quiet. It was a silence that had heard the whistle. One that knew Tuesday was coming. The rails still ticked and popped as they cooled from the engine's passage, small sounds in the settling air, and the platform smelled of coal and apples and new lumber — three scents that had never belonged here before and now did.

I walked to the apple crate. Picked one up, turned it in my palm. The weight of it was cool and real, solid in a way that numbers on a page never are. I looked at my hands — the scars, the soil-dark lines, the split nail on my left thumb that had never healed right, the evidence of twenty years spent working ground that had worked back twice as hard. These hands had held plow handles and fence wire and the deed to the North Field and Sarah's face on the night we thought we'd lose the well. Now they held an apple.

I took a bite. The juice hit my tongue sharp and cold, the sweetest thing this land had offered me in longer than I could tally. The skin broke clean between my teeth and the flesh was white and firm and tasted like rain. I didn't think about the ledger. I didn't calculate the debt. I just stood on the platform in the settling dust with the juice running down my chin, thinking about the rain that would eventually come, and the fact that we were still here to see it. Sarah took the apple from my hand, bit into it, and handed it back.

We stood there passing it between us until there was nothing left but the core, and even that we saved — for the seeds.

Chapter 36: Rain

Elias

Three days the sky had been the color of a bruise — copper-dark, heavy, pressing the breath out of the valley. Not the clean weight of an approaching storm; more like the land itself was holding something in, the way a man holds in words he's afraid to say aloud. The air had gone flat and strange. The dust devils that had been working the North Field all week had stopped moving — they just dissolved, mid-twist, as if they'd been called off by something they could feel and I couldn't yet.

I stood on the porch with both hands on the rough cedar railing and watched the stillness. The grain of the wood was hot under my palms. Even the light was wrong — too yellow, too thick, falling heavy on the yard the way lamplight falls on a room with the windows shut. The cottonwood by the well had gone motionless, every leaf hanging limp, and the shadows underneath it were dense and purple instead of the usual thin grey. Something was different, and I couldn't name it yet, and that not-naming sat in me like a stone in a boot.

I stepped down from the porch. The cracked earth crunched under my boots, each step as dry and brittle as it had been for two years — that sound like walking on old paper. Even the cicadas had quit. That was the thing that got to me. Those tireless drummers of the drought, the ones I'd stopped hearing because they never stopped singing, gone still without warning. The quiet that replaced them wasn't peaceful. It was expectant. Held. Like the moment between the auctioneer's last call and the gavel.

I walked toward the North Field and stood in the middle of it, the way I'd stood a hundred times — a man in the center of his own debt, trying to read the terms. The soil was cracked into thousands of thirsty mouths, all gaping upward at a sky that had shown no mercy. I'd walked this ground so many times I knew every furrow by feel, knew where the old plow had caught a stone, knew where the runoff used to pool in wet years before the wet years stopped coming. I pressed the toe of my boot into one of the cracks and felt it give slightly — a faint underground moisture that hadn't been there last week. Something was already moving below. The soil knew before I did.

Then the scent hit me. Cold and sharp and old as stone — petrichor, the smell of water striking dry earth after a long absence. I knew that smell the way I knew the smell of Sarah's bread, the smell of the North Field in spring when it used to have a spring. My throat tightened around it. I tilted my head back. The clouds were slate-grey, low, their bellies swollen and dark, sagging with a weight you could almost see. I could taste it already — a clean mineral sweetness on the back of my tongue that made the dryness in my throat feel like a debt about to be forgiven.

The first drop hit me on the forehead. Heavy and cold. It didn't feel gentle. It felt like a finger pressing hard on my skin, insistent, demanding acknowledgment. It left a dark star on my brow. Another struck my shoulder. Another the bridge of my nose. I looked down at the dust at my feet and watched the drops punch into the silt, each one kicking up a tiny puff of powder before the earth swallowed it whole. Thud. Thud. Thud. Slow at first, like a pulse coming back to something that had been still too long. Each drop hit the ground and was gone in an instant — the soil drinking so fast you could watch the dark circles shrink and vanish. I held out my palm and felt the weight of it — real water, falling from a sky that had finally broken.

My hand was shaking. I watched the drops gather in the lines of my palm, filling the creases, running along the same channels where the dirt of the North Field had settled so deep it would never fully wash out. I closed my fist and opened it again and the water was still there. Still falling. Still real.

"Elias!"

Sarah was in the doorway, hands clutching her apron, face pale in the kitchen shadows. The lamp behind her threw her shape into silhouette — the curve of her shoulders, the tilt of her head, the way she held herself perfectly still as if moving would scatter the clouds back over the ridge. I raised my wet hand toward her. Showed her my palm. The water catching what grey light there was.

She ran. No shawl. No hat. She flew down the porch steps with her skirt bunched in one fist, boots kicking up the last of the dry dust until the sky opened in earnest and there was no more dust to kick. The rain overtook her between the porch and the yard — the sound of it changed, from scattered tapping to a hiss, and then from a hiss to a roar.

The rain became a grey curtain, solid and hammering against the barn roof. The noise of it drowned the world — drowned the creak of the windmill, drowned the cattle shifting in the paddock, drowned everything but the fact of the water itself. Sarah reached me in the center of the yard and grabbed my arms, fingers digging through my sleeves, and we stood in it as the deluge washed over us. It wasn't an angry storm — no lightning, no crack of thunder, just a steady soaking that seemed to press down through every layer of the past two years. The ridge labor. The canyon. The cold iron of the railroad stakes. The nights of pacing by the well with a lantern, listening for a trickle that never came. The debt that had lived in my shoulders so long I'd stopped noticing the weight of it, the way you stop noticing a wall until someone takes it down. All of it running off in rivulets, carrying the long bitterness of drought down through the cracked earth.

Sarah was laughing, head thrown back, mouth open to the rain. And she was crying. Both at once, the tears indistinguishable from the water on her face, and I don't know which sound was which — the laughter or the weeping — and it didn't matter because they meant the same thing. I pulled her to me, and something broke loose in my own chest — a sound I hadn't known was trapped there, something between a gasp and a word that wasn't a word. We stood in the mud forming beneath our feet and let it happen.

Her dress was heavy with water, clinging to her shoulders. My shirt was plastered to my ribs. The rain ran down between us where our bodies pressed together and pooled at our feet, turning the hard-packed yard into a soft, dark mirror. I could feel her heartbeat against my chest, fast and strong, and my own answering it.

"It's real, Elias," she whispered. Her lips were cold against my ear. "God remembered us."

I buried my face in her wet hair. Breathed her in and breathed the rain in with her — the soaked earth and the cold, the smell of the ground waking up, the scent of her soap and her skin underneath all the water. I held on. We stayed until we were cold through and through, until our skin had gone pale and our clothes were dead weight and the mud had crept up over the welts of our boots. Neither of us moved to go inside. To go inside would be to leave it, and we had waited too long for this to seek shelter now.

Somewhere out beyond the paddock I heard a shout — one of the Parker boys, maybe, or Jedediah's baritone carrying across the wet air. Other voices joined it. The town was waking up to the rain, the way people wake up to church bells on a morning they thought was ordinary. I imagined Rachel Parker standing on her porch the way Sarah had stood on ours, and Anders in his doorway above the Emporium, and old Jedediah just standing in it, letting it fall on his bare head, that weathered face tilted to the sky.

The fury of the downpour eased into a steady, persistent fall — the deep-soaking kind, the kind that goes down into the subsoil where the roots are waiting, the kind that saves a country. I stepped back from Sarah and wiped my eyes with the heel of my hand. The North Field looked different now: the harsh ochre and burnt umber muted by grey mist, the cracks already softening at the edges, the sharp geometry of drought blurring into something gentler. Puddles were forming in the furrows, small brown mirrors reflecting the heavy sky. I started walking toward the wheat section, my boots sinking into new mud, each step a sucking sound that felt like the earth trying to hold me in place. Sarah's hand rested on my lower back as she followed. Her fingers spread warm against my wet shirt.

I'd planted that wheat in defiance, back when the soil was dry as ash. Done it out of spite — a way to say to the bank and the railroad and the sky itself that I was still the master of my own furrows, even if I was planting seeds in a graveyard. I remember the way the dust had sifted over the kernels as I dropped them, the wind trying to scatter them before they could settle. I hadn't told Sarah what I was doing out there that morning. I think she knew. I think she watched from the kitchen window and let me have my stubbornness in peace.

I knelt down. The mud soaked through my trouser knees immediately — cold and thick, the kind of wet this ground hadn't felt in two years. I brushed away the top layer of silt with both hands, working through the cold muck, my fingers searching the way they search for the first potato in a hill, careful, not wanting to damage what might be there.

There.

Tucked into the wall of a melting clod, a sliver of green. Barely the size of a sewing needle. Translucent and fragile, bent slightly under the weight of a single raindrop — but upright. I touched it with my fingertip and felt the tiny resistance of it, that impossible strength that lives in a thing no thicker than a thread. My hand was shaking. It wasn't a weed. It was the wheat. Against the heat that should have baked it and the wind that should have scattered it and the drought that should have ended the argument entirely — the seed had held on in the dark, waiting. Doing what seeds do when there is nothing else to be done: holding still, keeping the germ alive, trusting that the terms would change.

Sarah knelt beside me. Her breath caught. She reached out and touched the tiny shoot with the tip of one finger, so gently it barely moved. Then she covered her mouth with her muddy hand and closed her eyes.

I raised my own eyes and looked across the field. Now that I knew what to look for, I could see them everywhere: tiny, defiant points of green breaking through the darkening earth, row after row, faint as candlelight but there. Hundreds of them. Maybe more. The pattern of the rows I'd planted was visible in the pattern of the sprouting — proof that the furrows had held, that the seeds had landed where I'd put them and stayed.

The crop wouldn't be grand. It wouldn't undo the scars the surveyors had left, or clear the debt in a single season. I could already do the arithmetic — half a stand at best, late germination, the yield would be thin. But it was there. Written in mud. A testament to everything that belongs to the soil if you give it time and water enough.

I looked at my hands — the North Field etched into every line of my palms, the dirt so deep in the cracks of my knuckles that the rain couldn't reach it. These hands had done everything I knew how to do, and most days it hadn't been enough. But they'd put the seed in the ground, and the seed had answered.

The ledger was still there. The train would come on Tuesday. The debt was real and the margins were thin and the winter ahead would test every calculation I'd made. But the land had spoken last, and it had said: *stay.* We had held on long enough for the roots to find their depth, and here was the proof of it, green and shaking in the rain, no bigger than a needle, no quieter than a shout.

Chapter 37: The Schoolhouse Wedding

Elias

My Sunday coat pulled tight across the shoulders — a remnant of a heavier man, or maybe I'd just grown narrow with the years of lean. The wool smelled of the cedar chest and the faint trace of Sarah's lavender sachets, scents that belonged to a quieter season, to the drawer where we kept the things we didn't use often enough. The metallic bite of the smithy that usually rode my skin was gone, scrubbed off for the occasion with lye soap and cold water at the basin, and the absence of it felt strange — like a field without its fence line. I stood on the porch and looked out toward the North Field. The green I'd seen days ago was no longer something I had to squint to believe. It was there, solid as seed money. Rows of wheat needles stitching the earth back together, even and unhurried, the way honest work tends to look once it's done. The morning light lay flat across them, and each tiny blade caught it and held it, and the whole field had a faint shimmer to it that was nothing like the old heat distortion — this was the shimmer of living things, of water still in the soil, of growth.

"Stop fussing, Elias." Sarah stepped out behind me, the screen door knocking softly on its frame. Her fingers found my lapels and straightened them without asking permission, the way she'd been straightening me for twenty years. She wore her good blue dress — the one she'd kept folded in tissue since before the surveyor's first stake appeared in my field — and her eyes were clear, the way they got after a long worry finally settled. The dress was pressed sharp, the buttons bright. She'd been up early. "You look like a man going to his own burial. It's a wedding."

"I know what it is," I muttered. My jaw was tight. I tugged at the collar, which had no give in it. "A wedding in a sod schoolhouse. It's a strange thing, Sarah. After everything."

"It's the right thing," she said, quieter now, her hand resting flat against my chest where the collar met the coat. I could feel the warmth of her palm through the fabric. "It's a planting. Same as the wheat. We're putting down roots where the railroad wanted to lay iron."

I didn't have an answer for that, so I covered her hand with mine and held it there for a moment. Then I helped her up onto the wagon seat.

The wagon wheels made their usual argument with the damp earth as we drove toward the settlement, a low, rhythmic groan that I'd stopped noticing years ago the way you stop noticing the creak of your own front door. The ground was still soft from the late rains, and the ruts held water in their bottoms — brown mirrors that reflected the sky back up at us as we passed over them. The grass along the track was green and thick, growing with a desperate energy, as if it knew the moisture wouldn't last and was trying to get as tall as it could before the dry came back. One late-season whiff of wet sage drifted up as we rounded the creek bend — I drew it in, held it, and let it go. Sarah's hand rested on my knee, a light, steady pressure. By the time the Little Red Schoolhouse came into view, we could already hear voices — a murmur of them carrying across the flat, the sound of a gathering with no dread in it.

Eleanor and the women had been at work since dawn, and the proof was in the doorframe: bunches of purple locoweed, yellow thermopsis, and white evening primrose twisted together with bits of twine and scrap ribbon, as if the land itself had been asked to dress up and had answered with what it had. The wildflowers had come up hard after the storm, the way things sometimes do when they know their window is short — blooming fast and bright, crowding the roadsides and the creek banks, throwing color against the green and brown like a debt being repaid all at once. I climbed down from the wagon and felt the ground take my weight — the honest, firm hold of living soil, not the treacherous powder we'd walked on all last summer.

There was give in it. Spring. The kind of ground you could trust to hold a post.

Titus was already posted near the entrance. He wore a clean white shirt that strained at the seams whenever he drew a full breath, the fabric pulling across his chest and shoulders in a way that made you aware of the size of the man inside it. His beard had been trimmed with the same care he gave a carriage spring — precise, deliberate, every cut considered. His hands — usually dark with soot and scored by the work of decades — were scrubbed to a raw, pink honesty that looked almost painful. He spotted me and gave a single, stiff nod. The man was more afraid than he'd been in the box canyon with the rustlers at his back. I knew the look. I'd worn it myself once, standing in a church back east with my knees going soft, waiting for a woman to walk toward me.

"You look like you're waiting for the anvil to fall," I said, stepping up beside him. I kept my voice low. The crowd was still gathering, wagons pulling up, people calling to each other across the yard. My fingers found the gold ring in my coat pocket — a simple band he'd hammered from a coin, carrying the marks of his own labor in the slight unevenness of its surface. I turned it between my thumb and finger and felt the warmth of it.

"The forge is easier, Elias." His voice vibrated low in his chest, barely above a murmur. "In the smithy, you know the heat. You know the iron. Here, the air feels too thin."

"That's just the lack of dust," I told him, and clapped a hand to his shoulder. The muscle underneath was rigid as oak. "Take a breath. You've earned this."

He didn't answer, but I saw his chest expand and his jaw unclench by a fraction. He looked toward the door of the schoolhouse, and something in his expression shifted — not softening, exactly, but settling. The way a beam settles into its notch when the fit is right.

Inside, the schoolhouse had been turned into something I didn't have a ledger entry for. The desks shoved to the walls, wildflowers pressed into every crevice of the whitewashed sod. Purple and yellow and white against the pale walls, the colors catching the light from the open windows. The room smelled of crushed stems, beeswax from the candles Eleanor had set along the window ledges, and the bread Rachel was cooling in the yard — that warm, yeasty scent drifting in through the door each time someone entered. That smell — bread cooling on a day with no particular dread attached — was not something I'd catalogued in a long while. It sat in me the way the first warmth of spring sits in frozen ground: slow, deep, changing things. The gathered folks murmured among themselves, their voices filling the low space without friction. Mrs.

Henderson was dabbing at her eyes already, and the ceremony hadn't started.

I glanced toward the back bench where Jedediah usually planted himself at any gathering — arms folded, spine against the wall, positioned where he could watch the door and the windows both. The bench was empty. His absence registered the way a missing fence post does: you don't stop walking, but your eye catches the gap. I looked once more toward the door, half expecting to see his lean shape filling it. He wasn't there. I let it go. It was a wedding, not a roll call.

Anders Larson came through the door just then, hat in both hands, and the murmur in the room dropped by half. Not silence, exactly — more like the sound a creek makes when it hits a stone and has to decide which way to go around it. Anders stood in the doorway with the light behind him, turning the brim of his hat in slow circles, his eyes finding no particular place to land. A few faces turned away. Rachel Parker's mouth thinned. The moment held — two, maybe three seconds of the room remembering things it hadn't yet decided how to file. Then Titus, who had come inside by now, crossed the room and extended his hand. Anders took it. The handshake was brief and firm and said what needed saying without words. The murmur came back, and Anders found a spot along the wall, and the room absorbed him the way soil absorbs a late rain — slowly, but all the way down.

Then Eleanor came through from the back quarters and the room went quiet.

She wore a dress of cream silk — Boston cloth, dismantled and remade to fit a different life. I could see where the seams had been taken in, where new stitching ran alongside old, the whole garment a record of two worlds joined. The lace at the throat was fine, the kind of work that belonged to a world where people had leisure to make beautiful things — needle lace, the kind you see in shop windows back east, delicate as frost on a pane. But the way she carried herself belonged here. This was the woman who had burned her own books to keep the schoolhouse warm, who had faced down the town council and the drought and her own grief and come through all of it upright. Her hair was pinned with a sprig of evening primrose — white against the dark — and her face was calm and open and certain.

Her eyes found Titus. The fear went out of him like air from a bellows. What came back in its place was steady and certain, and I could see it in the set of his shoulders, the way his hands unclenched and hung easy at his sides. Watching it, a tightness moved through my throat that had nothing to do with the collar.

I took my place beside him at the front of the room. Sarah found a seat near Rachel Parker, and I saw her reach over and take Rachel's hand.

Standing there, I thought about the canyon — the smell of gun oil and the cold patience of waiting for men who wanted us dead. The mud at the creek diversion, muscles burning through the last hour before the water finally went where we needed it. The long nights at the kitchen table with the ledger open and the lamp burning low, trying to make the numbers say something other than what they said. Titus had been there for all of it. The weight to my figuring, the hammer to my ledger. His forge had mended our plowshares and our resolve in equal measure. This wasn't just a man and a woman making a covenant before a preacher. It was Oak Haven binding its two pillars. Knowledge and iron. The teacher and the smith. Without either, we'd have been nothing but a name on a surveyor's map — a line to be drawn through and forgotten.

The ceremony was short, as it should be. A traveling preacher, arrived on Tuesday's train — a thin man with a loud voice and careful hands that held the Bible like it was something borrowed — said his words. They were the usual words, worn smooth by use, and they fit the room the way the wildflowers fit the crevices: simply, without pretension. When it came time for the vows, Titus set aside the script.

"I have spent my life breaking things and mending them," he said, his big hands reaching for hers. His voice was rough but it held. "I have seen what fire does to iron. I have seen what the wind does to the plains. I cannot promise you an easy path. But I promise to be the anvil. When the world strikes, lean on me. I will not break. I will keep the fire going when the winter comes. I am yours, as long as the hammer strikes."

The room was still. Not the held stillness of waiting, but the deep stillness of listening — every person in that room leaning forward slightly, drawn in by the weight of the words.

Eleanor's voice was a clean, steady note in the hush. "I came here looking for a story that was real, Titus. I found it in the dust and the rain. You are the strength that allows me to teach the children to look at the stars. I promise to keep the books, to remember our history, and to build a future with you that the drought cannot touch. I am yours, as long as there are words to tell it."

I reached into my pocket and put the ring in Titus's palm. The gold was warm from being held.

My hand was steady. As he slid the band onto her finger — a slow, careful movement, the precision of a man who handles fragile things with outsized hands every day — I looked around the room. Samuel Price was there, arm out of its sling, his face carrying a pride that made him look years older than the boy who'd arrived chasing dime novels. He was sitting up straight, his jaw set, and I saw him swallow hard when the ring went on. Anders Larson stood along the wall, nodding slow, the brim of his hat still turning in his grip. The Parker children watched with their mouths open, scrubbed faces and wide eyes, unaware they were witnessing the moment Oak Haven stopped being a collection of homesteads and became something more durable.

We were a scarred people. We had looked into the ditch of eviction and starvation and refused to climb in. The railroad, the lawyers, the Pinkertons — all of it had gone thin and distant, the way old debt looks once the balance is cleared. Not forgotten. Just settled.

"I pronounce you husband and wife."

The cheer that went up rattled the sod and shook the wildflowers in their twine. Mrs. Henderson was openly weeping. Samuel let out a whoop that belonged more to the boy he'd been than the man he was becoming, and nobody minded.

The reception moved outside. The sun was angling toward the ridge, pulling long shadows across the schoolyard and turning the grass gold. The community table held things I hadn't seen since before the drought took hold: crusty salt-rising bread with a crust that crackled when Rachel cut it, jars of preserved plums guarded like currency all winter and now brought out gleaming in the late light, crisp apples off the Tuesday train — a gift from the town to the couple, polished until they shone. The smell of roasted chicken and sage stuffing came in with the breeze, rich and heavy and honest, and my stomach answered before I could think about it — a plain, healthy hunger with nothing complicated attached to it. It had been a long time since hunger felt simple. Since it felt like appetite instead of fear.

I stood at the edge of the crowd, tin cup of cider in my hand, watching.

People were laughing — not the anxious kind, not the relief-laugh that comes after a scare passes. Real laughter, belly-deep and unhurried, the kind you can feel in the ground through your boot soles when a whole crowd makes it at once. Rachel Parker held court near the pies, her face flushed, her hands moving as she told a story I couldn't quite hear but could see the shape of in her gestures. Thomas Parker and the other boys ran shouts through the tall grass along the creek, their voices bouncing off the ridges, and nobody called them back to behave because there was nothing to behave for — no danger, no drought, no men on horses coming to take what was ours. The world that had felt like a fixed scarcity — every bushel counted, every gallon measured — had cracked open into something that felt like potential. Like a ledger with blank pages in it, waiting to be filled.

Then I heard it — a slow clap, deliberate and heavy, coming from the corner of the schoolhouse. Jedediah Stone rounded the building on foot, his buckskins dusty at the knees, that battered fur-lined coat open at the chest. He moved through the crowd with his long, unhurried stride, and people parted for him the way they always did, not out of fear but out of a kind of respect for the space a man like that carried with him. He found Titus and Eleanor and stopped. He didn't say much — just took Titus's hand in both of his, the missing fingers on his left making their own familiar shape against the blacksmith's knuckles, and gave Eleanor a nod so slight you'd miss it if you weren't watching. But Eleanor smiled at it, and Titus's shoulders eased a fraction I hadn't known they were still holding. Jedediah turned away and found himself a plate, and something in the afternoon settled into place — the last fence post driven, the line complete.

Sarah came to stand beside me, her arm sliding through mine. She leaned her head against my shoulder and for a moment neither of us spoke. The fiddle was warming up somewhere near the barn — a few exploratory notes, a string being tuned, the bow drawn slow across the gut.

"Look at them, Elias," she said. "We're still here."

"We are," I agreed. The cider was tart and sweet, tasting of autumn. "And the land is still ours."

"It's more than ours now." She was watching Titus and Eleanor, surrounded by well-wishers, Eleanor's hand resting on Titus's forearm. "Before, it was just a struggle. But today it feels like a home."

I looked at my hands. Calluses thick and familiar, the grain of the soil worked permanently into the lines of my palms. The same hands that had held the plow and the deed and the rifle and Sarah's face in the dark. I thought of the ledger on the kitchen table — the one I'd kept with grim precision, recording every loss, every debt, every inch of ground the drought tried to claim. Tonight I would open it again. I'd write the date. I'd write the names: Titus and Eleanor Croft, married this day in the schoolhouse. I'd record the rain and the green of the wheat and the way the sun sat over a town that had refused to quit. The ledger had always been a record of survival — debits and credits, losses and narrow margins. Tonight it would start being something else. A history of what we'd built.

Titus broke from the crowd with two plates balanced in his large hands, moving through the well-wishers with the careful tread of a big man in a tight space. He handed one to Sarah with a clumsy, careful bow that made her smile. "Rachel said if you don't eat, she'll come find me about it."

"In a minute, Titus," I said. "You did well. The vows. You meant every word."

He looked toward the horizon. The first stars were punching through the early dark, small and certain, the way they always were out here where there was nothing between you and the sky. "Iron and bone, Elias. It's all we've got out here." He paused. His jaw worked once. "But it's enough."

He turned back to Eleanor, his shadow long and steady on the grass. I watched them stand together as the night settled over Oak Haven — the teacher and the blacksmith, their silhouettes easy against the last of the light, her head tilted toward his shoulder, his hand at the small of her back. The fiddle found its tune and began to play — something slow and old, a waltz that carried across the yard with the breeze, thin and clear and sweet enough to ache.

I took Sarah's hand — her skin rough and known against mine, the familiar map of her — and we walked toward the table. The plates were full. The music was playing. The children were laughing in the tall grass.

The fear was cleared from the ledger. The starvation was a closed account. We had planted our seeds in ground that tried to kill them, and they had held. Whatever the next horizon asked of us, we had something we hadn't had before: proof that this ground was ours to keep, and people worth keeping it for.

Chapter 38: The Apprentice

Samuel

The lasso had been sitting on the same nail for three days, and every morning I looked at it and told myself today was the day I'd make up my mind. This morning I finally did.

I stood in the center of the stall — my stall, the one I'd called home since I first showed up at the Thorne homestead with more nerve than sense and a bedroll that smelled of freight cars — and coiled the rope one last time. The hemp was good and tight, the braid still clean, smelling of dry hay and the last traces of cattle that had long since moved on. The fibers scratched against my palms the way they always had, a familiar roughness that belonged to a different set of hands than the ones I was growing into. It was the rope I'd carried since I hopped my first freight east of the Missouri, back when I figured being a man meant the snap of a lariat and the thunder of a herd and a sunset exactly like the ones on the covers of the dime novels I'd worn through — those yellowed pages with the cowboys riding straight-backed against a sky that was always the same impossible shade of orange. I'd believed in those sunsets the way a congregation believes in the sermon. Every last word of it.

I looped the rope over the nail. It hung there like a question I was done asking, a circle of shadow against the sun-bleached wood of the stall post. I wasn't going to take it down again. Let it hang. Let the mice build nests in it for all I cared. The boy who'd needed that rope was as gone as the freight train that brought him here.

My bedroll, a spare shirt with a mended collar, Eleanor's battered book of poems with the spine cracked at her favorite page, a pocketknife with a chipped blade I kept meaning to sharpen and never did. I bundled it all up, tugged the straps hard until they bit into the canvas, and headed for the door without looking back at the stall. I couldn't. Looking back meant thinking about the boy I'd been before the Pinkerton's lead found my shoulder in that dark stretch near the canyon, before the fever that followed, before I woke up in Sarah's kitchen with my arm strapped to my chest and the certain knowledge that nothing in any book I'd ever read had prepared me for what a bullet actually feels like. The dime novels never mentioned the smell. The hot copper of it, and the way your own blood sounds hitting dirt.

Outside, the air was crisp and sharp and the woodsmoke from Sarah's stove cut right through it, warm and honest, carrying the scent of biscuits and bacon grease. My boots hit the path with a new steadiness, each step deliberate, my body finding its rhythm without the hitch I'd been carrying for weeks. The phantom itch in my healing shoulder was still there, quieter now, but enough of a reminder: things cost something. Every single thing you earn out here costs something.

I'd said my goodbyes to Sarah that morning over breakfast — she'd pressed a handkerchief into my hand and told me to keep my collar clean, which was the kind of thing she said when she meant something bigger — and I'd shaken Elias's hand on the porch, his grip hard and dry and holding a beat longer than usual. The word apprentice had always sat wrong in my mouth, like it meant waiting around for permission to be real. But walking that path toward the settlement with my bedroll over my good shoulder and the morning cold on my face, it started feeling different. It felt like standing on the first rung of a ladder that actually went somewhere. A real one, bolted to something solid.

I heard the smithy before I reached it — fifty yards out, the deep rhythmic sigh of the bellows, like the whole building was breathing. Then the smell: coal and hot iron and the scorched-hair bite of a fresh shoe, and something else underneath all of it that I couldn't name except to say it was serious. The open prairie smelled thin compared to this. This was a concentrated smell, a working smell. I stepped into the shadow of the cavernous structure and let my eyes adjust, blinking against the orange pulse at the center of the room.

Titus was there, his massive silhouette squared against the forge fire, already deep in the work as though the wedding had been a season ago and not yesterday. He wore the leather apron, scarred and darkened by years of sparks. His arms shone with the first sweat of the morning, the muscles in his forearms standing out like cables as he turned something in the coals with the long tongs. He didn't look up, but his shoulders shifted a fraction — I was registered, logged, and accounted for. That was how Titus worked. He knew where you were in his shop the way a captain knows where his crew is on the deck. You didn't need to announce yourself.

"Bedroll goes in the loft," he said, his voice settling into the floor and up through my boots. "Stairs are in the back. Mind the overhead beam. It's lower than it looks."

I nodded even though he wasn't watching and climbed the narrow wooden slats. The loft smelled of cedar and old smoke and was exactly big enough for a cot, my bundle, and not much else. A small window at the far end let in a square of morning light that fell across the cot like a blanket. I dropped everything, stood at the edge, and listened to the hammer below — that deep, steady pulse, harder and more demanding than the fiddle at the wedding, but with a promise in it I could feel in my sternum. My palms were damp against my trouser legs, and not from the morning cool.

Back down the stairs, the forge heat rose up to meet me at every step, growing thicker and heavier until by the bottom it was like walking into an oven with the door open. Titus was holding a bar of iron in the coals with the tongs, watching the color change with the patience of a man who had done this so many times the waiting itself had become a kind of work.

"Today you stop watching and start striking." He met my eyes for the first time and there was no softness in them and no meanness either, just that steady expectant pressure I'd been working toward since I first walked into this building months ago with my arm in a sling and my nerve not much better. He handed me a smaller sledge. The handle was worn smooth by years of someone else's grip — I could feel the contour of that other hand in the wood, the slight depression where their thumb had rested. My fingers closed around it and my forearms registered the weight immediately — more than I'd expected, and perfectly balanced, the head drawing my hands down in a way that felt like the tool wanted to swing. "I hold the tongs and the set-hammer. You follow my lead. When I tap the anvil, you strike the iron. Not the hammer, not the tongs. The iron. And you strike it like you mean to change its mind."

He positioned the glowing bar and I gripped the sledge and every nerve in my body lit up at once — my pulse kicking hard against my collar, my breath coming short and shallow and slightly stupid. I could feel the heat from the bar on my knuckles, could smell the particular sharpness of iron at temperature, that smell like lightning and stone. Titus tapped the anvil. A light, clean clink.

I swung.

The hammer bucked in my hands and the blow glanced off the edge of the bar with a jarring vibration that shot fire up my mending arm and rattled my back teeth. A piece of scale flew off and hissed against the dirt floor. The heat in my face had nothing to do with the forge. I looked at Titus, waiting for the sigh, the order to put it down and go back to carrying water where I couldn't hurt anything.

He didn't move. He adjusted the bar an inch to the left, calm as a man centering a plate on a table. "Again," he said, flat and patient. "Don't fight the hammer. Let the weight of the head do the work. Your arm is just the hinge."

Just the hinge. All the strength I'd been pouring into the grip, all the muscle I'd been trying to force through my shoulders — and what he was telling me was to let go of it. To trust the tool the way you trust a horse to know the trail.

Clink.

I took a breath and found the center of my own weight and swung at the brightest red of the bar. The hammer landed true. The sound was different: a dull, deep thud that felt like it went down through the anvil and into the earth and kept going. The iron gave, flattening a degree under the force, the surface dimpling where the hammer face had hit. A single spark flew up, a tiny gold star that died against Titus's apron without his noticing. Something jumped in my chest that wasn't panic. It was the opposite of panic. It was the feeling of the right thing happening for the first time.

We fell into it then, the clink-thud clink-thud of the master and the apprentice, and I stopped thinking about whether I was doing it right and just did it — my whole body locked into the rhythm, swinging from the hips, letting the weight drop, catching the handle on the rebound. My muscles began to burn — a deep, honest ache that spread from my shoulders into my back and down into my legs where I braced against the floor. My healing arm throbbed with every swing, a dull red reminder that ran from shoulder to elbow, but stopping wasn't a thought I had room for. There wasn't room for anything except the rhythm and the iron and the heat. The bar transformed under us, the raw stock thinning and bending to the will of two hammers working as one.

Titus didn't praise and he didn't correct, and in the heat and the noise of the smithy, that silence was trust.

The sun had shifted, cutting a hard rectangle of light through the open door, when a shadow fell across the threshold. I pulled the sledge back and wiped my eyes with my wrist — left a smear of black grease across my forehead that I didn't know about until later — and saw Elias Thorne standing at the door. Without his Sunday coat he looked more like himself: weathered and lean, the dust of the North Field already reclaiming the creases in his boots. He stood with his hands in his pockets, watching. I couldn't read the whole of his expression. But something sturdier and cleaner than what I expected was holding in it. He watched as I landed one last blow on the cooling iron before Titus plunged it hissing into the slack tub, a white curtain of steam rising between us.

"He's got the swing of it, Titus," Elias said, stepping into the shop. Quiet. He looked at my hands, which were trembling with exhaustion, the knuckles scraped, grease black in every crease.

"He's got the grit for it." Titus wiped his brow with a rag that was blacker than what it was wiping. A brief nod that landed like something heavy and good. "He doesn't shy from the heat. That's half the battle. The rest is time and repetition."

Elias crossed to the workbench and let his fingers trail over the tools — the punches, the drifts, the row of hammers from smallest to largest — the way a man touches things that belong to someone else's world, careful and respectful and just slightly out of place. He reached into his pocket and laid a small, crumpled sketch on the anvil. Drawn in his close, careful hand — a gate latch, a gravity-driven design with more complexity than anything we'd been working on. I could see the thought in the drawing, the way the weight of the latch arm would hold it closed, the pivot point, the catch.

"The North Field needs a proper gate," Elias said. His eyes came up to mine and held. "One that won't rattle when the wind comes up. One that stays shut when the stock gets restless. It's the first gate folks see when they come in on the south road, and I want it to look like this place is staying put." He stopped, worked something down in his throat. "Titus tells me you're looking for your first commission. I want you to forge this latch. I'll pay shop rate, plus a bit for the design."

I looked at the drawing. I looked at my hands — stained and already scraped, the skin across my knuckles raw where the hammer handle had rubbed, the hands of a laborer finding their calluses in a trade not his by birth. Something rose up behind my sternum and tried to close my throat. He wasn't just asking for a piece of hardware. He was handing me his blessing and the security of his land in the same gesture, and trusting me to deserve both. The North Field. The field he'd fought Voss for, fought the drought for, nearly died for. And he was putting a piece of it in these hands that couldn't hit the center of an iron bar two hours ago.

I looked at Titus, who watched me with a quiet gravity, arms crossed. Then back at Elias.

"I'll make it," I said, and my voice cracked slightly on the last word, which would have embarrassed me an hour ago but didn't now. "I'll make it so it never breaks. So the wind can't budge it."

Elias gave a short, stiff nod. The ghost of a smile touched his lips — not a grin, not even close, but the faintest softening around his eyes. He reached out and gripped my shoulder — the good one — his hand firm and staying a beat longer than it needed to. I could feel the strength in his fingers, the calluses, the years of work compressed into that grip. "I know you will, son. You've always been better at building than growing. It took me a while to see it. But I see it now." He turned to Titus. Between them passed a look that covered the canyon, the creek, the storm, and everything before and after — a whole history compressed into a second of eye contact. "Keep him honest, Titus. And don't let him burn the shop down."

"I'll keep him busy," Titus said. "That's usually enough."

I watched Elias walk out into the sunlight. His silhouette shrank as he headed back toward the farm, and he seemed lighter than I'd ever seen him — not in mood, exactly, but in load. Like a weight he'd been carrying for me had passed over into my own hands, where it belonged now, and the transfer had made us both stand straighter.

I looked down at the sketch on the anvil. The pencil lines were precise, each measurement noted in Elias's small, cramped numbers. I thought about the lasso on the barn nail and about the boy who'd carried it on a freight train heading west with the wind in his face, absolutely certain he knew what was waiting for him. He hadn't known anything. Not one single thing. But he'd gotten here — battered and shot and wiser than he'd ever planned on being — and here was the real thing. Not a story. A forge, and a commission, and a man's trust to live up to.

"Coal's getting low, Samuel," Titus said, already reaching for the bellows handle, his voice pulling me back into the present the way it always did — no nonsense, no sentiment, just the next thing that needed doing. "Heat the hearth. We've got work to do."

I reached for the handle, the worn wood familiar in my grip after three hours that felt like thirty, and began the long rhythmic pull that kept the fire alive. The bellows sighed deep and the coals brightened to a fierce, pulsing heat that pushed back against the cool air from the door. My shoulder ached and my arms burned and my hands were raw and I was grinning without meaning to — a stupid, wide grin I couldn't have stopped if I'd tried.

I wasn't a cowboy. I wasn't a farmer. I was a builder, and the gate for the North Field wasn't going to forge itself.

Chapter 39: The Ledger

Elias

The kerosene lamp sat in the center of the kitchen table, burning steady. Its flame held still in the windless room, a small yellow point that neither guttered nor climbed, and the light it threw was warm and close — the kind that draws the walls in and makes a room feel like the only room in the world. It caught the edges of my ledger: the cracks in the old leather spine, the frayed corners of pages turned a thousand times in dread, the faint ring where a cup of water had once sat too close. Outside, the evening air carried the smell of damp earth and the distant lowing of stock finally at rest — that low, settled sound cattle make when the day is done and the grass is in them and nothing is wrong. For years this book had been a tally of my losses. Inches lost to the dust. Bushels surrendered to the heat. The slow grinding of a man's margin until what's left is a number so thin you're afraid to look at it in good light. Every ink stroke a needle, stitching me tighter into a shroud of debt.

Tonight, the pen felt different. Lighter in the hand, or maybe my hand was lighter. Something had shifted.

I dipped the nib, the scratch of metal against glass sharp in the quiet room. A clean sound, precise, the kind that belongs to evening work when the house is still. Sarah's dishes were drying on the rack by the basin, and the smell of supper — salt pork and biscuits and the last of Rachel Parker's apple preserves — still hung in the air. The final column of the railroad easement agreement sat before me, the numbers clean and exact. The money from Voss and the company had cleared today. The sum was written on a receipt from the bank in town, the figures stamped in ink barely dry. I set the receipt beside the ledger and squared it with the edge of the page. Then I began to write.

First entry: the bank. I drew a single heavy line through the previous balance — a number that had lived in my sleep since Kansas, a number I could have recited faster than my own name — and in the space beside it wrote a zero. The nib scratched through the silence. I sat looking at that zero a long time. A zero is an odd thing. Hollow at its center, like a well seen from above. But this one had weight — the weight of my brother's memory, who'd lent me the down payment and died before I could repay it; the weight of a decade fighting to keep title to dirt that should have been mine outright; the weight of every night I'd sat at this table running the figures and coming up short. It meant the bank no longer owned the air I breathed or the soil under my boots. Not by blood or sweat alone now, but by law. The deed was clear. The title was mine. I ran my thumb across the zero and felt the slight ridge where the ink was still wet.

The taste of old dread was still at the back of my throat, faint and receding, like the last dust of a wind that's moved on. I let it sit there. It would go when it was ready. I moved to the next page and worked through the seed loans and credit lines — the spring seed on account, the wire, the coal oil, the sack of salt I'd been ashamed to ask for last February when the pantry was bare. One by one I balanced the accounts, each stroke of the pen a gate closing on the past. The columns zeroed. A knot in my chest — one I'd grown so accustomed to I'd stopped noticing, the way you stop noticing the weight of your own boots — eased open a turn. Then another. A breath went out of me, rough and ragged, the kind you don't know you've been holding until it leaves. It sounded loud in the empty kitchen. I pressed my palms flat on the table and let it finish.

The blank pages at the back no longer looked like the end of anything. They looked like unplanted ground. Clean and waiting. The kind of ground you walk across in spring with your hand in the seed bag, thinking about what might come up.

I turned to the last unmarred sheet. At the top, in my best script, I wrote a single word: Neighbors. The ledger had always been a solitary accounting. One man's production. One man's debt. One man against the sky and the dust and the bank, keeping his own score. But the land hadn't been saved by my hand alone, and it was past time the book reflected that. I began to list the names — every soul who had stood on the ridge or swung a shovel or brought a meal when pride would have let us starve. I wrote them together and apart, the way they'd come to me: in pairs, in families, alone. Each name brought its own freight — the sound of a hammer on the ridge, hands split from digging, a boy setting down his lasso and picking up a sledge. I wrote until the lamp guttered and steadied, the oil getting low, the flame dipping once and then recovering. Each name a small weight added to the right side of the balance.

The floorboard behind me creaked — the third board from the stove, the one with the knot in it that had been singing the same note for twelve years. A sound I knew the way I knew the wind direction from the tilt of the grass. Sarah. Her hand settled on my shoulder, fingers working into the muscle that always knotted when I kept the books — the left side, where the tension gathered, where the worry lived in the tissue. She leaned down, her breath warm at my temple, and looked at the pages. She smelled of soap and the lavender she kept in the drawer with her good dress, and underneath that the warm, bread-and-skin smell that was just her, the smell I'd known for twenty years and would know in the dark.

Her thumb traced the line where the bank debt had been. The heavy line I'd drawn through it. The zero beside it. The touch was light. She didn't need to speak. The silence between us was full and warm and complete, the silence of two people who have said everything already and can rest in what's been said.

She moved her hand to the list of names. Her face softened in the amber of the lamp — a small, tired smile, the kind that only comes after the storm has truly passed. Her lips shaped each name without speaking it, a quiet inventory of the people who had kept us alive.

I reached up and covered her hand with mine, my calloused palm against her skin. Her knuckles were rough from the wash and the garden and the years of making something from not enough, and they fit against my fingers the way they always had — the spaces between us exactly the right size for each other.

"It's a good book, Elias," she whispered. Her voice was low and steady, anchored in the quiet the way a fence post is anchored in the ground.

I squeezed her hand. The blank pages ahead had planting season written all over them — that feeling before the seed goes in, when the ground is ready and you know in your bones the yield is going to come. Not because you can see it. Because you've done the work.

I closed the ledger. The leather cover met with a soft thud — the sound of a gate latching shut.

Sarah's hand stayed on my shoulder. The lamp burned low.

Chapter 40: The Drifter's Departure

Elias

The morning was the kind of clear that makes the horizon look like a blade.

I stood by the corral gate, my boots sinking just slightly into the earth — still soft from the rains, still giving back what you pressed into it — and watched Jedediah Stone work the pack saddle. The scent of wet sage and curing grass was thick in the air, a sweetness that always felt like a promise, though this morning it carried something else underneath — the sharp edge of distance, of cold places and high passes and a country that still didn't have names for all its rivers. Jedediah moved with a methodical slowness, those leathery hands running over the worn leather the way a man does when he's making sure the work is right and he doesn't have to think about the leaving. Each buckle checked twice. Each strap tugged and tested. He looked different than the half-starved shadow that had first stumbled into Oak Haven — his face had filled out, the hollows no longer deep enough to hold shadows, and his eyes had lost the frantic glitter of a man running on fumes. Sarah had seen to it that his buckskins were scrubbed and mended, and the fur lining of his coat was brushed clean. He looked healthy.

He looked trapped.

I'd seen that look before, on myself, years back in Kansas when the fences started pressing in and the air began to carry the woodsmoke of too many neighbors. The itch of a man whose skin fits too tight for the room he's standing in. Jedediah tightened a cinch, the missing fingers on his left hand moving with their accustomed competence — a thing that always caught my eye, the way a man learns to do the work regardless. Those absent fingers had their own story, one he'd never told and I'd never asked about, and they moved through the task with a sureness that spoke of decades of compensation, the remaining fingers doing the work of five as if they'd never known another way. The mule, a soot-colored creature with a disposition like a county assessor, huffed a breath that went briefly white in the cool air and shook his head so the harness brasses rang out, hollow and light — the sound carrying across the quiet yard and coming back off the barn wall.

"He's well-fed," I said. My voice came out low and rough in the morning stillness, the way it did before I'd had enough coffee to smooth it. "The mule. He's got enough fat on him to carry you to the coast if that's where you're headed."

Jedediah gave the pack a final, sharp tug and turned toward me. His eyes went to the sky first, the way they always did — scanning, cataloguing, measuring wind and weather with the practiced eye of a man who'd lived outdoors long enough to read the air the way I read soil. He still carried the smell of the high places on him underneath Sarah's scrubbing — old smoke and cold stone and something mineral and wild. "Coast is too damp, Elias. Rusts a man's joints. I reckon I'll head where the wind don't have to navigate around telegraph poles."

I managed half a smile at that. It didn't hold.

The morning train from the east put out its long whistle. The sound rolled over the prairie — shrill, metallic, the voice of the new world doing its efficient work. I watched Jedediah's jaw tighten. A small movement, but it was there, visible in the cords of his neck and the way his hands went still on the mule's flank. He stood perfectly still until the echo faded and the homestead went back to just the sound of the mule breathing and the birds working the fence line. The quiet that returned was different from the quiet that had been there before — thinner, more fragile, like paper stretched over a hole.

"That sound," he said, and aimed a dark bead of tobacco juice at the dirt. It hit the ground and sat there, dark against the damp earth. "It's too loud for the space it's in. Like a scream in a church." He shook his head slowly, his eyes narrowing at the horizon. "This place is getting crowded. I can hear the neighbors thinking from five miles off. I can feel the law settling in like a frost that won't melt come noon. You got your tracks, your depot, your new laws. It's a fine thing for a man who wants to stay put. For a drifter, it's just a cage with a wider view."

I looked toward the North Field, the ground I'd near broken my back to hold. The rails had taken the south gap instead, a straight silver cut through that corner of the world—clean, efficient, catching the morning light as they ran east to west like a seam sewn through the prairie's belly. He was right. The wildness was being stitched shut. I'd fought for that — sacrificed my peace and nearly my blood for the right to hold this dirt — but watching Jedediah, something I couldn't enter in any ledger settled heavy across my shoulders. We'd traded the infinite for the measurable. The mystery of the horizon for the certainty of a schedule. Tuesday and Friday, Voss had said. The world arriving on a timetable.

My hand found the rough cedar of the fence post, splinters catching at my palm. Solid. Mine. But for the man across from me, that solidity was a different kind of sentence.

"You're leaving on good terms, Jed," I said. I wanted him to hear it, to carry it with him. "There isn't a soul in Oak Haven who doesn't owe you a debt. Titus, Eleanor, the Parkers — they all consider you family.

You don't have to run from a place that's finally learned your name."

He looked at me directly for the first time that morning. A ghost of a smile pulled at the corners of his beard — a smile that was more weather than warmth, more wind than fire. "That's exactly why I have to go. When people start knowing your name, they start expecting things. They build a version of you in their heads, and before you know it, you're just another piece of the furniture. I'd rather be a shadow in a canyon than a pillar in a town." He patted the mule's neck, and the animal leaned into his hand with a familiarity that told me the two of them had been having this conversation longer than I had. "Besides, this old thief is getting lazy. He needs a mountain to remind him he's alive."

I didn't argue. There was no arguing with a man who'd already left in his heart. The body was just catching up.

Jedediah reached into the deep pocket of his fur-lined coat. His hand rummaged a moment, the fabric rustling, and then he extended his arm toward me, fist closed. The knuckles were scarred and the skin was dark and cracked and the missing fingers made the fist look unfinished, like a hand that had been whittled down by use. When he opened it, a small nugget of dull yellow metal sat in his palm — no bigger than a dried pea, its surface pitted and raw, catching the light with a quiet, heavy gleam. Nothing like the polished gold in a jeweler's case. Something older and more honest, pulled straight from the cold teeth of the earth.

"Take this," he said.

I kept my hands at my sides. "Jedediah —"

"I found it years ago. Somewhere north of the Snake River, in a creek bed without a name." He held the nugget out steady, his arm not wavering. "I kept it because it was the only thing I ever found that I didn't spend on whiskey or beans. Twenty years I've carried it. It's been in my pocket through three territories and a flood and one knife fight I'd rather not discuss."

"I can't take that. If winter is hard or the hunt is thin —"

"I'm not giving it to you for money." The authority in his voice was the same flat certainty I'd heard when he tracked the rustlers — no argument expected, none taken. His eyes were hard and certain and a little fierce, the eyes of a man making a point he won't make twice. "It's a seed. For bad times. Every farm needs a seed that won't rot in the ground. If the drought comes back, or the bank starts looking at your ledger with hungry eyes again, you use it. It's a piece of the wild, and the wild don't care about interest rates or eminent domain."

I reached out and took the nugget. Dense and cold against my fingers — heavier than its size had any right to be, the weight of it sitting in my palm like a stone that had been compressed until it forgot how to be light. As my hand closed over his, I felt the hardness of his palm, a surface worn past leather into something closer to horn. The grip held for a moment — his hand and mine, the gold between us, the morning light falling across our joined fists. This wasn't a transaction. It was a covenant. He was handing me a piece of his history, a fragment of the life he was riding back into, and trusting me to keep it straight.

"I'll keep it safe," I said. My throat was working, the words having to push past something. "In the house. A reminder of the man who saw the shadows before the rest of us thought to look."

He nodded once — sharp and final, the nod of a man closing a deal he won't reopen — and swung himself up into the saddle with a grace that his years had no business granting him. The leather creaked under his weight and the mule shifted and set its feet and Jedediah settled into the seat the way water settles into a channel — naturally, without effort, as if he'd been born there. From up there he looked like a different order of creature, part of the mule and part of the land, already gone in some essential way. He turned his eyes west, toward the badlands rising in purple and gold tiers against the pale blue of the morning.

"Tell the schoolmarm to keep teaching them kids how to read maps," he said. His voice had already changed — looser, lighter, the voice of a man talking from the other side of a decision. "Maybe one of 'em will find that creek I was talking about." A pause. The mule tossed its head and he corrected it with a barely visible shift of the reins. "And tell Titus to keep his hammer swinging. The world needs things that are forged, not just manufactured."

I walked with him as far as the edge of the Thorne property. Neither of us spoke. The quiet between two men who have worked the same ground in the same hard weather doesn't need filling — it's already full, full of everything you both remember and neither of you has to say. Our boots crunched on the gravel track, and his mule's hooves made a softer sound in the damp earth beside it. At the boundary line — where the cultivated furrows of the North Field gave way to untamed grass, that sharp line between the tended and the wild — he paused. He didn't look back at the house or the town. He raised one hand: a brief, flat salute, palm outward, fingers spread. Then he was moving.

I stopped at the fence post. Wrapped my hand around its top and held on.

The steady thud of heavy boots announced Titus before he reached me. He smelled of coal smoke and quenching water, those scents so deep in his skin now they were part of him, and he took his place beside me, arms crossed, eyes fixed on the receding figure. The weight of him at my shoulder was a familiar thing — solid, unmoving, reliable. Neither of us spoke for a while. We just watched.

"He's gone then," Titus said. Not a question.

"Train whistle bothered him. Said he could feel the law settling in like a frost that wouldn't melt."

Titus let out a slow breath. "He's a man of the gaps. He lives in the spaces between things. We started filling those spaces with tracks and fences and deeds, and we took away his air." A pause. His jaw worked once. "He's headed west. Always west."

We watched until Jedediah became a single dark point against the vastness. The light was golden and young, the kind that makes the distance look like something you could walk to — close and shining and welcoming, a country without fences or schedules or names on a ledger. He didn't just move into that landscape; he merged with it, the way a fence post goes when you stop looking at it and look at the field instead. One moment he was a shape against the golden grass. The next, the light had taken him.

The point grew smaller. Then it was gone.

I worked the nugget between my thumb and forefinger. Still cold. A piece of the earth that refused to take on the warmth of my body, same as the man who'd carried it. I thought about the ledger in the house, the names I'd written in the back, the community built out of necessity and grit. We were the builders, the stayers. The ones who put down posts and strung wire and measured their ground and wrote it all down. Jedediah had been the wind that blew through us — the wildness that reminded us we were more than debt and duty, more than columns of figures in a leather-bound book.

"He won't be back," Titus said quietly. His voice was barely above a murmur, a sound meant for the air between us and no further. "Men like him don't return to the scene of a change. They just keep moving until they run out of world."

"The world's running out of space for them," I said.

Titus didn't answer. He didn't need to.

I looked at my hands — the soil of the Thorne homestead mapped into every line of my skin, indelible as a deed. Rooted. My story was written in the furrows and the well levels and the faces of my family, and that was the right accounting. The right reckoning. But turning back toward the house, back toward the breakfast Sarah would have waiting and the work that never stopped, I felt the particular weight of something that couldn't be balanced — what we'd gained, and what, in gaining it, we'd ended. The prairie behind me was still and wide and empty where a man had been a moment ago, and the emptiness had a shape to it, the shape of everything the fences couldn't hold.

I tucked the nugget into my watch pocket and walked back toward the North Field. The rails ran straight and silver through the ground I had fought for, catching the climbing sun. The next train wouldn't be long. Tuesday, Voss had said. Every Tuesday and Friday.

It was my land. It was right that it was my land.

I went inside. Sarah had coffee on. The kitchen smelled of bacon and biscuits and the warmth of the stove, and the ledger sat on the table where I'd left it, closed, its leather cover dark and familiar. Through the window I could see the North Field, green and stitched with wheat, and beyond it the tracks, and beyond the tracks the open country running west toward a horizon that Jedediah was already somewhere inside of, riding alone, the nugget's absence a small lightness in his coat pocket and the morning getting bigger around him with every step.

Chapter 41: Roots in the Dust

Elias

Sunday was half over before I noticed I hadn't checked the sky once.

I'd been mending the south gate since morning, fitting the new latch Samuel had forged — a clean piece of work, the tongue sliding home with a sound like a rifle bolt. I tested it a dozen times because the action pleased me. Open, shut. Open, shut. The iron was rough where he'd drawn it, but the thing held. It would hold through wind.

Sarah called from the porch. I couldn't hear the words, but I knew the pitch — company arriving, wash your hands.

Wagons in the yard. Horses at the rail. The Parker boys chasing a rooster around the barn. Laughter and roast beef through the kitchen window. I stood near the water trough and let the noise wash over me the way creek water moves over a flat stone — around, not through.

Titus sat on the porch in his iron chair, sleeves to his elbows, talking low to Larson. Eleanor beside him, one hand on her stomach, fingers spread — the way you hold your palm over soil to feel if there's warmth in it. She caught me looking and gave a small nod. That was all it needed.

Near the barn, Samuel was showing Thomas Parker how to grip a horseshoe for the throw. Patient. Shoulders square under the leather apron he hadn't bothered to take off. He looked like a man with nowhere else to be.

Sarah came out with a pitcher. Her forearm brushed mine as she passed, her fingers hooking the crook of my elbow for a step — two steps — before she let go and poured for Rachel. Her hair was damp at the temples from the stove.

After the wagons creaked away, I walked the fence line alone. Habit. Posts solid, wire taut. I liked the walk — boot leather on packed earth, the give of ground that still held moisture.

At the far corner, where the property met open grass, a killdeer had built a nest in the gravel between two posts. Four speckled eggs in a shallow scrape no bigger than my fist. The bird flushed when I got close, dragging one wing in that old trick, leading me off. I stepped back. Stood still until she circled and settled over the eggs, her bright eye fixed on me, body pressed flat to the ground.

I left her to it.

The air was cooling. The lamp was already lit in the kitchen window — a small yellow point against the blue dusk. Sarah's shape moved behind the glass.

I walked toward the light, and the gate latch clicked shut behind me.

Author's Note

Some books begin with an idea. This one began with my father's voice.

Melwood Christian Matson was not a man who announced things. He told stories the way the plains receive rain — quietly, without fanfare, as though the past were simply part of the weather. On an ordinary evening he might mention, almost in passing, that his grandmother had left a fishing village on the coast of Norway at sixteen years old, crossed an ocean alone, and somehow ended up on a ranch outside Laramie, Wyoming. He would say it the way you might describe a neighbor walking to the mailbox. As if courage on that scale were simply what people did.

I thought about her often while writing this book. A sixteen-year-old girl standing at a ship's rail, watching the only coastline she'd ever known disappear into the horizon. No certainty waiting on the other side. Only the decision, already made, to go.

My father also told me about a great-aunt who taught school in a sod schoolhouse in Nebraska. The building itself was cut from the earth — walls of stacked prairie sod, a dirt floor, light through a single window. She stood at the front of that room and taught children how to read and cipher and think, in a structure that was slowly, quietly returning to the ground it came from. She believed the work was worth doing anyway. That is Eleanor Croft, almost exactly.

And then there were the farmers. Generations of them, working the plains of Nebraska and Colorado, learning the discipline of planting in soil that offered no promises. They understood that the land did not owe them anything. They stayed anyway. They measured a good year not against what they'd hoped for, but against what they'd managed to hold onto. That stubbornness, that quiet refusal to quit, became Elias Thorne.

Titus Croft came from the ranchers and the craftsmen — the ones who fixed what broke, built what was needed, and said little about either. Men whose worth was visible in their work and nowhere else.

I did not set out to write about my ancestors. I set out to write about the high plains in the 1880s, about homesteaders under pressure and a community deciding what it was made of. But somewhere in the drafting I realized that the characters I kept returning to — the farmer who wouldn't surrender his land, the teacher who believed in the power of a well-run classroom, the craftsman who trusted his hands over his words — were people my father had already introduced me to. He just called them by different names.

He told me those stories for forty years. I spent the last few trying to write them down properly.

I'm not sure I've done them justice. But I know they deserved the attempt.

— Rocky Matson, 2026

www.ingramcontent.com/pod-product-compliance
Lightning Source LLC
LaVergne TN
LVHW100503110826
845146LV00002B/498

* 9 7 9 8 9 9 5 7 9 6 4 2 8 *